Praise for *The Rigel Affair*

★★★★★ "...Fans that enjoy reading stories written by Emily Baker Loring, and other wartime romance novels will also delight in reading *The Rigel Affair* by L M Hedrick. I love how the author explains in detail all of the main characters' beginnings, interweaving the different stories to skilfully tie them together at the finish... I loved this book! **5 Stars!!" Anthony E. for Readers' Favorite**

★★★★★ "...Most of my attention was taken up by the compelling narratives of the two protagonists. Easily my favorite part of the book was the detail given. It's obvious the author has great love for this time period, and it shows on every page. One of Charlie's missions will always stick out in my mind... **5 Stars!!" - Jo Niederhoff for San Francisco Book Review**

★★★★★ "The Rigel Affair is **very highly recommended** for its blossoming adventure, relationships, and characters that grow, change, and confront their worlds." **- Diane Donovan for Midwest Book Review**

★★★★★ "The Bottom Line: Based on a true story, this World War II adventure is the American answer to *All the Light We Cannot See*. Impeccably written and researched, *The Rigel Affair* is a big tent book that will appeal to readers from all walks of life. *Highly recommended!" - Best Thrillers*

★★★★★ "Hedrick is handing readers a perfect blend of Historical Fiction and Romance. The text itself is heavily laden with historical truths and gives fans of both genders something to appreciate and remember. **5 Stars!!" - Literary Titan**

THE
RIGEL
AFFAIR

L M HEDRICK

Chez Blanc Publishing

ISBN: 978-0-473-47487-4 (Paperback)
ISBN: 978-0-473-47488-1 (eBbook)
PUBLISHED BY CHEZ BLANC PUBLISHING 2019
www.lmhedrick.com

Cover Design by NZGraphics

Library of Congress Cataloging-In-Publication Data is available upon request
One previous edition was published by Black Rose Writing

The Rigel Affair is printed in Chaparral Pro

Printed in the United States of America

Dedicated to my dear mother, Mattie

ACKNOWLEDGEMENTS

Firstly, thank you to my beautiful mother, Mattie, for her countless stories about Charlie while she sat and fondled his letters. And especially thank you to my kind and understanding father, Syd, for accepting Mattie's long-lost love for Charlie.

Thank you to my wonderful Agent, James Fitzgerald, for his edits and expertise. Thank you to my expert editors, Gillian Tewsley, Hillel Black, and Kathryn Johnson for their invaluable advice in my transit through many revisions. I give special thanks my beta readers, Sally O'Neil, Jean Bartosh, and Mark Hurley for their patient travels and comments on my early drafts.

Our journey to this novel started with my husband Bud's idea and encouragement and endless efforts and support to write it. The next stop was Auckland's Central Library to harvest every account of 1940's history, especially daily newspapers. We had to know what Mattie knew. Thank you to New Zealand National Archives, and the fabulous museums in Auckland, Devonport, and Torpedo Bay Navy Museum. Additional pertinent Auckland historical information was supplied by Dale Court of George Courts, and Edward Bennett of the K Road Business Association. Huge thanks to the Australian Maritime Museums in Sydney and Brisbane for personal tours of their artifacts, records, and marvelous vessels. Thank you to the people of Nouméa and Vanuatu for guided tours throughout Charlie's territory, and sharing their records and life accounts.

I offer a special thank you to Charlie's shipmates, Leonard Anderson and Dave Jessup, for sharing a multitude of information on life aboard the USS Rigel, and its travels throughout the Pacific. I am forever grateful to Michael Dean, US Naval Sea Systems Command, for his total commitment to supply us with vast information on both the USS Rigel and Charlie Kincaid's activities.

Finally, in my pursuit to know and understand Tippah County, Mississippi, and Charlie's early life, I thank my now dear friends, Tommy Covington, Dennis Wolfe, Bobbie McDowell and Aunt Doris Butler. Their patient, endless interviews placed me at Charlie's side.

THE
RIGEL
AFFAIR

CHAPTER 1

Whenever Charlie caught a moment, he snuck aside his clothes, and dropped them behind the bushes down by the railings of the old bridge below the farmhouse in Falkner, Mississippi. It was the summer of 1937. He liked to watch the murky Muddy Creek waters ripple in the sunlight and bend their way towards town. Charlie waited for the wind to settle, just to catch that safe glimpse of the bottom in his favorite swimming hole. With a splash, he had the soft mud against his belly, a place of comfort, where for a short while nobody could find him or harm him. He pushed off the bottom, rising until he hovered in the warm top layer, with the sun on his back, washing aside the fears of yesterday. He gulped air, and headed back to the bottom. The soft mud soothed his wretched soul. Rising out of the water like a newborn seal, he scrambled up the steep bank and wriggled back into his overalls. His uncle would be looking for him.

His impoverished Ma could not provide for him so when he escaped from the fire at the Jackson orphanage in 1927, her sister and Uncle Dee had taken him in. They owned a cotton farm and a couple of shops downtown. He marched his uncle's fields, gliding the sharp steel hoe down dark earth rows in the hills northwest of Highway 15, the road straight through Falkner. The sweet dust clouded his senses, erased the days, and easily expanded weeks into months with each turn of the soil.

Charlie knelt behind the bush, giggled to himself, and watched Uncle Dee crane his neck like a turkey squinting into the midday sun. *Someday I'll see the last of that buzzard.*

"Boy... how long does it take to piss?" his uncle called with a big hollering voice.

Charlie trembled, stood up and ran towards him. He knew he was in trouble.

"Damn boy... you piss your pants?"

"I fell."

"Like hell you did, you lying little bastard. Boys like you ain't worth the day they were born," Dee muttered through half-shaven chubby cheeks, and spat his tobacco slime onto the parched ground.

Charlie heard the chaw spit whizz past his head, and stared at the splatter until it disappeared into dry clods. He rose up, grabbed the hot plow handles, and shook the worn leather reins across his mule. Charlie watched Dee waddle away, back across the field to the old wooden farmhouse and sit down on the porch.

.   .   .   .   .

Charlie was sixteen now and couldn't wait to get onto the school wagon that morning. The townsfolk rebuilt Falkner's twelve grade school after a tornado stripped it down in 1909. The State paid for only six months of the year and each family paid for the rest. Students attended about nine months each year, allowing for breaks at spring planting and fall harvest.

"Mind them wheels boy," chuckled the driver as Charlie jumped one stride onto the wagon bed. He perched on an empty seat and fixed his stare out in the rolling pastures, smiling to himself as the wagon rumbled onward, listening to the crack of the whip onto wet mule backs. The school wagon had seats on both sides and part canvas cover; most of the children huddled close under the canvas.

"Mind if I ride next to you?" It was a girl, much taller than he was.

"It's a free ride," said Charlie, keeping his gaze across the horizon.

"My Daddy says I can quit whenever I want. I hate this damn school thing."

"Then why go?" Charlie stared at her.

She shrugged.

"What you chewin'?" he asked her.

"Sweetgum."

Charlie grinned back out at the fields. *Bet she's trouble.*

"Here, have a bit." The girl put up her fingers, pulling some gum out of her mouth, rolling it roughly in her paws. She leaned around to catch his eye, "What? You don't think my spit's good enough for you?"

Charlie twisted to one side. The girl gave him a shove.

"What if I was to kiss ya? Then you'd have my spit all over you," she laughed.

Charlie looked round, snatched the gum, and popped it into his mouth. He watched her proud smile, but couldn't see past the missing tooth. Her gappy grin squibbed an unfortunate ornery look.

He tried to ignore her; he didn't need any girls hangin' about. He chewed her gum. The two of them sat facing the rambling pastures, watching the last of the children step into their seats. The wagon rolled its way along beside the railway track, past the cotton gin and old Leroy's repair store.

Dry dirt boiled up from the wheels as a steady reminder of that waiting hoe. Timber buildings, lonesome in the vast landscape, stood in a row parallel to the track. The last building was Bill Rogers' general merchandise store, adjoining the Bank of Falkner, with its wide-swept timber porch bearing the hopeful message of *Welcome* in the break of day.

The wagon came to a sudden stop.

"What's your name?" asked the girl, jumping away from the wagon.

"Owen, yarrr...Owen," replied Charlie chewing on her gum, knowing he'd be rid of her and graduate from school before long.

"My name's Roxy. I'm gonna be in your class, so you better be telling me the truth." She stood staring at him with hands on her hips. What hips? She didn't have any, but a straight up and down boy's figure, long legs and wild haystack hair.

Charlie leaped down and didn't answer, just walked past her. He found his place amongst the many white faces of the classroom.

. . . . .

Mr Reed was one of their teachers, a serious-faced, obese man with a fob watch hanging from a large chest. Charlie sat in the front of the class and fumbled his reading books, catching onto the words frothing from huge dentures that Mr. Reed seemed to have trouble keeping in place. Charlie learned without difficulty, but lunch was the highlight.

"Hurry along now, do ya hear? ...and don't leave any scraps," the kitchen lady scolded. She glared straight at Charlie. "You work for your lunch, Charlie Kincaid." She handed him an egg sandwich and a dish of baked beans without a smile. Charlie grabbed his sandwich and shoved a spoonful of beans into his mouth, walking to the tables. He took no notice of the sniggering amongst the other students. They all knew he was the poorest of the poor kids.

"I thought you said your name was Owen. Who's Charlie?"

It was Roxy, the tall girl, walking beside him, stuffing her mouth with a sandwich. Bits of egg poked out of her mouth, heaving outward with each chew.

"I have a brother. He's the paleface in the other classroom. I don't see him. I don't live with him."

"Why not?"

"Look... you ask too many questions, damn you."

"I heard things about your family..."

Charlie swung around at her, glaring as if his eyes had caught fire. He grabbed the collar of her blouse and stared right up against her, so close she leaned back.

"How 'bout I look in all *your* closets? Bet you got plenty to talk about."

"I'm not frightened of you. It's the sawmill, isn't it?"

"Drop it, will ya?" Charlie stormed off, ignoring her. That's why he kept to himself. He waited until they loaded the school wagon, then he began sweeping the classrooms to pay for his lunch. It wasn't long before the day's dust swept up between Charlie's racing feet. He cinched a belt over his books and darted out the door.

He skipped along the railway track, eyeing the boxcars, and headed down past the bridge towards the farmhouse. Charlie slowed his pace to watch the vivid yellow butterweed wave at him, as if to say goodbye as the breeze swept across the pastures in late afternoon shadows.

Around the coming bend and nestled in the trees, was the old farmhouse with its battered roof and white posts lining the covered wooden porch. It was in need of repair, but to Charlie it was almost stately.

This is beautiful land, he visualized... God's country they say round here. Even though I ain't no church goer... I jus' *know* God loves Falkner, and Miss Billie... an' Ma.

He went on walking towards the farmhouse, watching his feet stir into the dirt road, hands hanging in empty pockets. Gonna miss some of this place; no cryin'... it's here in my heart, it'll never leave me.

CHAPTER 2

It was summer and any hint of war didn't deter the gaiety of the Blanc family's celebrations. Their huge white villa was positioned on the crest of Pine Hill Road, Dunedin, New Zealand, deep in the South Pacific. From the road, it was a steep climb up schist stone steps, past treasured roses and onto a wide wooden veranda.

Mattie walked down the passageway to the sound of George thumping the piano. Mattie was a gentle soul, of slender build, in her late twenties. She stood at the entrance of the lounge, wearing a button-through striped cotton dress and beige cardigan. A gold pendant necklace hovered about her delicate neck. Her brilliant blue eyes scanned the smoke-filled room with its white paneled walls and mirrors that reflected flowers overflowing from crockery wall vases.

George stopped as he caught sight of her, "Hey Sis! Sing us that Suzie song."

Mattie clutched the handle of the lounge door at the thought of an audience. She smiled across at him. It was his night, but secretly she longed for success and a celebration of her own.

She glided over to join him. George led with a two-handed arpeggio, and her sweet soprano voice burst into song, "*If you knew Suzie, like I know Suzie...*"

Mattie's hips swung in perfect timing, "*Oh, oh, oh what a gal.*" Her ebony waves bounced atop her shoulders. She was no longer shy, but a confident, glistening performer. And when she finished, the room burst aloud with everyone's hoots and applause. George spun around, "You're a song's best friend, Mattie... tops."

A hot breath whispered into Mattie's ear, "How about a dance, Miss Suzie?" She spun to encounter Bernie.

There was something about Bernie that intrigued her. Was it his whimsical smile or was it something else? She was never sure of her brother's friends. They were well-educated pranksters. The kind of friends that visited their house, ate their food, sang their songs, and generally left behind hillocks of empty whisky bottles and cigarette butts.

Bernie swooped Mattie into a twirl. For a moment she tingled with delight when his strong fingers rounded her waist, allowing her to fall into his arms; her body gyrated exquisitely to the beat. She became the dance. Bernie sensed the end, and whirled Mattie into a deep backbend, with his leg between hers and his hand supporting just above her buttocks.

"Can I get you a little of our Otago punch?" he asked when the music stopped.

"I'm not much of a drinker," she replied, out of breath.

"Oh come on, Mattie… George wants us all juiced, you must be thirsty after all that dancing." He discreetly let go of her and walked over to the drinks table. He secretly slipped a vodka flask from an inside pocket, and splashed in some extra. *Bit of persuasion for those beautiful hips,* he imagined.

Mattie gulped the sweet drink and gazed everywhere in the room. She was sick of being the careful daughter. Audrey was sitting on the couch, preening herself, silk stocking legs crossed, her eyes locked on Bernie. Maybe she fancies him more than my brother John, Mattie surmised. Mattie saw Bernie saunter over to Audrey and whisper something in her ear. Audrey's lips curled up and her dark eyes crinkled. Mattie knew Audrey was trouble from the moment she met her. Audrey was one of her father's secretaries. She was smart, and although of similar build to Mattie, her dark eyes had no soul. Mattie guessed she had one motive and that was to marry money. John never suspected her real intentions, but Mattie knew. Mattie picked up a serviette and started fanning herself, but the floor was coming up to meet her. Voices blended into a louder hubbub. Mattie stared at the now moving carpet. It was all too much, her head was spinning. She noticed Bernie coming towards her. He must have been watching her; she looked in another direction.

Bernie crouched down beside her, "I'm sure with a bit of night air you'll be just fine," he said, rubbing her back. Mattie settled back. Bernie continued, "I've got the only '32 Chevy Roadster in the South Island. It's a Deluxe with radio, heater… the works! She'll do sixty no worries."

"My head's *already* doing sixty… but the cool night sounds good," Mattie reached for a cup from the tea trolley. The hot tea soothed her anxiety. She grabbed a biscuit from one of Mary's silver dishes and casually sipped a few mouthfuls trying to pretend nothing was wrong. She was tired of watching Audrey play her brother. *Perhaps if she went out.*

She glanced across at her mother. "I'm going for some fresh air," she said brushing the crumbs off her dress. Mattie stood up, trying to steady herself.

"Alone? Will you be alright?" Mary cautioned, staring across at Bernie.

"Yes, Mrs Blanc. She's with me. I'll take good care of her," Bernie said with his best smile. Mattie had to get out of the room. She accepted his arm and they walked out the backdoor. A sharp chill raced down her dress. She gripped her cardigan close and looked up at Bernie. Bernie's eyes sparkled in the nightlight above the wash-house, as he slipped his fingers into hers. Mattie felt safe and daring but there was something about his eyes.

"If we hurry, the best view in town's at the top of the hill," Bernie wide grinned.

She gripped his strong hand and ran with him. Their feet half-danced to the fading music, along the narrow pathway and up the hill to Bernie's roadster.

Mattie pulled apart from him, walking ahead to admire his car.

Bernie slowed a bit to enjoy the view of her swaying form, backlit by a streetlamp through her thin dress. *Delicious…*

The '32 Chevy sat gleaming like a polished cougar. She stood beside the passenger door, running her fingers over its mirror finish.

"Your carriage, Mademoiselle. Monsieur at your service." Bernie took a bow, swept his greasy hair across his forehead, and helped Mattie into the red leather seats. Mattie giggled, inhaling the beautiful, rich leather aroma. Bernie hopped around into the driver's door, smirking all the way.

Bernie reached up to pull over the convertible top. "Can't have Mademoiselle *cold* now can we?" He slipped it into neutral, stomped on the start pedal, and they raced to the hilltop.

Mattie's hair blew in the wind. She felt the power and the vibration of the engine beneath her thighs. Her button-through dress opened at the bottom, showing her legs with the sudden breeze through the window; but she welcomed the cool wind on her thighs and didn't think to push her dress back down.

The roadster's tires crunched over the gravel as they spun into a winding private road. A cityscape of twilight hills and puffing chimneys unfolded as they coasted into the parking area, and came to a stop on a slope overlooking Leith Stream. Gnarled Totara trees anchored the cliff beneath, with limbs and prickly leaves stretching upwards, as if waiting to catch a prize from the heavens.

Easing back into the pleated leather, Mattie enjoyed her favorite view of the winding shingle track into Woodhaugh Gardens below. She inhaled a deep breath and slowly released it.

Bernie switched the engine off and lit a cigarette. "Isn't this magic?" he said, offering her a cigarette.

Mattie half-grinned back at him, guiding his match to her cigarette. She relaxed back and breathed in the soothing smoke. She'd always dreamed of sitting on top of the world in a flash car with a handsome man.

Bernie's cigarette lit up with each puff in the dark; they shared the magic. Bernie stopped smiling as he admired her legs. He flicked his cigarette out the window and turned towards her. His movement bothered Mattie. He was staring at her bare knees. She started to move her dress back down her thighs, but froze, shocked, at the sight of the lust in Bernie's wide eyes. She remembered her mother's warnings about men.

He slid closer, put an arm around her and kiss-whispered into her ear, "You are beautiful."

She cringed sideways, pushing with her elbow, trying to put a bit of space between them, without appearing rude.

He gave her a testing squeeze. "Did you think we were going on a picnic?" He tightened his grip and pulled her closer, "Or is it *me* you don't like?"

Mattie didn't know what to say. She was out of her depth. But her senses sharpened and she instantly glanced outside. Could she outrun him? She was trapped. She stubbed out her cigarette and moved to open the door. But

Bernie's huge hand was too quick, now gliding over her bare thighs. She'd let him see her fear. Maybe he'd take pity.

Mattie scanned outside into the darkness, searching for help, but there was none; merely the rustle of the pine trees. She opened her mouth to scream, but he covered her mouth with one palm, while the other hand was now busy working up her thighs. Eyes wide open, Mattie bit his fingers but Bernie was ready and forced her mouth closed with his thumb under her chin. All she witnessed was the black fury in his eyes as he moved ever closer. Eyes of an animal and she was his prey. She fought like a cornered cat. She knew she couldn't let him do it to her. But Bernie's deft fingers were now ripping down her underwear, parting her knees. It was no use. She saw he had lowered his pants and his tumescence was waving, ready, wanting her. His giant size pinned her down against the side of the seat. Her muffled screams simply made it worse. She felt his hardness digging against her. Dreadful visions ran through her mind; she was going to die. The pain of his hard penetration was so intense. She convulsed and vomited through his fingers. But he didn't stop. Nothing would stop this maniac. No one would believe her. Bernie was inside her, pumping furiously. She heard his groans in horrible rhythm with his thrusts. Mattie seemed to drift in a half state near death, wishing that somehow mercifully, he would kill her. His thrusts now quickened and suddenly he came with a huge shuddering final deep thrust that made her wince in pain and revulsion. Bernie gradually, haughtily, raised himself and stumbled out the car door with a final groan of satisfaction.

Terrified, Mattie glared into his laughing face, "You animal… you'll be sorry."

Bernie looked down at his pants covered in blood, and stepped back on the gravel. "Sorry? I'm *never* sorry… sorry is for losers," he laughed. "If you tell anyone… no one will believe you. I'm the family friend, who everyone loves. Are we clear?"

Mattie drilled her eyes into him, wanting her message of revenge to burn… yes, to scar. She was hurting deeply now, but concentrated on her courage.

Heading towards a tree with his pants partway down, Bernie swerved and called back, "Nothing like a long piss after a good fuck."

Mattie watched him amble across the car park. Now was her chance to get away. She lurched up, and her knee crashed into the handbrake.

Off-balance, her hand slammed the free-wheeling button into the dashboard. The car shuddered, and started to glide towards the edge of the bank.

Bernie heard the gravel giving way. He glanced up in the darkness to see his 1932 Chevy Deluxe Roadster about to take wings. "What the bloody hell have you done?" The roadster was in midair, about to have its first drink in the Water of Leith below.

Pulling up his soiled pants over spouting urine, he panicked and ran.

CHAPTER 3

This hot summer had the bad manners to lapse with a sudden onset of frosts. Charlie and his family, like all families neighboring Ripley, rushed to their fields to pick the last of their crops, especially the delicate cotton.

One early morning Charlie made the mules ready for the usual run into town. There was plenty of cured hog meat down in the old backyard shed, now that the smoking was done. The warm smoke of the green hickory had slowly embedded its flavors through the hanging meat. Charlie couldn't wait till it was time to bring it into the kitchen and slice off a piece. It was the best taste in the whole world. Now was the season when food was plenty, and everyone had their bellies full.

Maybe enough food not to miss any, Charlie smiled to himself, and reckoned he'd sneak a bit.

He yanked on the reins, guided the mules into the road by the railway tracks, and stopped outside Miss Billie's store. He jumped down from the wagon, straightened the clothes she'd given him, and fumbled with his cap. There was something about Miss Billie that made him nervous. She could read his mind.

"Good morning to you, Miss Billie," said Charlie with his cap tucked under his arm, carrying a large bag of meat, as he walked up to her counter and thumped it loudly on the table.

"My, my young man, you're strong as well as handsome," said Miss Billie.

Charlie gave her his widest grin.

Now this boy is up to no good... bringing all this meat... he never does that. Miss Billie suspected to herself. *I bet this is the last time I see him.* Her heart sank when she set eyes on his poor feet.

"And... not too well heeled, I see," she raised her eyebrows. "What you got to smile about, eh?"

Pretending not to care, she opened up the flap of the counter and walked over to the corner of the store. Charlie smelled the leather from where he stood. He had never ventured over to that part of the store. He knew better. She swung around and beckoned him. There were boots of all kinds rowed in shelves in a tiny area tucked away. Miss Billie could tell he was nervous; she pushed him down onto a seat and shoved a pair of boots in his lap. She didn't want to think where these boots might take him. "Here, try these."

"But Ma'm?"

"Do as you're told. You know how to take orders." Miss Billie snatched a pair of heavy socks down from the shelf, and squatted down on the stool to help him. "Here's a pair of socks. Now get these on, Charlie." She touched his red swollen feet.

My word, this poor boy has suffered.

She hurriedly helped him into the boots.

Charlie eased his way deliberately into the solid, secure leather and stood up.

"Now you're ten feet tall, Charlie Kincaid."

Charlie noticed behind her round spectacles... there was a tear forming. He knew Miss Billie was saying goodbye to him.

"The world is waitin' for ya, son. Don't come back here. There's nothin' for you." She smiled serious this time. "Oh, been keepin' these out back. Take this jacket and sweater."

"Miss Billie, I'll never forget you... special place right here," he tapped his heart.

She watched him leave as he tipped his hat, just like always.

Yep, that boy's goin' places. Maybe I'll hear about him one day, she thought in silence.

That night, Charlie lay on his bed, listening to the owl's nightly serenade. He was seventeen and High School was done. The moment had come. He gripped his history book, a gift from his Ma, silently rolled out of bed, and pulled on his boots. *Miss Billie knows.* He scouted throughout the room, one last chance, grabbed his knapsack of meat and a few corn pones, opened the window and climbed onto the porch.

He hesitated, and drew in a deep breath of the night air. The owl gave another hoot. He hopped over the railings, landing on the ground securely with his new boots. Their thick soles steadied him. No longer feet fighting frost, he was determined and ready. He ran in the direction of the railway tracks, through the forest, his boots crackling on the crispy fallen leaves.

As he ran, his crunching footsteps echoed through the trees. He stopped for a moment. He sensed something. He waited, listening. Someone was following him.

CHAPTER 4

Mattie stirred and opened her eyes. She remembered falling out the car door. She stared down at her bloody dress, and screamed into the empty night. She struggled, but firmly wedged herself further between the brambly limbs of the Tōtara tree, trapping her. She pulled one leg free to steady herself, but a branch snapped from behind. Barbed needles speared into her back. She reached up and freed herself. Haltingly she pulled her bruised body over the clifftop. Exhausted, she clutched at her torn cardigan and limped up Pine Hill Road.

Reaching home, Mattie collapsed at the base of the steps, and sobbed away her hurt against the cold stone wall. Relief came as she blacked out.

Her short respite was shattered by the sound of voices.

"Mattie!... Mattie!"

She opened her eyes, trying to focus. She heard George's voice screaming in her ear.

"Mattie what's happened to you, you're covered in blood?"

But Mattie couldn't remember and wondered if she were in a dream. She stared at her dress. Her body started to tremble as it all came back to her. She clutched her brother's arm and stood up shaking.

"Can you promise me you won't tell Mother? I need to go in and take a bath. I'm not feeling well," Mattie whimpered.

George helped her and they eased up the steps to the front door.

"I don't know about all this, Sis. It looks damn suspicious to me."

"Shut up George... just shut up."

They both crept inside. Mattie knew she wasn't being fair to her brother, but Bernie was *his* friend. Murmuring voices came from the kitchen down the long hallway. The evening gaiety had subsided and Mattie heard her parents arguing above the other voices.

"Can you tell Mother I've gone to bed with a headache?"

George looked at her and her dress and didn't say anything further.

I bet he knows.

Mattie closed her bedroom door, desperately pulled off her bloodstained clothes and stuffed them inside a pillowcase. Opening her drawers, she pulled out a nightgown, slipped it on with her bathrobe, grabbed the pillowcase and ran to the bathroom. She watched the hot water wash blood and dirt from her clothes, and then she plugged the bath. Gingerly, she stepped into the warm water. She peeped over her shoulder in the mirror at the graze on her back. The nasty gash gnarled up red and swollen. She sank deeper into the bath, and winced as the rising water awakened wounds. She'd never tell. It would be her secret. Bernie could have his graduation, his success... his freedom. She wept into the washcloth, pressing it into her mouth to muffle the sobs.

"Mattie, are you alright?" asked Mary, knocking on the bathroom door.

Mattie, reeling from her mother's voice, pulled her knees towards her chest.

"Yes, I have a nasty headache. I'll be fine. I'm going to bed."

"Would you like some hot tea?"

"No thanks, Mother, truly... I'm fine." Mattie almost floated, stirring the water noisily with her fingers until she heard her mother's footsteps fade down the corridor.

Back in her room, she threw her wet clothes under the bed, flicked off the light switch and collapsed into bed.

The next morning, Mattie slipped on her bathrobe and peered out the doorway. A grandfather clock ticked down the hallway, echoing through a silent house. She crept past her parents' room and glanced through the door crack. There was time to grab the soiled clothes and make it outside to the toilet and washroom.

She squeaked open the back door into the fresh morning air, filled with a tui's squawk. In the washroom, she turned on the taps and scrubbed the garments, running the last of the filth and blood into the drain. She gave the dress a final wring, shuddering at the vision of where it had been. Her underwear was easy, but her cardigan was torn so severely she'd have to dispose of it. Hanging her dress up on the line inside the laundry, she stuffed her wet bra and panties into the bathrobe pocket and went to the toilet.

Opening the back door of the house, she came eye to eye with her mother.

"Oh...," Mattie drew her hand up to her face, "I thought you were asleep."

Mary looked down at Mattie's wet hands, "What are you doing?"

"I've just been to the toilet."

"I heard water running." Mary switched on the kettle and opened the door into the small dining room. "Doing your wash this early?"

"Mother... not now, please."

Mary stooped over the dining room fire, and gave the glowing embers several unnecessary shoves with her poker. She stood up, holding it as if it were a weapon. "I worry about you, that's all. Last night...."

Arthur's voice boomed from behind, "What's all this I hear? You pushed Bernie's car into the Leith last night?"

"It was Bernie... an accident," pleaded Mattie, almost in a whisper.

Arthur casually settled into his favorite chair by the fire, and lifted the wrinkled paper. Without looking up, he asked, "What were you doing with Bernie at the Leith?"

CHAPTER 5

Charlie froze as he stared down both barrels of a 12 gauge shotgun.

"What cha' want?" he said into the shadow. Charlie waited for an answer. "I got only a bit a' hog meat… and a few pennies," he called into the night.

A whistle blew, still a distance afar.

The shotgun moved in that direction. Charlie quickly jerked to one side and sprung around to take control of the butt. But his assailant stepped back just as fast.

"Quit fightin'. I'm coming with ya," a voice shouted. Then a tall, lanky figure, cap pulled down over the eyes, stepped out into the light. It was Roxy, his schoolmate, trembling, still pointing the gun straight at Charlie.

"You're only a girl. You think you're faster than me? Then catch me," Charlie dashed for the train.

He heard Roxy click back the hammer. *Bang!* Gunfire exploded into the air. Charlie braced and turned. "Can't you see…? I'm jumpin' a train."

She shoved past him. "Then we'd better run." She grinned her gappy smile and they scrambled down the tracks, flinging themselves into an open boxcar as it rattled past. They plopped down with their legs over the side, just as they'd done sometimes on the school wagon.

He knew she was trouble right from the start. They had both just finished high school, but Falkner, Mississippi, was dirt poor. It was June 1939— summer harvest coming. His bleak future, so long as he stayed, was plowing and picking Uncle Dee's cotton. Charlie couldn't wait to get the dust out of his nose. Uncle Dee would be in a rage finding him gone.

He shook his head and shifted to face Roxy. "Got some more of that Sweetgum?"

"Here…." She pulled some gum out of her mouth and held it out with a grin.

Charlie looked round, snatched the gum, and popped it into his mouth. "Trade ya a bit of hog later." He liked her smile, but he couldn't see past the missing tooth.

They sat chewing… watching the pastures slip by just like it was yesterday riding to school. The rumbling boxcar imperceptibly moved them closer until their shoulders touched in swing with the bogies' rhythm. Charlie put his arm around Roxy, but his mind was on freedom.

For Charlie, the air was already cleaner—no clouds of dirt boiling up from wagon wheels and plows. He shook his head and stared back at the life he'd left behind.

CHAPTER 6

The Leith sloshed ankle-deep past Bernie's roadster, as it grumbled bleakly to the winch on the tow truck ashore. Odd parts sloughed into the river... It lunged over rocks, rocks that seemed to be perfectly placed to attack the underbelly of this particular roadster.

•   •   •   •   •

Mattie knew she had to brace for her father. *What will I tell him?*

Arthur was in his usual place at the small dining room table with the paper up in front. Mattie settled warily into her seat. To her horror, a picture of Bernie's car crashed in the Leigh River was facing her. Arthur put the paper down and glared at her. Mattie's lip quivered. Mary broke the silence, pouring Mattie a cup of tea. Nobody spoke.

Mattie drank her tea and swallowed a bite of the toast Mary had buttered for her. She tried to pretend it would all disappear. She peered through the familiar lace curtains, fluttering in the morning breeze and remembered her sheltered childhood, so protected and loved. Nothing ever harmed her. But the gentle wind somehow snapped her back to the Roadster picture. She was damaged goods. She was so ashamed. So ashamed she couldn't even tell her own parents who loved her. She couldn't speak. The tears choked her throat. She leapt up and ran out of the room.

Mattie quietly wept in front of her mirror, tugging at tangled hair like it would somehow remove the horrible memory. Her mother opened the door. Mattie openly sobbed now into her mother's arms, looking with pleading eyes into her mother's kind face. How much she wanted to spill everything.

"Mother... I know father's angry because of me."

"Your father has a lot on his mind. I know you don't want to talk about it, but you have to for his sake. He loves you to bits, Mattie."

Mattie put an arm around her mother.

"Mother... I understand you want things to be right," Mattie spoke resolutely.

"Well then, act like you mean it, and go and confide in your father."

Bernie Baker was determined to protect his reputation, and filed charges with the Police against Mattie for damage to his Roadster.

·   ·   ·   ·   ·

The following morning, Mattie and Arthur went to the police station for her statement.

Mattie stared out the window at the same cliff top as they drove down the steep hill. She grimaced with her heart pounding in anticipation at what the police would ask. She had made up her mind... she wasn't going to tell. They walked up the steps of the police station. Arthur held the heavy door for her. The constable at the desk looked up above his glasses. Arthur introduced himself and Mattie.

"Mr. Blanc," said the constable standing up, "please take a seat." He glanced at Mattie. "Miss Blanc, follow me."

Mattie glanced at her father and fell in line behind the constable. Their footsteps echoed down a narrow corridor, until he stopped and ushered her into a small room with even smaller table and chairs. Mattie eased into her chair, and scanned the room. She found herself counting the footsteps to the door and then glanced up, through the window, across the corridor and into a similar room on the other side. She stared at the back of a man's head... Bernie's head. Mattie jumped at the sound of the detective's voice. A small man in plain clothes appeared, introduced himself and sat down opposite Mattie as he opened his notebook.

"Miss Blanc, Mr Baker tells us you drove his car off a cliff," the detective spoke and stared without a flinch.

Mattie sucked in a breath and blurted out, "I was a passenger. I didn't harm Mr Baker's car... he only harmed me."

The detective threw his pen down, "Harmed you...? In what way?"

Mattie's lower lip wavered uncontrollably, "He's an animal. He harmed me."

The detective flipped his notebook closed, "We'll see about this." The detective rushed to the room opposite, slamming all doors on the way.

Mattie watched him throw his notebook onto the table in front of Bernie. She could not hear their voices, but she could tell by the motion of the detective's finger that Bernie was getting a lecture. The detective paced and then leaned into Bernie, never dropping his finger or stare. Mattie watched Bernie lift both hands. The detective grabbed his notebook and stormed away. Mattie stared at the floor as he returned, dreading the outcome.

"Miss Blanc... Mr Baker has agreed to drop all charges... but I have a little advice. In the future, if you have any ideas about wandering to a cliff top with some man in a thin dress, you need to think about it. Watch what you wear and where you place yourself. Are we clear?"

"Oh my God...," Mattie sobbed hysterically. She pulled out her handkerchief, wiped her nose and kept her head down. She forced herself, "Can I go?"

"You are free... follow me."

They walked down the corridor towards Arthur, "Mr Blanc, the charges have been dropped. Your daughter is free to go."

Arthur's lips tightened, "That man needs to be held accountable!"

Mattie knew a scene was coming. She grabbed his arm, "Father please... No... I don't want to relive this... it is over... please."

They walked from the building in silence.

CHAPTER 7

The boxcar jostled on into the night, travelling south. Charlie managed to lean against the heavy door to pull it closed a bit. Some figures were running down the track but not in the direction of the train. They waved their arms over their heads. Charlie wondered why. Was it a warning?

Roxy rested, slumped over her shotgun. She hadn't moved since the railcar lulled her to sleep. Charlie jostled upright against the boxcar door, as his eyes drifted downward to her dirt-stained face. Her eyes were closed, her head bouncing to the steady clang of the iron wheels as they rode over track seams and jerked ahead with the force of the engine. It was a frightening sound; one Charlie was still not used to.

A sudden tug of hunger urged him to reach inside his knapsack. The meat he had taken was still warm and pulled apart readily with two fingers. A bite of hickory-flavored hog meat sent a sudden rush of homesickness right down to the depth of his belly. He almost choked, coughing and wiping the flowing juices from his mouth. Roxy stirred and opened her eyes.

She sniffed and jerked up, grabbed her shotgun, and put out her hand.

"If you think you're gonna use that there gun on me every time you want something, missy, I'm a gunna shove you off this train." Charlie glared at her.

"No, you're not. I'll scream rape. Yep. I'll scream and screeeeeam."

Charlie stuck his greasy palm over her mouth and grabbed the shotgun.

"No, you're not," he shouted.

"I'm pregnant. You can't touch me," she muffled under Charlie's grasp.

He pushed her back. "What the hell?"

"That's why I ran away. I... I didn't want my folks knowing. They'd beat me."

Roxy wiped a dirty backhand across her dripping nose and stuffed it back in her pocket. "It was Joe. I used to follow you down there to the sand pit.

One night, there was more than a fight when we grabbed a jar of that bootleg whisky. I woke up and all my clothes were lying in the pit. I swear that's the truth."

"You wouldn't know truth if it hit you in the face."

"I had to leave. I—"

"You did something, didn't you?" He shook her until her teeth rattled to the sound of the tracks. "Tell, or I'll ditch you."

"I shot the doctor!" she screamed. "Shot him dead. I'm on the run."

"Roxy! Now you've dragged me into this. I don't want no trouble with the law…," Charlie gave her a gentle nudge, plainly agitated and unsure what to do.

"I'm sorry. I didn't have anyone else to turn to. I tried to get rid of the kid. The doctor wouldn't. I…it was an accident. I only meant to—aw, hell." Roxy shuddered and wept with her recollection.

Charlie handed her a piece of meat with a corn pone, and stared out into the night through the crack of the door. She was his friend. He gazed back into her sad eyes. *This was bad luck*, he realized.

"I won't be a nuisance. I know how to cook, and clean, and work. I'll find a job," Roxy pleaded weakly, fidgeting with her clothes.

"You don't even know where I'm headed. Look at you, you're just a girl."

Roxy lifted her cap. "I can disguise myself. See. I cut my hair."

Charlie looked at her pathetic form. She was tall for her age and now her hair was cropped short like a boy's. All he knew was, she was just like him… alone, afraid.

It's too late now. I have to think.

The eerie darkness sent a chill down Charlie's back. He latched on to the rest of the meat and handed it to her. "Cheer up kid, you got two to feed. Cuddle up. Rest." Charlie liked the feel of Roxy. There was something about her. He moved his hips apart from hers.

"You won't be sorry." Snatching the meat and pone, she shoved it in her mouth. The moon wasn't up yet, leaving the boxcar ink-black, except for the occasional light flashing past. Charlie's mind progressively dulled and drifted from exhaustion. With his belly full, nudged barely by the rhythm of the train, his eyelids fell, and his head soon after.

The train gave a sudden jolt, followed by a booming voice of authority. A light shone wildly in the crack of the door. The boxcar door was flung back, and a figure jumped inside from the side ladder. A pull on his shirt front, and Charlie was swinging under a stinking breath, staring into his half-shaven cheeks and crooked, yellow teeth. The beam of the flashlight nearly blinded him, but he saw the fist coming. He ducked. The man hit him with the flashlight, almost knocking him out.

"Got you, you nasty little hobo." He threw Charlie against the boxcar's wall. "Riding for free eh?" Charlie struggled to see past the pain. "This railroad bull's gonna teach you." He kicked him in the stomach with his boots.

The man drew out a pistol from his tattered blue uniform and aimed it at Charlie." "Gimme your money and those new boots."

"Not so fast Mister," Roxy roared in a deep voice. She stepped out from the back of the boxcar, her cap down to hide her face.

"Two of ya, is there… with a shotgun." The bull waved the torch into her eyes.

Charlie took his chance and seized the man's pistol. The train gave a lurch. He stumbled backward, off balance, into Roxy. The shotgun stock slammed down and fired right through the bull's belly, blasting him back toward the open door. He hung there for a moment, like today's laundry, teetering at the edge of the car.

The train leaned into a bend, and with a shocked yell, the wounded man fell out into the night. There was a dull thud and sickening crunch. Charlie closed his eyes, imagining the man had fallen beneath the thundering train wheels.

"We're gonna get it now," called out Roxy, her eyes gleaming in the darkness.

"No," said Charlie grabbing the shotgun. "We're heading east. We'll ride another hour, and then we'll jump down by the bayou. They'll never find us."

"How do you know where to go?"

"Shut up and do as I say. Get some rest."

The train rumbled and rocked them as Roxy dozed, but Charlie focused solely on the passing scenery. After awhile, the steam whistle blew as the train slowed to round another curve. He smelled it, no mistaking; they were at the bayou.

Roxy, wake up." He shook her until her eyes opened in fright. "We're jumpin'. Roll when you hit; don't try to catch yourself."

Charlie pushed Roxy toward the door then grabbed the gun, torch, and knapsack. Hands held, they leapt far from the moving cars and fell onto the soft muck of the bayou. He led Roxy towards the water to hide. The thickness of the mud reminded Charlie of his escape down that dreaded river at the orphanage. Roxy screamed. Charlie shoved the gun up her back.

"If you scream once more, I'll leave you to the 'gators."

"Huh?"

"This swamp is thick with 'em... huge slimy jaws, just waiting. I'm telling you. You wanted to follow me. Don't say I didn't warn you."

They crouched by the water's edge, listening. "We'll wait here till the moon comes up."

They heard something in the water. Charlie pointed the flashlight. Roxy muzzled a scream and stared. Charlie saw it too—eyes gleaming red, peering just above the surface. Their human scent must have attracted the beast.

Roxy stepped back abruptly and stumbled as she tripped over a slimy root. She shrieked again and fell backwards. The creature raced toward them at lightning speed. Charlie fired the shotgun at its head. They both fell back with the kick of the shotgun. The giant animal sank down into the swamp. Bleeding or just scared off, Charlie didn't care. He pulled Roxy out of the goo and back up the bank.

Charlie set her down and saw the worst. There was an open gash, the muscle exposed, and blood pulsed onto the soil.

"My leg," she cried, "I can't walk."

"Gotta get you outa' here," said Charlie.

He ripped a piece from his shirt and wrapped it around Roxy's leg as a tourniquet. He pulled it tight just until the blood stopped pulsing. He knew that Roxy must get to a hospital, and fast. *But what about the gun?* Charlie scanned the area and spotted a place. The large tree had a hole and cavity in the trunk... *musta been struck by lightnin'.* He cleared out the tree hole.

"You see this tree? Here, I'll mark it." He gripped his knife and scraped a heart into the tree bark.

Roxy grinned, "You gonna put our names in it?"

Charlie shook his head, eased the gun into the trunk, and grabbed her under his arm. "There's a clearing further down, but we'll have to stay back from the tracks."

There was no other way if he were to survive. Already he had killed a railroad bull and shot a 'gator. He was starting to think he was some kind of warrior.

Jackson Township brought back all those childhood memories of the merciless orphanage. Charlie wanted no part of the place. Nevertheless, he had to get Roxy to the local hospital. He couldn't just think of himself. He felt responsible for her; he'd take care of her.

•   •   •   •   •

The hospital smelled of alcohol… and death. Charlie gave a false name at the admission desk after they'd taken Roxy for treatment. He dipped into the leather pouch in his tattered pocket. It held coins gleaned from years of odd jobs and gambling at the pool hall. Charlie knew the value of the coins by touch and slipped two onto the counter.

He settled down to wait. Someone came after awhile and beckoned to him. They went down the passageway to where Roxy rested; her form displayed a deathly gray-white paleness and motionless foreboding. She didn't respond when he said her name. He placed his hand on hers, then withdrew to leave.

"You never did tell me what happened to your daddy."

Charlie whirled back around. Roxy's half-closed eyes locked onto his. He leaned into to her side.

"No, I never did." He paused. "You want to know why?"

Roxy nodded.

Charlie leaned closer. "How would you feel, if you were eight years old, and you watched your daddy's brains spill out when the saw cut his head off, right in front of you?"

Roxy screwed up her eyes and tears trickled out.

"You were right about the sawmill. He did work there, sawing all those trees for that goddamn track we rode down on."

"You're leaving me here, aren't you?"

"Only place you'll be safe. Go to sleep." He walked back to the reception desk and asked for a piece of paper. It was the best way. She'd never understand. But writing a letter was something he'd never done before.

She's one tough little bird. Be seeing her again... that's for sure.

He returned to the desk and handed in the note for Roxy.

"By the way, she's gonna have a kid," Charlie said.

"We know." The girl smiled.

Charlie walked towards the station flicking his knapsack, but bolted to a run at the sound of train whistles.

CHAPTER 8

It was no surprise to the Blanc family when another war was finally declared in September 1939. New Zealand and the rest of the Commonwealth Nations joined Great Britain in a declaration of war against Germany.

Mary remained calm, but Mattie knew what she was thinking. Young men had a different attitude in their eyes. This was real war, and it might be voluntary for now, but just over the horizon was conscription and a quiet send-off to distant battles. New Zealand and her men were expected to join the battlefields in Europe and North Africa.

George had already left for the Papakura camp, just out of Auckland, sporting the epaulettes of a lieutenant that his Bachelor of Dentistry degree earned him. John's internship had been cut short, finishing his six years of medical school at the end of the year.

Everywhere, people were taking their lives seriously, both in mind and spirit, waiting for Germany to arrive on their doorsteps. But they had other enemies to consider, as the news of war spread like a shot. New Zealand was a vulnerable and isolated nation. Even though its vast neighbor, Australia, loomed just across the Tasman Sea, that couldn't stop the rumors of a Japanese invasion. Both countries were at risk.

Mary's anxious pleas for Mattie to wed were too late, but young brother John was marrying Audrey, the secretary. A quick wedding before he departed for Auckland. It all seemed so cynical. Mattie wished she were anywhere but in a church, far off from the sound of her mother's choir and the sight of Audrey swishing past in white tulle.

Mattie left the reception at the botanical gardens with her father. Mary was staying on with members of the choir and didn't seem to mind. They drove up Pine Hill Road, beside the trickling Leith stream.

Mattie refused to let the memories abate her determination to get away, particularly now that war was declared. She blurted out, "Mother says I have to get married or else I'll have to work in a factory or chop cabbages."

"No you won't, there's plenty of nice men your brothers' know."

"I want a career… maybe a hairdresser. I've seen ads in magazines." She kept her gaze on her father, but his eyes never left the road. He didn't say anymore. Mattie decided to wait. She'd think of something to say after they arrived home.

Arthur parked the car in the single garage sliced into the hill. Mattie wanted a response, but there was silence until they sat down at the dining room table by the window. Arthur removed his hat, and studied Mattie's slumped posture and restless hands.

"You can light up," he said opening the window. "I know a lot of things you think I don't know." Leaning forward, he lit her cigarette with the lighter that was kept on the mantelpiece. "For one… you've taken up smoking."

Mattie inhaled, "and what else?"

Arthur sparked a second lighting his pipe, until the glowing embers filled the room with the sweet smell just from pipe tobacco. "Well, I guess we could blame all the things that go wrong on the war… the First World War, I mean. I met your mother well before, when I was naïve to things."

Mattie knew he was searching for the right words, words that would comfort her.

Arthur continued, "Thirty-three years ago I began my career as an engineer and married your mother." He drew in another puff. "By the time you and your brothers were born, war had broken out. With the construction of the tramway in place, my job was considered critical and I couldn't enlist... plus your mother needed me, even though she came from strong stock. The Shetland Islands are remote from Scotland. Tough people endure brutal Shetland winters. We met when she was very young."

Mattie wondered why he was bringing up his marriage. Was it to comfort her? Was it his way of drawing her out?

But Arthur continued nonchalantly, "Your generation will never know what hardships we went through. Our parents were the pioneers. They brought with them the memories of their lost homelands and we bore their burdens. I told you because I thought it would help you." He paused.

Mattie knew she could never get close to him. He was too stoic. But she somehow knew his love.

He pulled out his watch. "That's enough on this matter. I have important work to do. I must go out again."

Mattie stubbed out her cigarette in the ashtray, and went into the kitchen to wash aside the ashes and the tears welling up inside her. She wanted so much to hold her mother for whatever secrets lurked. It had to be so bitterly sad. Maybe she had a horrible childhood.

I need to get away.

CHAPTER 9

By now Charlie knew how to dodge the box-car bulls. He rode for free, sometimes sneaking a glimpse out the slates of the boxcar. Outside was mostly never-ending moonlit farmland with ramshackle houses. The boxcar rattled into the night till Charlie felt a thump as the brakes and bogies growled to a slower speed.

Dawn was breaking and he saw the sign: *New Orleans*. He grabbed his knapsack and jumped, scrambling across the railway tracks. He made his way decisively towards the dockyards to get a closer inspection of the Mississippi river. He stood for a moment shoving his hands in his pockets like he always did as he watched the wide river flowing past.

The docks, on the Gulf of Mexico, were crowded with ships of all kinds. Charlie learned in short order to watch for cargo operators. Led by their sweet aroma, it was easy to spot the bananas, piled high beside a huge boat from South America. They wouldn't miss a couple a bananas. Charlie shoveled down his breakfast in two gulps.

He heard men shouting. One of them called out, "Hey you."

"I'm looking for someone who can learn and take orders," said the older man.

The old man limped towards him. He had a weather-beaten face; everything about him was worn, including his Captain's cap. But his voice was loud and gruff. He looked Charlie up and down. "There's not much of you."

Charlie stood for awhile, thinking. "I'll work hard." Charlie beamed.

"You'll load bags of flour and ask no questions."

"I'll work harder than anybody," he said again. *Damn it. I'm going.*

Charlie grabbed his knapsack and followed him. They walked on down the docks until the old man ascended the gangplank of a steamboat.

A steamboat to Charlie was a whole new experience.

"Doesn't look as if you've been on one of these before." The old man puffed and chewed on his pipe.

"No, Captain."

"We dodge the sandbars up and down the Mississippi River," said the old Captain proudly. "Yessiree, the old Mississippi won't do nobody any harm. Jes' remember the river is boss. You sleep down here," he pointed to a hatch. Charlie peered down to the tiny bulkhead and scrambled down the ladder. It was a place to sleep, read his Ma's history book, and stay out of trouble. The old Captain, he'd come round.

CHAPTER 10

Waking up in the dark, early the next morning, felt like a nightmare to Mattie. John's wedding and her father's conversation. Why he wanted to talk... her mother... it all came flooding back to her. She slipped into a robe, looked in the mirror, speared fingers through tangled hair, and glanced down the passageway to the clock. Closing the door behind her, she meandered around the side of the house and up to the mailbox for the morning paper; then went and relaxed in warm sunlight on the window seat in the dining room.

George appeared, rubbing his head. "Where did you get to last night, Sis?" he asked, sitting down to light a cigarette.

"What do you mean?" Mattie went on looking for jobs at the situations vacant pages.

"Thought you might have frolicked off somewhere."

Mattie leaned over and George lit her cigarette. They both settled back for that first long draw, and stared at one another.

"You know what?" Mattie said sharply, "I'm leaving this place." She ground her cigarette out with a vengeance, her gaze burning through the newspaper.

George put down the paper, "Look... Why on earth didn't you confide in Mum?"

"She's got her own troubles."

"Nothing a daughter can't talk about, for Christ's sake," said George, taking a glance at his watch. "You know, last night was so much fun. I saw you leave with Dad. Why didn't you join us?" He started to laugh, bending over, his shoulders shaking. "Oh Mattie," he leaned back, "you're so serious about everything. Loosen up girl. Tell you what... you need a damn good screw." Then he started laughing again.

Mattie stood up, rolling up the newspaper and whacked him. "Yes, and you need that too."

"Bugger the war, I'd say, old girl. Move to Auckland with us."

"I might just do that," Mattie's tone was serious. She sank back down and conspicuously straightened the paper.

"What's in the work force for you anyway, Sis?"

"I've been out looking, but there's not many openings... not in Dunedin."

"What?"

Mattie stood up, "Well I'm not going to join the army, if that's what you think. I want a career. I want to make something of myself, like you have."

George jumped up, "Good show, Sis. Go for it. I'm departing tomorrow... up to Auckland. By the way, Irene's an Auckland girl; maybe she can find you a job." He put an arm around her, "Talk to Mum, they'll help."

CHAPTER 11

During the winter Charlie learned to handle the freight and stay out of trouble. He read his page-worn book from front to back in the hours he perched tucked undetected in a part of the steamboat nobody cared to visit. Charlie was used to sleeping anywhere.

They'd set off along the Mississippi River, delivering cargo to the ports up and downstream, and along the intercoastal Gulf. Charlie kept his mouth shut and memorized the ship's rules. His first grip of the wheel set him dreaming to sail the oceans of the world. The old Captain worked him hard, and Charlie responded with his best. Steadily the radio blared out news of the war in Europe, but Charlie could simply dream and listen.

February 1940 the Mardi Gras embraced New Orleans. It was a tradition, a transformation into a fantasy world. Working his shifts restricted Charlie's chance to go ashore, but on this one occasion, the city had gone crazy. He made his way through the crowd, searching the faces of clowns, feathers hiding faces, masks, dancing to the carnival calypso sounds of the music. It made him forget who he was, until a shove sent him flying. One of the figures, dressed in a cloak of feathers with an ornate mask threw Charlie onto the sidewalk. The tall, lean bird-creature glared at him through the mask eyes.

"Deserter."

Charlie picked himself up, staring into the mask.

"We're even now," said the figure.

Above the music, her voice was strong, "See, I can be anything I like." Turning around, the figure cast away the mask.

"Roxy, how did you get here?" Charlie was stunned at her reappearance.

"I got out of the hospital. I lost the kid. I knew you were heading south and came lookin'." Roxy started to move towards Charlie.

A man grabbed her, dragging her into the crowd. "Watch it, you tramp. Get back to work or I'll carve you up."

Charlie made a dive at the man, trying to pull him apart from Roxy.

The man glared at Charlie and laughed, "Who's this wise guy...?" He punched Charlie in the belly.

Roxy leaped in front of the man, her long arms outstretched, "He's my friend. Leave him be. I'll go with ya."

"We'll see about that." Charlie punched him, knocking him into the crowd. Something smashed over Charlie's head.

•　　•　　•　　•　　•

Charlie woke to quiet streets and an icy wind from the North. He stirred, and bolted up with a jolt when he saw the figure lying alongside him. He lifted up the feathers to see Roxy. It reminded him of her devotion in the box car. She peered up at him in the morning light, and placed his fingers on her breast, "Did ya miss me?"

Charlie felt her softness and instantly wanted another taste. He licked his lips. His gaze lingered deep into Roxy's eyes. She leaned up and kissed him. It all came back to him just as if they were on the school wagon; innocent Roxy leaning on him with her cheeky smile.

This opportunity Charlie could not control. He reached for a canvas tarp and rolled them into it. Roxy knew he was ready. Charlie lowered his pants and entered her, gently at first, then thrusting.

"Yes, come to me Charlie." Roxy pulled him into her and felt the explosion.

Charlie immediately regretted but savored this first taste of Roxy. The love and agony were equal.

"Roxy, I will never forget this," he panted, and rolled to one side.

His mind now pulled him elsewhere.

"Here, I got something for ya." She pulled out a piece of paper. "I saw it posted up in the streets. I went back for the shotgun, pawned it, and bought ya a ticket. It's a bus ticket... to go make war. Take it." Charlie frowned at the ticket; no one cared for him this way.

"What are you talking about?"

"It's what you wanted to do, go fight."

Charlie studied her. He caressed her wilted feathers, choking with emotion.

"Roxy. Criminee, what have you done with yourself?"

"You're my hero. I want to be with you."

"Listen, stupid. You take those feathers off, and go make something of yourself. Following me is not the answer." Charlie stuffed the paper into his pocket, seized Roxy by the hand, and they walked towards the river.

He stood looking up at her tall slender form. "Don't sell yourself short."

"But I'm nobody."

He pulled the history book out of his pocket and handed it to her, "Here, I've read this a dozen times. Learn about the world. Go do your best."

"But, Charlie, I love you. I want to be with you."

"You can't love me. Love is maybe not for us. We're great pals... my love now is the wide open sea."

"You got another, is that why you work on a boat?

"No. I don't have anyone. Here, take the bus ticket. I can get my own."

"Damn you, Charlie Kincaid, I hate you." She threw the book over the dock into a crate, and screamed, "Just you wait, I'll show you." Roxy ripped apart handfuls of feathers and threw them at Charlie.

Charlie jumped under the wharf, "Get along, Roxy. There's plenty of good men out there." He fished the book out of the crate.

"I hate you."

Charlie just grinned, "No you don't. Like I say, we're best pals. You're a survivor, just like me. Be seein' ya."

"You'll never see me again." Roxy ran, half stumbling over piles of cargo.

Charlie watched her go. *Damn girl's got a will,* he felt, *she'll make it.*

He opened up the notice Roxy had given him: Calling for able-bodied men. Report to the US Navy Recruiting Station, New Orleans no later than 1800 hours March 9th, 1940.

Charlie watched Roxy down the docks, half wondering what would happen to her. Then he cast his eyes to the moving waters. *Roxy, dear Roxy... you have shown me the way.*

•　　•　　•　　•　　•

The old Captain had given Charlie many a turn at the wheel. Under his strict orders they had maneuvered up and down the Mississippi. Charlie stood at the wheel, now lost in his memories. He knew he had to say what was on his mind. He looked into the old man's eyes.

"What's with you, son?"

"I want to join the Navy."

The old Captain laughed aloud.

"I thought I should let you know."

"Huh, you're just a greenhorn."

"I can learn. I can sail. You've taught me everything I know."

"That I did, son." The old man squinted out the bridge's dirty window. "That I did." He pushed his collar up against the bite of the wind off the sea and filled his pipe with tobacco. He pulled in hard and handed it to Charlie.

"Here. If you're going to be a Navy man, take a puff."

Charlie's eyes lit up. Determined to measure up, he dragged with gusto and immediately wheezed and coughed non-stop.

The old man gave him a big thump on the back. "Come on, my boy. Let's get you signed up."

After docking that morning, they walked together down the road towards the township and into the Courthouse. The Chief was familiar with the routine and led Charlie through the procedure. He was to become an Able Seaman, United States Navy.

Charlie smiled to himself. *Soon gonna be a long way from Falkner. This is my chance.*

CHAPTER 12

The following day Mattie felt better after talking to George. She'd get a job and save up her money. Somehow, she was sure her family would help her get to Auckland. George was her best friend. He always knew her inner secrets.

She put on a lace blouse, stepped into a pleated skirt, gleaming black heels, and rolled her hair into a chignon. She was determined not to let this endless turmoil of war get the better of her.

Mattie joined her father in the dining room with her tea. Mary stood by the kitchen doorway, wiping a hand on a worn apron, holding the teapot in the other.

"I've been thinking," Arthur put the paper down. "Why don't you both look into a booking to join George in Auckland, before he leaves for the war zone?"

Mattie gulped her tea, almost choking. "What?" she said. Her teacup rattled into its saucer, almost spilling. *He must have been reading my mind.*

"I may have to take a trip," Arthur held the paper up while he spoke.

"When?'

"Soon... next couple of months. You've plenty of time to prepare."

Arthur rolled the paper up, tucked it under his arm and stood up. He followed Mary into the kitchen. Mattie waited, her heart pounding with excitement at the sudden news. She watched the two of them in hushed conversation.

After Arthur left for the day, Mattie and her mother cleared the breakfast plates and settled in the dining room to finish their morning tea.

Mattie seized the moment, "Mother can I search in Auckland for a job, training, maybe Hairdressing?"

Mary then confided in Mattie that she and Arthur had been actively looking for opportunities in Auckland for her.

Mary went on, "Your father hasn't told you, but there is imminent danger out there. Hitler is planning attacks beyond Europe—even here in New Zealand."

"I know… I've read the newspapers," replied Mattie, steeling herself.

Mary went on to explain that Arthur is sailing to Vancouver in the *Niagara,* and they are planning to see him off in Auckland. He's traveling across Canada and the Atlantic, back to England on business.

"Isn't that dangerous?" exclaimed Mattie.

"Everything's dangerous in wartime." Mary rubbed Mattie's hand as she continued to explain they had found out, under the war regulations that Mattie was not going to end up in any ammunition factory. Hairdressing was a critical skill that was needed for women's morale.

Mattie leaped up and held her mother in a full hug, "Oh mother, you're the best! And here's me going on about my career… and you knew."

But work regulations were changing. Mary revealed there was an exclusive Auckland hair academy, run by a married couple, the O'Hara's.

"In Auckland?" Mattie shrieked.

"Yes, we have an appointment at O'Hara's Hairdressing Academy in Auckland." Mary smiled with her best Cheshire smile.

"But Mother… you did all this for me?" Mattie held her mother close, hard, making sure her mother would never forget. Mother and daughter… never to dismiss this moment of love and devotion, knowing that the future would bring opportunity, but separation. Both sons were off to war, and now Mattie.

Assuredly, Mary broke the silence, "But I have your father to look after. Isn't that enough?"

•　　　•　　　•　　　•　　　•

Arthur slipped into his Masonic Lodge headquarters, past its entrance between huge pillars with their reed-like Grecian fluting. He was the Grand Master. Events were never shared with the world outside; Arthur never spoke of his fraternity with the Masons. They were a fraternity all of their own. A small gentleman came towards him, offered the secret handshake, and led him into an adjacent chamber.

"Have a seat," said the man.

Arthur removed his thick overcoat, placed his hat on the stand, and eased into the black leather seat opposite. He glanced at the Freemasons coat of arms on the wall, filled his pipe, lit it, and relaxed back.

"We have everything in place, Mr Blanc," said the man, lighting his cigar and puffing it to a red glow. "We are depending on your discretion with the oversight of the gold bullion. Every box will contain two bars of gold, weighing four hundred ounces each, as you know. Britain desperately needs this consignment to help fund the war. It is a call to arms."

"Yes, I am aware of that," said Arthur gravely. "There have been sightings of German submarines in the Hauraki Gulf? If Britain gets wind of this, there'll be no sailing."

"I understand, sir, but the *Achilles* and *Hector* are in port; there shouldn't be any interference."

He reassured him, placing his hand on Arthur's arm and wished him a safe journey.

CHAPTER 13

Charlie sailed through Basic Training, Carpenter School, and couldn't wait to board the Greyhound bus. He settled down in his seat, stared at his orders, and dreamed of his new life as a Navy Diver.

It was a cold winter's day when the bus arrived at the entrance to the Navy Deep Sea Diving School after hours of being on the road. With nothing else but a seabag and his history book, Washington DC would be a big change for Charlie from Falkner, Mississippi.

Charlie stepped out into the icy cold and faced into the brutal wind. He stopped, and stretched one kinked leg, then the other. Iron-strong fingers buttoned his pea coat up square over his lean silhouette, and he hoisted a seabag over his shoulder.

Charlie scanned the mass of Navy-grey concrete and weatherboard buildings, and paused as he read the words Experimental Diving Unit. A spark of anxiety raced into his mind, but he in a flash quelled it to calm. *I can do this.*

He strode towards a spot where two other seamen from the bus stood waiting, and tipped his cap at them. They gave him a nod. He remembered his belly sliding across the warm, soft bottom of Muddy Creek, but knew the swimming here would be neither warm nor soft. They walked in silence towards the black iron gates, each balancing their own heavy loads.

A Petty Officer directed them inside, and after a lengthy orientation, Charlie was assigned his locker and bunk. The barracks were nothing more than a glorified tin shed with too many windows and cracks in the wooden floorboards that allowed the winter winds into the iron bunks, stacked two high. But that was fine with Charlie. Compared to his straw bed, this bunk was destined to be paradise.

Charlie and the other seamen paraded towards the chow hall. He was starving after the long ride and smelled the feast before he saw it. Steaming hot pans of beefsteak, chicken, pork, potatoes, and heaps of beans and greens, boiled up before them. Every man grinned as a large helping of each hit his plate.

Beans... just like home, Charlie remembered as he eased himself into one of the chairs. He ate with his head down low, as he listened to the rest of the table hubbub.

"Hey you, handicap," one of the voices called out but Charlie ignored it. He went on shoveling in his steak and beans. "I'm Victor Houston," the voice chuckled, "in the making."

A fist banged the table.

Charlie dropped the fork into his beans. He clenched his fists; he always faced his problems head on. He looked up at Victor's square-jawed face and imagined his knuckles busting his chin.

"What's your name? Aren't you gonna say somethin'? Or them beans gonna say it for you?" Victor said, elbowing the seaman adjacent to him.

"Kincaid," answered Charlie.

"Kin-caid, heh?"Victor grinned, raising an eyebrow.

Charlie kicked his chair back and stood up, rocking the table with his jerked knee, and stared into Victor's laughing brown eyes.

"What's so funny?"

"You, that's what!" Victor said.

Leaning across the table, Charlie grabbed Victor by his collar, pulling his thick shiny head forward with tousled popcorn fair hair.

Victor's grin widened.

A whistle interrupted the faceoff and the Petty Officer in charge of the mess hall yelled across the room, "Newcomers at table number four prepare for kitchen patrol." The Petty Officer ordered the group into the galley.

His meal not finished, Charlie glared at Victor.

For the rest of the afternoon, the new seamen groveled, scrubbing scorched dirty pots, and disposing of food scraps in the heavy-duty grinder.

"You owe us for this," a sailor alongside Charlie said.

Charlie caught a backlash of discontent from a couple of men. It wasn't his fault; it was Victor's for instigating the trouble. Victor hovered over a large stainless sink, busy scrubbing dishes and murmuring something to another seaman. Charlie wasn't sure what they were talking about, but he figured it was totally further grief. Victor might be trouble. Boot camp was no different from this.

• • • • •

Next morning, the bugle sounded reveille. Charlie leapt down from his bunk in rumpled long johns, searching for his uniform under the flailing arms and legs of his fellow seamen.

A figure appeared at the entranceway, shouting, "AttennnHut!"

Charlie stood stiff, eyes straight ahead. The Master Chief had a neat moustache, his hat firmly planted—or more like glued on his head. The Chief stopped in front of Charlie, tapping a riding crop against his leg.

"OK sea slug, Name and Rate."

"Carpenter's Mate Kincaid, reporting for Deep Sea Dive Training, Chief."

"Deep Sea Diving, eh?" the Chief poked his crop into Charlie's chest and hauled him around to oppose the team. "Is there anyone else who wants to be the class clown here today?"

No one answered. All faces stared directly ahead.

"So, we have our first lady for tank duty." He shoved Charlie against his bunk, and flailed his stick midair as if to use it. "I am Master Chief Petty Officer O'Shea." He walked as he spoke. Reaching the doorway, he swung around, "In case any of you are thinking this is some sort of fishing party, guess again… there's a war on in Europe!"

Charlie was dying to say, "*No, This is a riding course.*" The Chief stomped back towards him.

Charlie imagined he was back in the circus; he remembered the elephant and the trainer whipping his poor flesh until blood oozed in buckets. *Maybe this jerk needs a whipping*, he thought.

"Wipe that smirk off, Kincaid." He twitched his crop. "None of you, and I repeat, none of you, have the balls to become a Navy Diver." He paced and slapped the riding crop against his thigh, "That's my job—to give you balls and turn you into the best. We will soon uncover the pussies." The Chief pivoted again to Charlie, "Why did you come here?"

"The Navy's my home." Charlie answered, and promptly wanted to erase the words.

"Your home?" the Chief cut in laughing. "This ain't no homecoming. You men are in for the most brutal and dangerous job in the Navy."

The Chief slapped his crop against the bunk. "You all have survived your specialty schools. But diving is where we separate the chaff; it's all brains and bodies here. The depths will bury your bullshit. *Am I clear?*"

"Aye, Aye Chief!" filled the room.

Charlie stood stiffly, eyes aimed straight ahead. He didn't want to draw any extra attention to himself.

"Double-time to breakfast, and then report to the diving tank 0800 sharp." The Chief stormed out of the barracks.

Charlie and the other seamen inhaled their sausage and eggs, and barreled back to their barracks to get ready for the tank.

Victor stood in front of Charlie. "Kinky, that's what I'm a-gonna call you," Victor said, flinging a clump of sodden clothes at Charlie. "And Vic's the name."

Charlie lunged at him.

"Wow, too much bean power, eh son?" Vic grinned as he dodged Charlie.

Charlie had had enough insults. Vic towered over Charlie's lean frame, but Charlie had pool hall training. He took a swing at his tormenter. Vic ducked and fell into the squeaking bunk, sagging almost to floor level.

A voice then boomed from a speaker, "Now hear this. Now hear this. Seamen from number four barracks report to the main building for tank training." The loudspeaker repeated the message, and the men scattered.

Charlie straightened what was left of his uniform and tore out through the door. He almost knocked over Chief O'Shea, who was still holding his bullhorn. Charlie stopped and saluted.

"Don't salute me, Kincaid. I'm a workin' man," O'Shea said, and walked on towards the tank shed. Charlie followed him down the path, aware and nervous now. *Nice job Kincaid.* He might as well have painted a target on his shirt. "I'm ready, dead ready," Charlie said to himself. He held his head high and followed.

Inside the experimental tank shed were two main water tanks, with a wooden ladder hung over the sides and several diving suits, hung in a line on a platform beside the tanks.

O'Shea had put on his full-length foul weather gear, with fingers clutching the Diving Manifold.

Charlie had read about these machines in the library, but had never seen one. Two huge tanks filled the shed with their looming pipes and gauges. But the mammoth wheels at the bottom caught his attention.

"Here we have the Helium-Oxygen Diving Manifold. You ladies will learn the meaning of gas mixtures, pressure, and how to not die from exploding lungs." He kept a grip on the wheel, his Irish brogue echoing off the concrete and steel. "Learn to control your breathing, and you'll live inside the ocean," he said louder as he cranked up the machine.

"That ocean is more your home than the bed on your ship." He caught Charlie's eye. "Maybe Kincaid wants to be a Naked Diver. Eh?"

Nobody commented. The steady clicking of the machinery made every man stare across at the water.

"Move it, you pussies, no good staring at the water. Tell me, who's a Naked Diver?"

There was a murmur. "A sea scout, Chief."

"Who said that?"

"I did Chief," said an unseen voice, behind Charlie.

"Who?"

The man stepped out. "Seaman Holland, Chief," said a small man with elf-like ears underneath disheveled hair. He lifted his arm.

"Good God, can hardly see you," O'Shea notably ignored him.

"A naked diver separates the men from the boys. In your first week of training here, you *will* learn the value of friendship, loyalty, and the meaning of war. He kept his gaze on Seaman Holland, now standing in view.

O'Shea likes to pick on the little guys, Charlie realized. He'd try to befriend Holland, if the man was willing.

Taking his grip off the wheel, O'Shea moved towards the diving section. "Can anyone tell me what this is?" he asked, pointing to the large copper headpiece.

"A hard hat, Chief," the seamen all replied.

He swung the suit on the line, towards Charlie. "Of course it's a fuckin' hat."

"A Mark V Mod 1,"Charlie said in a low tone.

"Excellent. Let's see it on. Tenders, dress the diver."

Charlie stripped to his long johns, and stepped into the rubberized canvas suit, in Navy terms, a dress.

This jerk might be trouble, he thought to himself, as he felt the hardness of the canvas suit over his sinewy form and forced his feet into the thirty-six-pound, lead-soled shoes. He glanced across at O'Shea, who was still watching him while hanging onto the wheel of the Manifold.

"Get the lead out, we haven't got all day. There's a war on, but you ladies wouldn't know." He fiddled with the dials, "This clown here can sound like the clown he is, with a mixture of too much helium. Am I right?"

"Yes, Chief," said the group.

Pointing to Vic, "Help dress Kincaid."

Charlie squatted on the diver's stool, facing his future team players, wondering why he was chosen to be the first. *Can I trust this prick, O'Shea*? He wondered what his game was.

Vic and the other tenders bolted the heavy brass breastplate to Charlie's suit. He hesitantly put his arms through the shoulder straps of the eighty-pound lead-weighted belt. A sudden feeling consumed him. *Fear*. He was going to be sick.

This was it. This was what he had wanted to be. But Charlie's small frame made him a target. The son-of-a-bitch. He was hoping Charlie would collapse in front of all his classmates, fail the test, then he'd send him back to Falkner.

Charlie breathed steadily. His tree-climbing days held him sturdy. He rose, held his head proud, and gestured toward the heavy copper helmet. A lifting ring steadied him, keeping the weight off as the helmet swung towards his head.

He watched Vic through the glass, unflinching, as they secured the helmet to the breastplate with a twisting motion and motioned him towards the water.

With ease and confidence, Charlie climbed down the wooden ladder into the depths of the fifty-foot tank, sinking into the chilled silence of the water chamber, his vision restricted to the view from the small glass ports of his helmet.

"He won't know how this feels," O'Shea yelled over the engines, as he spun the wheel. "After he's been compressed at the thirty-foot mark, we'll see if he's still the team's clown."

To demonstrate a problem, O'Shea reduced the helium admixture, but without warning the valve slammed shut, switching the breathing mixture to pure compressed air.

It was too sudden.

Charlie scarcely heard O'Shea's muffled Irish brogue, *he won't know...* Charlie knew the mixtures had gone wrong, nitrogen narcosis; he'd read about it but it was too late. He felt dizzy, euphoric, and buckled over. He began to sink. "*Nitrogen narcosis. Get your mixtures right, O'Shea,*" Charlie bellowed into the microphone.

The lifeline rope went slack as Charlie collapsed to the tank bottom.

O'Shea ran to the edge, yelling at Vic to give the wire two pulls; but there was no response. The men pulled Charlie up, wobbling and swaying. The tenders helped him to the stool, with Vic's large hands unscrewing the helmet. They lifted the rest of the heavy equipment to one side, and Charlie inhaled a deep breath of fresh air.

Water poured out over the feet of the anguished seamen trying to get a closer look at the action. Charlie pretended to slump forward.

Vic bent down, whispering in his ear, "Sorry Kinks, you made a star of yourself." He patted Charlie on the back.

Charlie spluttered.

Helping him to his feet, Vic added, "Keep that up, and you'll be in for a medal."

Charlie winked at Vic as the two men exchanged glances.

There was a look of concern on O'Shea's face as he shouldered his way in front of the seamen to get a closer view. "How exactly do you feel?"

Charlie didn't answer him, but gasped a gulp of air, and paused to eyeball the men. He squashed his cheeks together, his features distorted, and swayed in an uncontrolled manner. There was silence.

Vic caught his eye. Charlie braved another wink at him.

O'Shea banged at the equipment in frustration, until his face reddened like a radish gone berserk. Charlie suspected that experiment had gone wrong.

The Chief yelled, "Class dismissed."

Charlie and Vic left together, relieved the first day of tank training was over.

•   •   •   •   •

Liberty came as a relief from the constant tests. The promise of a beer and warm hospitality was an inviting idea as the bus pulled up outside a group of shops and hotels in Washington DC. Charlie had noticed mainly the beautiful parks. It was the land he missed and the smell of hog meat in the smoker. But still, the lure and power of massive buildings and proud statues reminded him of his duty and mission.

Charlie and Vic leapt off the bus but scurried in separate directions. Charlie reached for his buttons, as springtime in Washington was no stranger to icy winds.

A few of the men had gone into the shops, their white hats bobbing amongst the shelves of a store across from him. He caught site of Vic opening the door of a beauty salon, and then hugging a bodacious black girl. It looked as if they knew each other by the way she hugged him.

Charlie crossed the street at the corner, leaning into the biting wind blasting his head. He stood outside one of the saloons listening to the raised voices. He spotted through the windows that this place could be a fight or a frolic in five minutes, just like Falkner.

Charlie swung open the saloon doors, eased inside, and stopped to savor the smell and commotion. *Bit busier than home.* He couldn't wait to grab a cue and separate some locals from their money.

Thick cigarette smoke curled up from the pool tables, punctuated by the hard sound of balls clicking together. He found a table, grabbed a cue, and chalked it. Charlie was soon winning game after game. Across the table Vic appeared. He jerked his head in the direction of the music in the other room. Charlie gathered up his stakes, and the two of them left.

"Hey you, sailor boys, get your asses back here with that money," a man slurred and tipped half his beer onto Charlie's boots.

Another local made a lunge at them.

"We don't owe you nothin'," said Vic, standing tall over the man.

"You owe us to stay. We wanna chance to win our money back, jerkheads," the drunk said.

"Let's go, Kinks, give him nothing. Don't fuck with divers." Vic elbowed the man back hard.

The drunk winced, holding his bruised rib. Charlie and Vic walked out of the saloon.

Vic put his fingers into his jacket and pulled out a shiny case. "Here have one of these." Vic tapped a pencil-slim cigarette on top of the shiny lid.

"Needed your help. I was out-gunned in there."

"For a southern boy, you don't miss with that cue, do ya?

Charlie grinned. "Nope."

●   ●   ●   ●   ●

During their serious studies in the classroom, Charlie sometimes drifted to reflect on his childhood. He had trouble sharing much of his life with members of the team. He knew he had to trust them. They'd be on missions together. But with so much hurt inside, solely the depths of the sea brought him relief. Now there was so much additional to overcome.

"I don't know why I'm standing here, when you men only get half what we teach," Lt. Barrows said in front of the classroom of seamen, breaking Charlie's study.

Lt. Burrows wasn't much of a comfort when the test results came back, with an average of fifty percent. Charlie's palms sweated as his fingers slid down the pencil at the tone of the officer's words.

The man was an intellectual, further removed from the military than Charlie could imagine. He had an arrogant air about him, and a habit of running a finger down the right side of his nose, like he was chasing something excess.

Charlie was distracted during the lecture, and Burrows' eyes rested on him.

"You, Kincaid, with the vacant stare. Why is Boyle's Law so important?"

Charlie stood up. "It describes the behavior of gases, sir."

"That's obvious, what else?"Burrows sneered.

"If a diver holds his breath at a hundred feet and keeps on rising to ten feet, the pressure in his lungs increases four times as much. If he forgets to exhale, his lungs will explode."

"So," Burrows leaned on his desk, and with the slightest nod for Charlie to sit, he went on in his slow tone. "We've had some incidents that have gone horribly wrong but we've learned from them." He pointed to Seaman Smith in the front row. "Name a recent disaster."

The seaman replied, "The war."

"You idiot."

"Sorry, sir, but isn't that why we're here?"

Burrows went back to his desk and removed a file of papers, not answering.

Charlie stood up. "Sir, what about the USS *Squalus*?"

Burrows eyed Charlie. "Well, Seaman Kincaid, you should know that answer, especially after the mix-up with your first dive." He paused, rocking back on his heels. "Kind of preys on your mind, doesn't it, when things go wrong?"

Charlie didn't answer him. Instead, he sank back down, shocked by Burrows' words.

Burrows continued to walk amongst the men, in between tables, handing out papers as he spoke. "In this particular test dive, just two years ago, the USS *Squalus* sank in 243 feet and twenty-six men died. A McCann Rescue Chamber, specially fitted to connect with the submarine's deck hatch, rescued the other thirty-three men. Analyze this experiment and think about a better way for a rescue. Make up your own design as a practice run. We need to learn from all these tragic incidents. Loss of lives must be minimized, whether it's war or not. New ways to mix gas are continually being developed and improved. You men will leave here with the right knowledge to fight, save lives, and repair ships."

Burrows continued to lecture them on equipment, and the history of diving. Charlie tuned out again. He was already thinking of how he could improve upon the McCann Rescue team's approach.

•　　•　　•　　•　　•

Charlie had left the classroom deep in theorization when Vic appeared, shaking his head, "So what ya think about all that technical stuff? Kinda blows your brains out, doesn't it?"

Charlie frowned, "We're all having a bit o' trouble."

Vic shrugged and spat on to the concrete as they continued towards the barracks.

Charlie's outlook on life had been shaped by grief and hard work since the orphanage. He considered being alone forever, but trust was becoming a new friend. He turned to Vic, "Look, ain't nothin' wrong sharing some ideas on a design. Why don't we do this rescue chamber together?"

Vic's eyes lit up. "Swell." Charlie detected Vic was pleased.

A few weeks later Burrows announced, "The results are on the notice board. Well done, A team." He smiled and left the classroom. Nobody knew the 'A team' and all raced for the notice board.

Charlie grinned at Vic as he read the notice – *Top Honors A Team – Kincaid & Houston.* "We did it, we passed the salvage test." They smashed knuckles and sauntered out into the sunshine.

Charlie gave Vic a knowing glance from inside the view port before the copper helmet was bolted shut onto his breastplate. No more hesitation. No more practice. The deep sea was waiting to teach or kill. Exhaustion became his friend.

•   •   •   •   •

After months of training, Burrows and Chief O'Shea stood in front of the classroom.

"Class, we are now at a crossroads, and I am turning this session over to Chief O'Shea to complete your indoctrination," Burrows said. "Chief?"

"Men, you have read and signed your Top Secret agreement to continue training," said O'Shea, his voice serious. "You might wonder why I carry a riding crop in the Navy. The fact is I started my military career in the Army as an Engineer. I am not just a qualified US Navy Diver... I'm also an expert in explosives from my Army training. You are the first class to enter into Top Secret training. You will become the most lethal weapon in the military. The agreement you signed states you will talk to no one about any content of the following course and training. That means your family, your priest, everybody in your life except me and the members of this unit. Are we clear?"

"Yes, Chief!" roared the men.

"Any of you who choose to blab about this course to any unauthorized persons will not be subjected some crap court martial. I will personally hunt you down, rip your head off, and shit in your neck. *Are. We. Clear?*"

Charlie gulped.

"Yes, Chief," repeated the men.

"Anyone wanting to leave, do so now. You can successfully continue your career as a US Navy Salvage Diver. Leavers, step out and pick up your orders."

Charlie noticed nobody moved.

"Excellent. Let's begin. I'm an expert Navy Diver, but you will be better. You will train to dive anywhere in the world. You will be experts in explosives, able to make what you need in the field for any assignment. Lt. Burrows is an Engineer, also trained in explosives. We have a vision and the authority to train you as the first Naked Warriors to silently enter enemy territory and gather intelligence, destroy assets, remove obstacles, or assassinate enemy commanders. You have demonstrated your ability as top swimmers with a team spirit, and you're smart. The only thing left is bravery and guts. Are you with me?"

"Yes, Chief!"

Over the following eight weeks, Charlie became skillful in analyzing structures and crafting explosives for their destruction. He was the best at swimming. Charlie felt his diver's knife become an extension of his hand that could build bombs or equally slide between ribs into an enemy heart. They studied anatomy and medicine to both treat their wounded buddies, and assassinate in silence.

Intense close combat training charged his dreams and instilled confidence. Charlie learned to trust his touch, like a blind man feeling his way into the silent, dark world of the ocean. To Charlie the murky waters offered peace and security just like Muddy Creek in Falkner. But he knew dreaded unseen dangers could be inches or miles distant, just waiting to snare a sleeper. Calculation was the key, he surmised. *Gotta outthink 'em every step of the way.*

•   •   •   •   •

"All right, men," O'Shea said to the class. "You have completed your six months of training. You will be transported by train across country. You'll arrive in San Diego for further dive training on the submarine rescue vessel, USS *Ortolan*, and Camp Pendleton for live-fire explosives and hand-to-hand combat with the Marines. These aren't drills. Your ship of designation is the USS *Rigel*, originally the SS *Edgecombe,* an old cargo ship for flour and bananas. She's in Bremerton for conversion, and then on to Pearl Harbor for final refit.

"The *Rigel*'s an old beauty. Just missed the first war. She's one of a kind. No fancy array of battleship armor, but big as a Cruiser. Silent, proud, and the best repair ship on water."

Visions of massive ships raced through Charlie's mind, mixed with sweat and underwater swirls. He clenched his fist to regain concentration. *I have a job, a real job*, he thought with a smile.

O'Shea roared, "You men are in top form and our secret weapon to save thousands of lives, and don't you ever think otherwise. We are counting on you. Do you hear me?"

"Yes, Chief."

"I didn't hear that. Do the Navy proud!"

"Yes, Chief!" the men shouted back.

"After West Coast training, you'll report to the *Rigel*, Pearl Harbor, southeast dockside." He wailed around in his usual bulldog manner. "No fuckin' island paradise where you're assigned. Pack your sea bags and report to head office for ticketing and departure." He watched the group as they were leaving.

Charlie moved past him and caught his eye. "Don't forget to look for a four-leaf clover on that island shoreline, son." He winked at Charlie.

"I'll look, Chief, but I may have to make my own clover." He grinned and shook hands with the Chief he'd never forget.

CHAPTER 14

It was June of 1940 when Mattie and her parents made their long journey by train and by sea from quiet Dunedin in the deep South Island, to bustling Auckland in the North Island.

Mattie hardly noticed George and Irene waving from amongst the huge crowd. Irene appeared so gorgeous with her blonde hair rolled to perfection under a black pillbox hat, standing waving; she was taller than George, especially in her black heels. George gave Mattie a brotherly hug and started teasing her about her pale complexion. Mattie didn't have the energy to smile. She was glad when Irene put her hand out. She had a gentleness about her when she spoke. Mattie hardly heard her soft voice over the crowds. George was due back at his camp and wanted to get Arthur down to the wharf.

Mattie dodged the oncoming masses on the train station platform, *relishing* her chance of a new life.

Irene slipped her gloved arm inside Mattie's. "A good night's sleep and a bath will do you good. My flat's not far from your hairdressing school. You're staying with me tonight. It's more welcoming than a hotel, don't you think?"

"Are you sure? We can make other arrangements," said Mary.

"You can stay a couple of nights. Look in this area while you're here, why don't you?"

"I've arranged an open ticket return, so of course Mary, see how you feel," said Arthur, leading them outside to a waiting taxi, and helping everyone in.

The taxi swerved into Quay Street, and stopped at the corner of Queen Street, waiting for the traffic officer on his pedestal to give a signal to turn. The Ferry Building stood to their right with its orange brick archways, fairy-like pinnacle clock tower and pillars, all glowing against the evening sky. At the signal, the taxi turned and stopped outside the wrought-iron gates that lined the wharves on Quay Street. Stepping out of the taxi, Mattie marveled at the cityscape up Queen Street, and realized how different it was to Dunedin. A light rain brushed against her cheeks.

"Come on Mattie, stop daydreaming," called George. He poked his head inside the taxi window and looked at the driver, "We'll be seeing my dad off on the ship, but please wait… the rest of us and luggage will go on to the top of Queen Street."

"No worries, sir," replied the taxi driver.

The *Niagara* towered above them as they walked towards her, amazed at her size and opulence. People were gathering closeby the gangway, carrying bursting suitcases, shopping bags, and stumbling into each other to gain access to a porter.

"I'm going aboard to see what time she sails. I'll be back," said Arthur. He ascended the gangway. Stepping onto the quarterdeck, he followed the ship's purser to the bridge of the ship.

"Welcome aboard," said the Captain, shaking Arthur's hand.

"Pleased to meet you, Captain."

"This way, we have business to discuss."

Arthur followed the Captain to his cabin. This captain's cabin smelled of wax and leather as they entered its sumptuous interior. Shelves of books in carved wooden bookcases stood behind a large walnut desk with green leather inlays, polished to perfection.

"Please, have a seat," said the Captain, motioning to the two leather-studded swivel chairs. The Captain offered to light Arthur's pipe and sat back, sucking on his own pipe.

"Tell me about the *Niagara*," Arthur began.

"Never missed a port yet sir… safe as the day she was launched. She's even sailed through the Great War, you know. They call her the *Lucky Niagara*," replied the captain.

"You have the bullion?" Arthur asked, wanting to get to the point.

"Yes, we've packed them, on D-deck, all 295 wooden boxes," the Captain winked at Arthur, "alongside the Chief Purser's office. He is responsible, and will answer to me personally."

"Well, actually he will answer to me on the bullion."

"Yes, apologies, sir…"

They shook hands. Arthur left the quarterdeck and descended the gangway.

"Everything go alright?" asked Mary, as he came towards her.

"Yes, don't worry. I've sailed many times before."

"I know Arthur, but… "

"This is just another business trip to everyone." He spoke in a low voice to her. "Nothing to worry about. I'm going to England… that is all." Arthur acknowledged the rest of the family, "I'll be checking the engineer's report on the triple-expansion engines. I'm an engineer myself, don't forget."

"We certainly won't forget that one, Dad," said George, shaking his father's hand.

Arthur stepped to Mattie, "Now, don't let me down, my dear… this is your chance to excel."

"I won't, Father, and thank you. I will do my best, as always."

"It's a late sailing. I don't want you to wait," said Arthur, giving Mary a hug and a peck on the lips. Mary stepped aside and clutched Mattie's arm. She looks tired, Mattie judged.

"Sensible," said George, "I'll look after the womenfolk until you return."

"Not for very long, my son. You'll be off yourself soon," warned Arthur.

Irene glanced at George, and he shrugged his shoulders.

"Yes. Fiji. Can't wait... Please ladies, taxi's waiting with your luggage," he replied.

Arthur ascended the gangway. He signaled to his family, and watched them waving back. He turned from their view and descended to his quarters, past the magnificent first-class dining room. It had been a long day. He ordered a full dinner to be delivered to his cabin, and retired for the evening.

•   •   •   •   •

As the German merchant raider *Orion* approached the New Zealand coast, her radio operators were astonished to receive local commercial radio broadcasts reporting all the daily shipping and aircraft movements. New Zealand, so remote from the havoc in Europe, was still in a blissful sense of security, unaware that a deadly enemy was entering their coastal waters.

They used their radio direction finder to flawlessly home in on Hauraki Gulf. Through the night of June 13th, 1940, the *Orion* painstakingly laced *all* the approaches to the Hauraki Gulf with its cargo of 228 mines. Navigating and also revealed by blazing lighthouses, they laid their barrage of mines from Great Mercury to Cuvier to Great Barrier to Mokohinau Islands, and eventually northeast towards the mainland.

Orion's mines lay moored at deadly depths, deep enough for just big ships, lurking, as their detonator caps dissolved to become active... waiting for the ocean to deliver its prey.

CHAPTER 15

Charlie and Vic relaxed at the back of the undulating railcar, the coal smoke from the steam engines seeping through the cracks surrounding the windows and creating a dingy haze inside.

In Charlie's mind, nothing much had changed from the boxcar days when he ran away from Falkner with his schoolmate Roxy. He grinned, chuckling to himself... *Roxy, you li'l beauty. Good thing she showed up with that shotgun.*

The whistle blew, jolting Charlie back to reality. He slumped back into the dark-red padded, leather upholstery. The train stretched its bogies up a hill, behind powerful steam pistons, heading west. Trains to Charlie would always feel dirty and noisy, but they clacked with the sound of freedom.

After shifting trains in Los Angeles, Charlie soaked up his first sight of the Pacific Ocean as they approached San Diego. The warm sea breeze hit him as the train slowed to a halt. He grabbed his seabag and headed off the train, and then out of the station where he and the other men caught a bus to the foot of Broadway pier.

He reported to the USS *Ortolan* for the continuation of his dive training. Through some mishap in the Navy, there was also another group of eight second-class divers on board for training. Charlie and the other men were far greater experienced, so after just a week of diving, they were transferred to Camp Pendalton for further demolition and combat training. Their real mission was unclear, even the USS *Rigel* remained a mystery, but Charlie had a feeling the Navy had plans. Big plans.

•　　　•　　　•　　　•　　　•

In July 1941, Charlie received his orders for Honolulu, Hawaii. He and the other men travelled by train up the west coast, winding through the massive rugged coastline to San Francisco, just in time to board the USS *Henderson* bound for Hawaii.

Charlie marveled at the powerful currents and eddies as they passed Fort Point and headed under the Golden Gate Bridge. The confusing seas soon had the *Henderson*'s bow pitching to the heavens and dropping hard into pounding seas. Charlie went astern and watched the coastline disappear as they left the main ship channel.

Amidst a groaning mass of nauseous, homesick sailors, Charlie drew in the sea air and admired the power of the mighty Pacific Ocean. The ship moved along at eighteen knots, and Charlie imagined he was on a speedboat.

Hawaii: the very name excited the troops onboard, and the constant bouts of vomiting were soon forgotten as early morning brought the shores of Waikiki rising above the horizon off the port bow. A green land, thick with vegetation, ablaze with hazy pink and chocolate-colored mountains, drastically changed as the ship rounded the corner of Pearl Harbor and slowed to five knots.

Charlie ogled the first fleet of battleships that circled Ford Island. The USS *California* gave reason to their mission. A feeling of respect unexpectedly fell upon him as he stood there in amazement, his eyes fixed on the strength and the size of the battleships. A symphony of whoops and hollers lifted from the decks surrounding him, men proud at the power before them. The USS *Henderson* sailed past amassed battleships docked in the harbor—the USS *Maryland* with USS *Oklahoma* nested to port side. Their Captain maneuvered and docked their ship abreast the USS *Rigel*.

The orders were clipped out fast in military fashion, and Charlie didn't have a moment for any idle gawking at monster battleships. He could not wait to board this old destroyer tender being converted to a repair ship. His new home, the USS *Rigel*.

Charlie stood still on the dock under the clear blue Hawaiian sky, holding his seabag and gazing up at the old hull towering above him. He winced at the rust-bucket appearance of his first permanent assignment. Fancy the USS *Rigel*, an old cargo ship for flour and bananas, now converted for war. *Well, I'll be damned*, he said to himself, shaking his head. He remembered his first job in New Orleans on an old steamboat.

He stood for a bit, watching his shipmates climb the gangway to the quarterdeck, overwhelmed by the mass of steel, the tank-like shape, with its two cranes towering above.

"Changed your mind, Kinky?" yelled Vic, waving at him. "Can't keep the Captain waiting."

Charlie hitched up his seabag and hopped onto the bouncing gangway. Hanging onto the ropes, swaying on the steel rungs of the ladder gangway as he stepped upward, he said, "Well, old girl, you'll do me."

Getting to the end of the gangway, Charlie said, "Permission to come aboard, sir?" He saluted the flag at the stern and the Officer of the Deck, who stood stiffly in command, his eyes motionless.

"Permission granted," said the man. "I'm Ensign Hall. Welcome aboard the USS *Rigel*." The Ensign paused, and shifted his feet to a more relaxed pose.

Charlie liked the glint he saw in the man's eyes. "The bosun will show you to your quarters. Get your gear secured, and report back to the Wardroom at 1100. All ten of you have a meeting with the Captain and Exec, and—" he smiled, "—don't fall down the open holes. Big works underway here. Keep your eyes peeled. I don't want any injuries."

"Aye, aye, sir."

Charlie studied the gaping holes amidships, opened for installation of new boilers and other machinery. Twisted clumps of painted pipes lay all over the decks. Sailors and civilians with helmets and welding machines added to the noise of the machinery working in the access hole. Other sailors used a brush and pick, scraping at the paint on the decks. The familiar smell of oil and paint reminded Charlie of his first ships.

The men kept in single file adjacent to the steel railings. Dodging fixed funnels, working sheds, boats, and ropes, he and the other men followed the bosun through the hatch, down the ladder in Number 2 Hold to Deck 2, and then down to Deck 3, along the passageways. Charlie sensed the closeness of the vessel, the steel bulkhead cold to his touch, the overheads strung with every pipe and armored cable imaginable, twisting and turning in line with the passageway, the crowding of the men—everything was so confined. And he noticed the bosun kept his head low.

After stowing their gear down below, he and the divers entered the Wardroom and removed their caps. Charlie rapidly cast his eye at the plush, dark blue carpet underneath the red leather buttoned couch, stretched along the bulkheads.

"Attention on Deck!" called Ensign Hall.

"At ease, men," said Captain Dudley, coming through the side door, papers under his arm. "You have trained hard, and the Executive Officer, Commander McClendon, and I have been made aware of your special capabilities by Chief O'Shea and Lieutenant Burrows. You will be assigned normal Navy diving routines or other duties within your rating. But from here on, only the Exec or I will be consulted on your demolition and sabotage qualifications. You will have regular opportunities to improve your skills with explosives and hand-to-hand combat. You men are the vision. I can assure you, it is merely a matter of time until we are in a big-ass shootin' war, and you will be desperately needed to pave the way for our Marines. Your mission remains top secret. But we are also a repair ship, and divers are in short supply, so you will be busy every day. Any questions on this matter?" Captain Dudley's face was narrow and piercing. Everything about him was lean.

The men had been as deliberately chosen as the *Rigel* itself. Their rough edges were about to be chiseled to perfection, like the hull of their ship. They would be the protectors of the Navy. Charlie was looking ahead to the challenge.

"I want you to feel a part of this ship," Dudley said, unrolling a set of plans he had clutched in his hand, laying them out on the table. "New boilers are being installed through the holes topside, you've no doubt noticed. The conversions and repairs will bring this tub up to be the best ship repair unit the Navy's ever seen."

Dudley inspected every man and asked, "Are there any questions?"

"Do we have a diving tender?" asked Charlie.

"No. One will be provided for you in the next few days." Dudley paused, looking concerned. "Your special skills will not be needed until we get to a war zone. But train you will, train hard. That is all."

"Aye, aye, Captain," the men responded in unison.

"Oh, and liberty," Dudley continued, glancing at the sparkling ocean between the two destroyers docked near them. His smile was cynical, exposing small teeth. "Liberty's cancelled just now. There'll be no leave for any excursions into the city until you've earned it."

The men saluted, and Captain Dudley left for the bridge.

The men hurried down the hatch and raced along the passageway towards their assigned area. BANG!

"Shit a brick," Vic rubbed his head and wiped fingertips over his blood-smeared forehead. One of the unseen valve handles attached to the pipes running the full length of the overheads, jutted out, and had caught Vic's head. "Gotta learn to duck, eh?"

Vic walked on with his head bent down. "Watch those handles, and watch out for old Dudley."

"Bit of a hard man. Not one to cross, I'd say," said Charlie, narrowly missing the oncoming handle himself.

"He comes at you like a tame seal, but he's got a bite worse than a shark. Be careful."

"Where'd you hear that?" asked Charlie.

Vic shrugged. "Overheard the men talking, that's all." Catching hold of Charlie, Vic asked, "Want a little fun?" His eyes twinkled in the darkness of the passageway.

They stood by, waiting for the rest of the crew to follow, racing down the ladder. *Bang!* "Fuck it." Moult, the tallest member of the team, had caught the blow.

Charlie moved onwards, pretending not to notice.

Moult glared at Vic, rubbing his head. "You asshole, you..." he said. With a thump worse than the handle, Moult's horse-powered muscle sent Vic sliding along the narrow passageway.

"Anyone else?" Moult smirked as the rest of the crew barreled down the ladder. Picking up Vic, Moult shoved him further down the passageway. They paused, waiting for the rest of the men to catch up.

Red was next down the hatch. Charlie gave Red an extra shove. "We survived O'Shea; we'll survive anything 'round here."

Charlie and the other men assembled amongst the rows of lockers as Ensign Hall rounded the corner. "You'll store your cots in the tool area each day. They're foldable. When we depart, we'll be carrying troops, so all the ship's company will be bunking on cots in their workspace."

Taking one of the canvas-laced metal folding frames, Ensign Hall snapped it shut and crossed the room. "The lockers divide the shipfitter shop from the carpenter shop. It's partitioned off with a door at the far end into the shipfitter and sheet metal shops."

The smell of wood and machinery in the carpenter shop gave Charlie a warm message, it was home to him: the workbenches with power tools, lathe, drill press, shaping and finishing tools.

Another officer arrived. The men snapped to attention.

"At ease, men," the new arrival said. "I'm Repair Officer Wilkes. Ensign Hall here has shown you around."

Charlie sensed the officer's nervousness. Was this his first assignment? He had a plump, young face, and small brown eyes that narrowed and darted as he stared at them.

He walked without deviation over to Charlie. "Kincaid, you'll be the team's Petty Officer, promoted to Petty Officer Second Class as of now, operating the diving team. Captain's orders."

"Thank you, sir," answered Charlie.

Not returning the look at Charlie, Wilkes said, "That is all. Ensign Hall, take the men topside and turn to."

"Told ya you'd be picked, Kinky," whispered Vic.

They followed Hall through the maze of shops. The passageways led through a maze of shop bulkheads, rather than being one straight line from fore to aft. It was confusing as they zigzagged their way, bending, dodging and awaiting headaches, trying to keep up with the Ensign.

Nearby to their central tool room and connecting machine shops, the other shops were set up with electrical and battery equipment, radio and radar, engineering, dental and medical facilities. There was even a post office, barbershop, tailor shop and general store. The USS *Rigel*, Charlie determined, was a fix-it ship, and might even be the most valuable ship in the US Navy. He was itching to get started, and couldn't wait to make his divers the best in the Navy.

CHAPTER 16

The peaceful waters of the Gulf Harbor offered little disturbance as the crew and passengers relaxed, knowing yet another voyage of *Niagara* was underway. Arthur walked down the hand carved staircase to the first-class dining room. Tall Grecian pillars supported high studded ceilings, dotted with silver light fittings. There were white starched tablecloths with silver trays awaiting the evening meal. He decided it would be a long wait to be served and went back to his cabin. He ordered a meal to be delivered and reclined on his bed to relax.

BOOM!—a mammoth explosion. The ship shuddered violently, throwing Arthur's suitcase across the cabin. He sat up, grabbing the side of his bunk. Then he stood up, and nimbly pulled down the lifejacket from above the wardrobe. He slipped into his overcoat, stuffed his wallet and a few letters of importance into his briefcase, and put on his hat. Carrying his lifejacket, he opened the cabin door and looked out. The ship's steam whistle blew repeatedly in distress.

"All passengers report to the boat deck," called the steward as he passed Arthur. "All hands to the boat deck."

A full-bodied matron waddled precariously up the stairs outside Arthur's cabin. "I want my furs and luggage," she wailed, with a pomposity mastered uniquely by the truly rich.

Arthur joined the other confused passengers ascending the central staircase to the boat deck. The steward was several steps above him, carrying a small child, and sobbing, "I want my teddy."

Arthur noticed strange creaking sounds coming from below. The ship was pitching downwards at the bow. He caught up with the steward and tapped him on the shoulder, "Excuse me, but are you aware of that sound?

It's getting louder from below. Shouldn't we be doing more to get everyone's attention?"

The steward swung around facing Arthur, "Sir... that sound is from the Number 2 hold. We're doing the best we can to fix it. Please keep moving with the rest of the passengers. Wait your turn up on the boat deck. We are abandoning ship."

The steward went on up the stairs, calling out to everyone, "Keep moving to the boat deck. There's nothing to be concerned about. Rescue is on the way."

"I'd say there was," remarked two women who were struggling up the stairs. They were both wearing heavy coats over their nightgowns, dragging their lifejackets woefully behind.

On the boat deck, the passengers stood motionless, shocked, staring at the dark and mysteriously ocean portentously lapping against the side of the ship. Surely this must be a drill.

Speeding up the launching of the lifeboats was essential, now that the listing became more severe. Arthur gave his name for a lifeboat. He was among the last of the passengers lowered into the water. With the creaking of strained ropes, the small boat lurched bow-down, not quite meeting the water.

"Everybody stay calm and sit still," barked the bosun. He yelled to his mate on the ship's deck, "Hey Sam, unleash the cable... We can drop... it's okay. We need to get clear."

"I can't stand this," a woman called. "I'm going to..."

"Sit down, madam... now. We will get you out of here," snapped the bosun.

"But I'm..."

"Madam," Arthur leaned over and clutched her arm firmly, his expression severe in the darkness, "You could capsize this lifeboat."

The woman stared back at him and then at the other members of the small boat. She bowed her head. Her two children whimpered.

The man called Sam pulled the release lever for the lifeboat winch, and suddenly it dropped to the sea with a thud. They were on the ocean, with Sam grappling down the lines to join them. He heaved the oars and rowed the lifeboat swiftly away from the ship. They huddled together in the soft light of the moon, watching the ship slowly amble onwards.

In a short time, the *Orion*'s mines had claimed their first prey, the *Niagara,* Queen of the Pacific. At 0343 hours, she fought to reach shallow waters, pointing towards Auckland... desperately she tried, but she sank pitifully into the waiting ocean. The Captain and a few crew were the last to leave. The *Niagara*'s SOS had been acknowledged and all passengers and crew were picked up by rescue boats.

CHAPTER 17

The arrival of the diving tender gave the men their sanity back, after being cloistered in the carpenter shop. The dives were long and hard. Charlie's slim build afforded little protection from long hours in the cooler winter waters. It was lowering his blood pressure, causing him to feel numb in the water.

They departed on a small boat to salvage a broken propeller from a destroyer-minelayer. Charlie suited up and braved the first dive. The propeller had to be tied off to a lifting cable and dynamited loose from the shaft.

Ascending from the first dive, Charlie undressed and grabbed an air-fed facemask to give him extra freedom of movement. He re-entered the water several times, determined to complete the job, but his world of underwater comfort transformed into an uncontrollable nightmare when he lost the feeling in his legs. Grabbing the tie-rope, he hauled himself out of the water and pulled off his mask, looking around to see if anyone had noticed his distress. His work was the sea, and to fail in the ocean would mean the end for him. He lay on his back, baking on the warm wooden deck, facing the Pacific sun. He'd have to report his condition. Even though the deep water was low 70's, the cold was a killer.

Charlie didn't trust Wilkes and knew he had to go direct to the Captain. His secret mission permitted this. After an official invitation, he entered the Captain's quarters.

"You're one of the best divers we've ever had," said Captain Dudley, offering Charlie a seat. "You're also very lean. Not much meat on those bones, boy. I'd say a snort or two of this will get your blood boosted. Hide it for later." Dudley handed Charlie a flask of whisky.

"Thank you, Captain," said Charlie, tucking the flask into his pocket.

"Don't thank me, thank the US Navy." He handed Charlie a shot glass of whisky and poured one himself, taking a mouthful. "Now son, no bragging about this, otherwise I'll have the whole crew wanting whisky. It'll be drunk like water. Do I make myself clear?"

"Yes sir," Charlie stood up, downed his whisky and handed Dudley the empty glass. "But, sir, I'd rather not. I can't be above the other men."

"Captain's orders. You report to the ship's doctor for a checkup and whiskey ration. We'll arrange it that way."

"I appreciate that, sir."

"I'm not here to make you feel good. You're here for a purpose, and that's to get these ships fit and ready for war. That is all."

Charlie stood to attention, saluted and left the office. He removed the flask from his pocket and placed it in his locker; then made his way to the ship's medical room, located forward on the starboard side of the second deck. The medical department wasn't busy. There were eighteen starch-white beds, but they were empty. The Corpsman measured his blood pressure. The Doc was on shore leave. Charlie said he would return another time.

Prolonged days were spent in their hull shop, applying the hydrostatic tests for refitting of the huge boiler, to be installed in the lower deck of the boiler shop. The carpenter and shipfitter's shops were located forward on the starboard side of the ship. They were frequently shared and Charlie had familiarized himself with both, for when he needed extra parts.

"I'm Petty Officer Kincaid from the carpenter shop, requiring a fitter," said Charlie to one of the sheet metal workers, who was sitting at a desk working on a set of plans. "Can you help out?"

The man stood up with his back to the papers.

"Don't get up," said Charlie, inadvertently glancing at the desk.

"Oh no, I'm finished," said the man, folding up the plans. He walked over to his locker, opened it and put the plans inside. He removed a mask. He didn't act as if he was in any kind of hurry. "You're from the diving team?"

"Yes, I am. Why?"

"I'm Andy. Second name's Adolf in case you find out. But I'm no German. I'm named after a Swedish king." He smiled, putting his hand out to shake Charlie's.

"Pleased to meet ya." Charlie scratched his head. "Just as well you're not Hitler's cousin." Andy didn't fit the standard rough exterior of a shipfitter, he imagined, with his schoolboy face, rounded jaw and pleasant smile.

"I've instructions to make a ton of these," said Andy, handing Charlie the mask. "Here, see what you think."

Charlie put on the mask. It covered his whole face. "Fantastic, I'd say. Who're ya making all these for?"

"You divers… so you have greater freedom on the shallow dives."

"Great work, can't wait to get it wet." Charlie handed the mask back to Andy as he went on, "Can you make me a rubber suit? It's iceberg cold down there."

"You shouldn't complain. The Captain's been giving you the good stuff."

Charlie stared at Andy. "How'd you know that?"

"Nothing's a secret on this old tub. You'll have your suit."

The men worked the rounds to the constant burr of the sanding and milling machines, then grabbing a hearty meal, and going topside for a quick smoke and fresh air. The night air had a smell all its own—a mix of the sea, and the barnacles attached to the wharves. Casting his gaze across the yard as he leaned on the thin metal rails of the *Rigel*, Charlie examined Ford Island and rows of mighty battleships. The closest in view were the USS *California* and USS *Oklahoma*. Off the starboard bow, down Pier 1010, was the cruiser USS *Helena*. Past her in dry dock Number One was the battleship USS *Pennsylvania* with the destroyers *Cassin* and *Downes* forward.

"What a view, eh?" said Vic bending down on the rails.

Charlie lit a cigarette and drew hard on the warm smoke. "Yerr. Somethin's going down… all this metal in one small place. We'd never sail out in a hurry, that's for sure," he said, straightening up. "We've got the cruiser *New Orleans* off the port quarter, and an oiler to stern. Goddamn, we'd go up in smoke if there was an attack. We're just sittin' ducks out here," pondered Charlie. He swiveled to watch Crow coming towards them.

Vic scanned across at the battleships. "Nah", that's why they're all here, best defense in the world."

Charlie cringed at the idea of this tub ever going to war. He still didn't agree with Vic. Something was horribly wrong about the whole set up.

"Who's for a game?" said Crow, jiggling a pair of dice.

"Come on, Kinks, let's play," Vic coaxed.

The deck was quiet… punctuated with just the sounds of gulls and lapping seas. They stood among the tangled mass of heavy pipes that disappeared into the deck below. Everything about the *Rigel* was cumbersome with her rebuild in process, all four hundred and twenty-three feet of her. The wing of the bridge had fine-arched supports, running amidships, reminding Charlie again of New Orleans. Spans of grey iron wrapped around the bridge in a triple deck. Its gunnery platform at the fantail had been stripped of all armament, which made it a perfect hideout for a game, hidden from the prying eyes of any guard on duty.

Crow threw the dice, and the men hunched over, casting their bets. They gambled compulsively—with cards, dice or anything they found for a bet. The dice were cold this night. Charlie preferred poker, notably stud poker so he could count the cards. Crow pulled his well-used cards out of his pocket, offering a cut to Charlie sitting on his right. Red, without a hint of expression, watched the cards hit the table.

"Goddamn, Kinky, I don't know why we bother playing. One day I'm gonna have your luck," complained Vic as he saw Charlie's ace.

A loudspeaker blared, "Now hear this. The smoking lamp is out. Clear the decks."

"What? At this time of the night? What the hell are they doing?" said Vic standing up looking any which way. He signaled quiet as footsteps roused their attention.

"Who gave you permission to be here?" yelled Wilkes, coming down the ladder from the gunnery platform. The man had a habit of appearing unexpectedly, as if he had hawk eyes, Charlie reckoned.

"We were just—" began Crow.

"Get your asses below. Fuel's being transferred. You know the rules: smokin' lamp is out." Wilkes spat over the side. "If Dudley spots you, your ass'll be in the brig," he said, looking towards the bridge.

"It's disarmed. No ammo here, sir," grumbled Crow.

"Don't argue," ordered Charlie. "Game's over."

The men descended to their quarters, pulled out their cots from the lockers and stripped to their undershorts and T-shirts for relief from the sticky heat. It was a nightly routine. A few went to the trouble of putting up family photos; others preferred to lie or sit on their cots and chat. Charlie had bought writing paper from the ship's post office on the second deck.

Dear Ma, he wrote, staring into the room, oblivious of the mass of machinery and bodies lying on the cots, *how you doin'? Life here is so hard to write you about…*

He put the writing paper down and recoiled to stare at the metal bulkhead, frowning into the night; he didn't know what to write to her. He closed his eyes and remembered his lumpy straw bed back home. In his visions, the words came to him, but exhaustion took over.

The following morning, Charlie waited until Vic left for the divers' shop and then hastily slipped through the entrance to find Andy.

"Hey, here's a new project for ya," he yelled into Andy's welding helmet.

Andy snatched away his gloves and helmet, and looked intently at Charlie, "Fuck! Don't do that when I got a stick in my hand. Whatcha want?"

"A still." Charlie grinned.

"No sweat, but it'll take some doin' to side-track the metal," Andy chuckled.

Whisky was short rationed. A cure for this catastrophe was to build a still. Andy knew how. Charlie had seen the other documents Andy was drawing—plans to skim oil off the sea—and had wondered why the air-fed masks were required, when all they were doing out here was diving with bells and tanks. He decided to keep quiet.

"Listen, you get that still built, I'm gonna make you the best bootleg whisky your boss has ever seen. Then he won't complain about losing a bit of copper tubing. First liberty I'll get the fixin's for some killer sour mash whisky," said Charlie, patting Andy on the back.

Charlie headed back to his work, sporting a smile that came from knowing comfort from home was about to arrive.

"Where've you been?" asked Crow. "Wilkes came in looking for you. Says he wants you topside on the double."

Charlie scrambled up the narrow ladder, puzzled about Wilkes. He could not possibly have heard about the still.

"Reporting for orders, sir," Charlie said, saluting.

Wilkes's baby face relaxed into a smirk, "0700 hours tomorrow your men are granted shore liberty. Report back no later than 2200 hours. I will be on leave for a few days. Don't be surprised if I see you downtown."

"Yes, sir." Charlie saluted, pivoted and, grabbing the ladder, slid down, almost landing on one of the deckhands. He was eager to tell the news.

"We're out of here tomorrow. Liberty! Young Wilkes might join us, if he can find us."

•　　•　　•　　•　　•

The bus crunched and spun over rough gravel passing Hickam Airfield, rounding the bay to Honolulu and the golden sands of Waikiki beach. Native girls in a thatch-roofed curio shop caught sight of the bus and raced to catch them, holding out their leis.

"Now we're talking," said Vic, exasperated and hoarse from leaning out the window, whooping back at the girls.

Charlie hunkered down in his seat, laughing at Vic and all the sex-starved yelps of his companions. He didn't mind; he'd become a part of a fraternity.

The bus stopped downtown, and they jumped to the sidewalk welcomed by a gush of warm tropical air. All the latest models of cars blazed past both ways—everything from Willys Coupes to Cadillac convertibles.

Vic offered Charlie a cigarette and lit one himself. "Time to taste the brown sugar, Kinky." He grinned, tucking his lighter in his pocket. "Let's get to the action." They walked across the street and into the shade of the expensive-looking shop façades. They veered down a side street and the hidden wealth dwindled totally to squalor; the sidewalks and buildings oozed a smell of dope.

A girl was leaning up against a brick pillar. "Yankee dollar," she called out to them. She repeated herself, coming towards the men. Vic, in the lead, thrust his hands into bursting pockets, then bent down and put his arm around the girl's bare waist and stuffed a dollar into her bra top, grinning at the rest of the men.

"How much to park it?" he whispered to her. "What's your name, sweet pea?"

"Daisy," she said smiling up at him, hips pressing his, as she placed a lei over his neck. Her graceful body lured them into a decrepit building down Hotel Street.

"A neon sign that read 'Hubba Hubba' lit the dark entrance. The sound of drums grew louder as they entered the dimly lit clubroom.

"Hello, sailors," said a young woman, her smile and manner as alluring as Daisy's. "I'm Rose." She beckoned them to a table by the dance floor. Charlie stared at the beautiful girls with their oriental smiles, leis of tropical flowers about their delicate necks, carrying trays of drinks. They swayed to the pounding beat of the Hawaiian ipu gourds, sharkskin-covered pahu drums, and guitars.

"I could get used to this," said Red, his face florid at the adoration.

"Yes, but not for long. Look behind ya," said Vic.

The bar was filling up with other sailors, pushing their way towards the dance floor.

"Hubba Hubba," called out a group of dark-skinned men in grass skirts, beating on drums, with jiggling straw leggings.

The spotlight fell on a line of female dancers. Their ample breasts jiggled like Jello, scantily contained by coconut bras, underneath richly perfumed frangipani leis. The beat of the drums, guitars, ukuleles, and the girls' oscillating hips sent the men crazy. Their table rumbled across the floor, with the sailors all rapping and shouting. As the tempo increased, the men's frenzied hollers echoed back.

A tall, lean woman appeared at the rear of the stage, wearing a red-and-yellow headdress of thatched beadwork, sparkling shorts. Small half-coconuts cupped her firm breasts. Layers of frangipani, laced with pikake jasmine and maile vines, draped around her neck. She led the dancers undulating throughout the dance floor. The men began to throw coins at the dancers as they came towards the front of the stage.

Charlie felt shockwaves run through him when he recognized the tall dancer. *Roxy?* It couldn't be!

Gulping down his beer, he glanced quickly at the others to see if they'd noticed his sudden reaction, but all eyes were on the bouncing hips and breasts of the dancers. Everyone in the club was now cheering and clapping. Roxy led the dancers towards Charlie.

"Don't you forget where you've come from," she said, leaning close enough so that everyone heard her, staring straight at him, her flowers flooding sweet aromas over the sailors.

Vic's mouth flew open. "Goddamn, Kinky! Where've you been hiding this beautiful creature?"

Roxy laughed, curling her legs around a pole in front of them, leaning towards Vic.

"He never wanted to—" she twisted on the pole, dangling inches from Vic, "—find me." She pouted her lips, and they all jeered at Charlie.

"Hey Kinky, what's the game?"

"Okay, okay." Charlie stood up, kicking back his chair in rage. "Okay." He raised his hands. "Joke's on me."

"That's more like it," called out Vic to the others. "And I'm next." Vic gave a wink to Roxy as Charlie grabbed her by the arm, briskly walking her backstage.

"What the hell are you doing here?" said Charlie.

"Don't you yell at me," said Roxy, grabbing a robe off a hook near the door. "Has it ever occurred to you to say *hello*." She clutched at his uniform, pulling him close to her, "Like… how are you? What have you been doing all this time?" She began to cry, "What about me?"

Still the pathetic Roxy, Charlie flinched as he watched her. He didn't say anything; his thoughts were too confused at the sudden shock of seeing her again. She pushed him for fun and, before he could speak, she slipped behind the exit doors. Charlie followed her.

A woman flung back a tatty green curtain—yelling, "Get out, sailor boy. This area is off limits."

Back inside the club, Charlie searched for his men, but could barely see Vic's head bobbing above the others' on the dance floor. The band had struck up a fast beat and Vic swirled to the jitterbug, swinging an island girl through his legs. Charlie stood watching awhile, feeling the beat, wanting to hold a woman. Instead, he raced across the dance floor and slipped out into the daylight, passing thirsty sailors waiting in line. A voice called to him. He noticed a woman in a large floppy hat, standing across the road waving at him.

"Hey, what about us?" yelled the sailors at the woman. Charlie crossed the road shoving his hands in his pockets, and joking back at the sailors. "Hey, go for the hula girls, guys, not a hat."

He walked a block, until a parked car door flew open. The woman in the hat called to him, "Get in."

Charlie sat in silence staring out the front window. He rustled inside his top pocket, offered Roxy a cigarette, and lit one for himself. He fidgeted, tapping his ash out the car window.

"So how'd you get here?"

"I jumped on a ship… just like the boxcars we used to ride."

"Always the same Roxy, never changed." He twisted towards her. "Who fixed your teeth?"

"A dentist here in Hawaii." She flashed him a full toothy grin. "And you. Look at you."

"There's a lot of look-alikes out here, girl. Why pick on me? You're doing all right for yourself."

She sneaked her hem a bit higher, with the cigarette hanging out of her mouth, and plucked off her hat. Charlie noticed she'd grown her hair. Thick golden brown tresses looped up, in a pompadour style, glistening in the sunlight. He hadn't noticed the color of her hair before.

"Still the old stubborn Roxy," said Charlie taking no notice of her attempts to act sophisticated. "Who gave you the car? Some stooge?" She leaned over and thumped him. Charlie lightly poked her back... and they both burst into welcome laughter.

Charlie sensed she was thinking about the old times from her expression, even though she was buried in perfume and glamour. She wore red lipstick and a red halter-neck dress splattered with white hibiscus flowers. The fabric clung to her lean body, breasts mounding ready to erupt from the neckline.

Charlie gave her a wink.

"No, I earned the money. I'm taking you somewhere." Her face lost its smile. "Stand by, we'll get you your first taste of a real pineapple." Roxy started up the car.

They drove onward on the main highway from Honolulu, towards the rich vegetation of the hill country. Rows of pineapples plants spread for miles. Roxy and Charlie kept driving until they came to a clearing of thatched huts and Jeeps parked near a shaded coconut grove. She stopped the car and reached over to the back seat, grabbing a grass skirt and top.

Roxy opened the car door, turned her back on Charlie, threw off her dress and instantly stepped into the grass skirt. She clipped on a bikini halter-neck, which suited her long straight back. Grabbing a camera out of the car door pocket, she walked around to join Charlie and handed the camera to him.

"Here, take a picture for your wall," she said, pointing to the button on the camera. "Point and click, see? Here." She picked up two pineapples from a row on the ground by the entrance to one of the huts. She posed her glistening body to one side, holding the two pineapples with bent elbows, exposing her bare midriff.

"You can throw darts at me, or get your friends to bid on a date," she said, smiling into the camera. Charlie clicked the button several times, watching her seductive pose.

"Boy, you sure came into the money. How much did this baby cost?" said Charlie, turning the camera over.

"Careful, don't you know you can't open it, silly." Roxy threw down the pineapples and snatched the camera. Her naked midriff brushed his body as she reached for the camera.

They stared at each other under the shade of the trees. Clutching the camera, Roxy leaned against the trunk of the coconut tree, never taking her eyes from his. Charlie eased nearby, inhaling her floral fragrance. A single ray of sunshine glistened across the top of her oiled breasts. He couldn't resist kissing her. Her sweet-tasting lips melded to his.

Roxy kissed him back, passionately, thrusting her hips into his hardness. "Ohhh...,"

Without warning, a plantation worker appeared from one of the huts. "I peel for you?" he asked innocently.

They both fell silent. He was Japanese.

Charlie reached for his knife. It was an instant reaction. He sucked in a deep breath, calmed himself and took out two cents to give to the man. "Yes. Two pineapples please."

The man didn't look up. He vigorously chopped chunks of pineapple and dropped them into a small woven dish that he carried. Charlie watched him closely because he didn't smile.

"Thank you," said Roxy, taking the dish and racing the engine. "Let's git, I've something to show you."

They ate the sweet pineapple pieces while Roxy drove. Juice dribbled across her skirt. Charlie grabbed a towel and mopped across her lap.

"I like your touch, big boy." She smiled.

Charlie glanced across at her, remembering the meat in the boxcar. He closed his eyes and let the rumble of the car lull his mind. He awoke to a soft hand brushing up his thigh. He opened his eyes to Roxy's beautiful face. He breathed easy and rubbernecked out the car window, as she coasted into an opening and shut off the engine. White sands made their way along a tiny beach before them. Prevailing winds swept the palm-tree canopy in the beautiful inlet. To their right a high hill faced north,

"Wow, what a beach, Roxy. I got the blanket… race you!"

They settled into their private paradise. She leaned over and started fiddling with his collar, her eyes fixed on his, her other hand moving on his leg. Charlie was aroused again, now even harder than before. They rolled together on the blanket. It was like feeling fire. Charlie couldn't stop. He slipped off her bikini top and undid the hula skirt to expose her fully. Roxy beamed, never taking her eyes from his and ripped away his clothes. She playfully ran down to the shoreline and plunged into the waves. Charlie was seconds behind her and dove into her splash. Roxy was waiting and pulled his bare form into hers. She felt him respond, but decided to tease and swam off to the end of the cove abutting a rocky point. Charlie laid on his back in the sand and lowered Roxy onto his tumescence.

"Oh Charlie… my love… give it to me," as she undulated her hips.

Charlie felt Roxy's insides—smooth as silk, but tight as a button. They both groaned together with each beautiful thrust penetrating deeply, banging into flesh against flesh. Roxy felt the pleasure and quickened her pace, harder… bucking. She slowed almost to a pause as their eyes locked, both grinning in fuming lust. Then Roxy quickened the pace even faster. But Charlie didn't last long and groaned, "Roxy… jump off… I'm gonna come!"

Roxy bounded up and they held each other tightly as Charlie spilled his seed, two chests heaving, reveling in their newfound bond.

Charlie half-whispered, "Roxy darlin', that was amazing… don't know what got into me." Somehow he awkwardly regretted taking Roxy, but at the same instant felt a burning desire fulfilled. He was ashamed and proud but also perplexed.

Roxy looked square into his eyes, "Charlie… it is you… only you for me, ever since grade school." She silently dropped tears onto his chest.

Charlie caressed her tenderly, and Roxy softly squeezed back praying that Charlie would be hers. But Charlie's feelings were slowly, dreadfully, changing from glee to remorse.

"Roxy… you are beautiful beyond words. I will never forget this… but I am going off to war. Life is so cruel right now." Charlie regretted these words the moment he said them, but he did not have any answers for Roxy or know how to respond better. He was lost, except to his love, the sea.

He felt he should change the subject. Something was not right, not for her, not for him.

He clinched her hand. "Roxy. I'd like nothin' better than to climb up your skirt every day, all day long, but—"

Roxy interrupted, "You think I'm no good. OK, I've had a bit of help with my finances. But it's not what you think." Roxy lurched upright, withdrawing from him.

Charlie could tell by her face that something *was* wrong. "You don't have to explain."

She shifted herself back towards him, and crossed her legs with a look of concern bordering on anger. Charlie didn't say anything. He watched her sit up with her legs pulled close as she glared out into the ocean

Finally Roxy spoke with anger in her voice, "OK Charlie Kincaid, ditch the romance! But there's something happening here with the Japs that's not right."

Charlie rubbed her arm. "The Japs certainly make their presence felt here, that's for sure," he coaxed.

"Yeah. Many have become citizens, but a lot come and go. My job has been to listen and learn about anyone suspicious coming into Hubba Hubba, and to get information. Intimacy is the only way to get close to them." Her voice was quiet. "I'm not a total spy. I report to my boss and he pays me well. I'm good at what I do."

"You'll get yourself shot if you don't watch out."

"You don't listen, do you?" Roxy pointed out to sea. "Look out there; local Japs are taking pictures and pretending to be fishing when they're not. My friend Daisy's brother was involved; I followed him out here several times. I watched him while I swam. One day he entirely disappeared, left Hawaii, and someone else arrived in his place. Trouble is they all appear the same to us, so nobody notices. Daisy said her brother went back to Japan to visit their uncle, but I don't believe her. I pretend they're my boyfriends and take pictures of them. Then I give the pictures to Navy Intelligence." Roxy twisted to front onto Charlie.

"You what... give to whom?"

"I don't know. Usually a guy in a suit, but sometimes a Navy officer. What's it all about?"

"Look, I'd say it's none of your business. You shot that doctor. Now you're getting involved in espionage and you're dragging me into it." He shook his head.

"I'd say it's every bit your business if you want to stop a war. Don't judge me. I just told you, that's all." Roxy stood up and walked up the beach, snatched her clothes on and threw his at him. She started the car and revved the engine. "I'll drive you back. You go off to war, Charlie Kincaid. I'll be here when you get back."

Roxy didn't speak to him. She stopped at the depot for Charlie to catch a bus, and switched the engine off.

They lingered without saying anything, and then Charlie spoke. "Roxy...," he rubbed her neck, "I've told you before. Don't sell yourself short. Get rid of that camera." He touched her cheek and brushed aside a long strand of hair. Roxy's fuming expression held her unspoken words.

Roxy whisked up her skirt, exposing white lace panties against oiled bronze dancer's legs. "You see these beautiful legs, Charlie?" she grinned.

"They're beauties all right," he smiled broadly.

"They're gonna take me places, but not by spreadin'. I'll be on a dead run." She glared at him.

"We'll get more liberty soon. I'll hunt you up." Charlie slid out, tapped lightly at the window. Turning the car, Roxy sped away at top speed without looking back.

Around the corner by the bus depot, Charlie caught site of a general store. His glorious vision of white lace against brown flesh gradually morphed into a memory of what he was meant to get for the whisky still—a bag of barley, box of raisins, sugar, and a couple tins of pineapple juice. With all packed into a large paper bag, he left for the bus.

The bus had picked up a few straggling sailors and pulled into the dock, where they were greeted by a motley, and pickled, crew recovering from liberty. Charlie spotted Moult holding up Wilkes. Moult called out to Charlie as he walked towards them, "Hey, did you do this to him?"

"Never saw him," said Charlie helping with one free arm to steady the legless Wilkes, who was blathering some girl's name that sounded like Daisy… and slobbering down his whites.

Charlie shook his head, thinking of Vic. With the help of Moult's strength, they carried Wilkes up the gangway. The guard stopped them at the top, and was about to peer inside Charlie's paper bag, when Wilkes involuntarily puked down the guard's pant leg.

"Holy shit... You assholes get the fuck to your quarters," screamed the guard.

They made it amidships to Wilkes' quarters. Charlie threw back the curtain of the bunk, and rolled Wilkes towards the wall.

"Someone's going to catch hell, when he wakes up," said Moult as they left.

"Yerrr… I'm in charge. I'll cop it," said Charlie.

CHAPTER 18

When Arthur and the rest of the passengers arrived back in Auckland, there was a cold sober concern among the on-lookers. How did this ship sink? Was New Zealand under attack? Nothing was making sense.

Arthur wished he'd been more cautious. He was sure he'd never spoken about this. His Masons were sworn to secrecy. There was no evidence of any spies. He'd go and speak with the Captain, but before he did, he knew the family would be waiting for his news. Arthur called Irene's flat from the Union Steam Ship Company to a barrage of anxious voices. In his usual calm manner, he assured them he was safe. Taking Irene's address, he promised he'd catch a taxi very soon. But first, the Captain was waiting in an office in the Union Steam Ship Company.

The Captain's offices were regal by any standard, embellished with carved oak paneling and shelves to mimic the finest stateroom on the seas. Arthur stopped momentarily at the windows to view the wharf where they had embarked the previous night. He entered the office and took a seat, looking at the Captain. He summarily launched into a heated conversation, frowning as he spoke, asking if the mine was German. The Captain replied in a brash way, that the Navy was sweeping the channels and they would soon know. Arthur wasn't convinced.

"The *Niagara* arrives without a scratch, loads up with a fortune in gold, and then hits the mines on the way out? No accident... deliver a list to my office of every person in your company who had knowledge of the gold."

The captain leapt to his feet, "Mr Blanc, surely you do not suspect my company?"

Arthur rose from his chair also and sharply growled, "Captain... Hitler had help from somewhere. The Navy Department will be here later today. What about salvage?" Arthur noticed sweat beading down the side of the Captain's face.

"Yes, sir. We will cooperate fully. Salvage from sixty fathoms is extremely difficult... but not impossible. We'll report back in confidence."

"Thank you," said Arthur. "Now I need to return home immediately."

"I'll arrange transport. There's a daily flight to Dunedin."

Arthur walked out into the crisp morning air, and caught a waiting taxi to Irene's flat, situated on Symonds Street. He knocked at Irene's door.

"Thank God," said Irene, ushering Arthur inside. Mary stood up from her chair, and Mattie rushed to hug her father.

"What happened?" the three woman all asked at once.

Arthur calmly lowered his exhausted body into a chair at the dining table as Irene poured him a cup of tea.

He was in no mood to explain. He hastily told them the Union Steam Ship Company was tasked to handle everything. It was the best way... they would never understand. He had to get home to see if he'd missed anything. Arthur quietly and politely, in his usual manner, wished Mattie good luck with her interview and thanked Irene for taking care of them. He slipped back out to the waiting taxi.

When Arthur had left, Mary and Mattie rode the tram from Irene's down to O'Hara's Hair Academy on Karangahape Road. They climbed the long stairway.

The lighting in the stairwell gave a theatrical atmosphere to the arched ceilings and the white painted walls. At the first landing, they stood at the entranceway of the Savoy Reception Rooms and Dance Hall, and waited for Mary to catch her breath.

On the second floor was a door with a glass panel and a sign that read *O'Hara's Hair Academy*. A slice of morning sun shone on Mattie's feet through side windows.

On the far side, next to a dressmaker, was another door with *E. O'Hara* on it. They knocked and entered. A man stood up and walked towards them. He shook hands with them both. "Welcome to Auckland. I'm Mr O'Hara," his neat, closely clipped moustache bobbing as he spoke.

They took a seat. Mattie noticed his immaculate hands as he fingered a fob watch from his waistcoat. He handed Mary a few papers and began to explain the training. Mattie was excited to know there was just four students enrolled. She liked the sound of him conscientiously describing the curriculum. It all seemed to fit together, and Mattie knew Mary was happy listening. Mary looked over at Mattie.

"What about accommodation? Do your students stay close by?" asked Mary.

"Yes Madam, the girls from the country generally do. There are small dwellings nearby on Upper Queen Street and Greys Avenue. I can give you some addresses."

Mary shook her head, "I think a boarding house would be ideally suitable."

"Take a tram ride down Khyber Pass. You'll see many grand boarding villas up in the hills surrounding Newmarket."

"Thank you, we will," said Mary.

"Here, let me show you around," Mr O'Hara said, inviting them for a tour.

As they walked into the salon, Mattie caught her breath. Bright sunlight reflected from white walls, highlighting the Eugene perming stands suspended from the ceiling, with their cables ready to latch on to a waiting client.

"This is our salon, where eventually you will work with customers. Our top students stay on until the following intake." Mr O'Hara directed his conversation towards Mattie as he walked through the salon. "Students arrive at 9:30am sharp, and we have lectures for forty hours a week, as well as homework each night. If you don't mind my saying, you strike me as a mature student with an eye for meticulous detail... I'm quite sure you will succeed."

"Mr O'Hara," Mattie replied, "I can assure you I will do my very best. I am determined to pass with top marks."

"Excellent... That's what we like to hear, Mattie," Mr O'Hara smiled. He put his hand out to shake their hands.

Mattie and her mother stopped at the Savoy tearooms on their way back down the stairs. A fire was crackling cheerfully in an ornate brick fireplace with a rustic-looking chimney. Mattie lifted her mother's arm, and they stepped inside to seats at a table near the fireplace.

Adjacent to the tearooms, was a huge wooden dance floor, which ran all the way over towards the large set of windows facing the road. An upright piano waited over by the windows.

Mattie couldn't help wondering if she'd ever be asked to dance, but she didn't say anything. She sipped her tea with visions of her exciting new life. Mattie rubbed her Mother's hands, "Look at the glorious dance floor."

Mary pursed her lips. "Hmmm, your studies won't leave much time for dancing, my dear."

•   •   •   •   •

The next morning, Mattie eagerly watched out the tram window as she clutched Mary's arm. Not long after the tram started lumbering down Khyber Pass Road, Mattie's eyes widened and she exclaimed, "Mother, look... that huge villa. Oh, this so reminds me of Dunedin. Come... let's walk." They eased off the tram and walked up Huntly Avenue.

Huntly House, an enormous two-storied weatherboard villa, perched elegantly on a hilltop overlooking Newmarket. Its wide verandas surrounded both levels, protecting the sash windows from the unpredictable Auckland weather, and a random puff of smoke emanated from its solid brick chimneys. Exquisite gardens glistened in the sunlight after an early morning rain.

Mattie and Mary walked past the large tree close to the verandas that surrounded the house, and ascended the steps to the front door, sliding their hands up the smooth wooden baluster. Mattie gave the brass doorknocker a loud bang. It was answered by a sharp bark from within, and through the glass, she watched a shadow coming towards her.

A woman opened the door. "Yes?" she said, clutching a small dog with a probing wet nose. Her stack of blonde hair swished up into an officious French roll.

"Hello, I'm Mattie Blanc... I'm moving here from Dunedin and looking for accommodation. This is my mother, Mary."

Putting down the squirming dog, the woman offered her hand, "I'm so pleased to meet you Mattie... and Mary. I'm Mrs Frisken. Please, this way. We can talk in my office."

They followed her into a room with an arched alcove in front of a bay window. Mrs Frisken went to her seat behind a desk in the alcove, and asked them to sit. Mattie felt a bit uncomfortable for some reason. She surveyed the room, trying to act naturally. Then a soft brush of fur on her leg gently reminded her of home. *Maybe it will to be just fine here,* she thought. She leaned over in her chair to pat the little flat-faced dog, but it jumped back with an imperious bark.

"That's Bonny. She's a Pekinese. I hope you don't mind dogs."

"What a cute name. Of course I don't mind," said Mattie.

"Bonny, here," said Mrs Frisken, picking her up. She devotedly caressed the little dog and didn't look up as she continued. "We have one room available, our best... with views out the front. The basic rules here at Huntly House are respectable conduct..." She paused, and then spoke unequivocally: "Do you have any men-friends?"

"No—do you have any objection to visitors?"

Mrs Frisken raised one eyebrow. "Not if they're decent. Our boarders are working people. I don't tolerate any loud or raucous behavior."

Putting Bonny down, she motioned them to follow her into the grand passageway, "Perhaps best that you see the room first, please... follow me."

She led the way up the stairs. A long, rounded stained-glass window glowed over the first landing; outside leaves were swirling behind the red, green, and yellow-colored glass mosaic. Mattie and Mary continued up the stairs.

At the top landing, another wide passageway extended in both directions with windows at each end. Daylight streamed through the windows, highlighting the polished wood floors. Mrs Frisken walked the length of the passageway in a majestic strut past three bedroom doors, and opened the last room to the left.

"Of course there's a wartime blackout, but it's not dark yet." She drew back the curtains, opened the tall sash window and turned to face Mattie. For the first time, Mattie saw her smile. "Your view...," Mrs Frisken said.

"This is going to be just perfect," said Mattie, smiling wide at Mary.

"Well, we better settle and make the final arrangements," added Mary, putting her arm around Mattie.

"Then welcome to Huntly House. I trust it has everything you wish," Mrs Frisken said. "Dinner's at six o'clock every day."

Mattie wiggled gingerly on the bed, running her fingers over the soft satin of the rose-printed bedspread. She grinned at her reflection in the wardrobe mirror and gazed into the room, her own room.

CHAPTER 19

Charlie's crew were kept busy night and day. Any liberty they were granted was unexpectedly announced the day before; and then it was divided port and starboard with half the crew ashore each occasion.

On their next liberty, Charlie watched Vic catch a bus before he and the others could join him for the usual trip into town. Charlie wondered why this mysterious paradise had become such a playground for the officers in command, who scored the whole weekend off. The golf courses were packed. Jeeps barreled past them carrying beautiful laughing women, their hair flowing in the summer's breeze, white teeth blazing against a perpetual tan. Christmas was not far ahead and the buzz of celebrations for coming festivities filled the streets. Santa Claus, in his red fur-trimmed hat, bobbed down the decorated street, handing out candy to the children. Charlie stopped to watch their faces.

He crossed Hotel Street, shoved back the saloon doors and sauntered into Hubba Hubba. The familiar Hawaiian music was playing. A girl swayed to his table as he sat down, her tray balancing on her palm above his head.

"What would you like?" she asked.

"Is Roxy here?" he asked

"Who?"

"Roxy, she works here."

The girl shook her head, "Sorry sir, no Roxy here."

Charlie stood up, looked around and left. He had to find out where she was. He crossed the road, looking for her car. *Maybe she's in trouble*, he guessed to himself, as he searched the streets.

He just made it back in time at 2350 hours. Climbing the gangway, he noticed Vic ahead of him.

"Where were you?"

"Same question, Kinky," said Vic, walking on ahead.

"Look, what's up? And where's Roxy?"

"Who?"

"Roxy." Charlie grabbed his arm. "You know, the girl we met at the dance floor. My friend."

"Hey Kinks. Who's kidding who?" Vic walked on.

Charlie ran after him. Vic made his way towards the tool room. His long legs outstripped Charlie's, as they slid down the ladders to Deck 3.

Vic opened his locker and unpinned a photo.

"Recognize this? He shoved the picture of Roxy with the pineapples in Charlie's face. Charlie stared down, startled, "That's Roxy."

"It's not Roxy. Her name is Fran, buddy. And she's gone." Vic glared at Charlie, shoved the photo into Charlie's hand, closed his locker, and walked away.

Charlie viewed the photo again. They musta picked her up for protection, he suspected. *She's been discovered.*

CHAPTER 20

7th December 1941

Before sunrise, north of Oahu, at 0550 the Japanese aircraft carriers veered east into a thirty-knot wind. The flight decks rose and fell to the forty-foot waves, allowing no delays in a day of methodically laid plans. Waiting another fifteen minutes for the winds to settle down to twenty-four knots, the dedicated Japanese, the *hachimaki,* loyal to their emperor, impatiently sat with their white headbands, emblazoned with the rising sun, firmly tied around their foreheads.

Each aircraft was carrying a torpedo of unprecedented size and heaviness strapped to its belly, designed for shallow waters, ready for the signal to launch the first wave. The Zekes, emblazoned with their red *Kyokujitsu-ki,* were first in line, then the Kates, then the Vals. At 0620 hours, the men on the decks of the aircraft carriers held out their flags. Mightily, flags arced down through the icy wind. Men screamed above the racing engines. *"Tora Tora"* (tiger). *"Tora Tora,"* they kept calling.

All one hundred and eighty-three aircraft blazed successfully off the heaving deck, each plane superbly timed to pitch into the heavens in sequence as the carrier crested a wave. Squadrons amassed and climbed through the thick clouds to a cruising altitude of 13,100 feet. The Japanese— their humble lives depicting confinement, with their *ikebana,* their little dishes of food, their worlds of artful designs—had created the fastest and largest fleet of planes in the world.

The course was set: *Pearl Harbor, Oahu, Hawaii.*

•　　　•　　　•　　　•　　　•

As the watch ended at 0700, the two young US Army radio operators prepared to shut down the Opana Hawaiian radar set, when something caught their eye.

"What do you make of this?" one of them said, pointing to the radar screen. The other Private looked on with an equally puzzled expression. Flickering on the screen were about fifty dots, coming from the north.

"Couldn't be. There's too many of them," said the other, yawning and sitting upright trying to understand the screen.

"You better call the Lieutenant."

The other Private put a call in to the operator.

"Report from Opana Radar. Over fifty contacts north of Oahu at a range of 132 miles, sir," the operator said.

"Don't worry," said the Lieutenant. "There's a major flight of B-17 Flying Fortresses coming in from the mainland." The Lieutenant wasn't in the mood for any overreacting new radar boys. The beautiful sounds of Hawaiian music had been playing on his way to the Information Center, mesmerizing him into a sense of false security. He was in Hawaiian Christmas holiday mode. It was Sunday. Churches were preparing their best Christmas services. The city was sleeping. Most of the officers were on leave… and all was well with the world.

•　　　•　　　•　　　•　　　•

The *Rigel*, docked in Berth 13 of the US naval yard, was still undergoing massive repairs and conversions. Her crew were concentrating and oblivious to what was happening in the vicinity; she had no armament, and all her power, water, and services were supplied from dockside. Major work was still in progress with the replacement of boilers and generators. Besides, it was believed that she would be an unlikely target in any attack.

Charlie and his close diving buddies were working extended hours and hadn't been back in town since the last liberty. A feeling of uncertainty haunted Charlie. Roxy's photo remained in his locker. Everything, even the endless days of pleasure that the officers enjoyed, didn't seem right. Why were they in this paradise? All he knew was, the *Rigel* was a repair ship, and they were refurbishing her to protect others.

Sunday mornings at the mess hall had become a social gathering. Charlie and his shipmates hunkered over their trays of chow, all while planning a baseball game on the dock in the brilliant Hawaiian sunshine. It was a pleasant morning and half the officers were at yet another golf tournament, or perhaps hiking into the hills behind Aiea. One half of the crew was on liberty, while Charlie and most of deck 4 and 5 relaxed enjoying the last of their sausages and eggs, when someone hollered down the hatch.

"The Japs are coming!"

"So's Christmas," chuckled Vic, scooping up his eggs with ketchup, and crunching on a piece of toast.

Charlie gazed around to see if anyone else reacted, but nobody said anything, nothing but murmurs. A few seconds passed. At 7:55 am, a loud explosion jolted the mess hall, a shudder and detonation they'd never heard before. All twenty shipmates leapt up, left their trays and raced for the hatch, all fighting for the outside air. All hoping it was nothing serious.

Topside, a Japanese torpedo bomber zoomed over them, heading towards Battleship Row.

"He strafed us," yelled Vic, blindsiding Charlie. "Look out!" They both fell to the deck, face down, listening to the sounds of flying shrapnel, like somebody had mowed them with a Tommy gun.

"It's the Japs. I saw the Rising Sun on the plane."

"Keep your head down," yelled Vic, covering his ears. Shrapnel kept shattering down, like deadly hailstones. After a few minutes, Charlie peeped through his fingers. Vic risked a glimpse. Another round of bullets went thundering to the stern, pitting sounds, faster and faster, as a couple of deckhands came running across the deck, and split into hunks of flying limbs and flesh, before their eyes.

"Jesus… they just burst into pieces," Vic gripped Charlie as they lay still, watching their fellow sailors writhe in agony in the distance. Ferociously there were Jap planes all over the sky, dive-bombers and torpedo bombers, as the first wave continued.

"It's unbelievable. Look at all those planes." The "meatball" of the red Japanese Rising Sun was painted on every plane, swooping and diving in every direction. Charlie rose up staring at the planes, as if they were hanging on a spout of water that the torpedoes made.

"We have to do something. We have to get to the stern and help the men on the deck. We need rifles. Is the armory open?" he said, starting to make a move.

"You'll end up like the rest," Vic yelled, staring at the wounded men on the deck. After waiting another minute, they crawled on their hands and knees towards amidships when another bomb struck the *Rigel*, raising it up out of the water. It thundered back down, sending battered men flying into the sea. Another bomb landed between the piers and the bow but didn't go off. For a short while silence reigned. Charlie rushed to the stern. It was pitted by shrapnel and bullets. The two ships tied up nearby to the *Rigel* had been utterly decimated.

Andy appeared next to Charlie and Vic. He called out, "I have orders to take these men to sick bay. You guys are to stand by. You're not to leave the area. I'll get these men below. Shrapnel's even gone through the lockers. Nowhere's safe."

"Stand by for what?" yelled Charlie.

"For orders."

"Fuckin' orders for what?" said Vic. "The war will be over and we haven't done a thing. All our men will be shot. We need to find some fuckin' guns and ammunition. This old tub's not worth a goddamn thing. We're not armed, for Christ's sake." He grabbed a stretcher from off the wall.

"Stop. I knew this would happen. There's no use arguing," yelled Charlie, clutching Vic's arm. "Remember, we've orders." Just then, a deafening sound like hell itself exploded into the air. It was incredible. The sound of their own battleships firing back at last. It was screaming, chopping, thumping, banging, roaring all at once… smoke and fire everywhere.

Vic and Charlie stood helpless, watching. But they were together, brothers in arms; they stood, side by side. They felt the bond.

"Holy shit, it's brutal. Let's go get "em."

Lieutenant Commander Loar Mansbach was in charge until the Captain returned. He hollered orders for dispatch, assembling repair parties. Charlie and Vic raced to the quarterdeck as they listened.

"I want all divers on standby. The Captain expects to see the designated divers ready for dispatch. You know who you are. Get below, get your gear, and report back. On the *Double*. Chief O'Shea has been notified and will be arriving from the mainland later today on a seaplane. Stand by to board our small boats to rescue men overboard. This is not a drill," yelled Mansbach.

"Aye, aye sir."

Across the dock, BOOM. "They just torpedoed *Helena*," yelled Charlie. "Give us the rifles. I can kill a turkey a mile away. These fuckers are dead meat."

By now it was 0815. Mansbach ordered a volunteer crew, led by Ensign Hake, to head out to rescue crew off the *West Virginia*. The divers watched while *Rigel's* number 1 motor launch descended portside.

"Keep out of the direction of that wind and fire," yelled Mansbach. "Get those men out of that burning water. Just do it. Hurry!" The motor launch surged ahead, engines screaming.

The number 2 motor launch with Ensign Bienia and crew was just getting underway. There was a dreaded whistling sound overhead and a man topside yelled, "Watch out." Too late. Ensign Bienia's launch was horribly splintered by a bomb that cut the planking from capping to keel, exploding and throwing the crew overboard.

"My God, get those men. The boat's destroyed. Move out!" yelled the Captain, running up the ladder. "And someone get those hammerhead cranes moving. Get those torpedo boats off the docks and into the water. We've just lost our launch, for Christ's sake."

The bombs didn't stop.

"Captain, sir?" Andy spoke in a calm voice, coming up behind him.

"What is it?" snapped the Captain whipping around, his combination cap tilting, his face screwed up in a torturous glare.

"I can drive the crane, sir," exclaimed Andy calmly.

"Well, don't just stand there, do it."

"Yes, sir." Andy saluted, pivoted and ran down the gangway.

Another bomb struck at the *Rigel's* stern. One of the crew yelled. "A bomb's gone off between Piers 13 and 14."

Dodging the flying splinters and fragments, Charlie raced to the stern to see what happened.

"A bomb exploded on contact with the water," said one of the deckhands, covered in oil, standing alongside Charlie, wiping his eyes with a dirty rag.

"Damage?" asked Charlie leaning over the stern.

"Holes of just over two inches in diameter." The man put his fingers apart to describe the distance. "It blasted the port quarter," he said pointing, "just above the waterline." They bent over. "I'm sorry, you divers must be—" he shook his head, "so wanting to—"

"Yep, we're gonna get 'em," said Charlie gripping the railing.

"Yerr, well they've gone below to open the armory, get hold of all the ammo, guns, anything. We'll be getting them to you."

"Hurry! Fuckin' war will be over before I can fire my first shot."

"The rest of the crew will be back soon, but there's one hell of a big traffic jam out there. Some dumbass Jap truck driver parked his truck to block cars in the middle of the street, stood up on his cab waving, cheering the invaders, for Christ's sake," he hollered. "They shot him dead on the spot. No prisoners."

The thick, black smoke rapidly filled the Hawaiian skies. Random tracer bullets climactically found their mark. A few Japanese planes tumbled into the bay. Charlie ran for the quarterdeck to join his team.

"Vic's been looking for you," hollered Red.

Then before their eyes, a massive explosion blew the *Arizona*'s entire bow out of the water. Its mighty turrets crumpled like a toy against the dark and angry sky. Charlie, choked with emotion, caught a glance from Vic.

"Where the hell did you get to?" Vic said.

Charlie didn't answer. They stared at the next casualty. The destroyer *Shaw* blew up hardly 500 yards abreast, hit by two bombs; then over in the entrance to the harbor, the *Nevada* ran aground and dreadfully settled to the bottom.

By now the second wave of Japanese planes struck not far from where they were standing, blasting the battleship *Pennsylvania* twice in dry dock Number 1, and demolished the two adjacent destroyers, *Cassin* and *Downes*. The dry dock was now flooded and the massively hit *Downes* leaned against the *Cassin* like a wounded duck.

Across the waters, another mighty battleship became the victim of the Japanese. The *California* had most of its hatches open for inspection, and now lay drastically listing to port with seas rushing into immense torpedo holes.

On board the *Rigel*, everything from regulation rifles and Colt .45 pistols to privately owned hunting rifles were being passed all over. Charlie said a prayer under his breath and held his rifle. The difference that small, impotent weapon made as he raised it to the Jap planes was hard to say. But shooting that rifle helped ease all the anguish of the past few hours. He was sure his bullets nailed a few, but with so many planes barreling past at top speed, it was hard to tell which fell into the ocean on purpose or by accident.

Ultimately, Charlie and his men had orders to board the submarine rescue vessel, *Widgeon*. The rescue had begun. Their mission was far beyond the call of the *Rigel*. Their dive equipment was cautiously loaded onto the deck of the adjacent the *Widgeon*. Now was the careful hour; their role was critical. Charlie and his divers rehearsed all their training through determined minds as they descended from the *Rigel* in silence.

It was mid-morning and the sun was hidden behind the massive rage of fire and black smoke. Slippery filth and oil was under their feet, and knotted iron was everywhere they looked. The sweet, putrid smell of burned human flesh was hardly relieved by the occasional whiff of flaming Bunker C fuel oil, the bottom-of-the-barrel heavy fuel oil with its bilge aroma. Ships, once imperious, lay bleeding in the ebony-colored, oil-reeking waters. The Japanese had vanished; solely fire and misery remained.

America was at war.

CHAPTER 21

"Divers reporting for duty, sir." Charlie and the crew saluted.

"Stow your gear and get ready for a long day," said the Captain from the *Widgeon,* as it slowly edged down the port side of the *Rigel.*

"Kincaid, we've orders for an inspection of the torpedo damage to the *California.* We'll be dispatching you and your tenders first, and then departing with the other divers for the *Oklahoma.*" The Captain surveyed across the harbor, then swiveled and addressed the crew. "What you see, men, is the devastation that war brings. You're assigned to go beneath the problem, listen for trapped men, assess and measure the damage. Lives and our country depend on you."

They stood on the deck watching and listening. The *California* was a sorry sight as the *Widgeon* inched heedfully towards her huge exterior. None of the men had been up close to such a mighty battleship, now laced with black smoke gushing densely into the air, mixed terribly with the acrid smell of fuel, burning rubber, the putrid embers. The heat and oil were beginning to spell out their worst fears. What if there were no survivors?

"This is a dangerous mission. Are you up to it, Kincaid?"

"Can't wait, sir," spat out Charlie, glancing sideways at Vic.

With assistance from the diving team, Charlie and his tenders left the *Widgeon* for a diving barge alongside the *California*'s listing deck. It was noon as Charlie perched on the diver's chair, watching his crew stare at him. Charlie signaled thumbs up. Vic gave him thumbs up in response, mouthing something and nodding. Charlie knew he'd said, "I'd sink with you any day." The feeling of loyalty, comradeship, everything they had been taught, boldly hit him. This was why he was a Navy diver.

"Welcome aboard the *California*," yelled the officer on the deck.

Charlie was listening while his diving tenders lowered the breastplate over his head.

"She's listing heavily to port, and slowly settling. If "Abandon ship" is whistled out, it means get clear. Your mission will be over, got that?"

"Aye, aye, sir,"

"You have to be precise. There's nothing but thick black soup down there. You'll see nothing. Measure the damaged area, so we can build a cofferdam or rivet a patch to prevent her from sinking further." The officer hollered louder, "She's been hit forward and aft, and we don't know how badly."

"Ready to dive. Lower away," said Charlie, taking a final scan across the water at the *Widgeon* now settling close by to the *Oklahoma*

Charlie smiled through the glass port on his helmet, now screwed down securely, and lifted himself with the aid of his tenders. He gave the thumbs up and was helped down onto a diving platform dangling from a wire rope cable. The platform swung in mid-air. His circus days were back. It was his moment; he was reliant on training and pure guts from here on.

Steadily he descended. A strange sensation of nothingness came over him as his body became buoyant. Breathing in the forced air, he relaxed, spreading out his clumsy rubber gloves into every groove of the *California*'s structure, guiding himself cautiously along the hull towards amidships. The eerie silence, once his salvation, was now a harrowing corridor of debris. All he distinguished through his faceplate were solid dark shapes that appeared like body parts and personal belongings in a deathly flotilla. Distracted by the horror of it, he gasped at open eyes staring into his glass port. A sailor's lifeless head bobbed across his helmet. Charlie jolted back, pushing the sailor free; the body floated like a mysterious sea monster further along the hull. His hand ran over a gaping torpedo hole. *Holy Shit!*

He spoke into his helmet transceiver, "I've found the hole. It's huge. I'm going in to measure, over," Charlie said.

"Excellent. The edges will be razor sharp, over," replied topside.

"I see that, out."

Charlie edged around the perimeter of the ragged hole, carefully keeping his diving suit clear of the edges as he attached and pulled his measuring tape.

"Measures seventy feet wide, by thirty feet high, over," he reported back. Charlie circled in the area. "I'm going inside for a look."

He sensed a massive vibration. Vic's words, "*I'd sink with you any day*," rang hauntingly in his ear. A large interior bulkhead gave way, and the

California was sinking hard. Before he could brace himself, a torrent of water with the force of Niagara Falls sucked Charlie inside, pulling him thirty to forty feet into the hull. In the dark murky waters, he slumped, lifeless and unconscious.

When Charlie twitched back into consciousness, he found he was stuck fast. He could hardly feel his limbs. Seawater sloshed inside his helmet just below his nose, kept there by the pressure. *I must not panic...*

"Kincaid... Kincaid... report, over," topside blared.

They pulled on his lines, but he was stuck fast.

"We can't just leave him down there," screamed Vic.

"Everyone's life is in danger. We've radioed for another diver," yelled O'Shea. "Don't pull hard on those lines. You'll cut his air hose."

Unable to speak to topside with his helmet flooded, Charlie's communications were cut. His Navy training raced into action. Instinctively grabbing his lifeline and air hose, he coiled it over his arm, and began to crawl inch by inch through the slippery mud.

Slimy, sticky mud, it brought back memories of his escape from the orphanage. He clung to life like a dying seagull coated in oil, flapping its failed wings. He crept prudently along the line. Chunks of bodies and debris bounced into him with the sloshing currents. Then, dull light from the surface filtered into his range of sight. The diving platform swayed into view in the depths. He crawled onto it and pulled the signal rope.

"He's on the platform! Heave away smartly," blared Vic.

The compressed air rushed through as kinks in his air line were straightened. Struggling to control his terror, gulping for air, Charlie felt a strong grip pull sideways, almost drowning him. His faceplate opened, gushing foul air and water onto the deck. Charlie drew in a breath—even the smell of battle didn't bother him. He was still alive. He vomited buckets of oily water. A blurred figure wiped Charlie's face with a rag, pulling him up against the diving rig.

"He's gonna be okay," yelled a deep southern voice.

"He'd better be," said O'Shea, bending down to inspect Charlie's blackened head. "Gave us a fright. Bit more than the diving tank, eh mah boy?" He called to a tender, "Get him into decompression. He's not done diving, not by a long shot."

CHAPTER 22

The bombing of Pearl Harbor was still fresh in everyone's minds. Arthur sent word to George, congratulating him and explaining why he and Mary could not attend the wedding. With the world in conflict, travelling was dangerous and he was extremely worried. He'd heard serious talks had begun in Washington about Australia and New Zealand being abandoned. He was alarmed, after the *Niagara* had been so efficiently and precipitately driven to the deep by a German mine. New Zealand's position abruptly changed to serious battle mode, with rationing, and a quiet dread that the Japanese were headed their way.

And now Mattie was in danger. Auckland would be the first landing of the Japanese. Sightings of a Jap plane over Auckland had been announced, and additional sightings of Japanese submarines were reported in coastal waters. He put an urgent call through to George at the officer's mess in Papakura.

"Congratulations."

"Gosh Dad, I dreaded this was an emergency," said George, trying to listen through the bad connection.

"It is. I want Mattie back in Dunedin. I could send her home by seaplane. It's not safe up there."

"But Dad, everyone's in danger anywhere in New Zealand."

"Well, I don't see it that way. My family comes first."

"The Americans will not let us down."

"The lines are bad.' Arthur snapped. "Just see to it she arrives safely."

George and Irene's marriage was a very small affair… attended merely by Irene's parents, Mattie and Irene's sister as bridesmaids, and John and Audrey. It was held under the scalloped arches in St David's Presbyterian Church on Khyber Pass Road. George stood alongside Irene, looking cavalier in his officer's uniform.

Despite all the wartime uncertainty, Irene was a picture of serenity, like an angel draped in white satin. It was her day. *God bless her*, Mattie envisioned as a tear tried to form.

The bells rang out as the wedding party bounded down the steps. Irene turned around and the soft summer breeze blew aside her veil. She smiled back at Mattie, and threw her bouquet, calling out to her, "You'll be next."

Mattie caught it midair. She laughed as the flowers descended against her, their gentle petals brushing her nose and cheeks. She noticed Audrey scowling at her, but Mattie could not scowl back. She summed up pity, more like sorrow for Audrey. Mattie stood there, smiling and waving at Irene... how happy she was. All Mattie's ambitions were coming true; she loved her work, and she wonderfully loved being free, free to live her own life.

Angst over George's imminent departure to fix decayed teeth in Fiji was punctuated by daily media reports that the war was inching closer to New Zealand. There were growing numbers of people who believed that the sound of gunfire was not far over the horizon.

·　　·　　·　　·　　·

Soon after the wedding, Irene invited Mattie to her place for their usual chats, but she was surprised when George answered the door.

"Mattie... here, please sit," said George. His face was glum. Maybe it is the prospect of leaving for war, Mattie thought. George lit a cigarette and offered one to Mattie, sat back and took a deep draw. "I'll get to the point... Dad wants you home."

Mattie glared at George, "No... Absolutely *not*. You're posted offshore to some warzone, and I'm being ordered home?" Her fingers trembled, as she stubbed out her cigarette. "Father has always had his way, always."

"Hey, it's your life. He's simply trying to protect you," explained George.

"I have a career. I can look after myself," Mattie insisted.

"I'd say, let's head down to Mechanics Bay and send you to Dunedin," said George.

"The only one who's going anywhere is you, brother. Now get to the phone. You're so good at taking orders," Mattie replied, now frowning.

"No... you can tell him," grinned George.

"Go on Mattie," said Irene. "Ask him to your graduation."

Mattie hesitated, then jumped up and stabbed the numbers around the phone, as if the phone were the problem.

"Father, I'm not coming home. Not right now. I have my graduation," she spoke respectfully but firmly.

George and Irene remained silent, watching.

The line went dead, and Mattie hard-dropped the phone to its cradle.

"They're not coming," said Mattie. She lit another cigarette, her hands now moist. "Are you coming, or are you deserting me too?" Mattie raised an eyebrow at George.

"Wouldn't miss it for the world, my dear sister." Stretching out, he put his hand on Irene's clasped hands. "Got to support our family. Anyway...," he looked keenly at Mattie, "Why's Dad so worried? The Americans are coming."

"Maybe that's why he's worried," Irene interrupted, giggling, and then covering her mouth.

•　　　•　　　•　　　•　　　•

Mattie's graduation was held in the tearooms on the fourth floor of George Courts. Reaching the top floor, they made their way up four steps and through glass panel doors into the tearooms, with their convex ceilings over dozens of tables, draped with brilliant white coverings, surrounded by bentwood chairs. On three sides of the room were small alcoves, separated by carved oak partitions, each sheltering a table with padded leather bench seats. Nearby windows and doors opened out onto a terrace, which had spectacular panoramic views of the city and harbor. John and George were already chuckling together over matters uniquely men would dare discuss. The evening opened with speeches.

"Now, ladies and gentlemen," said Mr O'Hara, holding the last certificate. He smiled to his wife, "My wife Esmeralda would like to say a few words."

Mattie noticed Audrey glaring at the glamorous woman, as she lifted up folds of brocade. Mrs O'Hara's hair swirled across a high forehead. Her diamond earrings caught the light from the crystal chandeliers as she rose to speak.

"My husband has always told me our students give him great joy." She spoke steadfastly, calmly gazing at the audience. "Excellent staff are like gold, which is why we have saved our best student till last."

Mattie watched Audrey settle back in her chair, her mouth turned down as if she'd swallowed something vile. Mattie squeezed Irene's hand under the table.

"Miss Blanc. Rarely do we get a student with one hundred percent... perfect top marks!"

A mutter swept across the room—then a hush. Mrs O'Hara signaled Mattie to rise. Mattie didn't acknowledge anyone as she walked over to receive her certificate. Mrs O'Hara put a soft hand on her arm. "Miss Blanc, despite the onset of war, you have excelled in your studies. We are so proud of you. Well done."

Mattie looked into her eyes and smiled. She turned and spoke to the audience, "Thank you so much, and especially to my family for making this possible."

The room resounded with clapping and loud cheering. George stood up as Mattie came back to the table, and began to sing, "For she's a jolly good fellow...".

Supper was served along with tea and champagne, and everyone began to mingle.

"Congratulations Mattie," said Audrey, swilling down a glass of champagne. "We won't know ourselves, what with John a doctor and you a...," she paused to dab a blob of cream from her lips, "...hairdresser. We'll all be so busy serving the public." Audrey grabbed another glass of champagne from the passing waiter.

Miss Shearer opportunely appeared.

Mattie introduced her, "Miss Shearer, this is my sister-in-law, Audrey..."

"Pleased to meet you," said Audrey, tossing back another mouthful of champagne. Her voice deepened with a slur, "I was just saying to Mattie, what a wonderful achievement."

"I know. I've decided to offer Mattie a full-time position."

"Well, I suppose it's a relief not to have to go out in the fields and chop cabbages," Audrey parried.

"Mattie is both talented and hard-working... a rare combination," retorted Miss Shearer.

"Thank you, Miss Shearer. I'll be delighted to keep working at the salon," Mattie accepted quickly.

"Well... I'll be a busy Mrs Doctor Blanc in June, when my husband graduates," Audrey boasted.

"Perhaps you could help Doctor Blanc change bandages on all those injured soldiers," said Miss Shearer. She excused herself, and beckoned Mattie to one side. "I'm sorry, that was most inappropriate. I should have asked you privately how you felt about working for us. Your sister-in-law...," she glared over her shoulder. "Apologies, but her bovine behavior riles me..."

"Don't worry, Miss Shearer," Mattie held her arm, "I'd love to work for you."

But Mattie wasn't about to convince her to calm down. Miss Shearer's eyes were fixed hard on Audrey. Mattie grinned, "Audrey's not herself. It must be the war and the strain... and all her husband's traumas."

Miss Shearer's eyes narrowed. "Absolute... *rubbish*. We'll talk later."

Mattie watched her high chignon disappear into the crowded room. *I bet she's had heaps of Audrey's to deal with*, she smiled to herself. She picked up a sandwich from one of the three-tiered cake stands. I'm not just somebody's secretary, she foresaw for herself. I'm a *success*.

•　　•　　•　　•　　•

The following day Mattie and Irene stood on the dockside, blowing kisses at George as he loftily posed on the deck of the *Rangatira*. One prolonged blast of her steam whistle, and the ship eased away from the wharf, destined for Fiji; with the destroyer *Leander* close aside as escort. Mattie had mixed feelings, watching her brother steadily disappear around North Head. How much had changed in their small world. She was so glad they had their wedding day; even if their parents couldn't make it, she was there for them. She'd never forget that day. She and Irene walked down the dock arm in arm, in silence. Neither wanted to share their dread, not just yet—now their family had gone to war.

CHAPTER 23

Sweat snaked down Charlie's oil-stained face as he lay against the cold metal bulkhead. Someone had thankfully placed him outside the decompression chamber to recover and he must have dozed off. Charlie pushed himself up and searched around. He knew he was on the *Widgeon*. He heard O'Shea's voice over on the starboard side, calling out to the rest of the crew on the *Oklahoma*. He picked up his diving mask, shook himself, and hurried over to report to O'Shea.

O'Shea didn't offer any sympathy to Charlie.

"You've met death. It's a nasty son of a bitch, Kincaid, but it's here to stay," O'Shea remarked, staring at the upturned hull as they came closer. "There's 500 men trapped inside, depending on your skills right now," he went on, his voice cracking. "Ten minutes and flooded. They didn't stand a chance."

Charlie had a new respect for O'Shea. He stepped into his tank suit, buttoned on the lightweight shallow-water belt, and adjusted the air-fed facemask. He noticed the communicators. Holding his two-inch manila rope lifeline tied to the oxygen hose, Charlie gave his best thumbs-up to the men as he prepared to descend the ladder.

Vic came running up, "Goddamn Kinks, you old bugger. We almost lost you. O'Shea was beside himself."

Charlie grinned through his face mask...

Suddenly a civilian diver came up to the surface yelling, "There's been an explosion." He threw down his oxy-hydrogen torch and removed his mask.

Charlie and Vic rushed over to the upset diver, who mumbled something like, "I can't do this anymore."

O'Shea was right behind them, walking towards the commotion.

"What the fuck happened?"

"Beats me… no idea," replied Charlie.

Vic helped the diver onto the diving chair and started taking off his diver's gear.

Blood ran out of the man's mouth and nose. They urgently grabbed the rest of the equipment.

"I want a full report back at the *Rigel* as swiftly as possible," said O'Shea. "And work out a plan. You boys are going to have to pick up the slack. Cancel your dive, Kincaid. We need answers on that explosion."

•   •   •   •   •

Back in the mess hall, the men were all fired up.

"We've lost a lot of men. I can't wait to throttle a Jap. I'll rip his head off and dropkick it to Tokyo," remarked Crow, as he shoveled in a pile of scrambled eggs.

Charlie looked up from his plate of beans and bacon, "Whoa... it's no good gettin' angry; a bullet or knife will do the trick plenty good. Get mad and you lose focus. Concentrate on our job and we'll get 'em. There'll be more dead Japs than you can count."

They left for another day on the *Oklahoma*. Topside the odor hit them. Nothing could describe the stench and filth of smoldering heavy oil, laced with the smell of rotting, burned flesh. Spare salvage divers had been called in to free survivors. O'Shea had determined that the explosion was caused by a collection of unburned torch gases that ignited when burning debris floated into the large gas pockets.

"I told you, you're the guinea pigs," said O'Shea, picking up the torch to demonstrate. "Those civilian pussies will blow themselves up if they're not careful. One piece of hot shit floats up in an air bubble to a gas pocket and—" he waved the torch, "—*woosh*, Pearl Harbor all over again. We won't be using any gas torches inside ships. One of our shipfitter welders was too lazy to go get his gas-cutting torch, and just cranked up the amps on his welding machine. He drew a long arc, and cut the steel like butter through your butthole. So we're all trying it today. Make a long arc with the electrode and cut the plate," said O'Shea, with a knowing grin. "All for some portholes, so you pussies can have fresh fuckin' air in your goddamn cot beds, I hear. Now get to your posts. You've got work to do."

"Yes, sir," barked the men.

Charlie was the first to call out, "Juice on," and a massive 600amps raged through his electrode.

"Goddamn, it cuts like crap through a tin goose," said Moult, his toned muscles bristling wet blue in the light.

Charlie reached quickly into the compartment. A hand, an arm came wriggling out. Moult switched off his gear and they all crowded round.

"Oh my God, you're not Jesus?" said the first sailor to be rescued.

"No sirree," cried out Charlie, "just plain ole sailors, come to get you out."

"Of Hell," said Vic, leaning over, helping another sailor out. They stood on the hull of the *Oklahoma* with the survivors, all thirty-two men glad to be alive, stumbling out into the fresh air.

Hardly days later other lurking tragedies unfolded. Unknown to the divers, saltwater mixed with man-made materials on the ships created deadly hydrogen sulphide gas. Under pressure, this gas was odorless, with no whiff of rotten eggs to warn an intruder. When a compartment was opened by two civilian divers, they succumbed on the spot to the awaiting doom.

Charlie and the others fell silent once again, when they heard O'Shea's voice booming across the ship's deck at the hopeless conditions.

"Nothing in this goddamn filthy war will free these trapped men. Now we have more dead bodies," said O'Shea, his head in his hands. "If we cut a hole, then the air pocket escapes and they all drown before we can get 'em out. Or our torches burn the asbestos or whatever and we kill them with poisonous gas."

They stood there, looking at the two civilian divers lying face down in the opening. They covered them respectfully with a tarp, and left to alert the somber stretcher details for removal.

•   •   •   •   •

News of the attack on Pearl Harbor had reached Washington. President Franklin Roosevelt declared war on the Imperial Government of Japan.

Beyond doubt, Pearl Harbor was a deliberate and planned attack. The deception by the Japanese government unveiled their exterior of benign, humble little men into underhanded evil manipulators of dirty tactics. President Roosevelt, told the nation in a radio address, "...*The Japanese have treacherously violated the long-standing peace between us. Many American soldiers and sailors have been killed... It is not a sacrifice for any man, old or young, to be in the Army or the Navy of the United States. Rather is it a privilege... I repeat that the United States can accept no result save victory, final and complete... We are going to win the war and we are going to win the peace that follows.*"

But the Führer in Germany, exultant at Japan's success, slapped his thighs and bounded across the room, yelling, "We will now win the war."

With the Tripartite Pact in place, Germany and Italy declared war on the United States.

The Japanese surged ahead, sweeping forthwith into Hong Kong, the Philippines and Malaya. But in their haste, they forgot the strategic Pearl Harbor oil storage tanks, the Navy dry docks, and the *Rigel*. America could repair and had plenty of fuel for the chase.

CHAPTER 24

When they subsequently returned to the *Rigel*, Charlie went down to check on his distillery. The bubbles had gotten out of control in the past weeks and things were fermenting briskly, not the way they were supposed to, not like back in the South.

"It might be the pineapple juice," said Vic with a sarcastic smile. "Did you piss in it?"

Charlie thumped him. "I'll piss on you if you don't get out of my way," he said, stirring the fermenting mash. "Might have a problem with this brew. Don't know if she's gonna hold a bead. You'll be glad of this shit if we head out of here."

"Yeah. Too many dives, not enough women." Vic kicked the pipe, leaving Charlie stirring.

Andy ducked his head round the corner. "Better put a lid on that. Wilkes' replacement, the new repair officer, is coming."

Charlie shook his head; he was secretly relieved but still mystified. Maybe one day when the shit cleared he'd find out what literally happened out there to Roxy and Wilkes.

After several days, O'Shea called the team into the wardroom. He paced about the wardroom, his head down. Then he paused and viewed his men. "Now you've had a taste of war." Resuming his pacing, he went on, "I am leaving. Roosevelt's appointed a commission of inquiry to investigate the Pearl Harbor bombing."

Lowering his voice he told the men, "Reconditioning work will increase on the *Rigel* until she is complete. She will be ready, like you men, to take on any work necessary, near any front lines, keeping our Navy ships ready for action. There'll be no need for vessels to make long trips back to Navy yards. You are the salvage team and the first demolition divers." He picked up the charred remains of a manual, and waved it around, "Navy divers never give up. Any questions?"

Red stepped ahead, "How do we make contact with our families?"

O'Shea answered, but his concern showed, "For now, all letters will be submitted to our Navy censors. At 1700 hours you will go on liberty. Any phone calls will be monitored. There is to be positively no mention of your whereabouts or the work you are doing. Tell 'em you love 'em and will write. Better yet, don't call, just write."

As they travelled in the bus past Hickam Field, they viewed the horrendous damage. Fighter planes were strewn like crippled geese with their tails or wings shot off. The big hangar was a twisted mass of burned steel. Charlie swayed in the bus, frowning into the last of the sunlight. No island girls greeted them, just a pulverized hut crumbled to the ground. His heart thumped, heavy with the vision of Roxy and what he might discover.

Vic was trying not to act serious, but his inner mood showed on his face, and he winced at Charlie, lighting a cigarette as they crossed the road and hurried into Hotel Street. The Hubba Hubba still stood, but blackout curtains covered the entrance. The wreckage that had been close-by buildings reminded them that the townsfolk were not spared from the dreadful Sunday morning.

Vic pushed the doors open to an empty bar. There was no one in sight, no music; the bar was deserted. An older woman came towards them, arms flailing, wanting to kill—angrily calling out obscenities.

Vic spoke, "Is Daisy here, ma'am, any of the ladies here?"

"No! No sailors, no girls, go home, you make trouble. Get out."

They walked towards the rubble of the upturned streets, heading back towards the bus. Men were digging trenches everywhere, tunnels for the raids; nothing was going to be the same. It was no use searching. Charlie refused to think about Roxy, and what he'd left behind.

Christmas seemed without purpose, and the New Year passed. The *Rigel* was grandly fitted with four three-inch guns.

"Something's in the wind," said Charlie topside one evening, when the sun was setting.

"Yes, she's changing her battle armor. The old girl's steaming to war," said Vic.

"Yeah?"

"Well, like I said before, haven't you noticed? What's with the R11 on the bow?"

"Yeah, and what's with the army units?" Crow joined in. "I heard we're taking them somewhere."

April 1942 and the conversion work was complete. Captain Dudley announced that the *Rigel* would be sailing out of Pearl. A short test and sea trial made everyone certain that departure was imminent. When they returned to the harbor entrance, it was all too déjà vu: no one wanted to relive the horror. Graves stretched for miles above the Hawaiian beaches, bearing the American flag. No, it was not a proud sight.

All liberty was cancelled, and the *Rigel* readied for departure. This time the army units and their materials were no secret. The *Rigel* shuddered under hundreds of boots pounding her decks and ladders. The soldiers, who knew no more than the crew, struggled up the gangway under their bulging packs.

With the destroyer USS *Gridley* as their escort, the *Rigel* headed south. She proudly pitched into frothing cobalt blue seas towards the South Pacific.

CHAPTER 25

Charlie felt the *Rigel's* steady strength as she cut through the heaving seas at twelve knots, powered by her new boilers. Charlie was on watch on the starboard-side main deck. He leaned over the railings and marveled at how the dark, midnight-blue ocean frothed and foamed into a blinding pure white, laced with iridescent greens and blues.

After duty the bet was on to guess their destination. Vic, Red and Crow huddled around Charlie's cot. Charlie shuffled the stack of cards, determined to beat Vic, and handed him the deck. The rest of the team gathered in groups, talking; others read, wrote letters, or just lay on their cots. The shop was long, but by the minute all the cots were out, there was little room to move.

"We haven't got all night." Vic nudged Charlie as he dealt the cards. "I'd say we're headin' to the Solomons... right in the thick of it, next to the big guns." It was early days, so the bets were small and winnings just pocket change. The night drew on and eventually quieted with lights out.

Moult lay on his side, legs bent, half asleep on his folded blanket. Without warning, he burbled a grotesque moan that built to a full holler. He flailed wildly and tumbled onto the floor.

"Sorry guys... nightmare."

Vic tipped Moult's cot upside down. "Do that again, and I'll throw ya overboard."

"Now settle down," said Charlie. "This isn't a circus."

"Something's going on... we're changing course," said Red. He leaped up and pulled on his pants.

A voice shrieked from the ship's speakers, "Torpedo wake off the port bow. General Quarters, man your battle stations. Standby for collision. This is NOT A DRILL."

The men and all loose equipment lurched sideways as the ship's right full rudder took hold and bit hard into the seas.

General Quarters sounded again, this time a long burst. *Ahoooga... Ahoooga...*

"What'd I tell ya?" Red ran for the hatch.

"What the hell... three days and we're in the war," yelled Vic, as he grabbed his clothes. "Let's get these fuckers." He shoved his cot to one side. All sleeping hands scrambled into their gear and bolted to their stations.

Up on deck, Mansbach grabbed the rails, staring into the darkness. "Our destroyer's launching depth charges."

BOOM... BOOM... BOOM

Charlie had never seen a destroyer at flank speed. She churned a gigantic effervescent plume like a proud rooster, with depth charges flying off the stern and exploding close enough to the *Rigel* to rattle every bone in his body. The full moon, which had been a gift at first for the sub, was now its nemesis: it was the hunted.

"This is the Captain speaking. Gunners stand by your guns," the loudspeaker roared.

"The *Gridley* has it under control. Kincaid, take your men and report to damage control battle stations... on the double," Mansbach yelled.

"The *Gridley*'s sunk the sub. There's debris and an oil slick off the stern," said Ensign Hall, racing past. He repeated himself along the deck, "Stand by your post."

The waves were colored black and red in the moonlit oil sheen, coating bits of debris bobbing everywhere.

"What a catch," hollered everyone.

"We got him," the quartermaster yelled down from the wing of the bridge.

"Good old *Gridley*—they'll be getting ice-cream for breakfast. Standby for transfer at sea from our stores at dawn," said Ensign Hall. "You boys get back to work. Show's over."

Two long, hot days at sea, and they had their first sight of land. The crew stared at the tiny islet coming towards them. It didn't resemble much like Hawaii. They soon learned it was a British cable and radio station, called

Fanning Island. The 150 US Army troops disembarked off the *Rigel*. The following day a rumble of different army units came aboard the *Rigel*.

The crew maintained a tool room topside for paint and repairs. Charlie was hunkered down near the quarterdeck, repairing their dive gear, when he noticed the group of men in strange uniforms march aboard; Charlie imagined they were probably some displaced British servicemen.

They set sail again the next day. The mess hall took on an interesting flavor when Vic walked past the newcomers at chow.

"This is fuckin' hilarious," said Vic, sitting down and picking up his fork. "Take a look. They're pushin' food up the backside of their forks, and—" he smirked "—that's not all. They talk real funny."

"So you think this is some sort of game?" asked Crow, his stack of hair scrambled and spiked on end.

Charlie burst out laughing, spraying milk all over the steel table. "I think the Navy's commissioned us to be a transport for stranded Brits."

"No kidding?" said Red. "Where'd you hear that?"

"Oh... I snoop around." Charlie stepped over the bench, picked up his tray, and turned. "Watch this." He swaggered ahead to the newcomers' table.

"Hi ya. I'm Petty Officer Kincaid. Welcome to the *Rigel*." Charlie put out his one free hand. A man in army uniform with stubble on his jaw and skin like leather dropped his knife and fork onto his tray. He shook hands with Charlie.

"Gidday, mate. Bill Smith, happy to meet you," he said.

"We've a bit to learn about you British boys, by the look of it." Charlie noticed the knife and fork on the tray and thought about trying the oddball backwards fork routine.

"No, no," one of the other men spoke up. "You got it wrong, mate. We're not Pommies, we're from New Zealand. Goin' home, to our missus."

"You mean that's where we're headed—New Zealand?"

"Only place I know." Bill stood up. "Listen, if you get ashore down there, I'll shout you a beer." He winked, and slapped Charlie on the back.

Charlie went and emptied his scraps into the disposal unit, then returned to his seat.

"What was that guy saying?" Vic asked.

Charlie grinned at Vic. "Those lucky boys are going home."

Curiosity spread full tilt when they dropped anchor at what appeared as another piece of paradise. Vic went headlong into the mass of white uniforms, racing down the ladder and onto the boats ferrying them to the shores of Pago Pago, American Samoa.

White sands graced the shores of this peaceful island. The waters were a clear turquoise blue, more beautiful than any they'd seen in Hawaii. Charlie climbed out onto the wooden wharf, following his fellow divers along the walkway.

A small group of island women gathered on the shoreline. The sweet scent of the frangipani leis encircling their necks wafted downwind, and heatedly the men imagined they were back at the Hubba Hubba in Pearl Harbor.

A large elderly woman held out a wrinkled paw, pointing to herself and calling out, "Yankee dollar, you pay me, boss, Yankee dollar." She beckoned to the growing crowd of sailors, calling out, "Nude show... follow me..."

"We're in," laughed Vic, stuffing a dollar between the woman's pendulous breasts. "This has to be better than fighting the Japs. We're on a cruise. Come on, guys. We're gonna get laid. Don't mind if I did lose my bet," he shouted, handing Charlie his flask.

Charlie downed a long swig, and followed the hundreds of other sailors across the white sands towards the haunting sounds of island music.

But when the show started, the women had more clothes on than they'd started with at the dockside. It ended in a short skit, as quickly as it began.

"That was some sort of scam, I bet." Vic shoved Charlie into a crowd of smiling women. "We'll make our own fun... spread this moonshine everywhere." They each took another swig from Vic's flask, and headed towards a group of huts.

The afternoon transformed to a tropical pink sky. A wild hallucination of flowers, skin and lips crowded Charlie's senses. He fondled her softness as he blacked out. He woke to find himself lying intertwined with a young woman. He leapt up, groping all over in the dark for his clothes. Panicking, he raced down the beach, dove into the ocean, swam towards the *Rigel* and climbed up the ladder.

"Goddamn! Kinky, that's the second time I've had to haul you out of trouble," said Vic, throwing him a set of undershorts.

"I'm not done with you… not by a long way," Charlie stood dripping wet on the deck, glaring at Vic.

"Can't take a joke? The guard's just left." Vic shoved his pants at him. "I saved your sorry ass, didn't I?"

Charlie grabbed Vic's shoulder. "Hey, whatever it was out there… was worth it."

"Musta been that bootleg whisky. You made it, not me," Vic laughed.

"You jokers had a bit of a fling last night?" Bill said to Charlie as they stood in line for chow. "Here," he handed Charlie a knife and fork. "Better learn proper eating habits, if you want to score with a sheila."

Charlie frowned, taking the utensils.

"Yep, Auckland's got the best sheilas in New Zealand."

"Is that a food bar?"

"You'll find out. Go tell your mates. My shout, remember."

Charlie returned to his table, thinking about Bill's strange dialect. Puzzled, he leaned in to his meal.

"What took you so long, Kinky?" said Vic, gurgling through his mug of milk.

"Don't say a word."

A snigger in the group broke the silence.

"Too much pussy… eh?"

Charlie's eyebrows rose. "I've got news." He dug the knife and fork into his chow and raised his elbows like a chicken. He clucked, "We're goin' to Owckland, Noo Zillun to meet some Sheas."

CHAPTER 26

As they made the second crossing of the International Date Line, the crew was beginning to think they were circling, until another island appeared with coconut palms swaying in the warm breeze. A day stop in Tonga, and then there was a turn for the worse as the sea churned violently. The *Rigel*'s bow buried itself in fifty-foot seas, and rose again relentlessly, then plunging like a falling elevator into the waiting trough. The ship groaned and shuddered with the pounding. Sailors desperately hunched over the nearest railing, their vomit broadcast back on deck by the wind.

Charlie hadn't seen much of Andy until a trip to the head led by bellering sounds in the corridor. He found Andy moaning, hugging one of the toilets.

"Come on," said Charlie.

"I can't. I'm sick," said Andy, hugging his sick bowl.

"Take that," a fountain of piss flew past Andy's open arms. "Goddamn pussy," said one of the new troops.

Charlie lifted the new troop up by the scruff of his neck and threw him against the bulkhead. "So is this what's comin'?"

"You're going to be in for a shock when you hit down-under, mate." The trooper kicked the toilet and left.

Charlie helped Andy upright, and dragged his shaking legs up the ladder to topside.

They stood on the deck, wedged into an alcove, the ocean spray in their faces.

"Be right back, Andy." Charlie rushed down to the mess hall and returned minutes later.

"Here… eat these soda crackers and drink this cola until your gut squares away."

"Do you think I'm over the worst of it?" asked Andy, wiping his wet mouth.

Charlie didn't like the look of Andy; there was despair in his eyes. He put his hand on Andy's shoulder. "This storm will settle, just like every other storm settles. Do ya know where we're going?"

Andy nodded. "My uncle told me. He's on the *San Francisco*. She'll be there soon after we get in." His face lit up; a hint of color returned to his cheeks. "The weather's cold, but I heard the folks are real nice."

"Can't wait. Here, have a cracker."

After several days in rough seas, a bright sun rose at last from the horizon. With this dawn came the land–orange and purple peaks that increasingly became islands, and then lush green hills dotted with perfect beaches. The *Rigel* altered course into Waitemata Harbor on Saturday May 16, 1942.

Charlie, along with all available ship's crew, lined the rails to witness the spectacle of this new country unfolding. We have big work to do here, he realized. I'd hate to see the Japs get their hands on this beautiful land.

"Look at all those red roofs. They look like tiles," said Charlie, pointing all over. "Holy cow! We must have passed forty islands on the way in."

Rows of women lined the wharf, waving frantically as the *Rigel*'s whistle announced her arrival. Casting off lines, she docked at Princes Wharf, Auckland, New Zealand.

"Hey, those women are doing semaphore to our guys on the signal bridge," Vic said, frantically trying to catch their attention. "Ladies, the good stuff is right here," he yelled.

"Those gals musta heard you were comin', Vic. I betcha Mansbach will have some sort of curfew planned," Red complained over the loud noise. Just then a brass band, struck up *Roll Out the Barrel*.

Charlie squinted into the sun, tapping his foot to the music.

"We're finally upside down, Kinky," said Vic, stubbing his cigarette on the rail.

"You gonna leave any gals for us?" Charlie gave him a shove.

"Ha! After your effort on the beach babe, you can talk."

They hollered and whistled to the laughter and happy faces of the Auckland crowd.

•   •   •   •   •

Mattie and Nan had been shopping in Queen Street when they heard the rumpus. One of their clients had told them a convoy of American troops and ships were arriving.

"I just can't believe all this is happening. Look at that huge ship lined with men," said Mattie. She remembered the *Niagara,* once sitting there.

"Looks like good fun to me," said Nan. "Mattie… let's have a closer look."

"No. Look at all the women. You'd think some Hollywood dreamboat has come to town," yelled Mattie.

"Well, maybe he has. Don't be such a prude." They raced past the red wrought-iron gates. The band struck up *Yankee Doodle.* They heard the sailors whistling up on the main deck.

"Can you see what they're throwing?" asked Nan.

Mattie squinted into the sun. Glistening coins showered the dock in a silver rain. Berserk women pushed past them into a crushing crowd, building to a full frenzy of beautiful screams. The passing traffic came to a halt as drivers gawked and waved.

"This is crazy. Let's get out of here," complained Mattie.

They turned and pushed their way through the riotous commotion, and walked back up Queen Street in a daze.

•   •   •   •   •

The *Rigel*'s loudspeakers blasted, "Now hear this, as you were. Report to your duty stations." Several hundred disappointed men scurried back to their posts.

Mansbach hollered above the booming noise, "Kincaid, prepare for a briefing. Captain's orders, report to the Wardroom at 1800 hours."

Captain Dudley strolled into the Wardroom. Charlie had never seen him so relaxed. He gestured for the men to take a seat on the leather couches. The captain remained standing.

"We have arrived in Auckland, New Zealand, and all men will be briefed on the customs of this country. However, next week—" he paused and began to pace across the huge room with his hands behind his back "—the *Rigel* is to become Vice-Admiral Ghormley's flagship."

Charlie leaned forward to concentrate in the hushed room.

Captain Dudley studied each man, as he kept pacing. "Admiral Ghormley has been appointed by Roosevelt to take over the command of the Allied forces in the South Pacific." He raised his voice. "We have a job to do down here and that is to protect these people and build infrastructure. Do you read me?"

"Aye, aye sir." Charlie instantly stood up and saluted.

"At ease, Kincaid. I understand your passion. Your team will be issued a diving tender, and assigned plenty of repair work. But nonetheless you will continue to train in explosives and hand combat so you are fightin' ready when we reach the front." The Captain settled down backwards on a chair, straddling it as he faced the men. "Liberty. You'll get plenty of it down here. Today we secure the *Rigel* and make ready with shore services available. Tomorrow, Sunday, will be your first liberty. All of you will get the day off." There was a flurry of excited smirks between the men.

"Monday, we get to work. After duty, liberty will be granted port and starboard with half the ship's company ashore each night. The Admiral's arriving this Friday, and I want all hands on deck, dress uniforms. Any questions?"

"How long are we here for, sir?" asked Red.

"As long as it takes. We've a job to do… transforming Auckland into the South Pacific's main operating, supply and hospital base. We'll be building hospitals, repairing ships and training these local men down here. You'll be using your diving skills constantly, with regular deployments to practice your special skills." He stood up, and walked towards the door. "The Admiral is regarded in naval circles as being a strategist of exceptional ability. He's a good man, humble but firm. He'll get the job done. Get ready to kick some Jap ass."

"Aye aye, sir." Everyone stood up.

"Oh, and…" Captain Dudley scratched his chin. "You boys watch your manners. The people here are of a reserved nature, above all the women."

He frowned and showed them the door.

Outside, Vic whispered with a gaping grin, "Not what I saw on the dock. Reckon they can hardly wait to get a piece of us."

·　　·　　·　　·　　·

Charlie and his men left the dockside for liberty the following day. "Goddamn. I could get used to this." Charlie grabbed Red as he was almost hit by an oncoming car along Quay Street. "Holy shit! They're driving on the wrong side of the road."

Jingling a bunch of loose coins in his pocket, Charlie decided to take a tram ride. He wanted to feel at home in this new country. Best way was to do what he always did—hit the streets, meet the people. He hopped on a stationary tram across the road in Queen Street, smiling at the young tram conductor in uniform, who was threading her way through the tramcar.

"Where are you going?" she asked.

"Anywhere, ma'am."

The girl blushed. "That will be three pence, one way to Symonds Street."

"Then that will be fine." Charlie stared at the coins in his hand. She picked out a three pence, and gave him a ticket. Two clangs of the bell, and the tram moved onward.

He stared out the window. *Cars parked on the wrong side of the street. We're upside-down and backwards.*

The tram purposely ascended Queen Street. The shops were closed, but the movie theatres were open. Maybe he'd get a local newspaper to find out what was playing.

At the top of the hill, the tram followed its tracks left and stopped at a street with a long, jumbled name that he couldn't pronounce. He decided to get off. Burrowing inside his pocket, he prized out a few of the strange coins and bought a newspaper and an apple from a corner store. Fresh fruit was a luxury after weeks aboard ship. The crisp, sweet apple disappeared down his gullet in just a few bites. Light rain started to fall, and he ducked under a veranda to watch a tram on the other side of the track stop at the raised platform in the center of the street. Careful to check both ways this time, he crossed the road, and hopped into the tram.

It was as if he'd seen a ghost. Charlie's heart raced: there she was, the girl of his dreams. He risked another glance. It was her delicate features; her glowing dark hair that tumbled elegantly around perfect alabaster skin, so tastefully accented with a red bow. *She is an angel.* He took a deep breath and moved towards her.

•　　•　　•　　•　　•

Mattie glanced up at the handsome young man. She moved closer to the window to make room, and caught her breath. She focused out the window, stunned by the split-second eye contact with this beautiful man. His piercing black eyes hovered over a polite smile and a dimpled chin. Why was her heart beating so fast? Not daring to raise her eyes, she glanced at the dark wool of his coat. Then came his glorious voice…

"Pardon me, ma'am, do you mind if I sit next to you?"

His tone was resonant, like slow syrup. It was that southern drawl she'd heard in the movies. It was the hardest thing to do, connecting again with his rich, dark eyes. She smiled, "Not at all. I'm getting off at the upcoming stop. I'm going to the movies."

As the tram veered into Queen Street and started its descent, she was pressed against him and sensed the soft warmth of his coat.

•　　•　　•　　•　　•

Charlie swallowed. His throat had seized up. Shifting in his seat, he knew it was purely a matter of seconds and he'd never see her again. He blurted out, "Apologies, ma'am, I'm new in town. I just arrived aboard the USS *Rigel*, and I'm not wanting to be forward, but could you tell me what movie is playing?"

"It's called *How Green Is My Valley*."

"I've heard of that back home, but never had a chance to see it." Before any interlude of silence allowed a sudden change of plan, "Allow me to introduce myself. I'm Charles Kincaid." He shook her gloved hand for a brief moment.

"I'm Mattie... Mattie Blanc." She looked outside, clutching her handbag. "Pardon me. This is my stop."

The tram stopped at the concrete platform outside the Century Picture Theatre.

Charlie continued, "I'd like to jump off here also. The movie sounds interesting."

He briefly held Mattie's arm, then respectfully stepped back as they descended onto the tram platform. Cars rushed past them.

"I'm sorry. I can't get used to your traffic. It goes the wrong direction," He smiled at her in the light of day. Her eyes were the softest color of the sea. "Mattie. What a beautiful name."

"I like the way you say my name. Ma-t-t-ie. You speak so… differently."

"That's my southern drawl, all the way from Mississippi." Charlie grinned. Taking a step along, he crossed the road with Mattie by his side. "Tell me about the movie."

Mattie waited till they'd crossed and went inside the theatre lobby.

"I'm trying to understand you." Mattie blushed, fumbling with her gloves. She remembered Mrs Frisken's warning and it made her nervous.

She looks scared. I have to be careful not frighten her, he thought, and spotted the billboard. "*How Green Is My Valley...* Maureen O'Hara and Walter Pidgeon. What a great pair," he offered freely.

"Yes, she's so pretty."

"So you understand me?"

Mattie smiled up at him. "Your accent is easier to understand when you speak slowly. I go to American movies all the time, but it's definitely harder to understand in person." Mattie didn't know what to else to say—it was all moving too fast.

Charlie bought two tickets and they went into the theatre.

What am I doing with him? Mattie wondered. "Thank you for buying my ticket, but I honestly did not expect that," she said, feeling ill at ease.

"Oh, my pleasure… I've been at sea and working hard. It's swell being ashore."

Sitting down next to her was like being in the movie itself, for Charlie.

The movie opened with the green pastures of the valleys he remembered as a boy. He imagined carrying her across the butterweed, setting her down under a walnut tree. He drew in a quick breath, shook himself out of his dreamy sentiment. He must stop this ridiculous carrying on: This woman, he knew nothing about her.

He fretted, wishing the movie would end, so he could find out if she was also attracted to him. And if not, how would he manage to say goodbye? He snuck a sideways glance in the dim light. Her profile was so serene. She turned with a warm smile, and their eyes met.

When the movie finished they walked outside to the dull light of the late afternoon. Charlie had to think boldly. This must not end now; he had to know.

"Can I offer you a ride home?"

"In the tram?" Mattie smiled. "I don't mind. I live only a short ride away and you can see more of our beautiful city." She accepted his arm, and they crossed the road to the platform. As the tram ascended the hill and rounded the corner he remembered the funny name.

"How do you say that street name? Looks like kangaroo, but it's not."

"Karangahape. It's a Maori name."

He watched her expression. He wanted to say so much to her, but couldn't. The tram rambled through a right turn and another to the left, before starting down the hill.

"I get off down this road." Mattie reached for the railing as the tram came to a stop. Charlie followed her. "You don't have to get off. You'll miss your tram ride back. It loops around, you know," she said stepping onto the footpath. "I live up there," Mattie pointed up at the huge villa nestled on the hill.

"Oh." Charlie's heart sank. What was he doing? She must have been laughing at him, he sensed. He wanted to turn and run as fast as he could. "I have to get back," he said, hastily taking a step off the tram to join her, almost tripping. "I errr… it was wonderful meeting you, ma'am. I have to go." He departed and left her standing, watching him.

Charlie kept on walking with his hands in his pockets to the end of the street. He'd never been this hesitant about anything in his life. He knew what he wanted and he went out and achieved it. He strived for everything.

You fool, Charlie Kincaid. The one thing you've ever dreamed about was her, and you let her go. You got no guts.

Charlie looked at his watch. He had to make a snap decision. He had forgotten what time curfew was, and cursed himself for his carelessness. He so desperately wanted to see her. He missed her already.

He whirled back and started running up the road. What if she was married with children? He'd knock at the door and pick one of them up and say hello. He'd think of something. By now the rain had set in, but he didn't care if he was drenched. He ran faster, up the hill and came to a stop at the bottom of the driveway.

My God! It was like one of the antebellum plantation homes back home. He'd never been in a house like this before. Buttoning up his peacoat, he walked nervously into the driveway, up the steps, and tapped with the brass knocker.

He heard a dog barking and someone coming; an older woman opened the door.

"Oh, we've no room for sailors," she said.

A little dog began sniffing at Charlie's trouser leg. He bent down, putting his fingers out gently, slowly stroking the little quivering body.

"Well, if this isn't some sort of miracle. Bonny doesn't do that to strangers."

"I've always loved animals." Charlie stood up. "They can be great friends." He read her eyes. An element of doubt crept into his mind; he didn't like her expression.

"I'm Mrs Frisken. How may I help you?"

"Pleased to meet you, ma'am. I'm Charles Kincaid."

"You must be from that ship that came in. Mattie was just telling me about you."

"Yes, ma'am. I'm a Navy diver on the USS *Rigel*."

"The *Rigel*... is that a Cruiser?"

"A repair ship, ma'am. Bit shorter than a Cruiser, but we keep all the warships runnin'".

"I see, interesting. I bet you brought the fleet with you," she said, still holding the door.

"No ma'am, just a Destroyer escort. Fleets up North givin' grief to the Japanese." Charlie didn't like the military questions and rushed to his purpose. "Mattie. I went to the movies with her. I just wanted to say—"

"Of course. Why don't you come in? I'll let her know you're here."

Charlie stood in the huge passageway. He heard voices in a distant room. A man's voice boomed louder. He told himself he must stay and be polite, meet the man of the house and pay his respects. Mrs Frisken had disappeared up the stairs; he heard Bonny barking. An older man came out of the adjacent room, carrying a newspaper, nodded at Charlie and also went up the stairs.

Charlie wondered what to think. He waited, listening to the clock tick in the hallway. He stepped towards a room so grand it took his breath away. This was how he'd imagined the grand old houses back home. A fire was flickering in the fireplace. He liked the comfortable couches placed about the fireplace. He went to take a closer look, and bent down to stoke the fire when he heard her voice.

"Mr Kincaid, you're here."

Charlie almost fell into the fireplace. He dropped the poker and stood up, turning around. She was standing there. With her coat aside, she was even more beautiful and delicate than he remembered. When she spoke he melted. He'd heard an English accent spoken in a few movies but nothing as romantic as her voice.

"Mr Kincaid, I didn't get the chance to thank you for taking me to the movies. You left in such a hurry."

"Call me Charlie, please. I'm sorry for intruding. I have to get back to the ship, but I wanted to see you again." Damn, he told himself, that all came out wrong. He bit his lip in anguish.

"Mrs Frisken told me you were here. Please take a seat by the fire." She moved towards him. "Let me take your coat; it's soaked. I'll get you a hot tea."

Charlie visualized sinking into the floral cushions, tea in hand.

"No, no, I have to get back. I wanted to thank you, for your company." He walked towards the door, restlessly squeezed his hat, and gazed around. "Is there—" Bonny pranced forward, energetically wagging her tail.

"I'm all wet, little guy." Charlie bent down to pat her.

"She likes you."

"You're leaving?" asked Mrs Frisken.

"Yes, well it was nice meeting you ma'am." Charlie put on his cap and tipped it at the two women. Mrs Frisken smiled and picked up Bonny, leaving for the kitchen.

"Thank you again for the movie. Here." Mattie pulled a card out of her pocket and handed it to Charlie. "When Mrs Frisken told me it was you at the front door... I thought maybe. Well, O'Hara's is where I work."

Charlie held the card and stared at the name, *O'Hara's Hair Academy*. "Mattie Blanc. You're a hairdresser?"

"Yes, I work in that street, the one with the funny name. Upstairs in the Melvern Building."

"You mean you live in this mansion, and yet you work for a living?"

"What did you think I'd be doing?"

Charlie studied the card, and then their eyes met again. A sick feeling swept into his gut. He swallowed and shuffled. *Get it out*, he said to himself. *Ask her, for Christ's sake.*

"Does your husband mind your working?"

"My husband?" Mattie put her hand over her mouth and giggled. She looked even prettier when she laughed. "You think I live in this big house with my husband? What about Mrs Frisken and Bonny?"

"Isn't she your mom?"

Mattie exploded. "Mum?... My mum's in Dunedin." Mattie could not control her laughter.

Charlie was puzzled and started to chuckle at Mattie's glee, although he didn't know why.

"Oh, Charlie, I'm so sorry. I board here. Mrs Frisken is my landlady."

Charlie heard her say his name. He wanted to holler to the heavens in relief, but contained himself.

"Miss Blanc, may I see you again?"

Mattie gripped the door handle and blushed. "I'd like that very much."

"I was thinking maybe we'd go dancing?"

Mattie's face gave her answer. He'd never seen such expression, such warmth all in one answer. "Mr Kincaid, I would much prefer to meet you for tea... and then maybe a walk through Myers Park and a chat. It would be far greater fun to go dancing with someone I know." Mattie grinned.

"I'll call you." He put the card in his pocket. "I get liberty every other night and then one whole day on the weekend." He stepped outside and back down the steps, grinning ear to ear as she closed the door. He almost fell into the garden, stumbling, skipping, hopping, and then running. By the time he'd caught the tram, he was smiling the biggest smile he could muster. As the tram rumbled onwards, he stuck his head halfway out the window to look for her salon in that street with the funny name.

·   ·   ·   ·   ·

Mattie closed the door and stood facing the passageway, her head spinning. She was glad no one could see her. She wanted to be alone in her own world, to ponder... to dream.

She climbed the staircase, looking up at the stained-glass window glistening in the evening moonlight. She couldn't stop smiling. She caressed the kauri banisters, swirled around the top railing as if she were on stage. She couldn't get him out of her head... his smile, his beautiful lips... those dark compelling eyes. How he said her name, so slowly, carefully... *Ma t t ie*.

She blushed at her mental image of him. She'd never felt this way before.

CHAPTER 27

Admiral Ghormley left Washington with his staff, and after several stops, arrived in New Zealand unannounced by seaplane, on Thursday 21 May 1942.

The bosun's whistle piped Admiral Ghormley aboard, as he ascended the steel steps of the *Rigel*'s ladder with his official party. Captain Roy Dudley awaited him with a fixed salute. The Admiral turned to salute the stern flag, then snapped about to return the salutes from the Captain, the Exec, and other officers on the quarterdeck. The signalman on the flag deck briskly raised the Admiral's flag, flapping in the cool harbor breeze.

Charlie was on watch, standing tall, saluting, his gaze set. Secretly a lump stabbed at his throat; they were here to protect this magnificent land and people. *God bless America*, he said to himself.

A scurry of naval personnel made way for the Admiral's inspection. Charlie heard his pleasant tone of voice, laughing, as he walked intentionally along the deck talking to the men.

"Well, I'm down under that's for sure." Everyone laughed and the crew gathered around. "I want to say, it's great to be here." The Admiral raised his voice. "You know, they wanted me to stay at the Auckland War Memorial Museum." He paused, taking a stroll to the stern, facing the southwest prevailing afternoon wind. He swiveled back smiling. "I told them no. Everybody'd think old Ghormley's a museum piece in Owckland, Noo Zeellun."

Everyone laughed again. It was a heartfelt welcome, as every man watched their superior make his way up the ladder to his new quarters topside.

Later that day, the Captain called for a quick informal meeting in the mess hall. Charlie and the other petty officers crowded near the benches.

"Attention on deck," bellowed the Sergeant-at-Arms as the Captain and officers entered.

"At ease men. I'm going to be brief. The *Rigel* will be flagship for the Admiral, at least at present. Tomorrow will be the official announcement to New Zealand. Planning will take place immediately for a large supply and ammunition depot here, base hospitals and a large fuel tank farm. We'll start work on the dockside down here next week. Sheds need to be erected, and I want orderly cooperation with the civilian workers. Some of the New Zealand dockworkers will need to be escorted throughout the *Rigel* and assisted in ship repairs. This is where our diving team is needed." Here he made eye contact with Charlie.

The Captain stepped behind a bench, reached over to a stack of booklets, and held one up. "These booklets have already been issued to every man on board. So far, most of you have been on liberty, and already have experienced the lack of a few home comforts." He paused with a mischievous smile. "Number one… coffee."

Everyone chuckled.

"They boil it hard here, in a big urn… a brew worth staying away from. There's no Bourbon and definitely no hamburgers. And the word, tea… beware of it. A tea break sometimes means a meal, or a snack, or just a cup of tea. Believe me, you'll be drowning in tea before we leave here."

Another burst of laughter, as the men had already seen the civilian workers drop tools for a tea break. Charlie felt nervous at the speculation of his first invitation for tea, and decided to keep quiet.

"I'd like each and every sailor on board this ship to be aware of your surroundings and most of all, to make the Admiral comfortable and proud. His time is crucial here, to get the job done correctly. Don't forget, you are US Navy... here to whip Jap ass. Live up to your reputation and let's get this show on the road. That is all."

"Aye, sir," shouted the men, saluting as they left the mess hall.

Charlie found Vic working at the machinery in the carpenters' shop.

"You old butthole," he said, shoving the booklet at Charlie. "You knew all along. Thought you'd trick me, did ya?"

Charlie looked at the open page and grinned back at him, "Relax Vic… those sheilas can hardly wait to get a piece of you."

"So where'd you disappear to? Out with a new dame?" Vic gave Charlie a mighty shove, and a huge stack of wood landed on the deck.

"Hey," yelled Moult at the other end of the bench, slamming a drill down. All you fuckheads think about is skirts." He glared across the room.

Charlie picked up the pile of wood, sliding it across the bench, "Pal, just because you prefer stargazing and no booze or women, doesn't wear with the rest of us." Pulling the booklet out, Charlie opened it to the page, *down under... as an American sees it.* "There's none of your stars, pal, read this."

"Here... that's mine," Vic snatched it.

Charlie had his in his back pocket, and threw it at Moult, "Have a read, big boy. All of you, live and let live. Save all that energy for the Japs."

The following morning when the Admiral arrived at the waterfront, a flash signaled his presence and the closely guarded secret was out. The Right Honorable J. G. Coates, a member of the War Cabinet, on behalf of the Prime Minister, was the first to step ahead and shake hands with the Admiral as he stepped ashore from the *Rigel*'s launch. It was history in the making, as this man of average height, with his wide-eyed sincere expression, listened and learned of their mission. A group of high-ranking Royal Navy officers crowded around him, surprised at his sudden undercover arrival, and honored by his presence. Newspaper reporters clicked their cameras, pushed forward to join in the pandemonium.

•　　•　　•　　•　　•

Back at Huntly House, the Auckland Star was spread across the table in the breakfast room. The paper carried full coverage of Admiral Ghormley's arrival. Mrs Frisken had been making scones in the coal range, singing through the kitchen. She wiped floury hands on her apron, and offered Mattie a scone.

"I thought you might be interested," said Mrs Frisken, pointing to an article about a US Commander's arrival, and across on the other page, a smiling photo of the man with headlines, "*Here To Do A Big Job.*"

"Thank you. This is big news," replied Mattie, pouring herself a cup of tea. She relaxed on the wooden bench reading the articles, her back warmed by the coal range, still aglow from baking. The old clock ticked rhythmically on the mantelpiece, interrupted simply by an occasional, careful sip of hot tea. By now Huntly House was home, and Mrs Frisken seemed almost as wonderful and caring as her own mother. Best of all, she wasn't judgmental.

"That handsome sailor rang."

Mattie looked up. Mrs Frisken broke into a smile. Mattie knew by her expression he must have charmed her.

"Oh?" She tried her best to act calm and went on reading the piece about how New Zealand was so unacquainted with war. She thought to herself, *Yes, and unacquainted with the most charming man in the world.* She swallowed another bite and a toss of tea.

The phone broke the silence with a startling ring.

"Hello," said Mrs Frisken. Her face broke into a smile, and she nodded at Mattie to take the phone.

"Well, hello there. Is that Mattie?"

"Yes," was all she could say, her heart pounding.

"I just got off duty, and I'm giving you a call to ask you where would you like to go for tea on Saturday?"

"How did you get this number?"

"I looked it up in the phone book. Not many Frisken's hereabouts."

Mattie blushed, clinging to the phone. "I don't mind," she blurted out. "Just pick out a spot on your way in the tram."

"Great. See you tomorrow. Bye," said Charlie.

Mattie hung up the phone and shifted her stance. "I didn't know what to say," she confided in Mrs Frisken.

"Don't say anything, my girl. Remember what I told you; watch your manners and you'll be fine."

Mattie drank the rest of her tea and carried her cup out to the kitchen.

"I think you better read up about American culture," said Mrs Frisken, wiping down the bench.

"Why? He seems fine to me."

"Well, they're not like other men. They already have a name for themselves, the Yanks. I'm betting when the Kiwi men get home and find their women all knocked up, there'll be hell to pay."

"Oh, Mrs Frisken, I hope you're not referring to me."

"Well, you said you didn't have a boyfriend." Mrs Frisken peered over at Mattie raising an eyebrow, handing her a tea towel.

Mattie frowned at her. That's odd, she mused. I've just met him. Why is Mrs Frisken being so mean? She felt a sudden tension in the air. She wondered if someone had hurt Mrs Frisken in the past. She never did say anything about her life before she became the landlady of Huntly House. But then, why would she?

"Mattie, I know what war does to people. Best to go slowly… carefully," said Mrs Frisken, with just a hint of a wobble in her voice.

"Don't worry, Mrs Frisken. He's so polite, he won't hurt me." Mattie watched her. She withdrew, seemingly on the verge of tears, and looked aside. For a moment Mattie wanted to hug her; but when she turned back around, Mattie noticed her look of concern.

Not wanting to spoil the moment, she tactfully excused herself and went up the stairs, mystified about Mrs Frisken.

CHAPTER 28

The next day was Saturday. Charlie left the *Rigel* unnoticed by his shipmates, crossed the road, and headed into lower Queen Street. The shops were open, packed with people, but just enough shoulders to allow room for another. He noticed a sign "Queen's Arcade", and on the corner, a restaurant called Cook's Restaurant, so he bounded up the stairs to the smell of freshly grilled steak.

A smiling waiter introduced himself. "Best place in town, sir, Cook's. What would you like?"

"The works... steak, eggs, and 'taters." Charlie smiled. This time it was easy picking. His nose knew what was on the menu without looking.

His meal arrived promptly—a sizzling, crusty steak grilled splendidly medium-rare, beside two fried farm eggs and potatoes. These guys sure know how to please us Yanks... bet they learned that in a hurry, Charlie imagined. He chewed moderately at first to cherish the familiar taste, grabbed the ketchup, and then devoured this feast like it was his last.

Leaving a tip, he sauntered out of the arcade, winding back into Queen Street.

"Whoa... chocolates," he exclaimed, gazing in the window of the Adams Bruce Confectionery store. A bulging box of Queen Anne chocolates gleamed in the window. He followed the chocolate aroma inside.

"I'll have the one with flowers on the cover, and the other with a house and garden, ma'am," he said. Already he imagined Mattie standing in the garden, waiting for him. He tucked the two boxes under his arm.

A picture theatre caught his eye across the street. He observed both ways to cross the road, not trusting his memory on car directions. Standing outside the theatre, he read *Upcoming musical smash hit, Moon over Miami, with spectacular dancing.*

"Can't wait for the dancing, pretty girl," Charlie breathed to himself as he walked up Queen Street. Ultimately at the top of the hill, Karangahape Road appeared. Charlie turned right, passed a few shops, and smiled at the rainbow of flowers poking into the footpath. "Now we're talkin'," he said out loud. It was the red roses tied with a red ribbon that caught his eye.

"I'll take those. They're beautiful, just like the gal I know."

"They all say that, lovie," said a woman's whisky-deep voice. She stooped down, picked up the bunch of roses out of a bucket, and hobbled back towards the counter. Inside the shop, the fragrance was overpowering. "Do you want a corsage?" The woman picked a spray of tiny rosebuds, nestled in white gypsophila, from beneath the counter. "She'll love this one."

"You betcha. I'll take 'em both."

The woman put her fingers out and grabbed half a crown from Charlie.

He went out of the shop, continued right and fortunately found Melvern's Homewares store. He gazed at the hubbub inside. Rows of assistants stood behind cash registers, busy serving customers. Looking around, he noticed a sign by the main doors: "O'Hara's Hair Academy"

Charlie jumped with excitement up the flight of stairs. It was still afternoon and maybe she hadn't left yet. He climbed to the first landing, and gazed curiously at all the tables and chairs and what looked like a dance floor. He sneaked up the rest of the stairs. It was quiet as he stood in front of the Academy door. He knocked, but no one came. He was sure he saw someone move behind the glass.

Just as he went to leave, a young woman poked her head through the door, "Sorry, we're closed."

"Thank you, ma'am." Charlie grinned at her and tipped his hat. Then, hugging the huge bunch of flowers against his thick peacoat, he raced down the stairs and kept walking, a little deflated at not finding Mattie. A butcher's shop, with the word *Economic* written across the window, reminded him to get a soup bone for Bonny. He joined a bunch of shoppers on the tram platform.

•　　•　　•　　•　　•

The phone rang. Percy, one of the boarders, tapped on Mattie's door. It must be him, guessed Mattie, racing for the phone.

"It's Nan," said a voice on the other end.

"What's wrong?" asked Mattie.

"You know the American sailor you were telling me about?"

Mattie's heart leapt. She didn't realize the effect he had on her. Something must be wrong, "Go on… yes?"

"Well, he… I'm sure it was him—"

"Nan, stop it. What's happened?"

"It's him…"

"Who?"

"He was here, at the salon looking for you, with a whole bunch of… Oops! I mean, I shouldn't have said."

"You're mumbling. Speak slowly." Mattie was now desperate to know.

"Never mind, he's gorgeous. I can see what you meant. Oh my God, are there any more like him?"

For an instant Mattie didn't answer. "He's too early. I wonder why he went to the shop?"

"When was he supposed to come for you?"

"I told him we'd go for tea. Oh!" Mattie flushed. "He must think afternoon tea."

"You silly, he wouldn't know one tea from another. You'd better get your face on. He's on his way."

"Oh my God!"

Just then there was a knock at the door. Mattie saw his shape through the glass panel. She froze, looked down at her slippers, and touched her hair. She almost burst into tears. This was a disaster. She wasn't ready to go out.

Her feet felt like jelly, as she and Bonny tripped over each other, racing towards the door. There was another knock. Mattie swung open the door. Bonny sniffed at the smell of the soup bone buried in a paper bag. Charlie grinned wide as he held the bag up, out of reach.

"You're early," Mattie gasped, staring at the bunch of roses beneath his glorious smile that made her quiver.

"I've come for tea," he said. But the look on her face made him take a step back. Maybe she had changed her mind.

She couldn't look at him. Her eyes were on the roses, pressed against the same peacoat she'd touched in the tram. How was she going to eye contact him, without powder on her nose, rouge on her cheeks, and lipstick on her lips?

"Oh no, I'm sorry... it's me, silly me. I'm—" She put her head down. "I'm not ready. I made a mistake. Supper in your country means our tea time."

"So that's what all the fuss is about. The Kiwi guys on the docks have tea every afternoon, but I guess you're not exactly a dock worker are you?" Charlie said with a hint of a smile. He handed her the roses. "Maybe a little water for these, before they wilt... like you."

They both burst out laughing. Charlie opened the bag, with Bonny anxiously sniffing and barking, easing the tension. Mrs Frisken came hurrying down the passageway at Bonny's loud barking.

"Well, what a nice thought, my dear man. But unfortunately, she's not a bloodhound. She's quite fussy."

"Maybe she'd like a bite of your chocolates, ma'am?" He handed her the box with flowers on the lid.

"Oh, you've no need to spoil me."

"Well, I hope you like nuts. Hickory nuts, just like we have back home." Charlie tucked the other box under Mattie's arm, and lowered the bone. Bonny raced proudly to the backyard with a prize as big as she was.

"Come on in. Mattie got the hour wrong. I'll make you that cup of tea she talked about. Have tea here before you go out." She turned to Mattie with a twinkle in her eye. "Hadn't you better go and curl your hair?"

Charlie lifted the roses, undoing the ribbon. "I'd love to fix these for you," he said.

Mattie acknowledged the picturesque chocolate box, taking it out from under her arm. "I... I don't know what to say."

"You'll find something." He winked at Mrs Frisken.

"Here, hang your coat on the coat stand and I'll get a vase for you," she said.

Hurrying up the stairs, Mattie put the chocolates beside her bed, blushing at the beauty of the gift. She dressed in her favorite white lace blouse, pulled on a check skirt with pleated front, and stepped into her new two-tone navy and white heels. Smiling in the mirror at her glowing image, she pursed her lips, flicked her hair into curls, and pinned the red bow on top of her head. She was ready.

Mrs Frisken had a large pot of simmering homemade soup on the range. "I'll be gone. I have errands to run. You can serve yourselves." Charlie heard Bonny's little feet scuffing on the wood of the stairs, following Mrs Frisken as she left.

Charlie hung his coat, tucking the corsage into his side pocket, careful not to bruise the tender petals.

He placed the roses in the vase. Their scent, the ticking clock, the warm afternoon sun warmed his back; he took a long deep breath and unwound there imagining how much joy it would be, just to be here in this house with her, to imagine the feeling of coming home to her. He jumped from his dreams at the sound of heels clicking. It startled him. She was coming down the stairs; he hurriedly straightened his uniform, and stood up, his face intense, but expectant.

She hadn't seen him in his Navy uniform; it gave her a sudden twinge at the reminder of who he was and where he was from. He appeared so... so different from anyone else in her world; the navy-blue uniform, the loose knotted tie, the white stripes around his collar. She clutched her tweed coat. Their eyes met. He came towards her. Being so close to him again sent shock waves coursing through her. Her knees went weak, everything went weak. She mustn't reveal how she felt. She dropped her gaze.

"Here let me take your coat. Are you going somewhere?" he teased bending down to recapture her eyes.

Mattie looked up. "You're teasing me again," she giggled. He made her laugh, his sensuous bottom lip curled into that cheeky grin, exposing those pearly white teeth she'd seen when she first met him. She focused onto his dark eyes, staring straight into her soul. She dared to look into them; one was slightly narrower, dreamier than the other. Thick dark eyebrows almost joined on the bridge of his perfect nose. She sparked at the feel of his touch as he folded her coat and hung it next to his. She was glowing with happiness. She secretly wondered what it would be like to kiss him. Kiss someone special, someone she genuinely loved. She'd never had a real boyfriend. It felt strange having all his attention.

"How do I look?" she did a twirl, and he grabbed her waist as she twirled around him.

His eyes pored over her, "Like a dream."

"You're full of compliments." She blushed shyly up at him. Their hands touched. Her eyes sparkled as he led her into the breakfast room. Charlie released his grip. She kept her gaze on him. She'd wished for, imagined a man just like him; he was perfect. "I love what you've done to the roses," she sighed.

"You're welcome. Can't wait to taste Mrs Frisken's soup. I'll serve." He grinned round at her.

"A man in the kitchen," said Mattie not wanting to take her eyes off his backside.

"Where I come from, ma'am, we help everywhere." He handed her a bowl across the table. He ladled out a portion for himself and slid with ease onto the bench opposite her.

Mrs Frisken had set a basket of bread on the table and wrapped the cutlery with the napkins. They unraveled their napkins in silence, and started to sip the hot broth.

Mattie waved her hand for the heat in her cheeks, put her spoon down, and dabbed her lips with the napkin, "The roses—"

"I found a—" Charlie said at the same moment. "Sorry, I interrupted you." He put his spoon down.

"No. I was merely saying thank you. Tell me about yourself, Charlie." Mattie smiled.

"Good golly, I'm from a little town you've never heard of, not even in the movies. Up top'a Mississippi. Falkner is cotton country, with lots of sorghum."

"What's sorghum?"

"Spent my young days choppin' sorghum cane. It grows to 'bout twice your height. Then gets boiled into the best molasses syrup you ever had."

"Wish I had some on my bread right now," said Mattie.

"Might have a bit in my pocket next time."

They both laughed. He couldn't wait to have her on his arm in town.

His lips curled into that grin, but each moment Mattie saw more; this time his eyes carried a soft glint, soft like velvet. She was getting used to him.

"Yes, you can tell me all about Charlie choppin' sorghum," Mattie mimicked his accent. It was so comfortable sitting, listening to this man and his distant life.

Mattie picked up the dishes and started to clear the table, humming a little tune. Charlie noticed the newspaper lying on the end of the bench by the roses and started to read.

"Isn't that exciting about your Admiral?" Mattie said, glad she had seen the article first.

Charlie's worried expression made her hesitate.

"Well, I mean your country's arrived here, to help us."

"I know. But it's a big job ahead, serious job." Charlie put down the paper and stared out the window.

Mattie went into the kitchen, relieved she hadn't offended him; but she sensed an element of mystery surrounding him. She carried the vase of roses up the stairs, thinking about his possible secret side. She placed the roses in her room, gave herself one last glance in the wardrobe mirror, arched on new lipstick, and gracefully descended the stairs.

Charlie was standing at the bottom, back to a full smile, hands behind his back.

"How 'bout I pin this on you and we go in to town?"

Mattie's mouth flew open. She stared at the tiny bunch of flowers resting in his hand. She couldn't answer him. Tears pricked her eyes; she felt her heart pounding. She tried not to cry and faked a sniffle instead. Was it time to trust?

She watched his beautiful hands finger the soft layers of the leaves of the corsage, as he pinned it on her blouse.

"There." He leaned back, admiring his workmanship. "You're all ready for the ball, princess. Now, can I call a cab?" he asked with his teasing smirk.

"The tram's just a block. I don't mind, truly."

Charlie did a swoop of her coat. "Your carriage awaits, ma'am."

He placed her arm in his, and they walked out into the night.

They sat in silence on the tram ride up the hill. It gave Mattie a chance to reflect. She felt relieved, and a lovely confidence. She watched her delicate spray of roses in the reflection of the window, bobbing to the rumble of the tram.

"You must have stopped in every shop on Queen Street. You spoil me. It's embarrassing."

"Don't worry. It makes me happy. I'm proud to put a smile on your face."

Mattie blushed, and they remained in silence again, each wondering how the other was feeling. The tram rambled into the Queen Street turn and it was soon the place to step off.

"Where's this Myers Park?" asked Charlie, taking her arm.

"Just down the street, but it's too dark."

"Sounds romantic."

"We can take in a dance if you prefer."

"Whoopee! I was hoping you'd say that. Can't wait to shake a leg," he replied.

"My friend Nan said Peter Pan Cabaret is the place for dancing. It's just a few blocks." Mattie smiled into the night air, her lips shining in the light. She liked his company more and more, and particularly his gentle manner.

The box office sign said: *Entry Three Shillings, No Alcohol.* They heard the band playing inside. Charlie dipped into his side pocket, paid their entry fee, and they walked into the smoked-filled dance hall. He was dying for a cigarette but he didn't want to risk his chances. He offered Mattie a piece of gum instead.

Charlie removed her coat, and ushered her into a dimly lit booth down the side of the hall. He hadn't been to a place like this before. Everything was happening so fast. Sailors, lots of them, crammed the dance floor, shuffling their partners round the huge ballroom, cigarettes dangling from their lips.

The band started belting out *Chattanooga Choo-choo*. Mattie's feet spontaneously began to tap.

Charlie jumped up, put his hand out. "Want to try? I'm a quick learner," he said, taking Mattie's cue. "That song was real popular back in Pearl Harbor," he shouted into her ear. "I watched my buddies on the dance floor." He grinned.

He held her, then let her spin, falling back in his arms. This is how it should be, Mattie visualized. Oh, his strong grip sent sparks through her body.

The trumpet took the lead with a change to the Andrews Sisters, *The Boogie Woogie Bugle Boy of Company B*. The crowd roared and clapped, as the singer started to tap dance. Mattie joined in, "a toot… a toot… "

Charlie stood beside her, watching her feet, nodding, then clipping his feet, tapping the beat, "a toot… a did-li-ar-dar toot". Suddenly he got it, "a toot…" He never missed a beat. They were stepping out together, almost like Fred Astaire and Ginger Rogers.

A few dancers clapped at them, cheering them on. Each step melded into the following, until the music lulled to the lead singer's sultry voice. Mattie sang along, when she heard some of her favorite tunes, "*You'll never know how much I love you.*"

They drifted back to their booth and eased into the soft cushions for a rest.

"Where'd you learn to sing and dance?" asked Charlie.

"At home, down south in Dunedin."

"We're both southerners. You're out with a Mississippi gentleman tonight, pretty gal."

Mattie rested her head against Charlie's shoulder. They both knew something strong had brought them together. Charlie held her, smelled her delicate perfume, and fingered the softness of her hair. He adored her already. He didn't have to imagine her anymore, she was in his arms. He tightened his grip, she responded, gripping his hand back, meeting his eyes. The lights dimmed. A foxtrot came on, and they sprang back to the dance floor.

"Oh, my feet are tangled. I'm trying but… Can you teach me?" Charlie asked.

They stopped, began again, staring at each other, their hands held tightly.

"Ignore the crowd. Relax, just feel the beat," Mattie said, trying to lead. "Try again. Slow, slow, quick, quick."

Charlie hated being out of step. He wanted to persist, but the lights came on.

"Darn. I was just gettin' it," he complained.

Supper was announced, and they followed the crowd into a separate room. Tables spread with cups and biscuits. They laughed secretly at the teacups.

"Now," Mattie paused, "this is a cup of tea." She picked up a round object. "This is a biscuit."

He crunched into the tangy lemon sweetness. "Hmmm... not bad. What's next?"

"How do you take your tea?"

Charlie shrugged. "Surprise me." He cordially swallowed the strange brew. "Can I come for tea, and get it right next time?"

Mattie almost spat out her tea, nodding and coughing, holding her chest. "I think it's better fun if you just surprise me. Be here when you like," she laughed out loud.

The lights were dimmed for the last hour. The night seemed endless. When they finally stepped into the cold outside air, it felt like a gentle reminder of evening's end.

They arrived at Huntly House by taxi, and Charlie instructed the driver to wait. They climbed the stairs and stood in the dark landing, glad of the blackout.

"Well, Miss Blanc, did you enjoy our night?" he asked, twirling a lock of her hair. "I loved that cute dance you did. You'll have to show me again sometime."

"The tap dance?" Mattie smiled up at him shyly, touching her bouquet. "I had such a good time. I shall never forget it."

"You don't have to, my..." Charlie couldn't stand it. He wanted to say darling, but instead he pulled her close and kissed her. Then kissed her again.

Mattie kissed him back. She felt his mouth on hers, his soft warm lips, the lips she'd watched and desired. Their lips melded. Then the gentle touch of his tongue so delicately, fleetingly, slid inside her mouth. They kissed till there was no breath inside her.

"Oh Charlie... Charlie," she moaned. She reached up to touch him, her fingers caressing, rounding his dimpled chin.

"Call me Kinky," he whispered, kissing her nose, her cheek, her neck.

Mattie leaned against him, his warm body engulfing her. The safety of his arms… Then she pulled back. Tears cascaded down her cheeks and onto his jacket.

"What's wrong?" asked Charlie.

"It's you. It's always been you. I've dreamed about you, and now I've found you—I'm scared."

"Don't be scared, my darlin'." It slipped out, he couldn't help it. He loved her, he knew it. He wanted to say it. He kissed her tears. Bending down, he nuzzled her face, gently touching her porcelain cheek with his fingers. "I'm just like you. I've dreamed about you too." He stared into her eyes, "When I saw you on the tram, it was as if I already knew you."

"Oh, Kinky, what are we going to do?"

"We will stay together… a long time together."

Mattie didn't answer. She drew back.

"It's curfew." Charlie leaned across her, opening the door. "I have to be back, darlin'."

They kissed once more, hungry for each other. Charlie held her tight. He bent down and cradled her soft cheeks in his hands, and gave her a tiny final kiss. "If only you knew how gorgeous you looked today at the door, in the sunlight with the roses against your beautiful skin."

Mattie flushed. She leaned up and kissed him back, "Tea's at six o'clock, don't be late."

"Save my place, darlin'."

CHAPTER 29

The *Rigel* shifted to a permanent berth at Hobson Wharf on 2 June, a familiar site for Aucklanders. Admiral Ghormley hauled down his flag on 10 June, moving his headquarters to a new building on the corner of Jean Batten Place and Shortland Street. His Divisions were assigned the top floors of the Dilworth Building across the street, on the corner of Queen Street. Senior officers' accommodation was provided by the Waverly and Grand Auckland hotels.

Ghormley formed the US Joint Purchasing Board, providing a pact between the United States and the United Kingdom to share each other's war resources, supplies, shipping space and manpower. A lend-lease agreement was signed and the United States took over the use of Princes and Hobson wharfs. A full format of functions was set out by Admiral Ghormley.

There was a lot happening. Hobson Wharf had a better feel, Charlie reckoned. It was a block from Queen Street and offered fabulous, busy seascapes to watch. The neighboring fuel tank farm bustled with trucks and barges, and the area across Quay Street was changing into a new hospital.

Charlie knew something was up when Mansbach called him into the Wardroom. "Good morning, sir," Charlie said, saluting.

Mansbach kept reading the papers he had on the table. Then he raised his eyes. "As you were. Grab a chair," he said, offering him a cigarette. "We're putting you in charge of setting up additional diving equipment and overseeing the diving operations for ship repairs. We may also need your divers as welders on the waterworks for the new hospital that's under construction across the road." He paused, "The Navy needs men like you." He broke into a smile. "Don't think you're some genius. There are lots of changes happening every day with this war. We need great leaders." He slid the papers towards Charlie. "Congratulations. You've been promoted to Warrant Officer."

Charlie picked up the papers.

Mansbach leaned back in his chair, smoking in silence for a minute. "Give you time to inform your men, shift quarters." Bending forward, he stubbed out his cigarette in the ashtray, "You'll be sharing a cabin with another Warrant Officer, commencing July 1st. The storekeeper has your new uniforms ready."

"But sir... my men..."

"Men will serve you on any level, once you gain their trust. Something you've obviously achieved."

"And may I ask, sir, does this mean we're leaving here?"

"Keen to get to war, boy? Or is there some other agenda?" said Mansbach, with a grin.

Charlie stubbed out his cigarette, and looked his Repair Officer in the eye, something he always did when he wanted to level with someone. "I'm getting to know the New Zealanders... beautiful people. Just wanted to leave them in good shape before we sail."

"That's the way." Mansbach handed him another sheet of paper. "You can look forward to a few island sunsets down here." He smiled. "We're having an Officers' Inauguration Supper at Hotel Auckland. Across the road, the Civic Wintergardens has been reserved for us. You can bring your lady along."

Charlie was stunned that Mansbach somehow knew about Mattie, but decided to keep his mouth shut.

•　　　•　　　•　　　•　　　•

The night sky in Auckland could be an array of magnificent color, or an angry black torrent. That evening it was a raging black hole; rain threatened. Charlie was not ready to tell his men about what had happened. A friendly voice gave a shout at Charlie and Vic as they finished another load of equipment for their diver's barge.

"'Bout time we had that shout," yelled Bill, screeching to a halt in his jeep.

Vic stopped work, "Here's trouble."

"Wouldn't say that. You didn't get to know Bill." Charlie waved.

"Nah… no need, heard enough about the men down here," growled Vic.

Bill hopped out, "What ya say we go across for a beer before closing?"

"Before the rain? We're not on liberty," said Vic.

"Wasn't talking to you, only me mate here. Charlie, isn't it?"

"Listen, don't try that dumb talk round 'ere. If it wasn't for us you'd have your nuts fried," Vic interrupted, folding his arms and standing with his legs apart.

"Settle down. Now!" Charlie glared at Vic. He walked to Bill, and shook his hand. "Vic and I were saying how great it was to work with you fellas."

Vic screwed his nose up at Charlie. "What crap."

"Get to know your fellow men," joked Charlie at Bill.

"That's right, mate." Bill patted Charlie on the back. "You blokes need a beer. I'm staying at Hotel Auckland, might want to have a nightcap. Got a lotta pretty sheilas over there with hungry eyes."

Vic's mouth went spontaneously from down to a full-toothy grin. "Come to think of it, Charlie old boy," he said, "haven't seen you in action yet."

"We have to sign out and change," said Charlie, pretending to chuckle.

"I've arranged it with the guard." Bill winked. "You'll have no trouble."

"Well then, we'll meet you dockside shortly."

"Meet us at the pub. It's just across the road."

They sauntered blithely over the road and up Queen Street to the local bar. Loud voices filled the room, where the scotch ration flowed from 5 to 6pm.

Bill's voice rose when he saw them enter the bar. "You Yanks have to match us Kiwis head on, I reckon," he yelled, his face already flushed beet red with scotch.

"Where you fellas going, anyway?" asked Charlie, poking an elbow into Bill's ribs.

Vic drank without commenting. Red had followed, and Crow was coming in the door.

"We're goin' up North, campsites everywhere. With you Yanks hitting the scene we can't move. Bloody artillery, machine guns, bloody buildings goin' up, water tanks for Christ's sake, bloody nineteen of the bastards, 20,000 gallons each. How you blokes go through the bloody water, for Christ's sake."

Bill swilled down another beer, and plonked his glass on the counter. Charlie threw down a few shillings on the bar.

"Six o'clock shutdown for scotch, last round," shouted the barman.

"Hey," Bill beckoned to a tall man walking in. "Give this man a drink," he yelled, his arm round the other man's neck. By now, Bill was in no hurry to leave. "I want you to meet our latest hero, Harry Jeffers."

Harry's rugged deadpan expression belied a reluctant handshake with Charlie and Vic.

"Good to meet a real hero," said Charlie amiably.

"Big deal. I lobbed a grenade into a Jap pillbox and then dislocated my shoulder running a bayonet into 'em," said Harry in a deep, somber voice.

"Give the man a scotch, my shout," yelled Bill. "Come on, we're moving up the road."

It was six o'clock closing, and the doors closed to the raucous shouts of mixed cultures. By now, a lot of the Americans had joined in, and it was a fun affair as they left in the rain, walking up Queen Street. Charlie pushed up the collar of his peacoat, shoving his hands in his pockets, enjoying the jaunt with his crew members, when a group of colored men pushed past, forcing them into the gutter.

Vic lunged at the uniformed island men, "Who the fuck you think you are? We don't go to war with no niggers."

A fist flew in the air and Vic landed off balance. From nowhere Moult appeared, wrenching his huge arm around the dark-skinned man's throat.

Bill gave a loud blast of orders to the men, and picked up Vic, shoving him along the road. Looking back at Moult, he growled, "You blokes got a lot to learn. The Maori Battalion's not to be fooled with. Our Maori folk over here are not niggers, never will be."

Charlie quickly caught up to walk beside Bill and Harry. "You'll have to excuse my buddy. He's not been out much since we came in. He doesn't understand your ways."

"We'll get him trained." Bill opened the door of the Hotel Auckland, headed briskly through to the bar. There was music playing and a billiard room visible in the adjacent room. Vic strolled over, picked up a cue, chiseled it with chalk, and glared hard at Harry.

Charlie put a dollar bill down on the bar and raised an eyebrow at Bill. Charlie had a long draw of smoke, and now recognized up close that Bill was a young man, but his skin had worn to leather.

"So tell me about your stay so far?" asked Bill. "I hear you've met a sheila?"

"Yes, but my mates don't know."

"That bad, eh?"

"Bad all right… so bad I can't talk about it."

Bill started laughing, shaking his head. "I'm proud of ya, mate. Picking one of our girls. Hope she's not taken by any of *our* blokes."

"Not a chance." Charlie grinned. "I want to marry her."

"Geeeez… if it's that serious, you should be telling your mates." Bill swayed alongside Charlie, like a dare, "You think they'll steal her?"

Charlie laughed, "No way, not my men. I just don't wanna be hassled."

Charlie scouted for Vic, but he'd gone. He stood up, craning his neck to find him. Over in the distant lounge corner he watched a blond stack of hair cuddling up to a pretty dark girl. Bill caught his glance and laughed.

"Doesn't take your bloke long. She's one of the barmaids here, nice Maori sheila. Better tell him to watch out, no more fighting with the Maoris. They'll put him in a pot. Just kidding, mate," Bill swilled back another beer.

"Listen, bring your sheila up to Warkworth. It'll be a nice drive for the two of ya… see some of the countryside. Bring old Casanova boy, we're all mates down here. I'll loan you one of our jeeps… We've dances goin' on. Here's me card."

Charlie picked up the card. *Bill Smith*, he smiled to himself, New Zealand Army Garrison, Fanning Island Cable Station.

"Don't take any notice of that guff."

Charlie was glad to have met Bill. He liked the New Zealand way.

"Thanks, Bill," he replied shoving the card in his pocket.

"Give me a call when you're coming." Bill twirled about on his barstool. "Well, look who's goin' home for a nightcap."

Vic walked past with the girl, winking, opening the hotel door.

"Hey, mate, the bedroom's that way," yelled Bill pointing upstairs.

Vic went on out the door.

"I thought you Yanks had all the humor."

Charlie reached into his hip pocket and pulled out the flask, "Hold your beer under the bar. You're about to get spiked with some of the best corn liquor Mother Nature can provide."

"Holy shit, Charlie, you boys put a still together on that ship? Tax man will getcha."

Bill and Charlie willingly spent the night blitzing one spiked beer after another, until Charlie patted Bill on the back and slid back from the bar. "Well, sir, it's been a pleasure to trade a whole night of each other's never-ending bullshit," he chuckled.

"Don't give me that Yankee charm." They both laughed. "You better scoot up to Warkworth, before the rest of your bloody country hits town," shouted Bill, as Charlie left.

Charlie buttoned up his peacoat to the evening air, and shuffled along the street, careful to watch for traffic. Passing the red iron gates, he heard a whistle. Charlie peered round, and caught sight of Vic.

"So, lover man, no score tonight?" said Vic, sauntering up to him.

"You did all right by the look of it."

"Yeer... got me a beautiful brown sugar."

"You have to be careful, they're different down here."

"You seem to know it all."

"Get to know the locals, respect their ways." Charlie kept walking towards the *Rigel*.

"Find you a Roxy in town?" teased Vic.

"You know, Roxy was never the one," replied Charlie sharply.

"What's that got to do with down here?"

Charlie put his foot on the *Rigel* gangway and whirled back to deal with Vic. "You think I'm a lousy cad, but I never did anything to hurt her."

Vic took a step back. "Oh wow, spit it out. Don't tell me you've fallen for some dame down here?"

"Don't make it sound like that. She's not like that."

"So you have, you son of a bitch. Gotcha a honey!" Vic stared at him.

Charlie softened his expression. "She's different than anyone I've ever met. She's classy."

"How'd you meet her?" asked Vic, acting uninterested as he climbed the gangway.

"On the tram, that first day we arrived into port," said Charlie, checking past the guard. They easily descended and opened their lockers. "I want you to meet her."

Vic laughed, "What, so I can be your stooge?"

Charlie grabbed him by the neck. "You just don't get it, do you? I never loved Roxy." He pulled out her photo. "Here, take it. Don't you ever understand friendship? I loved Roxy as a friend."

Vic stared at the photo. "You think 'cause I'm not as smart as you, I don't know anything. I know you didn't want her. I felt sorry for her. You made me mad, that's all. Here," he shoved the photo back into Charlie's locker, "she's your folk. I've got no business with it." Vic's tone softened. "Keep it... remind you where ya come from." He eyed Charlie long and slow.

Charlie kind of knew what Vic was getting at, but he didn't want to listen. They pulled their cots out and headed off to the shop to turn in for the night, when Vic said, in a softer voice, "I know why you're telling me about her. I'm no fool. I'll stand by you anywhere in this goddamn war. You're the best boss a man could ever have. But sounds like she's a dream, buddy." He shook his head. "In this rotten war, who can tell anyone what to hope for? I promise you—" his voice quivered, "—if you're not around, Kinky, I'll...I'll let her know. Give me her address before anything happens."

CHAPTER 30

Charlie couldn't wait to cross Quay Street and catch the tram up the hill in the five o'clock traffic. On the platform there was a sea of men's felt hats, all fighting for a seat on the trams. It felt like an American city. He wanted to find her before she left for home, and maybe surprise her. The anticipation of seeing her again churned his stomach.

He leaped from the tram and headed towards Melvern's. He passed another Adams Bruce and went in: he managed to grab the last tray of cream puffs. Careful not to drop the precious pastries, he climbed the two flights of stairs, reaching the top landing plainly to find not a soul anywhere. He peered in the windows of the empty, dark salon, before walking across to the dressmaker's shop. Then his heart missed a beat as he saw the wedding scenes on the far door of the photographer's. Out of the back windows in the dim light, trees swayed majestically in the wind across Myers Park.

Charlie caught the tram to the bottom of the hill. He gazed up at the magnificent Huntly House, its chimneys puffing smoke against the fading skyline. He let the brass knocker slowly drop.

Mrs Frisken came out, wiping her hands. "What have you brought this time?"

"Oh, just a little something for a cold night," said Charlie, putting down the package on the wooden bench in the breakfast room. Mrs Frisken opened the package.

"Cream puffs! So did they make these on the ship?"

"No ma'am, I just bought them in town." Charlie looked away to avoid any further ship talk, searching for Mattie. Mattie came down the stairs, carrying a coal bucket. "So glad we have the hour right," she said with a cheeky grin. "I'll just set this down. I was lighting a fire."

"Sounds dangerous."

"It is," Mattie answered smiling playfully, taking his arm. She showed him into the dining room. "Meet the rest of the household."

Mattie nodded at each person. "Gladys, she's a nurse. Her roommate Paddy isn't here tonight."

"And I'm Jean, I'm a trammie. I work on the trams," said Jean smiling broadly.

"Yes and we live around the corner upstairs," Burt said. Percy stood up. "Pleasure to meet a sailor," said Burt, shaking hands.

Mrs Frisken pulled out a chair for him, as Mattie moved to sit opposite. She glowed so regal he couldn't divert his eyes from her. He half-smiled, feeling a bit out of place, uncomfortable at the formal setting—the starched white tablecloth, the polished silverware.

Charlie noticed Mrs Frisken watching him.

Burt made the first polite introductory conversation, "So Mattie tells us you're on the *Rigel*?"

"Yes, sir. She's a repair ship."

"You can't miss her, she's huge. What a magnificent sight. I work not far from the wharf at the Chief Post Office in lower Queen Street," said Burt. He picked up the steaming vegetables in the oblong china serving dish and passed them to Charlie. "Must say, all this activity's good business for us."

Mrs Frisken had hovered in the room, and eventually asked Charlie, "What will the Rigel be repairing in Auckland?"

"We're here to build hospitals and accommodation for the troops." Charlie tried to water down the information best he could.

"That could take months. Mattie will be thrilled," replied Mrs Frisken.

"Yes ma'am, we'll be here a while." Charlie did not look at her, solely at Mattie.

Charlie helped himself to vegetables and slices of the roast lamb. He watched the others to see how they handled their silverware.

"Hmmm, is this the famous New Zealand lamb roast?" he said, thoughtfully knife-prodding a mouthful onto the upside-down fork like the locals.

"That's one thing we're proud of here, is our lamb," said Mrs Frisken. She didn't eat with them, but she served and supervised.

"If my Ma cooked like this, I would've never left home." Charlie grinned.

Everyone howled with laughter. Charlie was glad he made them laugh. Then, there was simply the quiet clicking of everyone's silverware. It was so quiet, Charlie wondered if it was him… or the great meal.

"I hope y'all like cream cakes," he said, looking up when Mrs Frisken put a large silver tray of his dessert on the table.

"Our coupon supply doesn't allow for this very often," said Mrs Frisken, pouring out a cup of tea. She handed Charlie the sweet nectar. "Nor for sugar and tea," she sighed.

"How does that work?" said Charlie taking a sip of tea.

"Slowly," everyone muttered, almost in unison.

Percy hadn't said anything all night. Remarkably he spoke up, "It's a bloody pain. We even have petrol coupons; everything is rationed. But then you guys don't have that."

Mattie swiftly interrupted, "Oh, I'm sure there are a lot of extra supplies coming in now. Don't you think, Charlie?"

He glanced up and smiled, "Of course, maybe a bit might drift your way by accident."

It was Jean's turn for the kitchen cleanup, and she pushed her chair back as everyone started moving. Charlie picked his plate up, and followed her into the kitchen.

"Percy's taking the war a bit hard. Don't be offended," Jean whispered, taking Charlie's plate. She added discreetly, "You're not supposed to be in here."

"It's a habit," whispered Charlie, watching Mattie walking down the passageway.

"Go on." Jean gave a wink to Charlie, nodding, mouthing, *"She likes you."*

Smoke was rising from one of the large armchairs as Charlie passed the first room and walked into the one nearby. It was the same room where he'd first seen her delicate form appear in her house slippers. Why was he feeling so nervous? He so wanted to be alone with her, to take her in his arms. She was there, sitting on the couch with a magazine.

Mattie heard him enter. She pulled two cigarettes out from a packet, "Would you like one?"

With one step, Charlie eased down next to her and snuck out his lighter, "Good golly, didn't know you smoked."

"You never asked," said Mattie.

He leaned back, inhaling and turned to front onto her, "You tricked me."

"I most certainly did not, Mr Kincaid." She blew a puff of smoke in his direction.

Mattie watched his expression turn playful, his bottom lip twist into that familiar curl. A warm rush of excitement rushed through her veins, just with his smile. She relaxed; she edged herself up against him, inhaled and leaned back.

With her impish smile, she asked, "How did you make out with the cutlery?"

"You're messing with me."

"I saw you looking around with your fork upside-down... not very American."

"If you'd like to know," Charlie scratched his head, and tried to act the perfect gentleman. "I eat with my hands. We all do on the ship, I mean. We can't keep cutlery, it's not allowed. Shows up on Jap radar. This is top secret."

Mattie had a pained expression, drawing in the smoke. She viewed him peculiarly, wondering who was about to be the bigger fool.

He twisted towards her, trying to keep a straight face, "You see, we had a group of New Zealanders come aboard at Fanning Island on the way here, and they brought their cutlery with them. Half the Jap Navy steamed towards us until we threw it all overboard. But I did get to see the backside of the fork trick." His eyes twinkled.

Mattie stubbed her cigarette out, "You're teasing *me* now."

"I'm not. I wouldn't dare take advantage of you."

Mattie had never seen eyes like his before; they inveigled her into his heart as he spoke. She wanted to believe. She put her fingers up to touch him, tenderly caressing his nose, his lips. She hadn't been this close to him or to any man. She breathed in his earthy scent like beautiful clean linen but more worldly. *It must be his clothes, his after shave.* She slid her fingers down the side of his neck, and felt the rugged heat of his body; she wanted to explore everything, but she pulled away.

"We shouldn't be doing this. We've only just met."

Charlie sat upright again, clasping his hands. For once he couldn't understand. He wondered how many dates he'd need with this gorgeous woman before he would qualify to know her, to love her. He remembered Dudley's words. Maybe he had offended her.

"Now who's teasing who?" he said offering her another cigarette. He flicked out his lighter and leaned forward; he inhaled her floral perfume. His fingers twitched slightly, waiting for the will to touch her. She lit up, and sank back against the silky cushions. They remained in silence, smoking; each trying to understand what the other was thinking.

Mattie stubbed out her cigarette on the ash tray. "You know," she said, playing with his sailor's tie, her fingers moving up to his lips, "I loved the story about the cotton fields, the sorghum... but what about Charlie's life?"

"No, you tell me about Mattie," said Charlie, nibbling her fingers. "I have to know you, inside and out," he said in a teasing tone. "Miss Blanc... is your family French?"

"You're smart, but you first."

"I told you about sorghum. Be fair," pleaded Charlie.

"Well, my family is principally from Scotland with French ancestors. It's complicated; they came from the Shetland Islands north of Scotland. I have a brother up here in Auckland who's a doctor and one in the Fiji islands who's a dentist. As I've already told you, I'm from Dunedin, far south in the south of the South Island."

But Charlie detected a melancholy almost somber note in her voice.

"Tell me," she looked halfway serious, "why did you become a sailor?"

"To meet you."

Mattie rolled her eyes. He loved her expressions. He could read her by just saying something and watching.

Something triggered her face to lighten and then gradually fade, "You're not telling me anything. The real Charlie, inside and out."

"Okay." Charlie settled back. He put his arm around her as they watched the flames. "My Ma would rock on her chair and tell us stories." He leaned closer. He tensed at the next thought, forcing a cough, but willed himself on.

"Until one awful day when my Daddy had his accident... I shouldn't be telling you all this."

Mattie huddled closer. This was precisely what she wanted—the real, down-deep Charlie. "But you must, darling." She stroked a strand of hair from his forehead. "It's all right, please trust me. No secrets."

He felt safe in her touch; it was okay, he could trust her with his story. "He worked as a woodcutter and I used to go along sometimes. The saw he was using kicked back, and he slipped. I ran to help, but it was too late." Charlie softly wept at the memory. He swallowed hard. "His head rolled away down them hills. My Ma... then she had trouble. Big trouble. She couldn't feed all us kids. Make matters worse, she was so thin and tired. One day she fell off the hay platform down into the barn. She was never the same. I was the one that got sent to an orphanage." He stared into the flames. The fire crackled. "I'm never goin' back, Mattie. Not till I'm able enough to give her everything she never had."

Mattie sat there running her fingers delicately through his hair, kissing him gently, looking at him with tears in her eyes.

"Oh, Kinky, that touches my heart. It makes me so sad."

"Don't be sad." His face lit up. "I left, more like ran, from home and that's why I joined the Navy. I'm going to be a hero."

"If only you knew how many times I've wanted to run away." She flashed apprehensively at Charlie.

Charlie knew there was something behind those eyes, something she wanted desperately to tell. Why was she here in this boarding house, so distant from her family?

"You don't have to be afraid of nothin'. You're with me. We've all had our troubles." All of a sudden his life seemed simple; he waited, adoringly caressing her back, comforting her, consoling her.

"There's nothing to tell, but..." She stared down briefly at her lap. "My father, he wouldn't approve of us."

Tears welled in Charlie's eyes now. He didn't want to know anything further; he wanted to leave, like the first time. He was inadequate. All the doubt crept back in. She was ashamed of him; she didn't want him. He was just a sailor and he'd told her too much. He bit his lip; he was in too deep.

He did what he was good at. He faced her. "So what do you want from me?"

Mattie hesitated, then stood up and reached for his hand. "I've lit the fire upstairs."

Charlie crinkled up his forehead, "Really?"

"Shhh… it's okay." Mattie squeezed his fingers. Charlie was puzzled. He followed her up the polished wooden staircase, past the stained-glass window, down the huge passageway. They entered the end doorway on the left. Mattie went straight across to the fireplace and bent down to stoke it.

"Here, let me help you."

"No really, I like to do it. I so love a fire." She eased back in a chair, looking across at him. "Watch the fire fairies dance up the chimney. You might pick up a new step."

"We'll be dancing like hot charcoal all right."

She stood up, brushing herself. "I hope you didn't mind my asking you here," she said as she walked over to the bed, with its rose-printed bedspread, and the box of chocolates sitting in its pride of place on the night table.

"Seems a bit further than Myers Park and a cup of tea," said Charlie. They both laughed.

"I wanted to tell you about my world, from the inside," said Mattie, her heart thumping at the vision of his warm, naked body, nuzzling up to her.

"I understand," said Charlie. His throat went dry; he was sick with desire for her.

Mattie sat down on the bed.

"When you told me so much about your family…" Her voice was shaky. Charlie sensed something was wrong. Standing up against her, he ran his strong hands through her hair, and listened. "I… I didn't want you to think I wasn't listening."

She felt him, his hardness against her. Mattie pulled away and lay on the bed, sinking herself into the quilt.

He dropped alongside her. Tucking her hair deftly behind her ears, he whispered, "It's all right. I knew you were listening. Why wouldn't your father approve?"

"Haven't you figured it out?" She rose up, sobbing. She grabbed a handkerchief out of the bedside drawer, her hands trembling.

He took her in his arms, "It's not the first time a gal's felt like this."

"No, you just don't get it. Not if they've been…" She buried her face in her handkerchief, bawling, "…raped."

Charlie held her solidly. "You don't have to say anymore. You won't suffer again... ever." He delicately turned her over, brushing away the sodden hair from her eye, "Is that why you're up here in Auckland?"

Mattie nodded, her mouth pursed closed.

"Does your mother know?"

Mattie followed his eyes, nodding.

"I knew you'd get the wrong message, I could tell. My father knows. He's rich, and he doesn't care," Mattie sobbed uncontrollably.

"You're not making sense. Who's rich, your father?"

"No… the man. He was my brother's friend. Ohhh," she hid her face again, "why do I have to relive this?"

"Because you care enough to tell me, to share your grief." He held her for a long while, until she gradually calmed down. She let out a huge sigh. Charlie picked up a photo from the bedside table. "Is this your dog?"

"His name's Jerry," she whispered.

Charlie placed it back, effortlessly smiling at her, "Just as well Jerry's not here. He'd be jumping Bonny's bones."

Mattie's tear-stained face broke into a smile, searching his eyes, touching his neck with her outstretched fingers. She said in a whisper, "Will you make love to me?"

Charlie wiped the last of her tears, gazing at her for a long second. "You make me proud." He bent attentively down, to kiss her milk-white nose with a grin. "But first, I'm taking you out. We're going to celebrate."

He stood up, pulling her towards him. "I haven't told you, but I'm being promoted to Warrant Officer."

Mattie's eyes lit again with that wonderful glow he loved so much. He held her chin up, "When I make love to you, it will be for keeps. I'll never leave you. I want to get down on my knees—" he had tears in his eyes "—and pretend this war is over. I'll return, and…"

"I can't."

"Ma'am, you'd better believe me. I am here to honor you and your country," he said. "Your daddy." He pointed in the photo. "Is this him?"

She nodded.

Charlie twisted fluffy curls in his fingers, and then squeezed her hand. "He'll thank me one day for loving you but, we've got a ways to go."

"I love it when you say that," said Mattie smiling through her tears, "that southern accent... a ways to go."

"Get ready." He grabbed her and did a replay of the tap dance. "Now it's my turn to take you out, and you better show me all that stuff on etiquette. I've been given a book on it. You know... the silverware, we don't have."

Mattie giggled and they relaxed by the fire. Charlie sat cross-legged, like a Cherokee, grinning at her. "And another thing your daddy better get used to... I live in a tent. We call it a tepee."

Mattie shook her head. "I don't know when to believe you."

"I'm serious. I'm part Cherokee Indian. Does that bother you?"

"Nothing bothers me about you. Tell me, I want to know."

"Well, my darlin', that's another story. It'll have to wait until I'm in my buckskin and feathers."

CHAPTER 31

Irene arrived at the door of the salon at midday, and the two women went downstairs and picked a seat by the brick fireplace in the Savoy tearooms.

"Thank you for coming." Mattie looked earnestly at Irene.

"That's all right." Irene slipped her gloves into her handbag. "You look worried. Is something wrong?"

Mattie settled back into the warmth of the fire behind, fumbling with her napkin. *This is not going well.* The familiar room seemed like a prison.

"Mattie, what is it? You're not...?"

"Don't be silly, Irene, you know me better than that." Mattie swished her shoulders. "I'm in love."

"What? My word, this is sudden. Who's the lucky man?"

"If I tell you, will you promise not to tell George?" Mattie squirmed on her seat. She dreaded what was about to happen. Her brother George was always a tease; he'd be the first to tell. Irene raised an eyebrow. "I don't like the sound of this, it sounds illicit already. You're too much of a lady to get into trouble," she said, picking up the menu to order some food. Mattie was beginning to think there was a side of her that was quite strict, even controlling, and she wished she hadn't shared her secret with her, but it was too late.

"Just because you're married with a husband off to war, am I not allowed to fall in love? This is normal human nature, not trouble."

"You make it sound that way, Mattie."

"I've nothing to be ashamed of," said Mattie, lighting a cigarette and letting the match drop into the ashtray. Inhaling, she paused for effect. "I've met a sailor."

Irene's eyes widened and jaw dropped.

"You can look as horrified as you like, but I'm going to marry him," Mattie confided in a serious tone.

"What…?" Irene drew back in shock, both hands up to her mouth. "Oh my dear girl, I'm so glad you told me. Now I can reason with you, without anyone else finding out."

"I beg your pardon?"

Irene scrutinized the room, "Shhh. Don't raise your voice. Someone might know you." She eased forward whispering, "Have you told your parents?"

"No." Mattie felt resigned. What was the use—no one would understand. No one wanted her to be happy, not even Irene. Tears edged into her eyes, as if she should be ashamed of falling in love. Was it some disease, like the plague? Now her best friend, the one woman she looked up to, would shun her. She shook her head.

Irene softened her voice, "Look Mattie, I want you to be happy. Come on. I'm merely trying to protect you. Imagine what you're saying. What if sister-in-law Audrey finds out?"

"Yes, I know. Forget I said it." Mattie stared at her in silence, clenching her fist. She felt abandoned and angry, angry at people prying, controlling. But in her heart she knew, and allowed that calm to soothe, to cleanse her mind.

Irene ordered tea and sandwiches. "I'd like to meet him," she recanted.

"What made you change your mind?"

"It's the war. It does funny things to people."

"So what? Now I can tell you he's an American and he's just been promoted to Warrant Officer, and—"

"Mattie, does that make a difference? Are you trying to impress me? He's a sailor, a Yank sailor at that. That's all your father will hear. Not that he's an officer. He doesn't want you marrying an American."

Mattie dwelled upon her father's panicked phone call about Auckland being invaded, urging her to return home. What if Irene were right?

Irene continued, "Now you know why he wanted you home. The Yanks are here, and the Japs may not be far behind." She frowned as she needlessly wiped her hands into a napkin.

"No Japs will get past these Americans, Irene," Mattie countered, locking eyes with Irene.

"Hope you're right, Sister."

"Oh Irene, he's so polite." Mattie put her hand out to Irene. "He's kind and gentle, and—" she grinned into Irene's lovely, caring eyes "—he is so romantic and so-o-o good-looking."

Irene let go of Mattie's hand. She reached into her handbag, drew on her gloves. "Well, enough prattling. We'd better get those dancing lessons in. You have a partner now. But Kiwis are not going to like your American fling."

CHAPTER 32

Admiral Ghormley had taken control of the New Zealand ships *Achilles* and *Leander*. By mid-June, his plans for Auckland to become the major support base for operations against the Japanese were in place. The sight of the American ships, along with the *Rigel*, signaled a mighty force in the harbor, helping to relieve the New Zealanders' fears of the advancing Japanese.

Admiral Ghormley, with his US Joint Purchasing Board, continued a massive, unprecedented purchasing of supplies and equipment. Nothing was spared. The latest equipment, including forklifts, jitneys, cranes and flat-tops, arrived by the tons. A portion of it was transported over to Motutapu Island in the Gulf, where concrete and brick magazine stores were being rushed to completion. Almost overnight a 1500-bed hospital sprang up in Cornwall Park, and 750 army personnel were billeted on the Outer Domain. Campsites, crudely structured like chicken coops, arose both north and south of Auckland. The Americans were everywhere.

Charlie and his men had many tasks to complete, but silently wondered why they were building all these hospitals with thousands of beds. Crisp white sheets were soon to be soiled in a terrible way.

Andy gave a holler to Charlie, "Hey buddy, haven't seen you for awhile."

"No, there's been a bit going on," replied Charlie.

"Yeah." Andy put down his gear. "They have me welding up the steel beams for those sheds over there." He pointed across to the dockside. "I see you've cottoned on to the Kiwi smoko." He gestured to the other men: a few were getting down from their ladders; others were already sitting in the sun, munching their food, with steaming cups of tea.

Charlie laughed. He lit a cigarette. "Such relaxed folks."

"My uncle's here," said Andy looking across at Princes Wharf. "He's on the *San Francisco*." The heavy cruiser towered defiantly into the sky down the wharf.

"She's a beauty," said Charlie, admiring the huge ship.

"Got them giant Ohio Buckeyes on board," Andy went on. "They're lining up between the cargo sheds and marching down Quay Street to the railway station."

"Hmmm, that'll stir up the crowd."

"Yep, sure will. Then she's taking wounded back to Pearl and into the yards for a re-fit. I don't like the look of this one bit." Andy's grin faded into gloom. "There's too many shot-up men. Have you seen what's coming in? My uncle told me—"

"Andy, don't let it get it to you. Take a gander. You see this beautiful land, these proud people? You want Japs living here?" he said, looking out across the sparkling waters.

Andy's face tightened to a painful expression. He gripped hard on the railing.

The sun blazed against the surrounding hills, like a paradise. Charlie judged it looked all too inviting for an enemy invasion. *Duck soup.*

"Guts and manpower, that's what it takes." Charlie kicked at the equipment, staring out at sea again. "Met a gal yet?"

"My uncle invited me to someone's house, and there's this gal." Andy grinned mischievously. "She wants to go out on a date."

"Well then, go."

"Think I should?"

"Sure do. I've met a honey." Charlie smiled. "Wouldn't trade her for the world." He turned to look at Andy. "And I've been promoted," he confessed.

"You never used to be a bragger."

"No, I'm not. I've been putting off telling the men. Think they'll mind?"

"Not one bit." Andy's big smile came back. "Boy, I'm glad it's you. Couldn't have happened to a better guy. I'd say spit it out. Tell 'em." He picked up his welding mask. "Looks like smoko's over. Better get more of these frames done before sunset. Might see ya at a dance."

Charlie flicked his cigarette into the sea. There was a chill in the air with the last of the day behind them. He picked up his new uniform and was checking the day's inventory inside the shed when Vic strolled in.

"I have orders," Charlie blurted out.

"Who's in trouble?" asked Vic.

"No one; it's me. I've been promoted to Warrant Officer. I'm moving topside tonight."

"What?" Vic's jaw dropped. "Just like that?"

Charlie looked up. He realized he'd upset Vic. Later, he was not surprised when he went to pack his gear and found his clothes had been painted, his locker picked, and his homebrew whisky gone. He ignored the disaster and went about changing into his new uniform, whistling to himself. A flutter of footsteps behind startled him. Before he could turn around, he was blindfolded and hustled off the ship into a waiting vehicle.

·   ·   ·   ·   ·

Charlie perceived they were travelling uphill. There was no sound from the driver of the vehicle, until Charlie was thrown out on a sloping hillside, his head down in wet grass. He was picked up, carried into a building, and his blindfold removed.

His vision progressively adjusted in the smoky dark to a round-shaped bar glowing in the corner of a red-carpeted room. In another corner, a fat woman jiggled at a piano and pursed her thick lips at him, "Kiss me big boy... tonight." She beckoned to him with gyrating hips, "Tuck me into my little wooden bed...." Her fat fingers ran over the piano keys. Another woman lay on the top of the piano; her long, black-stockinged legs lifted and spread enticingly.

"Welcome to the Biltmore Club, Paritai Drive, best whorehouse in town!" Vic danced excitedly, giving Charlie a nudge. "Hmm, must be that fine officer's jacket. Got you in for a treat tonight, buddy." He grinned.

Charlie brushed at his new jacket, and snapped at Vic, "You peckerwood, you can't resist a—"

"Here, you forgot something." Vic slipped Charlie's flask into his pocket. "Come on, Kinky. The look on your face." He burst out laughing, well lubricated with his shipmates.

"Who're you clowns?" yelled a pug-faced man, sprawled across the bar, cigarette barely dangling from ugly lips. A bloated battleship tattoo flared on his fat arm.

"Shell shock special for Mr Kincaid," blathered Vic with one elbow on the bar. "I rigged his swearing-in party with the Exec from the *Rigel*. Didn't you get our official notice?"

"No I didn't, sonny Jim. This place is not for enlisted. I'm Jacko and you pretty boys better get lost."

"Not tonight, big boy." Vic was getting agitated. He slammed down a fistful of dollars. Crow and Red were standing behind him, draped with two busty women, ready to go.

"Can't you read the sign?" Jacko scowled, wiping a filthy towel through the bar grime.

"They're with me," said Charlie. "This is Officer Country. Drinks are on me." A soft arm snaked seductively around his middle. He swiveled and looked into the eyes of a small woman dressed in red satin, staring up at him with rock-steady eyeballs.

Vic leaned over and grabbed her waist, pushing her up against Charlie, "Hey Kinks, I'll get her warmed up for ya." He called over to the woman on the piano, "Play somethin' hot." The dance was on. Vic grabbed the small woman in the red dress, bending his knees, twisting, flinging her round the room.

"Best skirt in town," mumbled Jacko, as he snatched Charlie's dollars; then he poured out the whisky.

"Vic can handle the action." Charlie gazed down at Jacko's stubby fingers, laden with US Navy signet rings. He disliked this man.

"Hey…" Jacko leaned over the bar, tapping Charlie on the sleeve of his new jacket. Ashes shook off his sodden fag, "If I were you, I'd scram with your mates before the cops get here." His beady eyes darted through the room. "How'd your fuckin' buddy fix a deal here?"

"Easy, fat boy, you're on every billboard in town," Charlie joked. "Best whorehouse in town." He pretended to choke on his next shot. He'd get this son-of-a-bitch. "If I were you, I'd play it cool." Charlie looked around suspiciously. "A wild wind is about to blow." He nodded at Jacko. "Here's a tip…ever hear of the Ohio Buckeyes?"

Jacko went on uselessly rubbing the bar. "Your mouth's full of shit, sailor, you don't fool me." His fat tobacco-brown fingers squashed and rotated the last of a butt into a blackened ashtray.

Charlie wanted to punch his lights out. "Course, small fry like you… when them giant Ohio boys scramble up here tonight, there'll be nothing left of your skirts after they've been serviced by Buckeyes."

"You've just scored yourself a ticket to trouble." Jacko leaned towards Charlie, so close he tasted Jacko's foul breath. Charlie stared straight into Jacko's eyes as he drank the last of his whisky; eyes that were dead with greed.

"See these rings?" Jacko shoved a clenched fist in Charlie's face. "I didn't get them by playing fair with you dickheads."

Charlie had had enough. He growled, "Listen, you fat fuck—"

Glass shattered against the bar wall. Vic thumped Jacko clear across the room as the rest of the crew thumped into Jacko's men. Furniture crunched into kindling.

"You damn fool," yelled Vic. "Look what you've started."

"I didn't start anything," Charlie flung the glazed wooden bar doors open at the back, and walked out into the night air under a huge veranda. His head was spinning from the whisky, but he still heard the commotion behind him. The veranda surrounded a dome-shaped building with rows of small unlit windows. Beyond the veranda, two lion statues guarded the entranceway, but the grass became wild at the edges, and scattered into rocks and debris, disguising a sheer cliff drop.

Charlie turned around, held open the doors and glared at Vic. "I told you, don't fuck with the locals," he yelled. "You fuckin' idiot. If we get done on this, we'll get shipped out of here so fast we'll be smothered in Japs by sundown."

"Jus" lettin' off some steam, lover boy," slurred Vic.

"You're out of control. Fuckin' can't get laid, that's your problem!" He slammed the door shut.

The whisky was frying Charlie's brain. He stumbled across the grass, heaving in the cold air. The moon danced across Waitemata Harbor. Huge tangled trees now became the enemy. He tripped, wobbled and fell into dense foliage.

●   ●   ●   ●   ●

Mattie had organized dancing lessons for Charlie and invited Irene to join in. They huddled together after work, waiting for Charlie, watching the small group of people arrive. Irene started to fidget.

"Maybe he was caught up in that parade today," she said abruptly, breaking the silence.

"Or they shipped out," Mattie said nervously. "There are too many ships coming in."

"Well if it's anything like I saw today, there are armies of Yanks storming ashore. Someone was saying at the surgery that hundreds of them arrived this morning, parading down Quay Street. Biggest crowd there's ever been; kids waving American flags. Didn't your sailor tell you about it?"

Mattie shook her head. She didn't like Irene's tone. She was in no mood for a lecture. Irene could be so condescending. She tried to block her out, but Irene droned on, "So many hard hats. The papers never say who they are, but I know they're goddamn Yanks." Mattie noticed the clock... and then steadied her eye on the door. The beautiful music started and the few men began to partner up with the women.

"Go on, join in," Mattie said, looking in the direction of the entranceway. "A few dances will be good for you. I'll leave it tonight. I've been in dancing lessons since I could walk."

"Excuse me, Miss Blanc," said the instructor. "The lesson is starting."

"No, sorry, I've made a mistake," said Mattie, standing up. "I'll be ready another night. My apologies." She turned to Irene. "I know what you're thinking. It's the same story—it always will be." Mattie had tears in her eyes. "I don't want to talk about it."

Irene picked up her gloves to leave. "I'm sorry, Mattie. I'll leave with you."

"I don't want any pity. I'm going home."

Before Irene said anything more, Mattie rushed down the stairs, her heart pounding. She caught a tram back home, went to bed, and cried herself to sleep.

All the next day she couldn't concentrate on her work. She listened to Nan laughing about her missing the dancing at Peter Pan's. It made her mad. She was being made to look a fool. Why had he disappeared? She quietly chafed, pretending to smile as she combed out a client's thick permed hair.

He didn't want to go dancing and couldn't confront her. By lunch break she was boiling mad. She'd made up her mind: she'd confront *him*.

She grabbed her coat and raced down the stairs to catch the first tram on Queen Street.

All the way, she sat in the tram staring at the different places they'd been to. Why would he just vanish, she wondered. What if he had left? She'd find out if the *Rigel* was still there. She almost fell off the tram in her haste, raced around the corner and stopped dead in her tracks at sight of the magnificent two masts of the *Rigel* stabbing above the buildings. Fresh doubts set in.

No one was allowed near the ship. Mattie examined the workers, cranes, and machinery thumping across the dock. Maybe someone would help her if she walked closer—but it was no use.

The day never seemed to end, and dinner that evening was even worse. The empty chair opposite reminded her of Charlie. Everything reminded her of him. She left with her head down, climbed the stairs and flung herself on the bed, wishing he'd made love to her there. She longed for his tender kisses, his gentle touch.

Why doesn't he want me? What have I done to deserve this?

She fell asleep in her clothes.

Mattie woke an hour or so later to a soft knock. Mrs Frisken was standing in her dressing gown with little Bonny. "Someone on the *Rigel* called," she informed Mattie. "There's been an accident. Charlie's in Cornwall Hospital."

"Oh, my God!" Mattie gasped and bolted up.

"Isn't that where your brother works?" Mrs Frisken went on, trying to be helpful.

"Oh, Mrs Frisken," Mattie collapsed in her arms.

"There, there, child," she patted Mattie on the back. "Let's go downstairs and call... then go to him."

Mattie grabbed her coat and purse and raced downstairs to the phone. She dialed the hospital and spoke to the receptionist. "Yes, it's him," she blurted to Mrs Frisken, "he's there... being transferred. I must find my brother. He'll know."

"Be careful."

But Mattie didn't answer her. She dashed out the door and down the road to catch the tram to Greenlane.

The hospital was a single-storey field hospital for patients in transit. It was set back against the hillside in Cornwall Park, erupting almost overnight into full operation.

Mattie walked up to the nurse at the front desk. "My name's Blanc, Miss Blanc. I'm Dr Blanc's sister. I'm here to see a patient, Mr Kincaid."

The nurse looked up. "Someone rang here about him."

"Yes, that was me. Where is Dr Blanc, please?"

"Dr Blanc is busy with a patient."

"Well, I'm sorry, but this can't wait." Mattie swooped past her, towards the corridor.

"Excuse me, you can't go down there," the nurse called out.

Mattie ran down the open wards. She heard men groaning, and caught sight of a doctor in a white coat.

"Excuse me. Can you tell me where your patient Kincaid is? I'm Dr Blanc's sister," she pleaded.

"Sorry, but we don't have a Kincaid here," the doctor said.

"Mattie, what are you doing here?"

She spun around when she heard her brother's voice. They stared at each other.

"I think you have a little explaining to do," John said, picking up a clipboard at the end of the bed of the patient lying there. "These men have been through enough. Have you taken leave of your senses? Or are you wanting to get on a uniform and become a nurse?"

Mattie stared at the seemingly lifeless form on the bed. "I'm sorry, John, I must be mistaken… I… Kincaid." Her mouth flew open. "It's not him..."

"What's going on, Mattie?"

"I've been dancing with a sailor… Charlie Kincaid."

"For Christ's sake, Mattie, not you." John glared at her.

"What I do is not your concern," snapped Mattie. "If you don't want to help, then I'll find him myself." She scowled, furious at her brother.

"I have patients," John pivoted and walked onward.

Mattie followed him. "I was meaning to tell you," she told John, once they were out of the ward.

"Listen, old girl, take a good look around. In case you hadn't noticed, there's a war on. These poor bastards are the fodder. Riddled with malaria, dysentery, gaping wounds, burned flesh, amputated limbs. Go out with your sailor, while he's alive, Sis."

Mattie frowned, "What's that supposed to mean?"

"By the look on your face, you're in love with this guy Kincaid." Shaking his head, he departed, leaving her standing there.

Mattie went back down the long corridor and asked at the desk, "Excuse me, but where is patient Charles Kincaid?"

The nurse responded curtly, "Sorry, Miss Blanc, he has been transferred, but I cannot say where."

Mattie stormed, determined, into the cold night air.

CHAPTER 33

The following morning, Nan caught sight of a tall handsome figure standing at the door of the salon. She blushed as he tipped his hat.

"Excuse me ma'am, but is Miss Blanc at work today?"

"Of course, I'll get her for you." Nan almost knocked into Mattie, who appeared at the sound of an American accent.

"My my, you sure are pretty," Vic said, smiling apprehensively. "You see, ma'am, I've come to apologize for Charlie. I'm Vic, by the way," he said, putting out his hand.

Mattie politely shook hands. "Is everything all right?" She frowned, stepping out onto the landing and closing the salon door behind her.

"Yes, but… it's our fault. All of us pulled a prank to roast his promotion to Warrant. We were only having fun—his first night as an officer and all that. We'd have had him back in time to see you, but he fell down a cliff."

"Then where is he?"

"He's back at the ship's infirmary. The doc says he'll be as right as rain soon."

"He sent you up here?"

"No, ma'am, he didn't. I was just to call," he smiled, putting on his cap. "Just lookin' out for you, that's all, ma'am."

Mattie liked Vic instantly. There was something clumsy and reckless about him that reassured her he was a good friend of Charlie's. He had an eye for the ladies, she thought, as he winked at Nan through the window of the salon, tipping his hat. Nan saw; she dropped her scissors and bloomed burgundy red.

"Thank you, Vic. You're very kind to make this effort. Now I must return to my work," Mattie said, hoping her excitement would not show through. She smiled secretly to herself as she returned to the salon. She was so relieved at the news.

When she got home that night, Mrs Frisken was in the kitchen preparing the evening meal.

"I couldn't believe it when I walked in from shopping," Mrs Frisken said, whirling down the passageway. "Come and see this."

A huge carton was on display by the kitchen door. Mattie gasped at its contents. There was flour, sugar, tea, cakes, biscuits, tins of food... even soup bones. Mrs Frisken caught Mattie's expression. "Yes, that's what I thought," she said. "Percy said a few American sailors dropped it off this morning."

"I bet I know who they were," said Mattie, thinking of the charming Vic. "What do you make of these?" she asked, turning a tin around, trying to read the label.

"I'd say they were Charlie's black beans. He must be hoping for some southern cooking."

Mattie pursed her lips, put the tin back in the box, and picked up a pound of butter. "But all this butter?" she exclaimed. "Surely..."

"Here," Mrs Frisken snatched the butter. "Never complain about getting too much butter, my dear girl."

"It's like Christmas," said Mattie. "He's such a dear."

"Better see if it was him first," cautioned Mrs Frisken. "Your turn tonight for the dishes, Mattie. It will keep your mind busy."

Mattie helped Mrs Frisken place everything neatly inside the pantry. As she closed the door, Mattie supposed she seemed bothered.

"You can use the phone," Mrs Frisken told her. "I mean, if you want to call home."

"Thank you, Mrs Frisken." She smiled at the older woman. "I know I should tell my mother about Charlie." She grimaced at thought.

Mrs Frisken broke into a smile. "Hmmm, yes, I think so," she said, patting Mattie's arm.

Mattie picked up the phone and dialed home. Her mother answered. It was heartbreaking, hearing her voice.

"Mattie, oh my darling, I miss you so much. When are you coming home?"

Mattie rolled her eyes. "Mother, I knew you would say that."

"Your father's been worried about you," her mother went on. "We've heard you're seeing someone."

"What?" Mattie's mouth flew open, "Who told—"

"My dear, your family cares about you, that's all."

"Who told you, Mother?"

"Your brother's concerned."

Mattie was silent. She wanted to wring his neck. "He's no right to say anything, Mother. I was going to tell you and Father… I've met an American. He's an officer and a good man." Nothing was coming out right. Then she heard her father's voice in the background. "Father, is that you?"

"What's all this about an American?" asked Arthur.

"He's very respectful. He wants to meet you," Mattie offered.

"Well, I can't see that happening. There's a war on."

"He's helping set things up here. He's a Navy diver, a Warrant Officer…There's so much happening."

They were both silent for a moment, till Mattie tried to speak. "I'm… I'm sorry Father. I know this war is hard but…"

Her mother's voice came back on, "Listen dear, I think it's best you come home."

Dear Mother. She could just imagine her father breathing down her mother's neck, telling her what to say. Of course she would go home, but not now. She said her goodbyes and put the phone down, contemplating her next move.

•   •   •   •   •

Two days passed. Mattie answered the phone at the salon and heard Charlie's sweet southern drawl, "Well, how's my little sweetheart?"

"You disappeared." She spoke deliberately, trying to sound calm.

"Darlin'," I couldn't help it, I had a fall. The doc just let me out. I've spent days thinking about you. Best I could do was get Vic to call."

"Is this how it will be when your ship actually does leave?" asked Mattie. She couldn't help it; her agony over losing him was clouding everything.

"Gee, honey, you've just no idea how worried I've been about you… about us. I just gotta tell you."

Mattie gripped the thick black receiver. She felt her heart hammering as she listened to his voice. "Tell me what?" There was a pause; Mattie heard his breathing into the phone.

"I'm coming into town. I wanna catch those dancin' lessons."

"Well, they don't take too kindly to partners not showing up. Are you sure you'll appear this time?"

"Ma'am, it will be my privilege to be there."

"Please, no more rude behavior. I don't deserve it." Mattie hung up the phone. She realized she was shaking. She went into the bathroom to run cold water on her face, and stared at herself in the mirror. She was afraid, afraid of any fresh hurt in her life. This occasion she had to be strong, respect herself. She put on lipstick, patted rouge, and tied a red bow in her hair. Feeling calmer, she returned to work.

It was late afternoon when Mattie caught sight of Charlie at the salon door. She couldn't believe her eyes: he was her officer, standing there in his new uniform. He hadn't seen her. She darted into the changing room.

When she emerged, she looked ravishing, with the light catching her dark, tightly woven curls. Her Harris-tweed jacket nipped in at the waist, enhancing her perfect hourglass figure. She closed the door behind her, and locked with his loving eyes. They were alone in the silence.

"Hello, Charlie."

Charlie touched his hat. "Well, evenin', ma'am." He took her arm. "Mattie, I'm so sorry."

"Leave it till later," said Mattie, willing herself to stay calm. She pretended to act uninterested, when all the while she ached to hold him and tell him how handsome he looked in his uniform. They walked evenly down the stairs. Charlie paused at the first landing. There was a small alcove beside the door of the Savoy tearooms that was just room enough for a private huddle.

"Mattie, I..." Mattie averted her eyes. Charlie held her, forcing her to look at him.

Tears pooled in Mattie's eyes. She knew he could read her mind.

"Mattie, I know what you're thinking, that I'm a heel for leaving you stranded."

He peered round the corner into the tea rooms where he'd seen the dancing; "Hey, isn't this where the dancing lessons are?"

"They were, until you stood me up."

"I won't be doin' that again… will I?" Charlie was desperate to make it up to her. Mattie welcomed the adoration in his eyes.

"I hope not. Don't you break my heart, Charlie Kincaid," she replied softly.

Charlie clutched her hands, "Mattie, after being separated from you in the hospital, I mean…," he listened to himself beginning to stammer. Nothing came out right. He just had to go for it. "When I was lying there, unable to get to you, I knew. I knew when I first saw you, Mattie. I'm in love with you."

"Oh, Kinky, I love you too, but it's so fast… frightening." Mattie willed these words past the lump in her throat; it was all she had wanted to hear.

"Darlin' it's not frightening, it's natural as bees to honey." Charlie's bottom lip curled into his cute smile.

Mattie melted. That smile, how she'd missed it. She threw her arms around him and nuzzled into his neck, breathing in that familiar oaken scent, the same when they first held each other on the couch. She rested her damp cheeks against the soft, new wool of his jacket. Charlie gently rocked her, wiping her tears with his knuckles, stroking her hair. Then he leaned down, and with his fingers, lifted her face towards him and searched deep into her eyes.

"I'm here, baby, I'll always be right here." Without warning Charlie's mouth was on hers; he was kissing her. She kissed him back, his tumescence against her belly sending her crazy. She wanted him bad. She didn't know why she felt this way so completely. She let him slide his hand up her stockings, reaching the top of her bare thigh. His fingers massaged their way inside her panties.

"Ladies don't behave like this." She swallowed hard and pushed away, straightening her jacket. "Don't you think we'd better—"

"What, my darling, make love?" He grinned, playing with one of her long curls. He searched her eyes for answers.

"I can't do this here, Charlie, please…"

Charlie peered back into the tea rooms. "You up for tea, princess?" He broke into his quirky grin. "I'm starved."

The waiter showed them to a private alcove by the fireside, not far from where Mattie and Irene had waited that dreadful night Charlie went missing. Mattie sat staring across at the starlit dance floor, trying to imagine dancing with him. She desperately wanted romance, not some quick love affair; she was frightened of her own desires.

The light shining through the tall windows added a magical glow that haloed the piano player, as he deftly played "*Amapola*", a current Jimmy Dorsey hit. The waiter arrived with the tea service.

"What's on the menu?" Charlie asked.

"We serve small meals, sir, cottage pie and pudding," answered the waiter.

"We'll have two of each, please," replied Mattie graciously.

"And a couple dancin' lessons," added Charlie, with a cheeky grin.

"Sorry, officer, but they don't start till later."

Mattie whispered, "I could have told you that." She secretly wished Irene was here to witness.

Charlie didn't hesitate to devour his meal; good Navy training. When he had finished, he lit a cigarette and patiently watched Mattie catch up. After her last bite, he reached over and lit one for her.

Smoking helped Mattie's nerves. She noticed him dab a speck of crumb at the edge of his mouth. She presumed he was in a world of his own. He could be playful and capricious, but underneath it he was steeped in a bewildering solitude. She longed to unravel it and understand him better.

He remained silent, pensive, smoking for awhile. Leaning his head back, he blew a final puff of smoke, and then stubbed out his cigarette with a grimace.

Mattie reached and caressed his rough fingers, bringing her blue eyes into his.

He squeezed her hand back and broke into a smile. "You're so good for me, Mattie. You're the best." He sat back and sipped his tea. "You know what?" His eyebrows lifted seemingly to his hairline; he loved watching Mattie with his every move.

She nestled closer. Their knees touched under the table.

"I think this tea has something in it."

Mattie frowned up at him.

"Sugar. Yep, you're sweet as sugar," Charlie winked at her, and pulled a few coins out for the bill. He stood up and held her jacket, "Come on, sugar... We're goin' shopping."

"What... now? It's almost closing time."

"Don't worry, doll, we'll beat the bell, no sweat."

Mattie threaded into his arm, and they went down the stairs into the crowded street and crossed the road into George Court department store. The huge doors opened and they paused in front of the perfume and cosmetics counters.

"Wow. This is swell. Smells like every flower in the garden," he said, jiggling the coins in his pocket.

"What would you like to see?" Mattie asked, looking coy.

"You... in something special," he said, with a sexy gaze.

Mattie moved through the merchandise, towards the elevator. She couldn't believe she was inside her favorite shop with this gorgeous man.

"Going up?" said the elevator attendant, his white gloves pulling across the bronze scissor gate. "We have first floor... Curtains, furnishing and carpets... second floor, ladies sportswear and frocks, coats..."

"That's us," interrupted Charlie.

They walked through rows of beautiful ladies shoes, clustered in elegant displays. He stopped by the stairs, and turned to Mattie. "I want to buy you something special." He made his way over to the fur coats.

"Let's try on some style." He picked up a white fur cape. I'll take your jacket. Here, slip this on."

"No. You don't have to."

"I know what I have to do, Miss Blanc. If you'll allow me to take you out dancing, you're gonna need suitably warm attire, so we can walk the streets in comfort," he assured her.

Sometimes his attention was too much to take, especially in public. What will people think? Mattie imagined.

The soft fur brushed against her neck as Charlie slipped it on. Mattie clutched the elegant cape and did a slow pirouette in front of the mirror, ending with an alluring look into his beautiful eyes. She couldn't help herself. "Oh it feels so luxurious and soft," she whispered.

He watched her preen herself in the mirror; he loved what he saw, proud to take care of his sweetheart.

But somehow Mattie all at once felt ashamed at the opulence. She startled him, when she handed it back to him. "But honestly, I don't need this. I have a coat."

"Not this one." He winked at the assistant, burrowing in his pockets. "Wrap it up please."

"This is so kind of you," Mattie remarked, her face flushed, taking Charlie's arm.

"Why wouldn't I spoil my gal? Let's see what else is out there." He nudged her.

Outside, the air had chilled as the sun disappeared. They crossed the road.

"You might want to put the coat on… it's turned cold," Charlie said, as if genuinely worried.

Mattie liked the way he cared for her, she grinned up at him and shook her head, "I'm fine. It's late we should be getting back." They walked on down the street till Charlie heard the music from the radio shop on the corner. They stared in the window.

"What do you think of a radio for your room?" he asked, hugging her waist as they walked inside.

The music was playing from a radio sitting on a bench near the front door. He bowed for a closer once-over and asked, "How can we dance, if we don't have music?"

"Oh Charlie… this is all too much, please." Mattie's eyebrows arched upwards, almost pleading.

Charlie ran his fingers over its small, burled walnut case. "It's such a little beauty. It can go on the table by your bed." He noticed her foot was already tapping to the beat. Charlie couldn't wait to hold her in his arms.

A salesman made a beeline for them, "McCabe's Radios prides itself on the best selection," he touted. "This one is a Bell radio, the latest, excellent quality."

"How loud can she go," asked Charlie?

"Yes, well…," the man rotated the volume knob, "it will fill the room with your favorites."

"Swell, that's the story." Charlie grinned, putting his arm around Mattie. "What do you say, Mattie?"

Mattie's gaze was on the radio, and then she looked up at Charlie. "Okay, you buy the radio, and I'll teach you to dance."

"Deal! We'll take it."

They went back outside and caught a taxi back to Huntly House. They closed the front door to a clickety skelter of feet on the timber floor, and Bonny's officious bark.

"Bought the town out," exclaimed Charlie, placing the box on the table in the breakfast room.

Mrs Frisken appeared, dusted with her usual flour. "Well, well, look at this; Mr Kincaid, an officer in the US Navy. Aren't you a picture?"

"Yes, ma'am, Warrant Officer Charles Kincaid at your service," he replied graciously.

"You had us all worried," Mrs Frisken told him. "I don't know what we're going to do with you… and all those gifts."

"What gifts?" Charlie kibitzed.

Mrs Frisken blushed. It was the first moment Mattie had seen her flustered. "Go on with you, boy, you're messing with an old woman."

"I wouldn't mess with an old woman, but I would with an attractive lady," he said, putting an arm around her. "So you liked everything, did you?"

"Would you like me to make you some black beans and ham?"

"Yes ma'am, sure would." Charlie smiled and opened up the radio.

"I hope that won't disturb the household," Mrs Frisken frowned.

"No, ma'am not a chance. Mattie's going to teach me to dance… proper style." He grinned at Mattie for approval.

"Well, you'd better get all this upstairs and start dancing. Just remember… we have other boarders."

Clutching the two boxes, they climbed the stairs like excited children, and ran to open Mattie's door.

Mattie laid the fur box on her bed, and switched on the bedside light. Charlie carefully set the radio down on her bedside table. He plugged it in, and the dial lit up. He fiddled with the knobs till a blast of music filled the room.

Mattie put her hand up to her mouth. "Oh, Kinky, this is wonderful, but what about... Mrs Frisken?"

"Shhh, it's a big house; she'll never hear."

Mattie reached up and kissed him on the cheek. "Thank you, darling."

"Well, sweetheart, we'd better see what else we bought," said Charlie hovering over the glamorous wrapping paper of the box.

Mattie perched on the bed to open the box. She unfolded the white fur out of its tissue paper and laid across her lap. "It is beautiful."

He lit up with pleasure and pride. "Let me help you." She stood up, while Charlie draped the white fur onto her. She smiled back at their reflection, her man standing behind her. She felt his soft lips kiss her neck. A waltz came on the radio. Mattie swirled around, letting the fur coat drop against a chair.

Charlie picked up her right hand, and slid his other arm around her slender waist, "Teach me, Mattie... proper style," his eyes twinkling. A song came on the radio: *Dance...in the old fashioned way. Won't you stay in my arms?"*

Mattie twirled out of his arms, and danced about him. She began to sing along to the song; her face radiated a glow and her voice rang out *"If we just close our eyes, and, dance around the floor,"* she sang along till the song stopped.

"I just love your voice, Mattie, where'd you learn to sing like that?"

"Madame Riggiarno taught me when I was a little girl."

"You're still a little girl," he joked, and bent down to kiss her on her nose, "and we're dancin' just fine."

"No we're not." Mattie frowned with concentration, tightening her grip. "Here, get the footwork right. And a slow... quick, quick, slow... quick, quick," she repeated, her eyes fixed on his. They spun into the room, Mattie now following his lead, melding her body to his. Suddenly, her foot caught the edge of the bed, she fell back, and they both collapsed onto the bedspread.

"Geez Mattie, what's this? Are we still slow... quick, quick or what?"

Mattie burst into an uncontrollable nervous giggle, rolling over the bed. "I've a confession to make."

"What?"

"I can't teach you to dance, you're too gorgeous. I can't concentrate and now the radio has to go back."

Resting on one elbow, Charlie burst into laughter. "Nope, radio stays. Everything stays, darlin'."

Charlie smoothly brushed aside a strand of hair from her face. He couldn't believe she was lying here, the woman he'd dreamed of; and now he was touching her, caressing her. His fingers lightly skimmed across her lips. He studied her for a moment, and then he bent closer to kiss her nose, her neck, her soft cheek, moving ever so lightly with each kiss, to her waiting parted lips. His fingers moved down to the lace-covered buttons of her blouse; one by one they fell undone. He stroked her breasts, keeping his gaze on her. Mattie moaned. He felt the beat of her heart under his hands, as he exquisitely stroked her whole body.

Mattie feasted her eyes into his, now blazing with desire.

"Oh, Kinky, I want you. I want you so badly." He loosened the straps of her petticoat. Her heart pounding, she undid his tie and helped him take off his shirt. She reached up to caress him, to explore every crevice, the stunning face she had seen across the tram. She ran her fingers across his strong muscles, firm under her touch. She nestled up against his chest. It felt safe and warm.

How am I going to do this? She tightened her grip around him as if he were about to slip away... or budge too fast towards her. Tears spilled down her cheeks.

Charlie didn't have to guess what was wrong. "Shhh…." Gently he put a finger up to her lips, "Just relax. I love you, my precious darlin'. You'll be safe," he whispered. "It will be this way till we get married," he reassured her, slowly sliding down her panties. Charlie unbuckled his pants, removed them, and they crawled in between the soft sheets.

Mattie closed her eyes to the gentle lull of the music, while his fingers casually massaged their way back down her naked body to that familiar ache.

"Oh, Kinky … please … don't stop," Mattie gasped with pleasure.

"You're so… juicy darlin'," he whispered, playing with her hair and teasing her as he lay on top of her, and slid down her body, the roughness of his chin against her soft thigh. His tongue swirled inside her tiny parts. Her whole body was on fire.

"Oh, my God... ahhh... yes," she moaned.

Charlie pushed back up on his elbows, caressing her, he whispered, "You are beautiful darlin'. Don't be afraid. It's being in love, you've never felt this before." His hard erection slipped inside her, slowly at first, then thrusting deep inside her.

"I feel you... so deep inside... push harder... yes, deep... ohhh," Mattie moaned. She gnarled her fingers through his hair, pushing her hips up to meet his every stroke, wild with excitement.

Abruptly, Charlie safely withdrew and blurted, "Mattie, ohhh... ahhh... that was close." He cautiously eased off her, and looked over. "How was that?"

Mattie turned towards him, her face reddened; her smile blossomed as wide as he'd ever seen.

"It was wonderful. I feel alive. I can't believe it... I didn't know... I love you!" She was still catching her breath.

His drawl came soft and slow, "I'll love you forever, Mattie... and wouldn't I love to marry you. Arrive home to a fire burning. Watch our babies grow and run towards me when I'm back from work. I'd bend down, pick 'em up, and swing 'em 'round till they giggle."

He leaned over and kissed her. "This is what it's like... to love someone, unconditionally love someone."

Mattie kissed him back, her eyes closed. She whispered, "This is heaven."

CHAPTER 34

When Mattie woke the following morning he was gone. There was music playing faintly. She stared at the radio next to her bed, wondering if it had all been real. The light from the open curtains streamed across her bedspread, highlighting the fur draped on a chair. *It wasn't a dream. Oh my god, he made love to me...*

"We made love," she said aloud.

She rose up and hugged herself in front of the long mirror, smiling at her reflection. I'll love him for the rest of my life, she said to herself, no matter what my family says, nobody can take that from me. She was so excited she wanted to tell the world. She went over to the window and closed it. *He must have gone out the window... down the tree.* She put her fingers up to her mouth. *Mrs Frisken...* she blushed and bit her lip. *I'll have some explaining to do.*

Mrs Frisken was pouring out the tea for the two men when Mattie came into the breakfast room. They all had a smile on their faces.

"Well, Mattie," said Mrs Frisken, "there surely was a bit of ruckus at your end of the corridor last night."

Mattie felt the heat rising first and knew she was turning bright red. Burt rustled the paper.

"Gee, Mattie, did you hear that wind last night? It almost brought the house down," he rotated to the unsuspecting Percy spreading marmalade on his toast. "What about you Percy?"

"Uhh... only sound I heard was your snoring." Percy did not look up, but his grin said it all.

Mattie gulped her tea to wash down the last of her toast. She was glad the paper entertained the two men and she didn't have to view their faces. She stood up and carried her dishes into the kitchen.

"Mrs Frisken," said Mattie, "he left early. I'm sorry if the radio was a bit loud." Mattie was desperate for an explanation. But she could only visualize his naked body bounding in her bed.

"I didn't hear him or the music, but who knows what the others heard." Mrs Frisken raised one eyebrow.

"He was quiet." Mattie nodded; she didn't know what else to say.

"But I do have to keep a standard here for all boarders, you know that, my dear," Mrs Frisken said, with kindness in her voice. "He's done me proud, all this butter… all these supplies. I don't think there'll be too many nights we'll be complaining. Go on with you, girl, and don't be late for dinner tonight."

"I won't, Mrs Frisken." Mattie kissed her on the cheek. "And that's from Charlie."

"Tell him I like the nuts in the chocolates. Next time I'll make those beans for him." She winked.

"Charlie will be thrilled, Mrs Frisken."

After work Mattie caught the tram to Irene's. She wanted to explain what had happened the other night. She knocked on her door, but Irene didn't answer. She looked at her watch; it was almost six o'clock. Another tram came past and she jumped on it.

She rushed up the driveway of Huntly House. Delicious aromas were coming out of the kitchen. Everyone was in such a happy mood, when Mattie walked into the dining room. Mrs Frisken seemed pleased to see her. Mattie could not quite work her out; it was like treading on egg shells, sometimes friendly, other times difficult. Maybe something else was stressing her, she sensed.

After dinner Mattie dialed Irene's number and was relieved when she heard her voice.

"I have my partner for dancing," she told Irene. "It's a surprise."

"Is it him… is he okay?"

"Yes, he had an accident. I'll explain later. You'll meet him tomorrow night at eight at the Savoy lessons. We'll make it fun, shall we?"

"Can't wait! See you then," said Irene.

•　　•　　•　　•　　•

It was two long days before Charlie appeared at the door of the salon. Mattie had arranged the evening off from Huntly House and a dancing lesson for them, but she hadn't told him yet about Irene. When five o'clock came, she was ready with her two-tone shoes and glistening curled hair topped with a red bow. They went down the stairs.

"Darling, we can eat at the tea rooms across the street. We need to be back here to the Savoy by eight for the lessons," said Mattie.

"This time I wanna to treat you to dinner… American style. We'll be back no sweat, pretty gal," Charlie squeezed her waist.

The tram rattled down Queen Street till the last stop at the end of Queen Street. They departed at the platform and crossed the road to Cooks Tea Rooms. It had become Charlie's favorite. They climbed the stairs. A waitress appeared and showed them into a corner booth, and handed Charlie a menu. She was a tall slender blonde with an hourglass figure and ample breasts. She wore a white cap on her wavy shoulder-length hair, with big brown eyes, eyes plainly for Charlie. She pulled out a notepad from the front pocket of her white apron and waited with her pencil ready, her eyes still fixed on Charlie, blended with a pouty smile.

"What do you say, Mattie—two juicy steaks, potatoes, and ketchup?"

She shrugged. "And don't forget the peas," she added, smiling.

"Thank you." Charlie peeked up at the waitress, giving her one his cute grins, which she returned.

Mattie watched the waitress swivel down the aisle. She wanted to throttle her.

Charlie raised one eyebrow. "She seemed friendly."

"Too friendly," replied Mattie. "She looks like she could eat you."

"How about I eat *you*?" he said. He jostled closer, pressing his leg against hers, and gave her his slow sensuous smile. He slid his hands up her stocking leg. "Maybe I'll get you some real nylons and I can eat my way up your leg, nice and slow?"

Mattie blushed, looking around. "Stop it," she whispered, "someone might hear you."

"I love it when you get mad," but he didn't stop.

Mattie was hot with desire at the touch of his palm on her stockings. Then she felt embarrassed at her anticipation.

The waitress brought two steaming steaks. "Will that be all?" she asked Charlie, standing over him twirling her pencil, with her hips cocked towards him.

"Yes ma'am. You can bring the bill, please. We gotta dash." His voice was serious and he didn't look back up at her. She casually spun and left.

Charlie couldn't wait to tuck into his steak and potatoes. Mattie prodded at hers with her fork. She wasn't sure if she could eat or was it this place? The tables were full of Yanks—sailors surrounded by girlfriends. It made her bite her lip and wonder what she was doing. Would he remember her... positively remember?

They ate their meal nimbly, and then Charlie lit a cigarette and offered her one. It was times like these that Mattie worried whether she was connecting to the real Charlie, the whole Charlie. Regardless, she wanted him, almost desperately.

When they finished, Charlie left the waitress a tip and helped Mattie on with her coat.

"Did you want to take me home tonight?" he asked.

"What do you think? I'm still cooling down from last time." She locked arms and they walked back outside. "But first, you're in for a surprise."

"I love surprises," Charlie said, as they stepped on to the tram.

"Irene, my sister in law, I've told you about her. She's coming tonight."

"Great... can't wait to meet your family."

Mattie dreaded this moment. *...meet your family.* She knew they had a long road ahead of them.

"She's so nice, and she's an Auckland girl. I was her bridesmaid and..."

Their tram stopped near the Savoy, they jumped off, and Charlie guided her across the road. He looked down at her. He didn't say anything. He didn't need to; she saw the passion in his eyes. A spark hit her loins. *Ohhh... I could grab him... Mattie, stop,* she told herself. I wish I could take him home. I want to know his dark sexy side, she imagined. *Bet that waitress knows how to please him. Loosen up girl—let your feelings go.* She held Charlie's hand proudly as they walked into the Savoy. Everyone was lining up on the floor of the dance studio. Charlie stood at the far end by the piano, opposite Mattie, pleased that he was the one and only Navy officer among the other men. He smiled at each woman as she stood in line, wondering which one was Irene.

The sound of the piano interrupted his speculations. Mattie had seen Irene arrive but she didn't want to attract her attention. The piano struck up a tune. The instructor called for them to partner up. Charlie moved towards Mattie and grabbed her waist. The instructor called out, "and slow, quick, quick... turn, quick, quick... now keep dancing to the beat, keep your eyes on your partner." They danced till the piano stopped.

"Change partners now," he called out.

After two other dances, the instructor called out, "Take a quick break."

Charlie felt a tap on his shoulder. "So you're the famous Charlie." Charlie spun around to a woman's soft voice, "Hello, I'm Irene." She put out her hand. "I can see why you've captured my sister's heart."

"Irene, I've heard so much about you. Warrant Officer Charlie Kincaid reporting for a missed dance lesson," he said, taking her soft hand.

Irene smiled, "Oh, here she comes."

"So you two have met without me," interrupted Mattie.

"Got to be quick round here." Charlie grinned keeping his attention on Irene. "I was just telling Irene how much I love you and how lucky I am..."

Just then the instructor called out, "Take your partners." Charlie walked onto the floor with Irene and Mattie beamed a smile back at the two of them as they danced away.

Irene held his eyes. "We've not much time. Mattie is precious to me. Do not break her heart, Charlie." Irene did not take her eyes off him.

"No, ma'am, there will be no broken hearts on my watch, guaranteed. Don't be concerned, Irene. I love her." He grinned, but his voice was positively serious. He gripped her delicate hand. She was a good dancer, but she did not have Mattie's grace.

"I know you must," she replied. "It was so nice meeting you at last." They began their last steps about the room and ended alongside Mattie.

"The night's not over yet. We can have tea and Mattie and I will walk you home," offered Charlie.

Irene hesitated. "I have work in the morning, I'm sorry, another night."

The two women went for their coats. Irene gave Mattie a nudge, whispering in her ear, "He's a charmer, Mattie. Take every step carefully... but he loves you. Don't forget we love you too and we are family." She frowned as she gathered up her coat and walked down the stairs.

"Well," Charlie gave Mattie his whimsical smile, "Got a lot of practicing to do before the big night." nudging her down the stairs. "Shall we take in Peter Pans, keep on dancing, pretty girl?"

Mattie smiled widely. She didn't want to say goodnight. She was so in love with him. Just being with him was all that mattered. He understood her.

"Yes, let's."

CHAPTER 35

It was the night of Charlie's commission evening. He had the taxi wait at the driveway of Huntly House. He stood in the front veranda in his officer's Dinner Dress Blue Jacket, white shirt and black bow tie, holding a bouquet of white roses and a small oblong-shaped box, tied with a ribbon.

Footsteps and there she was, dressed in a long pink floating gown. The beautiful white fur floated around her shoulders.

"Do you like it?" she said, in a ballerina twirl.

It was the same twirl he knew. He beamed down at her. "You're one in a million, Mattie."

"It's Irene's bridesmaid's dress. I thought you'd like it."

He bent down and pinned the corsage on her dress and stood back to admire her, "I got you something."

"Ohhh... you spoil me, Mr Kincaid." She smiled up at him, deep into him, and untied the ribbon. "Where did you get these?"

"Shhh, they come from America. Slip them on those beautiful legs, and don't forget your toothbrush," he whispered. "Tonight we're goin' first class... the Auckland Hotel."

Charlie's ceremony was a formal event; the distinguished guests were members of the war cabinet and the NZ Army Quartermaster, Captain Dudley, and Admiral Ghormley with his staff members from the Jean Batten Building. Charlie caught site of Captain Dudley's wink as he and Mattie entered the conference room. He knew as she floated down the stairs, swaying at his side, that Mattie was the most stunning woman in the room.

Admiral Ghormley stood up to speak. "Good evening, fellow Navy men, and partners. It is my sincere pleasure tonight to congratulate our future officers. Every one of you has been chosen because of your leadership abilities and dedication to the war effort." There was a murmur in the audience. Ghormley paused and then went on, "The Japanese are determined suicidal maniacs, with solely one course... and that's to fight till the death. We need men like you...."

As she listened, Mattie studied Charlie's face; he had a bearing of courage, he would never give up. She wondered, as she glanced throughout the room, just how many of the women would be still sitting next to their partners in the years ahead. There would be empty seats, she knew, horribly empty.

Charlie accepted his promotion along with several other Navy officers. He was proud to be a Mustang, to become an officer the hard way, up through the enlisted ranks.

Charlie and Mattie left the hotel and walked up Queen Street, across Wellesley Street, and into the Wintergarden beneath the Civic Theatre.

"How did I do?" Charlie asked her.

"You did just fine," said Mattie, smiling up at him, patting him on the sleeve of his new jacket. Mattie caught sight of Irene hovering in the foyer with a tight grip on her little evening bag. She beamed delight as Irene came towards her.

They walked into the ballroom just as the sound of the famous Wurlitzer organ whirled down from the stage above.

Mattie grinned at Irene, and turned to Charlie. "Here, have the first dance with Irene; you can practice your new moves. I'll look for John." Charlie led Irene by her fingertips onto the dance floor.

Mattie wanted to find John before anything was said about the night at the hospital. She dreaded the introduction with Audrey—a disaster waiting to happen; she was sure of it.

The orchestra was playing in a golden barge. On either side of the stage, statues of lions featured with mysterious twinkling eyes. There were rows of Kentia palms in pots on shelves, and huge pillars behind the orchestra that reached up to a starlit ceiling of the theatre above. It was the grandest affair. Mattie watched the couples wind around the huge ballroom, stepping out to *Take the A Train*. She felt a ping of proud excitement that Auckland offered such style.

"There you are, Sis," said John, threading through the crowd. "Where's this Yank you're so crazy about?"

"Up dancing with Irene."

"No, he's not. I saw Irene dancing with one of her colleagues." They both eagerly searched the dancing couples. Mattie caught sight of a taffeta bustle and the back of Audrey's hair with a black bow set on top… dancing with Charlie.

"Who's the handsome officer?" John's face fell. "Looks like a real Prince Charming."

"He is. That's my Yank."

"Well…"

For once Mattie could tell her brother was speechless. They stood there for an awkward moment, and then John reached for Mattie's arm. "We can outdo them, Sis. You'll be the belle of the ball."

The music switched to a wild foxtrot as Mattie and her brother glided onto the polished timber floor. Mattie kept her eyes on John. "That night at the hospital," she began, "Charlie doesn't know I was there."

"Ethics, Mattie. I wouldn't be saying anything anyway. Can't help being concerned though."

"I know. I remember your lecture at the hospital."

Mattie searched the crowd for her Kinky; she wanted to stop dancing and find him. She hated the idea of Audrey being with him. The music thankfully ended and, as the floor cleared, she saw them. Audrey was standing beside Charlie, cooling herself with a small fan she had tied to her wrist, her cheeks blazing red.

"My word," said John, joining them. "So you're the famous Charlie."

"Yes, sir." Charlie smiled, reaching out to shake his hand. Mattie watched, proud of Charlie's stance and his elegance. He oozed a quality all his own, with his handsomely sculpted head poised, listening intently to everything John was saying. Charlie held onto his charm to deal with Audrey.

"You have a very beautiful wife," said Charlie, and he smiled at Audrey. Audrey fluttered her fan; breathless and, for once, silent. "I had the pleasure of meeting and dancing with both Mattie's sisters-in-law tonight. What more could a man want?"

"Oh, you must visit our new home," said Audrey, keen now to interrupt, fanning at top speed. "We'll show you Auckland style at its best."

"Ma'am, I wouldn't dream of putting you out. I must treat y'all for dinner one night." Charlie grinned down at Mattie, taking her arm. "My little sweetheart here is looking forward to this night out. If you'll excuse us, the next dance I promised to Mattie." He led Mattie onto the floor.

With careful footwork, searching each other's eyes, they danced... and kept dancing, Mattie with her ease of steps and Charlie with his new-found feet. Mattie gave Charlie's arm a squeeze and whispered up to him, "So proud of you. I can't wait to kiss you... all over."

Charlie took a step sideways and spun her, "Shall I start taking my clothes off? Hope Audrey's watching."

"Why?" questioned Mattie, bewildered, now worried about what she's started.

"Cause she's a man-eater. She pinched my butt."

Mattie burst out laughing.

Charlie and Mattie danced the floor, song after song, blending their bodies into one. They smiled into each other's eyes, unaware of anything but the music. Mattie visualized his strong naked body wrapped around hers and blurted, "Do you want to leave?"

Charlie grinned. "Just what I was thinking. I'll get your cape."

Mattie caught Irene's attention and whispered, "We're leaving. Hope you don't mind."

"You look so lovely in the dress... brings back memories," she said, eyes watering behind her gold-rimmed glasses. She put her gentle fingers on Mattie's arm. "Hope your dream comes true."

Charlie came back into the ballroom and gracefully draped the fur cape on Mattie. She stiffened when she saw Audrey coming towards them.

"You're leaving so soon?" Audrey was staring hard at the fur. "But of course, I should have realized—you sailors have curfew." She smirked.

"No, ma'am, not tonight. I have reservations at Hotel Auckland. All the new officers have the night off," Charlie explained. He winked at Mattie. "Ready to be spoiled, my darlin'?"

Audrey sucked in a deep breath and gave a stiff laugh. "Better make the most of it, I'd say. Don't you have a war to fight?"

"Yes, ma'am. I'll remember that when I'm shootin' the rumps off the Japs so they can't get to Auckland." He nodded to Mattie, "Shall we, princess?"

They excused themselves and exited into the night.

Charlie guided Mattie as they strolled down Queen Street till they came to the hotel. They climbed the stairs, and Charlie opened the door into a sumptuous room. As he lifted her white fur from her shoulders, Charlie bent down and nibbled her ear lobe, kissing her long, slender neck.

"Hmmm, I love your perfume."

Mattie turned and planted a kiss on his cheek, her red lipstick leaving a mark. "There. Now no Audrey's can pester you."

Charlie continued, taking aside his jacket, stretching out his muscular body, tantalizing her with his smile. "Didn't want me dancing with her, uh?"

"No, I hated it." Mattie pushed him back down on the bed; playfully she climbed on top of him and kissed him, snuggling into his neck, sticking her tongue into his ear.

"Wow what's brought this on?" He teased, picking her up, swinging her around. He let her down, gazing longingly at her in the mirror, running his hands down her silken dress. "You have a man who adores you."

Mattie stared straight into his dreamy eyes. He could tell by her expression she was ready; he unzipped the back and daintily eased the gown off her shoulders. Simultaneously, she unbuttoned his shirt and pushed it over his solid shoulders. Then she loosened his pants and coaxed them down until they fell to the floor, never taking her eyes from his.

Charlie slipped the gown down over her perfect hips; its soft folds fell to her feet. For a moment she stood there admiring herself, that same feeling coming back as an ache for him. He picked her up, planted a kiss full on her red lips, and eyes-locked, laid her down on the sheets. She was so beautiful, her eyes so wide and blue, so vulnerable and sweet. He caressed her whole body, lowered his lips to her breasts then her tender nipples. He continued down, kissing her navel, her thighs, gently parting her legs, and worked his tongue into her spot.

"Oh, Kinky," Mattie cried out, arching her back.

"Shhh, I'm all yours," he said, sliding back up, looking into her eyes.

He grabbed her buttocks, his erection at her opening. She threw her head back and gasped as he slid inside her. She cried out, "Ohhh… Kinky." She wrapped her legs around him, forcing him deeper.

"I love you, Mattie… all of you."

In sheer delight she came. She kept crying out at her joy. "Ohhh, Kinky, I'm coming... deeper."

Charlie pushed hard, but triggered his own climax. He had to pull out. "Arhhh... Mattie... yes, darlin'... together."

He kissed her over and over, tears choking him. He wanted her entirely so much. Oh God, how he wished he could come inside her. Instead he looked down at her belly, and wiped away the joy. He locked eyes with her, frowning, "That is so sad we can't make a baby," he said. "But one day..." He kissed her knowingly. "We'll turn these critters loose where they belong, won't we?"

Mattie smiled. "I can't wait, my precious."

She tucked her head under his chin, as he caressed her hair. Mattie cuddled up, glowing, satisfied yet becoming ready for unknowns.

Tonight was destined to be their night to watch the stars flicker out the window, to make love, to sleep for a while in each other's arms... and do it all over again.

CHAPTER 36

It was late October as the chill in the air gave way to spring. Charlie and Mattie strolled along beaches of white sands, brushed by relentless tides, and watched flocks of shorebirds fighting for the odd morsel. They sensed their time was coming to an end, and cherished every moment together.

The threat of war was receding in small doses from New Zealand's shores. The *Rigel* was completing her Auckland mission, and would now be needed much closer to the front. Charlie's heart was heavy as he made his way up Hobson Wharf and into Queen Street. There were rumors on the *Rigel* about Army units getting ready to embark, but he didn't want to tell Mattie. He slipped into Robert's Jewellery shop adjacent to the cinema where they had first met.

●　　●　　●　　●　　●

As Charlie climbed up the steps to Huntly House, he noticed the familiar huge pohutukawa that arched towards Mattie's veranda. There was a funny bird perched on a branch, with a white tuft quivering at its throat as it sang, or probably scolded. "This your turf, little fella?" He whistled back, then tapped at the door.

Mattie's gleaming face appeared. "Give me a hug, you beautiful man."

Charlie gathered her into his arms and stood holding her tight, as though it might be his last. "Where's everybody?" he quietly asked.

"Gone out. We have the whole place to ourselves. We can dance… play," she said in soft voice.

Charlie smiled down at her and closed the door. He leaned her against the wall of the passageway, and kissed her; he ran his fingers through her hair and gazed into her happy eyes.

"So how did you arrange that Miss Blanc?" he whispered, pulling up her dress, feeling his way into her panties. Mattie shook her head, dazed; she felt sick with passion.

"Got something for you," she mumbled in his ear, her arms around his neck.

"I got somethin' right here," he pointed to his trousers.

"Upstairs," she giggled and pulled him forward. They ran up the stairs, their feet pounding down the long passageway and into her room. A bunch of roses lay on her bed.

Charlie frowned. "Who gave you these?"

"They're for you, silly. Happy birthday, darling."

Charlie picked them up, burying his nose in their fragrance and he bent to kiss her, "Pretty as you," he said inhaling her jasmine perfume, his favorite. He loved everything about Mattie. He placed the roses on the table, settled onto the bed next to her, and kissed her flushed cheek.

"Oh, Kinky... I want you." She leaned and kissed him back on the lips. She removed his tie and unbuttoned his shirt. He loosened her blouse exposing her beautiful shoulders. They cast their clothes into the room with devilish smiles, flung back the covers and slid into bed. Charlie kissed her hard on the lips and then kissed his way down her neck to her alabaster breasts. Her nipples hardened to his tongue. She pulled him towards her, pushing her pelvis into his hardness. She craved him, all of him.

"Whoa, pretty gal... you're gonna pop my cork," Charlie stopped long enough to look up.

"Take me Charlie... now," she breathed.

He entered her, and she felt his body synchronize with hers, like the waves of the ocean. He pushed harder and deeper, thrusting into his sweetheart, feeling the tight sweetness.

"Ohhh, Kinky... yes... together... I'm coming... so fast."

Charlie wanted to control himself, but it was too good, his darling panting below him, her body shuddering. He pulled out abruptly. "Ahhh, Mattie..." and lay back, his eyes fixed to the ceiling. "That was fantastic."

They lay wordlessly stroking each other, not wanting this memory interrupted. Their heavy breathing ebbed to a beautiful whisper, but Charlie's pleasure was tormented. How could he lie to her? How could he tell her what he knew? His expressions vacillated between bliss and sorrow at the news of his departure. It felt like a bomb exploding. He'd tried to hide it from her, but it was crowding closer... ever closer.

Mattie sat up, somehow now aware this was beyond just silence. "Something's wrong isn't it?" she asked. Her eyes danced across his, but he didn't answer. Charlie diverted his eyes. "Kinky what's wrong? Oh my God... *no!*" She threw her hands up to her face. "You're leaving."

The grimace he gave her, told her the inevitable—how she hated that word. How she dreaded that word, suddenly it was here, taunting them, tearing them apart. "Oh no, no, my darling... please, no," she pleaded.

Charlie twisted towards her, silent, and just held her tight, real tight, for a long while. Then he did what he was good at, he faced her. "Mattie, darlin'," he spoke softly, tenderly wiping the strands of hair from her sudden tears. "I've heard rumors. No orders yet, but they may come soon." He kept his eyes on her; he knew these words were like a dagger in Mattie's chest.

Mattie's lower lip started quivering. *I must be strong... match his courage.* "Charlie Kincaid, we will outlast this war," she said through her tears.

"Mattie Blanc... you have my word." He gave her the biggest hug he could muster. They clung to each other.

Head spinning, Mattie stood up and reached for her handkerchief, her eyes glazed. She knew there was no use. He was leaving. *Don't be a coward,* she told herself. She quietly picked up her panties and began to dress as if it were the last seconds she'd ever see him.

Charlie pulled on his underwear, stared at the radio, and then reached over and rotated the dial. Mattie admired his streamlined body, wanting to capture this memory. Music filled the room; she placed her arms around his neck, and felt once again his warm naked body against her bare midriff. She looked into those deep dark twinkling eyes—how could she be thinking what she was thinking... sadness.

The radio started rollicking the song, "In the Mood." Charlie picked up a rose and stuck it between his teeth, "Hey Mattie, let's get gussied up. I'm taking you out."

"You better get dressed," she grinned back. "Downtown may not like us in our underwear."

They danced and tapped their way into the room, singing out loud, laughing and hugging till the song stopped. "Come on lover, we're going to get decent," Mattie led him to the bathroom to wash and fix the roses in a vase. She powdered her face and put on fresh lipstick, her favorite red.

Charlie and Mattie left Huntly House, holding hands as always to catch the tram into town. They stepped off at the corner of Victoria Street and Queen Street. Charlie grinned, "How about a movie... jus' like our first date, pretty girl?"

"Can't think of anything better, handsome man."

They dashed to the Civic and bought tickets for "Mr Deeds Goes to Town." Under the starlit theatre, they took their seats and cherished every second with fingers laced together. Charlie didn't have to wonder who she was anymore and Mattie didn't have to feel unsure. The movie made sense of their simple lives—do the right thing. Back out into the late afternoon light, it was warm and pleasant as they strolled up Queen Street, thinking about the movie.

"What did you think?" asked Mattie, looking up at him.

Charlie grinned down at her, "I'd say, everyone's pixilated, 'cept us baby."

"I agree. Good for Mr Deeds." She paused. "Charlie, let's go back to Huntly House for tea. I want time alone with you."

"Me too, darlin'... me too."

They slipped into their tram seat, and the memory of when he first heard her voice came flooding back to him; He felt the lump in his throat.

Mattie stared up at him, "I'm not going to let you go."

"Hmmm," his lip curled up. "You can tell the Navy I got pixilated and we eloped."

Mattie smiled into his eyes, "You make me laugh." But she wasn't laughing inside.

Back at Huntly House, Charlie followed Mattie into the dining room. Everyone stood up calling out *Happy Birthday, Charlie!* The table was laden with streamers and whistles. Vic must have been busy, Mattie suspected. There was no way Mrs Frisken could have arranged that herself. Perhaps that's why she had planned to be out for the day. They all joined in to feast on Mrs Frisken's attempt at Charlie's black beans, ham and cornbread. That night he left with some small gifts and his bunch of roses; he felt overwhelmed at the kindness and secretly chuckled at how he was going to climb the gangway. What if Vic were waiting for him?

CHAPTER 37

Admiral Ghormley's relief, Admiral Halsey—nicknamed "Bull" Halsey—was on his way to New Caledonia, and ordered the *Rigel* to be his flagship. He was hell-bent on withdrawing the *Rigel* from her safe haven in Auckland harbor. It was purely a matter of destiny and determination before it was the turn of the *Rigel* and the men that went with her to fight this vicious war.

On 8 November the *Rigel* embarked Army units; the rumors were correct. Her crew was given twenty-four hours to say goodbye. It was an impossible task.

Charlie was given his orders—the ones he'd dreaded—and his day of liberty. It was his last liberty in the sun with the girl of his dreams. He ran for the telephone.

"Mattie darlin', I got my orders. Sailing tomorrow... I'm coming now."

•   •   •   •   •

As he went up the Huntly House stairs, his feet felt like lead diving boots. He gave the door a knock and Mattie opened the door. He took a step back in awe of her beauty. She wore a black-and-white dotted halter-neck dress with a flared skirt and a beige linen jacket; a large black hat poised perfectly, canted just right on her head. With lace gloves, she was the vision of a real English lady. It made him feel sick with sudden hopelessness, unworthy. How had he fallen in love with this gorgeous woman? He put on his best smile.

"Whoa... Mattie Blanc, you do it to me every time." He didn't know how he would get everything into their last moments.

"I hope so." Mattie just beamed. She was determined to make this their best day, but fought for control with every word.

"Let's go, sweet pea." He offered his arm. "I thought we'd start off at the beach... no tellin' when we'll get back tonight."

"Wonderful, darling. I'll get into sandals, and bring stockings and shoes for tonight. Can't wait." Mattie rushed upstairs to change.

They travelled on the tram to the bottom of Queen Street and stepped into throngs of Saturday shoppers. Staying close to find a path, they crossed the road and caught the Eastern Bus along Tamaki Drive towards Saint Heliers beach. They squinted into the brilliant sunshine rippling over the water as they rounded the Eastern Bays. Saint Heliers beach unfolded before them, lined with small pohutukawa trees set along a grass verge bordering the fine sand.

"Look darlin', there's Bayside tea room. Let's get a bite before we walk."

But Mattie worried about their quiet ride around the waterfront. She had to bring Charlie back, back from his silence. She was used to his silence, but couldn't bear it today.

Charlie helped Mattie into a seat by the long window. The waitress brought a pot of hot tea, and they ordered their meals. Mattie slipped off her gloves and set them down with her hat.

Charlie held her hand. "It will be okay darlin', I promise."

"I know." Mattie grasped her handkerchief, "It's just... all so sudden."

Charlie felt her trembling and her beautiful smile was fading. He took a sip of tea, "Ummm... gonna miss this. Not much room on board for tea."

"I'll put some tea in your letters." Mattie tried to appear happy.

A plate of potatoes and steak and kidney pie arrived for Charlie, but Mattie hardly wanted a small sandwich. She had no appetite. She watched him take a bite of potatoes, but mostly he just pushed them about. Mattie wondered if she would be pushed aside like the potatoes. *This is not going well,* she determined. *I must fight for him.*

"Kinky, we're not hungry, darling. We need to walk on the beach and talk. Lots of talk." She caressed his hand, and he knew she was right.

"You know me well, Mattie. Let's go."

They paused on the grass, cast aside their shoes, and smiled big smiles as their feet hit the soothing sand, cresting its heat over their toes as they walked. The tide was out, so the normal Saturday beach crowds were thin, but that didn't matter. Charlie and Mattie saw no one but each other.

"Kinky." She stopped. "Don't lose hope. I'm not afraid. I know you'll return."

Charlie's forehead creased. "Promise me you'll convince your father we can be married."

"I'll do everything I can. You know that." Mattie stepped back. "But you have to return for me."

Charlie clasped her hands; his eyes were dark and serious. "When I come back to you, there will be a ring for your finger, if you'll still have me. Will you marry me, Mattie Blanc?"

"Yes. There will never be anyone else, Charlie." She threw her arms around him.

"Yes, Mattie... *yes!*" Her hat flew away with a gush of wind. The sunlight now radiated off her hair. He stooped, picked up her hat, and buried other fingers in his pocket. He'd been fiddling with his little gift, while he worried if they would survive the separation. Did she truly want him for keeps? Now he was certain.

"Got a present for ya." He held it out.

Mattie looked down at the object glistening in the sun. It was an anchor with USN across it. He flipped it over and read, W*ith love, Kinky.* He pinned it on her jacket.

"Remember when you first pinned the corsage on me?" she asked.

"You don't have to remind me, Mattie. I remember all our times, just like they were yesterday."

"But memories can fade," Mattie replied tensely. She regretted these words almost immediately. This was their unspoken fear... the final fear. But she knew it needed to be said.

"Oh Mattie... dear Mattie. No time, no war, no *nothing* will cause me to forget you, my darlin'." He pulled her close and they hugged hard, feeling each other's body and breath, rocking, lulled into serenity by the warm sand and gentle wind.

Lovingly, Charlie put his arm around her and they went on walking along the beach.

"What say we head back to Cooks, darlin'? Hungry yet?" Charlie gave her a squeeze.

"Yes, feeling better, darling. Let's go out on the town." Mattie smiled.

They left the beach and went back to the hustle and bustle of downtown Auckland. At Cooks, Charlie ushered Mattie into their usual booth.

Charlie felt a casual hand on his shoulder. He lifted his eyes to Vic's smiling face.

"Well, well… if it isn't the two lovebirds."

"This is my sweetheart, Mattie. You two never met before?"

Mattie blushed and smiled up at Vic.

"Only when I needed a haircut." Vic winked. "Say, we're all heading up to the dance club. Where you two goin'?"

Charlie looked across at Mattie, "Are your dancing shoes workin', princess?"

Mattie could feel herself burst alive and she grinned back, "We're coming too."

They watched Vic and the other men leave the tea rooms.

"He's a nice guy," she said smiling after him. "He'll be good for you, Kinky."

"You sure got that right, Mattie."

"Let's show them how to boogie." Mattie grabbed Charlie's arm and they walked up Queen Street into Peter Pans.

"Here darlin', let's grab this booth by the dance floor."

The place was exploding with sailors, and Vic's head was above everybody else; the laughter and the music never seemed to end. Charlie and Mattie wasted no seconds and jumped into each other's arms, swinging all over the floor. They hardly missed a dance. Charlie now just needed to give Mattie the slightest signal, and she followed like she was part of him.

"You dance like the wind, pretty girl." Charlie was in heaven.

"Just following your lead, handsome man," Mattie replied between steps.

It was late when they crept down the dark and silent passageway of Huntly House. They walked softly up the stairs and opened the bedroom door. Everything was the same, the beautiful bedspread, the window, the radio. It was all so surreal, Mattie visualized as she cautiously came back to reality. Charlie took her in his arms and kissed her.

"Didn't we have a ball tonight, darlin'?" he whispered.

"I had the best night ever," she whispered back, but her eyes were on the room.

He noticed her quivering. Lovingly, Charlie coaxed her to the bed and they undressed and lay in silence, each thinking of the inevitable.

"Just gonna close my eyes for a quick nap, darlin'. Be right by midnight…"

Mattie listened to his soft breathing on her pillow, and watched him sleeping. If only she could keep him safe from harm.

They stirred and awoke, panicked that they'd wasted precious moments—they were still together. They wrapped themselves around each other, feeling the other's heartbeat in the darkness of the night. Charlie rolled on top of her and kissed her soft lips; she felt his lips trembling on hers. Mattie kissed him back hard, wanting to wish away his fears.

Charlie held her cheeks in his hands and thrust his tongue deep inside her mouth, as if to show her how deep his love was for her. Mattie's heart beat faster. She pulled him towards her, running her fingers desperately now through his hair. He buried himself inside her. She came so quickly; it made her moan bitterly into the night. When would she know this again?

"Don't be sad," he said. "It's not going to be our last."

They focused on each other, deep and steady—their eyes told the story of their months together. There was nothing else to say, it was war… that was why they had met, and that was why they would part.

Everyone was gone when they came down the stairs to the breakfast room.

Mrs Frisken came out of the kitchen carrying a pot of tea. "Charlie my boy." Her face lit up. "We're sending you on your way with a first-class breakfast", she winked. "Where you off to?"

Charlie put a hand on Mrs Frisken's arm. *She's at it again*, he reckoned. "Not sailing far. Save my place till I get back, Mrs Frisken. Much obliged for everything."

"There'll always be a place for you. Look after yourself, Charlie. There are some hearts here wanting you back. Meantime, I know Mattie will be waiting on your letters."

Charlie and Mattie locked eyes—Charlie eased closer and took Mattie's hand across the table.

Mattie smiled forlornly, trying to control her emotions and searched for her handkerchief just in case.

"Be strong, girl." Mrs Frisken patted her shoulder and winked at Charlie. "He won't let you down."

Charlie thanked Mrs Frisken for everything and they closed the door to Huntly House. It felt strange walking down the pathway. He hung his head and gripped Mattie's arm, swallowed and turned once more to gaze at the house, the tree, the door knocker, and lastly at her window.

Their last tram ride was the worst. The tram seats rumbled into them. Mattie stared out the window. She was upset, bruised this time, shoved not soothed.

Charlie knew. "Darlin', I'll be back before you know it. You must not worry." He grasped her hand, rubbing it with his other.

"Kinky, I know you have a big job to do, a terrible job. But we have our life together. Please... don't be reckless." She fought back tears, determined that her last moments with him were to be the best.

The tram lurched to a stop at the bottom of Queen Street. He helped her from her seat, and they descended the wooden tram steps onto the concrete pavement, turning towards Hobson Wharf.

Mattie clung to him desperately now, resting her head against his chest as they slowed their steps and stopped. Mattie clenched his hand, but that could not stop her shoulders shaking in uncontrollable sorrow. *I must be strong... courage!* Mattie composed herself.

She held out a little heart-shaped silver pendant, and put it in his palm, wrapping hers over his. "It's from Scotland." She unfolded their hands and read the words, "*Mizpah. God watch between me and thee.*" Mattie paused, "Keep yourself safe and come back to me, Charlie Kincaid."

Charlie tilted her chin up, and Mattie warmed to his smile in the morning sunlight. "Why Mattie, it's beautiful. But you shouldn't part with it; it's yours... your heritage. You shouldn't be giving it to me."

"Charlie, you *must* take it," she said, now staring intently into his whole being. "Take part of me with you. It will keep you well..." Mattie could not finish, *till you come back to me.*

"I'll wear it with pride. Here... let's string it with my Dog Tags. I want this right on my heart," he fumbled with his chain and threaded on the pendant. He didn't want to break down. The little pendant tipped him over with grief. He set the chain beneath his collar and stood reverently to love and absorb the woman of his dreams.

Choosing his words, "My darlin' love, I know it's hard beyond words. But I will be back. They will not get this Cherokee warrior, no way."

"Oh, Kinky, I love you so much. I will wait. Please, please write to me."

"Darlin', I'll write you every day, pages and pages. I'll tell you how much I love you." With a final squeeze, he dropped her hand. Charlie stared at her one last moment. He turned away, and strode towards the gangway, choking back the lump in his throat.

The superstructure of the *Rigel* loomed above him. Charlie gripped the rails of the gangway, and put a foot on the step. He scanned the dock and there she was. Charlie memorized the sight of her hair falling around her face, loose in the wind, as she clutched the railings, waving at him. He wanted with all his heart to just run back and pick her up. Fighting back tears, he ascended, and gave a final wave.

•   •   •   •   •

Mattie left Hobson Wharf in a trance. The tears wouldn't stop falling and she wondered how she was going to go back to work. How could she endure a tram ride? Sit on a seat and gaze out the same window. Live without him, without his smile, his kiss, the smell of his coat. She wept, sobbing into her handkerchief. It seemed everyone else was busy walking along in the bright daylight, talking, laughing, reading. They all had a purpose. But had her purpose just sailed out the harbor?

I must get control… be strong, like Charlie, she told herself, trying to get a grip. She wiped back her tears, and forced herself onto the tram.

Work will be a necessary distraction. Every day would blend into another day. She had to learn to live with the memories.

CHAPTER 38

Climbing on board the *Rigel* made Charlie unsettled. He had never felt this way before. He wondered what he'd done to deserve meeting Mattie. He lay in his bunk staring at the bulkhead, worried at the huge responsibility that faced him. A cigarette lit handily and he puffed it into the cabin, watching its smoke disappear like the times they'd shared.

As they sailed down the harbor, he went topside and watched as they passed the beaches where he'd gone with Mattie, past Rangitoto Island and out to sea. A sick pang of regret came over him, a longing to hold her, to smell her skin, to kiss her. He flicked his cigarette butt into the frothing wake and walked back to his cabin, glad of the break to be alone.

Charlie picked up his pen to write, but instead collapsed onto the desk in despair. The words would not surface.

•　　•　　•　　•　　•

After the devastating defeat at Pearl Harbor, the Americans failed to anticipate how deftly the Japanese would overtake the Philippines and push their eastern front into the Dutch East Indies. The Imperial Japanese Navy wasted no time establishing naval bases at Rabaul, Papua New Guinea, and into the Solomon Islands. News promptly spread of the atrocities they were committing against prisoners and civilians: bayonetings and beheadings were their preferred methods, as bullets were precious.

But in June 1942, the Americans had a break. They cracked the Japanese naval code and learned their fleet was headed to invade Midway Island. The American carriers converged, attacked—but all torpedo bombers in the initial raid were shot down. A lost group of dive-bombers from the carrier *Enterprise* stumbled onto the undefended Jap carriers, whose fighter planes were far afield shooting down the American torpedo bombers. These thirty-seven Dauntless SBD bombers sank or disabled every Jap carrier. The Battle of Midway became a turning point in the war.

The New Hebrides lay northeast of the Loyalty Islands. Because of the archipelago's safe location in the Pacific, Admiral Halsey had chosen these islands for the navy and army support bases. Following the raging battles of Guadalcanal and Santa Cruz, rumors flew among the *Rigel's* crew that the fleet was to secure the Solomons to the north.

After two days at sea they glided past the tip of the Segond Channel of Espiritu Santo at five knots and entered the channel. All eyes searched the waters for the missing troop ship *President Coolidge*.

Vic was at the rail, drawing hard and quick on his cigarette. He tossed it into the ocean after lighting another, exhaled with a deep sigh, and lamented to Charlie, "Well, Kinks, there's gonna be none of them hot sheilas up here." He stared out at the mountainous, wooded land, and snickered as he caught sight of a cluster of natives waving. "Only bare-breasted hot chocolate."

"Cut your complainin'. Knowing you, you'll make do." Charlie smirked. "You seem to like brown sugar, eh?"

"Well," Vic took off his cap and scratched at his thick locks, "I ain't hankering after no steady dame—just a taste."

Charlie's dark eyes narrowed.

Vic licked his lips and flashed his best toothy smile at all the jiggling brown breasts lining the dusty dockside as they drew nearer.

"Shut your face, will ya," Charlie said.

"Don't fuss, Kinks, it's all there, waiting to be properly serviced by the US Navy."

"Well, go service the lot. Your dick is runnin' your brain."

Charlie's heart sank. It was hopeless talking to Vic. It was even more hopeless trying to get Vic to accept the daily Atabrine tablets the Doc had insisted would prevent or mitigate the inevitable malaria. His other men reluctantly accepted the pills, but Vic had heard rumors they turned your skin yellow and caused the ultimate evil—sterility.

"I'm gonna plow some pussy before we start blasting the balls off the fuckin' Japs," Vic said, spitting out the foul-tasting yellow pill as soon as the medic walked away.

Charlie shoved Vic up against the bulkhead. "We need you on deck, not moanin' in sick bay with mozzie fever."

"No mozzie's gonna get me. Never caused me no problem back home. We're here. Ready for action," said Vic, pushing Charlie and scrambling down the ladder. "No damn pills for me, I need my strength and a big hard dick shootin' live ammo."

Charlie stood on the dockside watching him and the rest of the crew clamber down the ladder, the flow of men being close to a stampede. He frowned and inspected the panorama of this rocky coral land. Espiritu Santo. First landfall... and already he felt homesick for Auckland.

Santo was a confusion of rough structures, trucks, machinery—an unimaginable aggregation heaped into a depository of artillery and supplies. Rocks and mud surrounded the depot. But everything was dwarfed by masses of trees and jungle bush.

The Field Post Office swiftly became the largest base, with an exploding population of 100,000 forces. The *Rigel* spent several weeks there in constant heat, dust, and never-ending work. Day and night blended into a morass of misery for the men. Charlie figured it must have been his punishment—*definitely a long way from Falkner now.*

·　　·　　·　　·　　·

By May 1942, the Japanese had overrun Guadalcanal and started construction of an airfield. Both sides realized the advantages if they placed long-range bombers there. The Japanese could seal off and attack Australia. But the Americans could equally wreak havoc on the Japanese in Rabaul and northward.

The Americans reacted swiftly on 7 August, and landed 10,000 Marines at Guadalcanal and straightaway captured the airbase and Japanese equipment. But there were additional formidable enemies for both sides: the jungle terrain and disease. For the coming six months, Guadalcanal would be the scene of the most bitter and protracted naval and land battles of the Pacific War.

The Japanese were not solely cunning naval strategists, they'd spent the interwar years developing a "Long Lance" torpedo. It had greater range, speed, firepower, and accuracy than anything available to the Americans. On 9 August, the Battle of Savo Island cost the Allied forces four heavy cruisers, leaving nothing but two Japanese cruisers moderately damaged. But the Americans were quick learners. The subsequent battles at Cape Esperance and Guadalcanal cost both sides dearly, creating "Iron Bottom Bay." Sunken ships lined the seabed between Guadalcanal and Tulagi. By November the local Japanese fleet had been reduced to just destroyers and submarines.

The Battle of Tassafaronga on 30 November taught the Americans a huge lesson. Eight Japanese destroyers made a night-time run down "The Slot" towards Iron Bottom Bay to resupply their troops on Guadalcanal. They had learned to hug the Guadalcanal coast to evade American radar. The Japanese lookouts were alert, spotted the American fleet, and two Jap destroyers wheeled about and launched salvos of Long Lances at the American cruisers.

●　　●　　●　　●　　●

The next day, Charlie and his diving crew and Andy's shipfitters were summoned abruptly to the wardroom. Captain Dudley stepped out with his hands clasped behind his back, waiting till the chosen few all stood before him.

"At ease, men," Captain Dudley began. "We have classified information from Tassafaronga." He paused. "The good news is—we've given the Japs a big taste of trouble at Guadalcanal."

Vic gave a hoot.

Dudley raised an eyebrow and went on, "The bad news is—the damage. By our radar reports, at 0306 the heavy cruiser *Northampton* went down in Iron Bottom Bay, but the rest of the ships are salvageable. This is your first mission." He looked stern, and Charlie reckoned they were about to get a lesson in war.

"You're heading for Tulagi. The Japs got lucky there. We can't take the *Rigel* up there; she's far too important to risk near the front line. This is what you have trained for. The destroyer *Thornton* has just tied up alongside. Load her up with structural and plate steel, timber, and your welding and diving gear. You'll leave 0500 hours at flank speed. Get the cruisers *Minneapolis* and *New Orleans* patched up and ride them back here before the Japs figure out what we've done. We'll have air cover to keep the Jap spotter planes distant, but you are right in the mouth of the dragon. Do your job right, and do it quick. That will be all. Good luck and God speed."

CHAPTER 39

The USS *Thornton* sliced through waves like a streamlined shark, sailing north at 34 knots. There was a buzz of excitement; every man knew the true test of war was upon them.

Two days into the journey, the *Thornton* neared their target. She hugged Lengo Channel on the Guadalcanal coast line, a mountainous land with dormant volcanoes in every direction. Virgin jungle cascaded in dense layers down to the sea's edge. The surface SG radar operators searched vigilantly for enemy ships. Air search radar operators scoured the skies for Jap spotter planes and "Washing Machine Charlie"—a twin-engine Jap nuisance bomber, its engines out of sync and creating a terrible racket in the dead of night.

They crossed Sealark Channel, eased into Tulagi Bay, and straightaway caught sight of the *Minneapolis*. The wounded ship was moored portside along the beach at Sasapi, tied to coconut trees and stumps under a heavy pile of camouflage nets and jungle foliage. The men gawked at the sight as they tied up abreast to her.

"Holy shit," Charlie said out loud, "have we got some work to do."

Everyone leaned closer to inspect her crumpled bow, dipping into the sea.

Across the bay, the *New Orleans* was tied up between the destroyer *Maury*, which had to supply her steam and power, and the Patrol Torpedo boat tender *Jamestown* on the other side. Charlie wondered at how New Orleans kept appearing in his life. Maybe it was a message from his past: Don't forget where you came from. There she was, looking the worst of the three with her bow blown off past the first turret. Everything forward gone—hull, turret, anchors, chains, the lot. Charlie felt overwhelmed by the massive job ahead.

They stepped aboard the *Minneapolis* to take a better look. All hands were silent, staring at the damage until someone spoke.

"She put up one hell of a fight," one of the deckhands said, standing with his hands on his hips.

"What happened?" asked Vic.

"What didn't happen?" Another man moved along. "We didn't get the order to bloody fire on the bastards till it was too late. Our destroyers had moved up the bay to Savo Island, chasing the Tokyo Express, but all four of us cruisers were left like sitting ducks for the Jap torpedoes."

"Yeah, but we nailed the yellow bastards. They didn't get their drums to no one. We fired on them, blew their rice and ammo to smithereens. Teach them to sneak around. We'll get 'em," said a little short guy, kicking the buckled bow.

"We'll get y'all fixed up. Won't we, boys?" Vic crowed, with a wide grin.

Charlie barked orders: "Break out the diving gear and let's get below for a survey. First dive is with our tapes and noteboards to record the damage. Then we'll go back down with torches to trim this baby back and start the repair."

Charlie and his team put on their gear, sank into the murky waters, and began working underwater. They trimmed away mangled steel with their cutting torches. When Charlie finally emerged, his team followed. They assembled on deck.

"It's no use going any further," exclaimed Charlie removing his face mask. "We don't have the equipment to put a false bow on below the waterline."

"She'll just have to make it back on five knots," said one of the ship's crew, banging nails into the timber frame holding the false bow of coconut logs across the ship front.

"I've got jungle rot just being in this putrid water," said Red, climbing up, dripping oily residue on the deck.

"You're damn lucky you have legs! Some of our men got their legs shattered when the deck exploded. Quit your moaning," said the bosun mate, swinging his hammer in Red's face.

"Nobody's breaking till we've made this ship safe to sail," hollered Charlie, throwing down his mask. "We'll be sitting ducks if the Japs attack."

"We've checked the number 2 Fire Room. Both engine rooms have plenty of steam, but it's open to the sea where the torpedo hit," said Andy, wiping his hands on a filthy cloth. "With a bit of reinforcing behind the new steel plates, she'll hold."

"Always the boy with the bright ideas," Charlie said. "Take the rest of the day off."

Everyone made hooting noises.

Andy went on, "You have huge work to do in the boiler room. We'll need those metal plates riveted to patch up the hole. Then we gotta dewater that compartment."

The men were aware of the periodic sound of airplanes overhead, but had no idea whether they were friendly or deadly Japs. They worked long, hot days, frustrated at jury-rigged patches, but knew every minute was simply a short gift before the next, inevitable Jap bombing. Charlie's team was in no mood to share the anguish of the *Minneapolis*'s crew.

The *New Orleans* was able to get her own power and steam restored, so the destroyer *Maury* shifted to an anchorage in Tulagi Harbor to add to the anti-aircraft batteries ashore. Destroyers were their protectors. *Now that's a comforting sight*, Charlie said to himself as he watched the *Maury* underway. He stood there over the cesspool of troublesome waters laced with an oil sheen, and judged to himself, *what a hell of a place*.

Ultimately, the *Minneapolis* was ready for sea. They slowly got underway for Espiritu Santo with the *Thornton* as escort. Charlie's men, aboard the *Minneapolis*, rotated constant watches in the hot, damaged compartments, because the bulkheads were not meant to be exposed to a relentless sea, even at five knots.

Arriving back in Santo now seemed like luxury compared to the filth and danger of Tulagi; they slowly steamed into Segond Channel and tied up abreast to the *Rigel*. Even the smells and the familiar sounds on board the *Rigel* felt good, as Charlie and his men wearily unloaded.

When Charlie subsequently returned to his bunk; a note from the ship's post office was placed there. His heart missed a beat. He threw down his dirty gear, almost tripping over the threshold, as if he'd never been on a ship before, and raced down the hatch to the post office.

All out of breath, he said his name and rank to the clerk.

"Looks like you received all your Christmases at once." The clerk handed him a large parcel.

Charlie signed for the package but then the clerk called him back, "Wait… another three letters came today."

Charlie held the paper package and clutched the letters, two in Mattie's handwriting…with the familiar stamps and address. Huntly House came back to him, perched on the hill like a castle, as clear as if he were standing there. But one letter from New York.

He looked up. "Almost forgot… it's Christmas, isn't it?"

"Well, if you want it to be," said the clerk, looking puzzled.

"Been away... lost track of time."

The clerk cleared his throat and smiled. "Post office hours are 0800 to 1130. We'll be open for another hour, if you want to post a letter. Don't date it. It might take a while. Censors. Nothing about what you're doing here. You know the rules."

"I understand."

"Put your return address, your name, USS *Rigel* and care of Fleet Post Office, San Francisco, California.

"Thank you," replied Charlie, almost saluting.

Hurrying back to his cabin, he tore open the New York letter, curious. "Roxy!" he said out loud. *How did she know my address?*, he thought. *Vic?*

Charlie read Roxy's few words and crumpled her letter in his hands. He walked outside to the rail and threw her letter overboard. *Poor, precious Roxy… I cannot, not just now*, he decided.

He raced back to his cabin and tore apart the brown paper. He smiled to himself at the books; he loved the smell of the new pages. He read one of the titles: *Gone with the Wind.* He knew how much Mattie loved the movie. With swift but trembling hands, he opened her letters and grinned through wet eyes, reading her words, reminiscing about the times they had laughed and loved. It was all there. It had never left him.

He sat stony still for a moment in deep reflection. The clerk had given him a plain page and an envelope. He picked up his black fountain pen. The words flowed easily, taking him away from the Tulagi stench—into welcome moments in Mattie's arms.

Dearest Mattie, I hope you haven't missed my letters too much. I've been so busy since we got where we're at now that I haven't had time to write. I'm still alright except for being homesick for the good times we had together. Those were the good old days. I sure don't like the place we're at now, but a guy can get used to anything. If you think we were busy back there you should see us now. Thanks for the books. I'll read them the first chance I get. I'm sorry but we didn't stop at your brother's station. Tell Mrs Frisken hello from me. Answer soon for I enjoy your letters very much, love, Kinky,

Charlie Thomas Kincaid p.s.—Merry Christmas.

It was just a single page… on simple plain paper. Merry Christmas seemed like an afterthought, but he had no energy for regrets. Hurriedly he made his way back to the Post Office and picked up a few sheets of paper. He remembered what he'd said to her that last day. He couldn't wait to write again.

CHAPTER 40

The sun poured through the window of the little dining area at Huntly House, warming the letter in Mattie's hands.

"PS Merry Christmas," said Mattie looking up at Mrs Frisken.

"Now don't start that, Mattie. I told you before not to read into things, you'll only frustrate yourself. He has a war to fight," she said, turning the pages of the newspaper. "Just look on the bright side. You're going to get married, and have...," peering around the paper, "how many children?"

Mattie blushed. "Yes, a basket of babies, but first I must contend with Father."

"I wouldn't talk to him about Charlie if I were you. I'd wait for a while. See how the war goes."

"You're right. Father's up to something. I know when I don't hear from him."

"Well, he's probably concerned you didn't go home for Christmas."

Mattie said nothing. She concentrated on reading the back of Mrs. Frisken's newspaper with marked-up maps of the Pacific. She excused herself to run upstairs and reread his letter.

She couldn't wait to tell Irene.

· · · · ·

Irene raised her eyebrows when she opened the door. Mattie fumbled in her bag, pulling out the letter.

"You better come in," Irene smiled, but Mattie noticed she promptly looked away. Mattie followed Irene into the kitchen, and they sat at the kitchen table.

"A letter from Charlie?" Irene asked.

"Well," Mattie paused. "He said he was sorry he missed seeing George. The *Rigel* didn't stop in Fiji."

"And?"

"He wished me a Merry Christmas."

"I should hope so," said Irene sitting back in her chair, crossing her arms.

"He can't say much. Censors, you know." Mattie tried to smile. "But he had a good time in Auckland."

Irene gave a slight smirk, sighed and rose up. Mattie watched her rattle the cups as if on purpose. It was that same feeling of disapproval. Sadly the letter no longer seemed important.

"Listen, I know it's going to be hard, Mattie," said Irene, reaching across to touch her. "I didn't mean to…"

"Didn't mean to what?" Mattie pulled her lips together, to stop her voice from quivering. She stood to oppose Irene.

"Listen, you have to realize no one knows what's actually happening out there. It's all a—"

"All a what?" Mattie spun, glaring at Irene. "A dream?" Her voice rang strong and true. "Yes, and when the Japs storm up your street? Forget the men who are out there to stop them? I will not forget."

She shook her head and slammed the door behind her.

CHAPTER 41

Charlie didn't know if it was the heat or the Tulagi mosquitoes bringing their fever to cloud his mind. He slipped across the *Rigel* and poked his head round the corner of the Captain's cabin.

Dudley noticed him immediately. "Come in, Kincaid. At ease. Pour you a coffee." He grinned, gesturing him to take a seat. "Well done at Tulagi. We have some new jobs for you and your men," he said, rapping his fingers on the desk.

Dudley reached across for his whisky. "Here, put a shot in," he said, taking a seat, sipping on his coffee. "You boys are needed back up at the front. The shipfitters can take over the repairs down here."

The familiar smooth taste warmed Charlie's gullet. He listened as Dudley went on.

"You'll be glad to know the secretary of the Navy, Knox himself, is coming to see the action. We don't know when, Top Secret of course, but he'll be here in Santo with Halsey. Halsey's got the greatest respect for the Coastwatchers. Just like you boys." He smiled. Swallowing the last of his coffee, he went on. "We're fixing you up with a small landing craft, won't be a PT (Patrol Torpedo) boat, but there's enough grunt in the engine to high-tail it out." His gaze intensified as he stepped ahead. "Anything you want to share with me? Is the water warm enough?"

"Yes, sir," Charlie said. He bit his lip, and then blurted out, "Do we get any rehabilitation leave, sir?"

"What's that?" said Dudley, lighting his pipe.

"Sickness leave, sir."

Smoke billowed, entirely filling the room as Dudley's eyes narrowed. "It doesn't exist. This goddamn war is a terrible animal; there's no getting to one side. Go see Doc. You and your men are heading back North in the morning. Get your gear loaded on the supply ship abreast. That is all."

Charlie left, but paused by the port railing with Dudley's words echoing in his head.

• • • • •

Charlie lay in his bunk and noticed a different rhythm as the ship changed course and sea swells now pounded the bow. He rose and walked outside to the rail. He could smell land.

The sun was showing signs of dropping in the western sky when their supply ship vigilantly passed through the Sealark Channel off Guadalcanal and docked at Sesapi, Tulagi.

Tulagi was a tiny island lying southwest across the channel from Guadalcanal, well protected from the enemy by its tall jungle canopy dripping with humidity. The symphony of evening songs from white cockatoos, mynahs, and macaws, laced with the sweet smell of tropical fruits and flowers, was mesmerizing. They lured a man into a false illusion of paradise.

Charlie noticed a marked difference after their few weeks' absence. Two essential PT-boat floating dry docks had been assembled from pontoons; and thatched huts were cropping up everywhere. Native men were working along the dockside.

A voice caught his attention; the accent sounded familiar.

"Am I glad to see you blokes." A worker in sweat-stained khakis put out a dirty hand. "Spike, they call me. I'm from Downunder."

"Another one," said Vic.

Spike laughed, "You think I'm a Kiwi bloke?"

"Yeah, how'd ya guess?"

"They're here... out there coastwatchin' the joint, like us," Spike said, with a cigarette bouncing in the corner of his mouth, through an untidy beard. "But we're fair dinkum Aussies," he snorted, bending downwards, untying the ropes of the Higgins boat. "This yours?"

Charlie noticed Spike's large biceps rippling in the setting sunlight and worried about Vic making trouble. He answered with a curt nod.

"Dinkum... Dunkum I say," said Vic with a smirk.

"I don't take to smart talk, Yank."

"As you were, boys. Save all that energy for the Japs." Charlie noticed the dark rings round Spike's eyes, and remembered what the Captain had told him about Coastwatchers.

They left the Aussie to fuel up the boat, and walked up to the spreading torpedo base by way of the makeshift bamboo pathway.

"I'd say we need all the help we can get from these locals. Don't piss off the help," growled Charlie to Vic.

No one said anything, after that. The night air brought a swarm of mosquitoes diving onto any bare skin, giving them a collection of itchy, red welts, like the last trip.

"Insect-infested hole," said Vic, scratching his butt. "I'm still not taking those goddamn pills."

Charlie shrugged; he was too busy learning the territory to worry about Vic's attitude.

They entered a thatched hut marked "Operations Officer, Motor Torpedo Base Tulagi."

"Welcome back, Kincaid." The officer beckoned them to bamboo chairs on the dirt floor. Charlie sat down, scratching a new blister above his wrist. A poster hung above the doorway: it featured a mosquito riding a torpedo. How ironic, he realized.

"We've rigged up some tents for you boys to catch a few hours' sack time. Smoking lamp is out on the shoreline—fuel storage," the officer said, sucking on his pipe. "You'll be out every night, patrolling with dynamite and dive gear. Patch up the damaged ships so we can move 'em, just like last time you were up here. The *Ortolan* is here for dive support when you need it. Tonight we need you in your Higgins to transport these two Coastwatchers with their natives and equipment. They're heading to Guadalcanal."

Just then a native wearing a dirty white sleeveless tee and shorts poked his woolly head around the corner.

"This is Coco. Malaitans are our best workers," said the officer, smiling at the boy. "He works for the Coasties. He'll help you carry arms and ammo down to your Higgins. We're starvin' out the Japs, but they can still bring a pile of trouble. That is all."

They walked outside. Coco said nothing as he trotted to the armory. Charlie and his men were issued weapons and ammo, and were glad to have Coco's help to lug it all back down to the waterfront.

Spike saw them coming and yelled, "The natives hate the Japs." Then he said something in Pidgin to Coco. Charlie noticed the fear in the boy's face.

A small man raised his head out of the Higgins and spoke in a British accent, "Hello boys, welcome to paradise. I'm Briggs, pleased to meet you." He put out his hand with a smile. He had a theatrical face, with a dimple in one cheek, and tight curls that sprang out from cropped sideburns. He made for a huge contrast to Spike, Charlie thought.

"Watch it, we'll outnumber ya," joked Spike to Vic. Vic opened his mouth as if to comment but Charlie nudged him.

"You're taking us on this run," Spike went on to Charlie. "One of our Coasties has just reported an eight-ship Tokyo Express, highballing it down the Slot."

"I need to study the charts," said Charlie.

"Memorize the chart. You'll be too busy to be lookin' at any roadmaps. We'll go out with the PTs. While they're chasing Japs, we'll slip up the river near Lunga," said Spike, as he loaded the stretchers. "We're going in to get a stranded Coastie."

They worked till dusk, eventually departing in a convoy from the wharves.

Spike stood alongside Charlie but had to yell above the engine noise, "There's some shit comin' down tonight. Our PTs are about to pounce on a Jap rat run." Charlie watched the phosphorescent spray of the four PT boats ahead. His gut clenched. There was every possibility they'd run into the enemy tonight.

Silhouetted in the fading twilight was Guadalcanal, with its oval land mass, twisting north at the western end and south at the eastern end, like a dragon with its spine of mountains running right down its middle. Cactus, they called it; it had abruptly become the most hellish place on earth, with the stench of lives lost on Bloody Ridge. Yet the American public didn't even know where it was on the map.

The men braced against the lunging Higgins, listening to the motor grind its way towards the mouth of the Matanikau River. They idled back to dead slow as the PT boats abruptly changed course and charged north at full speed.

Spike yelled, "Now's our chance. We'll slip upriver while the Japs are busy dodgin' torpedoes. Go that way."

"No sweat, we'll get you ashore," replied Charlie.

The PT boats slid into action, turning their torpedoes into the black night towards the Jap convoy to the north. "Japs are about to swallow some Yank fish. Max it out!" screamed Spike. The Higgins ramped up to full speed towards land.

Suddenly a moonlit Zeke bomber screamed overhead, and the sea around them erupted into a mass of froth and fire. Their eyeballs instantly stung from warm salt spray, but worse, the momentary deafness brought a dangerous feeling of isolated safety, as if they'd become impervious to the bullets and shrapnel whizzing past.

"Holy Mother of Jesus," said Vic. Charlie caught the look of terror in his eyes.

"Keep your heads down. We're almost to the river. Fuckin' phosphorescence gave us away," he bellowed, as he leaned hard on the throttle to coax the last knot out of their engine.

The men watched the Zeke peel to the north, unknowingly coming within range of the PT's. They opened fire with their .50 calibers. Sparks flew from the Zeke as it cartwheeled into a wet grave.

"Un-fuckin-believable! Those heroes just shot a plane down with their .50's," yelled Vic proudly.

"Bullseye! We gotta take those boys on a turkey shoot." Charlie smiled.

Two Jap supply ships lit the horizon, silhouetted in the light of explosions. A Jap destroyer danced its searchlights across the sea, and changed course ominously towards the PTs.

"The PTs'll outrun 'em easy. Get us up this river," yelled Spike, as they powered up the Matanikau. "There. Put us on that bank."

Charlie idled back and pulled in against the muddy bank under a dripping primeval canopy. Mosquito swarms patiently hovered, and then clouded amidst the evening meal that was stepping ashore.

Spike hurried down the ramp first, clutching his walkie-talkie, pack jostling on his back. He motioned to Briggs as he scanned the swaying palm trees, backlit by the moon. "We've got company," he whispered.

He pointed his well-oiled Springfield rifle up the tree and fired. *Crack*! A body tumbled lifeless to the ground. Charlie and his gang stared at the distorted form, lying motionless in the sand.

"They're little bastards," exclaimed Red.

"The best fighters ever; must have slipped out of his sling. Let's move out," said Briggs, moving ahead.

Distant Japanese voices filled the air. Spike whispered, "I'll go on ahead. Briggs, get these supplies up the flank." They waited. Briggs signaled and everyone left the riverbed, climbing the hill of tall kunai grass, the coarse edges cutting into their flesh. Red whimpered.

"Shut up," said Vic, shoving his rifle about in frustration.

Scrambling up the flank with the others, Charlie saw Spike standing in the clear.

"I'll be damned," said Vic.

A dead one-armed Jap was lying nose down in the grass.

"They do that," said Spike. "Bloody barbarians! Japs send body parts home if they're dyin', but eat the livers of their enemy. They believe it makes 'em strong." His dark-rimmed eyes glowed with hatred.

A rustle in the grass made Vic rear about and ready his weapon. "Look out," he yelled, pointing his gun at black faces armed with rifles.

Spike pushed Vic's rifle to one side as if it were a toy.

"Tojo… kill," said one of the natives, pointing up the hill. They were loaded down with the huge transmitter radio boxes for Spike and Briggs.

"No Japs live." A native smiled and wiggled a bamboo pole with a Jap head jammed on top, still oozing the last drops of black-red blood down the bamboo.

Spike's face wrinkled up with pleasure, "They eat 'em, then stake out the heads to terrorize the Japs."

"Thanks for your help," said Briggs, taking the stretchers and passing them to the natives.

"We're heading up the hill to Gold Ridge. Coastwatcher Hay is still stuck up there," said Spike, looking up, "cause he's too fuckin' fat to outrun the Jap patrols. An old nun is keepin' him company. Japs nabbed the other missionaries and chopped their heads off, samurai style."

"No shortage of loose heads around here," Charlie said. "Call on your radio when you're ready for pickup. We'll take the trail back the way we came." He was anxious to get a move on. He indicated to Moult and Red to pass their bundles to the waiting natives. He watched Spike's huge arms tackle the radio boxes and sort out the supplies. The brave men from Downunder, Charlie reckoned.

They left and headed across the valley to a chorus of night creatures chirping in the jungle. Fiercely Charlie slapped at a searing pain on the back of his neck, and drew back bloody fingers. "What the fuck do I have on my neck?" he hissed.

Moult ripped at the back of Charlie's neck, grabbed his hair, whipped out his knife. "Don't fuckin' move, sir." He expertly scraped aside a dark, bloody blob. "Fuckin' blood-sucking leech. They drop out of the trees."

A spray of shrapnel hit the air as a grenade exploded too close. Gunfire erupted from behind them. Shrill screams filled the air followed by sounds of water splashing as Japanese soldiers rushed them. Spike and two natives lunged forward. The murky water churned to red.

"You boys are clear now," said Spike, wiping the bayonet. "Here, have a souvenir." He threw a dead soldier's sword into the water. Vic picked it up.

"Drop it," said Charlie. "We've had enough fun for the night." He glared at Vic. "We're not Marines. Spike and Briggs had to come back to save our butts. Let's get out of here... let 'em do their job."

They made it back to their Higgins, pitched the mosquito netting overhead, and grabbed a couple of hours sleep till morning light.

•   •   •   •   •

Red vomited non-stop all the way back to Tulagi. Charlie and Vic helped him up to sickbay.

"You have dengue fever," said Doc.

Red looked bewildered. A deep pang of sympathy came over Charlie; his men were like his children, and he'd rather suffer himself. He viewed the sickbay with cot after cot of wounded.

"Is there anything we can do, Doc?"

"Keep covered up, sleep in mosquito nets, and take your Atrabine," he said, casting a glance through bushy brows. Charlie glared at Vic. Vic fumbled in his pocket, pulling out the yellow pill.

"What happens if you forget to take it, Doc?"

"You die."

They walked out of the sickbay in silence. Vic was the first to say something. "Holy fuck, Kinks, I only meant—"

"Shut up, don't say anymore. Just take the goddamn pills, that's all."

Charlie walked onwards smiling, thinking to himself how good ole Doc's scare tactics had done the trick.

Charlie began to appreciate the ways of the natives but invariably running into bare-breasted women disturbed him. The native women quickly learned they were a top attraction at Tulagi. Charlie reckoned he had a brilliant solution to their bobbing distraction. Supplies were plentiful including clothing. He sweet-talked the base storekeeper out of a box of white T-shirts. After loading them up in the landing craft he headed off with his diving gang across the harbor. They landed near the Coastwatchers' quarters and approached the local tribal chief with their gift for his women.

"Got some supplies," he said to one of the Coastwatchers with a grin.

"Well, we always know when you're coming," said Major Carson.

Vic glanced at the rest of the gang, eager to see the reaction of the women standing by the men, with their shining dark torsos contrasting over white skirts. Charlie felt sorry for the younger ones with their bare breasts standing upright.

Charlie walked up to the women and handed them the white tees. "Put these on."

They grabbed them and left giggling.

•　　•　　•　　•　　•

The following day, Vic pushed up his welding helmet and scanned the shoreline. "Oohhweeee! Charlie, you're going to be in bi-i-i-ig trouble."

Along the trail, a collection of native women promenaded in white T-shirts, with two round holes cut out, and supple, soft-brown glistening breasts basking beautifully in the sun.

"Well, I'll be dammed," said Charlie standing with his hands on his hips looking back at Vic. Vic burst out laughing. "We'd better get out of here."

•　　　•　　　•　　　•　　　•

The loudspeaker blared, "PBY's in from Santo. Mail call in one hour."

All Charlie's heartache and fear subsided when he opened Mattie's two letters.

Dearest Kinky,

I love you, that's all I can think of. I know I have to wait but there's rehabilitation leave. You should apply for it. I haven't heard from you and I read all these things in the paper. What am I to think?

A piece of newspaper fell out; Charlie picked it up. The headlines read: "Nine Japanese Vessels Sunk." Reading the article, Charlie clearly sensed the propaganda was beginning to take its toll on his poor darling. He wanted to hold her and comfort her. Picking up his pen, his eyes wet, he wrote as fast as he could to console her, as if it were his arms embracing her.

Darling, I'm just back from awful days up at the front and I was overjoyed to find two letters waiting from you. This sure is a hell of a hole to be stuck in, but it seems nice to get back to after a few days up there. At least you don't have the noise of bursting bombs and gun fire grating on your nerves and the stench of death all around you. On the last trip I was with some Aussies. They were swell fellows and the best fighters I've ever seen.

Yes I've heard about 30 day's rehabilitation leave, but they refuse to give it to any of the boys in this area. We can't get anything in this outfit. We can't even get back to the States except with a medical discharge. I would give anything, Mattie, to be with you. To hold you in my arms and kiss you, but it looks like fate doesn't intend for me to have a wife, home, and children. Every time I go up to the front I have a feeling I won't be coming back, but my luck keeps holding out. Remember me to all and keep your chin up. Write often, for your letters are the only thing I enjoy. Love always, Kinky. Charlie Thomas Kincaid

He leaned back in his chair and reread the newspaper article she'd sent him and gulped with pride. She knew. He grinned to himself, folding the pages away, ready for another day.

CHAPTER 42

The Japanese had been making their nightly rat runs down "The Slot" to resupply Guadalcanal. Both sides had managed to amass about 20,000 troops each, but starvation was taking a huge toll on the Japanese. Drums full of supplies floated ashore from their destroyers and submarines, though this was merely a fraction of the food required for thousands. But they fought on, desperately—as did the Americans.

A strategic land airbase was like gold. Aircraft carriers could be bombed or torpedoed, put out of commission for months or longer, or sent to the bottom. A land airbase could be bombed, and Henderson airfield was a regular Jap target, but it was repaired within hours or days. This would be a fight to the last man.

Sesapi, Tulagi, with its rickety buildings crowding the little hillside, was beginning to feel familiar.

Before the Marines had landed back in August and wiped out the Japanese garrison, it was a bustling Chinese trading village, complete with a dock and marine railway for hauling out ships. Now it had become a complete PT boat base with mini dry docks for repairs—right next to their hunting grounds, Iron Bottom Bay.

When Charlie arrived with his crew, he watched the Base Commander walking around Sesapi shouting orders to his men. As soon as the officer saw them, he came straight to the dockside.

"Get your men and equipment ready. You're leaving on a patrol immediately," he commanded.

Charlie dropped his gear and looked over at the rest of the crew, "Very well, sir, but—"

"No buts about this mission," he said, pointing to the corvette docked by the PT boats. "You know the Kiwis. I want my best divers on board."

"Aye aye, sir," they all said.

The commander hesitated then came back, walking up to speak in a low voice. "Thought you'd like to know, Halsey brought the Secretary of the Navy Knox up here with Nimitz a few days ago, the three of them in a tender. It will be the talk of the Navy. Damn place put on a right show. Knox wanted to see for himself, but somehow the enemy must have got the word. Nearly took them out." He shook his head, walked further, and turned again. "We have to stop them," he hollered, his face flushed in anger.

"They won't get past us, sir," Charlie saluted and smiled.

•   •   •   •   •

Charlie saluted the Officer of the Deck as they boarded the New Zealand *Moa*.

"Permission to come aboard, sir?"

"Welcome aboard, Mister Kincaid," said the officer. "We're glad to have you."

Charlie grinned and gathered his men to help load their diving gear aboard. They didn't waste time heading out into the bay for orientation.

A storm rumbled in the skies. Buckets of rain hit the deck, making it harder to see the advancing Cape. The constant, heavy rainfall brought dampness and mist as deck puddles glowed eerily in the night. The rain stopped, and the ebony night opened to dazzling stars. The corvette *Kiwi* slowed her engines ahead of them. A radio message from the captain of the *Kiwi* blared on the *Moa*, "Sighted phosphorescent outline of Jap cruiser sub below us. Commencing depth charge attack at flank speed."

Charlie spotted an outline of what appeared as a mammoth glowing shape, gliding stilly under the sea. Without warning, the *Kiwi* belched out six depth charges, and then came about and spewed six more. They watched in horror as out of the clear tropical waters rose the devil itself—an enormous black Japanese submarine, like a waking giant, angry and disturbed by the two little boats. The *Kiwi* now fired its 4-inch and 20mm Oerlikon guns.

"Stand by to ram," the *Kiwi* blasted a message on the *Moa* radio.

"What the hell do you mean by that?" responded the *Moa*.

"I don't know, I've never done it before, but this should get us a weekend's leave in Auckland."

The *Kiwi* rode up on the sub's port side as her guns blasted the conning tower, killing all the Japanese sailors manning the helm.

Charlie watched the *Kiwi* ram the sub two further times. "This one's for a month's leave," blared the *Moa* radio.

The sub appeared to be getting underway, but much to everyone's amazement, the *Kiwi* wasn't giving up. From the *Moa*, they watched the *Kiwi*'s determination; she was out there riding onto the huge submarine, sliding her bow down the sub's portside deck, rupturing its oil tanks. The sub gushed burbling globs of oil.

"Got the lights on her," yelled the signalman from the flying bridge, swaying in the night air. "Ram that son of a bitch."

"Yerrrr," yelled the men in unison, "ram her." No one seemed aware of the danger of their attack. Adrenalin kicked in and both ships went in for the kill. The *Kiwi* made a third run with signalman Buchanan holding the searchlight. A sniper fired from the sub and Buchanan slumped to the deck.

The *Kiwi,* now hugely damaged herself, backed full astern and radioed, "*Moa*, we're crippled, take up the hunt."

Taking advantage, the sub slipped silently into the dark on its one remaining diesel engine, now unable to submerge.

The *Moa* revved its engines, chasing the smoking sub. "We'll getcha," the Captain yelled. The *Moa*'s engines reverberated. Charlie wished they could follow in silence, stalking this huge submarine.

Hours passed. In a futile maneuver, the sub ran aground on Fish Reef, 330 yards off the Kamimbo Coast, with her bow pointing out of the water. They waited till dawn, exhausted, watching their prey unload its crew into small boats and head for the Guadalcanal beach.

The *Moa*'s Captain spoke to Charlie. "We need you divers to go aboard the sub and retrieve their code machine, code books, charts, logs and every other scrap of information that could help us. There will most likely be a few enemy stragglers on board. You'll enter through the aft submerged hatch and work your way forward to the air pockets. Stay together. You'll only have your knives."

Charlie and his diving gang jumped into a small boat and raced forward to circle around the wreck. They started the compressor. Charlie gave a signal, dove down, and opened the sub's hatch. It was a tight squeeze. He couldn't see; he felt his way into the narrow opening, down the passageway, and up into a partially flooded compartment. Suddenly something sharp slid past him from above, almost cutting off his mask. Charlie saw a Rising Sun… slashing. He whipped aside his mask. Charlie felt the Jap's strong grip pushing him down, underwater to the depths of the sub. Vic came in behind him and fiercely sliced the Jap's throat, opening his neck to a pulsing red torrent. They eased the body aside and moved on through the compartment.

"Fuckin' hell, Kinks… you were shark bait," gasped Vic.

"Good one, Vic. We're goin' forward."

They searched for the submarine's secret documents and charts. Charlie and Vic scoured the captain's cabin, grabbed documents and the code machine, sealed them into watertight containers, and made it to the surface before any unseen enemy could stop them.

They surfaced, relieved, but knew to race at top speed back to the safety of the *Moa*. The *Moa* caught up with the *Kiwi* as they entered Tulagi harbor. A lot was at stake. Buchanan's wound was bleeding terrifically.

Back on land Buchanan was rushed to Tulagi's hospital, but no operation could save him. A silence hung over the base that day. Every death brought sadness and respect, but also fuelled the men's determination. No one had any need to dwell on their own mortality—they had a job to do. Charlie and his men left Guadalcanal with an even greater appreciation of the Kiwis and their bravery.

•   •   •   •   •

Charlie was dead weary as he climbed aboard the *Rigel;* but the *Kiwi* victory spurred him to reach for his new set of airmail paper, purchased at the post office. He poised his black fountain pen and pulled Mattie's photo out from his top pocket; warm from his chest and weather beaten from the living hell of the past few days. He heaved a sigh of relief. He couldn't smell the Guadalcanal cadavers anymore—although some said they could, even when they were an ocean away; the stench never left their memories. He lovingly set the photo down, staring into his stateroom. He gave a quick remembrance for the men he'd left behind, the Kiwis and the Coastwatchers from the last trip up to the front.

And then he began to write…

My Dearest Mattie, Here I'm at long last with another letter. I hope you'll forgive me for not writing to you more often. It's not that I don't like writing; it's that I'm so damn tired when I get off that I usually try to get a little rest before turning to it again. I've worked six days and nights without rest one time and I've come near that several times. I haven't had a single day off since I saw you last. Hell is continually popping off around here.

Do you remember that news item you sent me? I was in on that and quite a bit since. That's what comes of being a diver. Darling, even though I haven't written to you very often is no reason to think I've forgotten you. I knew that soon we would be leaving and that it would be heartache for both parties concerned. I seemed to be drawn to you by some invisible force. I could no more help what I did than the man in the moon.

I'm not sorry for any of it, for now, looking back, those days were the happiest days of my life. If God's willing someday I'll be coming back to you, although it looks awfully hopeless now with the road I've got to travel. If I live through what is ahead and come back to you in one piece I'll be the happiest man alive. Love always, Kinky.

CHAPTER 43

With the New Year, there was plenty to prepare for the new students at O'Hara's Hair Academy. Everyone loved Mattie; her constant beauty radiated a glorious example during difficult times. But her flare came from her love for Charlie; and when his two letters arrived, with money tucked inside, it was as though he snuggled beside her talking in his sweet Southern drawl. The letter had been opened; *I hate these censors*, she fumed.

Mattie held his letter and repeated to herself, *someday I'll be coming back to you…* Teary-eyed, she read his words of warning *I'm rather nervous today so I had better knock off until I can hold a pen better. I'll write more later. Love always, Kinky.*

I must get another photo taken, Mattie said to herself. She was sitting in the sun outside the salon, adjacent to Nan on their lunch break. Nan was good company and seemed interested in her letters. Mattie read aloud, "Three hundred dollars a month, we can live pretty good." She grinned at Nan. "What do you think of that!"

Nan gobbled the last bite of her sandwich and wiped her mouth on a hanky. "Bloody marvelous. Wish I had a sailor."

"Did you ever go out with Kinky's friend, you know, the tall blond one?"

"Na, he stood me up at Peter Pan's. I saw him with someone else."

Mattie shoved the two letters into her uniform, feeling uncomfortable. "Well, there's plenty others."

Nan stood up, shook the crumbs from her uniform, and stepped back through the window. She turned around, "If you don't mind my saying so, doesn't that apply to you as well?"

Mattie was shocked at her reaction but realized she'd offended the young woman. "Apologies Nan, I understand. I wish we had a giant bomb to end this war. We need our men back."

Nan half-smiled and returned to the salon without another word. Mattie winced. Her relationships with her friends at work had become strained in recent weeks.

The next day, she set out to walk the length of Karangahape Road, determined to find another job. Passing Peter Pan's Studio, she stopped. She couldn't resist taking another glimpse at the wall covered with photos, predominantly sailors smiling with their girlfriends. She visualized her photos, and fingered the little cameo necklace hanging around her neck, until tears brimmed in her eyes again.

Mr Pan saw her and came towards her, "Madam, I seem to remember you. Are you still working upstairs?"

"Well in reality, I'm looking for another position. I've graduated... "

"Ah, I know just the place," he said. "Such a nice lady runs the salon on the corner of Great North Road—a Mrs Marshall. I went in to take photos. Go and see her, and tell her I said hello."

"Oh, I will. You're very kind to help. I wonder... will you take a photo of me, a very special one?"

He moved the camera and tripod, adjusting it with care. "All photographs are special. Smile now, that's it," he said.

She thanked him and deliberately walked up Karangahape Road to where it met Great North Road. She crossed the road to the McLaughlin Building with its cute little turrets rowed along like a gingerbread house. One of the small shops in the building, tucked near the corner, was marked 'Mrs Marshall'. She peered in the window and saw a hairdresser bending over an elderly lady, relaxing in a salon chair; the lady smiled up at Mattie. It was a small shop and Mattie doubted there would be any positions available. She entered.

"Can I help you?" the hairdresser asked.

Mattie shook her head, unsure how to start.

"What a brisk morning," the hairdresser said, coming towards her, shrugging her shoulders. "Is there a shampoo or a powder we can offer you today, madam?"

"I was wondering..." Mattie hesitated, glancing about again. "I'd like to see the person in charge."

"Certainly. Kath's my name, please take a seat."

Mattie rested on the cane chair, watching Kath disappear into the back room.

An older woman appeared and Kath returned to finish brushing her client's hair.

"I'm Mrs Marshall."

"Mattie," she said, offering her hand. "Mattie Blanc. I'm looking for work but I see you're…"

"Yes, we're small," interrupted Mrs Marshall. "But we're moving into the front corner shop, beside the tobacconist. I'm looking for another hairdresser, but it won't be till August. I already have two girls. You've met Kathleen."

Mattie presented a folded copy of her certificate.

"O'Hara's has such a good name," said Mrs Marshall. "Goodness, my dear—a top student." She grinned. Medium-length brown curls fell beside her face, reminding Mattie of her mother. "If you leave your details, I'll be in touch."

"Thank you, Mrs Marshall. I will do my best for you. O'Hara's won't mind my staying on until August."

It made her feel better as she walked back down Karangahape Road. She had a place to go, a top salon. She stopped by Mr Pan to see about her proof for the photo.

CHAPTER 44

The secret documents from the Japanese submarine revealed Japan's belief that the Guadalcanal Campaign was over. Fortunately they had given up too readily. Many Marines were ill with dysentery, fever, fungus infections, and almost everyone was blood-sucked into malaria. If only the enemy had known...

Charlie, his fever spiking, refused to give in to the disease. He studied Mattie's photos and wondered, was this a hallucination? He picked up his pen and wrote.

My Darling, I just received your letter with the snapshots. I think the one of you is the best. It looks so natural. Gosh! Mattie you are the most beautiful and sweetest girl I've ever known.

He put his pen down and closed his eyes. He imagined her sitting right alongside him, touching him, her sweet lips... oh, how he could dream...

If I had never met you and just saw that picture I still would have fallen in love with you. Even when I was a kid I always dreamed of falling for a girl who had blue eyes and black curly hair. A girl who looked remarkably like you. That's why I acted so strangely when I met you. I'll always remember the days that followed as the happiest of my life. Love always, Kinky.

Exhausted, he flopped onto his desk. The words had just poured out of him like warm honey. He'd seen her in his dreams running across the butterweed, her long black hair in the wind, cascading about her head just like when they'd said goodbye.

He jerked up, everything a blur. A stabbing pain hit behind his eyes, his heart throbbing, his body breaking into a cold sweat. He felt totally confused. Disoriented. Maybe this girl was a...what? A hallucination? *Is... is she just a dream?*

Mattie's image streamed back through his mind: *No... no... Goddamn it, she is real.*

•   •   •   •   •

The *Rigel* departed Santo and sailed south for Efate the following morning. No reason was given. They arrived in Havannah Harbor, a deep horseshoe bay sheltered by coral masses and a barren, rocky landscape. There was not a hint ashore of any supple, shiny, bare-breasted natives.

"Why the fuck would we want to be here? Can't concentrate without pussy," complained Vic.

"A deep harbor for battleship repair, remote from the Japs. We'll send you into town by seaplane every night for servicing," joked Charlie.

"Fuck off... sir."

Charlie had a message; it must be another letter. He rushed to the post office. The letter he was handed bore a New Zealand stamp, postmarked December. Shoving it in his pocket, he jolted at the sound of his name booming over the loudspeaker, requesting him to report to the wardroom at once.

He opened the wardroom door and saluted Captain Dudley.

"Captain Benson," said Dudley to a senior officer standing next to him, "I want you to meet Warrant Officer Kincaid."

Charlie stiffened, his heart racing. He saluted, then stared respectfully at Captain Benson's medals and blazing gold shoulder boards.

"Mr Kincaid," said Dudley in his usual manner, "the Captain has a request."

Charlie noted Captain Benson's unusually intense eyes.

"I've heard so much about you, son... your great work here in the islands. We want you to share your experiences. You know, boost morale. Would you speak to my crew?"

Charlie's mouth flew open. His reaction changed from surprise to pleasure.

"Captain's from the *Washington*," Dudley explained.

Charlie noticed Dudley's puffed-out chest. Fortunately he realized who was in the wardroom. He swallowed. This was the captain of the battleship USS *Washington,* just arrived.

"Aye, aye, Captain. Nothing would make me prouder," said Charlie, saluting.

"I'll see you on our bridge at 0800 hours tomorrow. That is all," Benson replied. He saluted back to Charlie, and left the wardroom.

Dudley lit a cigarette, his arm leaning over the chair, watching Charlie. He slid a pile of papers across the table. "An outline of the required speech. You know the rest, it's your call. I'm proud of you, son. One thing though, can we leave out the part about native girls in your navy-issue T-shirts?"

Charlie couldn't speak.

"Oh, and there's something else..."

Charlie cringed, *here it comes...*

"The *Rigel*'s leaving for Australia. Tell your men they've earned a bit of leave." Dudley focused on him with a wry smile.

Charlie snatched up the papers and stood. "Great news, sir. My men will be doing cartwheels down the main deck."

"I'll pray for the Aussie women."

•   •   •   •   •

The following morning, Charlie boarded the biggest vessel in the world, bristling with 16-inch guns that towered above him. He stood before the two-thousand crew. There and then, everything he'd fought for fell into place, all of the sunken and shot-up ships. The story of his experiences was a way of honoring the achievements of every unknown sailor, and of his men, the divers. This crew needed to know they were not alone and that anything was possible... even right on Japan's doorstep.

After the excitement of meeting Captain Benson, Charlie and his men continued to dive, not much caring for their appearance until it was time to sail. No one knew where they were bound for except Charlie.

The repair ship *USS Medussa* arrived on schedule in Havannah Harbor. It was confirmation the *Rigel* was leaving her post. As if on cue, the *Rigel* sailed with a full convoy into the waters of the Coral Sea.

Standing on the deck and looking down, Charlie rode with the *Rigel* as she plodded and lunged into the southern swells at 12 knots. *Not exactly high-balling like the destroyers to Tulagi*, he envisioned. The ocean brandished a seascape today as if it were made by a designer of South Pacific post cards, accented by the stately column of supply and war ships. Through the clear water Charlie viewed the coral reefs teaming with brilliant fish. In the distance rose the peaceful, green islands.

We don't have much protection astern... wish they'd put the Rigel in the middle of the convoy, he worried. The salt spray whooshed past, and his mind drifted back to memories of their departure from Auckland.

CHAPTER 45

Mrs Frisken opened the door with a smile on her face. "Yes, two letters from him."

Mattie held the envelopes in her trembling hand and looked up at Mrs Frisken, who continued, "I'll go and make a cup of tea. I can see you have some reading to do."

"Yes, can't wait. Oh, these are a bit damp. Poor postie must have been caught in a downpour."

Mattie relaxed in the same room where they had shared their first moments; her eyes scanning, caressing each word...

My Dearest Mattie, How is the world treating you these days, fine I hope? Did you ever find another job? I sure wish I was there and you didn't have to work. The diving gang and I are still working every day. It sure is a miserable old life. We are beginning to look like a rugged bunch of individuals. I'm wondering how long we can last at this pace. We did a couple of jobs right under the Japs' noses that are the talk of the Navy around here. They would make interesting writing, but you know censorship regulations. You'll hear about them soon. I know now that I love you and if I live through this thing I'm going to try and do something about it. Love always, Kinky. P.S. – answer soon.

Mattie set the first letter down and smiled into the room. Yes, she had found another job. He would be pleased for her. She imagined a mammoth ship and her sweetheart standing there. She felt a swelling of pride in Charlie's achievements. Smiling to herself, she anxiously opened the next letter.

Darling, I finally received your letter with the photos. It took quite a while for them to reach me because they went all the way back to the States. You still look very beautiful.

She loved the way he praised her and always kept her informed. Perhaps he liked the one Mr Pan had taken, she remembered with a cheeky grin. A warm fuzzy prickle of happiness trickled through her, like a small reminder of her desires. She remembered where he had touched her, how he had kissed her, and how his beautiful words did things to her. She crossed her legs at the memory, and flushed with rekindled craving.

I miss you something awful and can hardly wait until we are together again. I have never wanted anything as bad as I want you. After a fellow has been away for a while he usually loses interest in the girl he left behind but instead my love for you has increased each day until my one ambition is for you and I to be together again and this time for keeps. There is one regulation I plan to break when I do see you. If you still love me we'll be married in spite of everything they say.

His words choked her. *'If you still love me?'* He can't hear me, he can't see me... *I'll never stop loving you, Charlie.* Her eyes blurred with tears as she read on,

There will never be anyone who can take your place and if God is willing I'll come back to you and, if I can't, I'll send for you. Could you get permission to travel to Australia to marry me if I were there? If you could I would catch the clipper; it's safer by air and much faster. If you can let me know I'll send you enough money to cover all expenses. In case you can't I'll try and get some leave and arrive down there. I can't plan on anything though. I sure wish this damn war would end soon. Love always, Kinky. C T Kincaid.

She stared at the money folded inside another page and read the words again, wiping her eyes.

"What's wrong?" asked Mrs Frisken, appearing as if from nowhere. She set down two teacups and a plate of freshly baked scones.

"He's asked me to go to Australia... and to get married."

"My goodness, Mattie! Oh my dear girl..."

Mattie held onto the money, as if it were his presence tugging her towards him. She frowned, startled. "He says Australia, but which city? He doesn't say."

"Well... he could be confused."

Mattie finished her tea and put the money on the table, shaking her head. "He's not crazy," she said firmly. "He's not shell-shocked. He loves me and I love him. Damn it..." She stood up. "I'm leaving. Next stop... Australia."

"No—wait." Mrs Frisken stood up, and put an arm on her shoulder. "Don't be foolish, girl. Your parents, what will they think?"

Mattie flew back at her. "My family wants him to return here. To wait until the war is over. My God, that might be an eternity."

"No... no. Please, Mattie, think about it. There's a protocol that has to be followed. And all sorts of Navy red tape. At least visit the Navy Chaplain and find out the rules. Then talk to your family. You can't just rush off when you don't even know where to meet him."

"How do you know all this?"

"Never mind what I know. Just go and do it."

By the next morning, Mattie had calmed down. She was glad she had Mrs Frisken in her life. But she wondered about her so-called knowledge of military protocol. And her subtle hints about men. Was she hiding something? But Mrs Frisken was her friend, she cared about her and she trusted her.

It turned out she was right; when Mattie inquired she discovered there were rules about becoming engaged to a Navy Officer. Mattie had to place two advertisements in her local paper, and get full permission from her family. It was time to go home and encounter her father.

She finished her last day at O'Hara's with the obligatory pastries washed down by buckets of hot tea. It was perfect timing to let the memories fade, like the fading sun across fallen leaves outside in Myers Park.

The following day, she took a stroll, remembering her lover's words: *Darlin' love... I will be back.* She could hear his voice as if he were walking beside her. A brass band was approaching up Queen Street. Mattie danced down the steps and caught sight of the musicians. They were marching in front of four Officers striding before columns of sailors. She watched them advance and stop outside the Town Hall.

Someone in the crowd remarked, "That's the Kiwis. They sunk a huge Jap submarine in the islands up north."

Another person said, "Such brave men."

Mattie stood with tears in her eyes, listening to the mayor, Mr Allum, speak in admiration of their job well done. They were men of a small Corvette; heroes who outgunned and rammed a colossal enemy submarine. Packed streets echoed jubilant with cheers as the men entered the Town Hall.

Mattie watched the sailors' faces. They showed no emotion. It was their duty.

She walked on towards Huntly House. She too had a job to do. She smiled to herself, and ran up the street towards the tram to Huntly House.

CHAPTER 46

It was the 2nd of May when the *Rigel* glided into Sydney Harbor with every sailor hooting at the sight. They arrived dockside at Cockatoo Island, a huge shipyard which had been an imperial prison for decades. To Charlie's surprise, there was the *New Orleans*, berthed adjacent to them, reminding him yet again of his heritage.

Vic was out of control, running, stretching his neck in all directions, hollering, "Where's the sheilas?"

Charlie had just one thing on his mind—Mattie—but he responded, "You and the men have liberty. The Captain wants to see me about something. I'll be along in a little while." He watched his men happily bound down the gangway on a dead run towards the perfumed women waiting just outside the base. New men raced ashore, with money in their pockets and free nylons bulging from their waistbands.

But Captain Dudley had something else planned.

The wardroom was strangely quiet with the *Rigel* now on shore power, and the sound of men's chatter fading in the distance. Charlie sensed his fate before he stepped inside.

"Something's come up. We have an urgent training exercise up the coast." Dudley looked grave. "It's serious. The Japs have been bombing the living shit out of Darwin, and now they've landed men and equipment just on the outskirts. We have to stop the invasion. The fleet is mobilizing up north to cut off their supply lines." He paused as if to put his ideas in order. "We reckon they've overstretched their reach. No doubt counting on operating from captured fuel and food, but that's not going to happen. The Aussies will torch everything before they can get it. All livestock are being moved south."

"What do you need from my divers?" asked Charlie.

"The Aussies are well into training men to sneak behind Jap lines and wreak havoc. This is your mission. You and your men will depart on the double for Camp Z, Cowan Creek. Train with the Aussies, share ideas, learn from each other. We have big plans for you up north. Muster your men."

"But sir, they've left on leave."

"Recall them. The Aussie assassins won't be around for long. You can have your leave another day."

"But sir, we only have a few weeks here. Do we get liberty on return from Camp Z?"

Dudley squinted up through his cigar smoke. "Mr Kincaid, I detect a certain urgency in you that is not entirely focused on your position as a Warrant Officer and a leader." He stood up from his chair to make his point and chewed hard on his cigar.

Charlie sensed Dudley knew more than he was saying. Maybe he had read his letters to Mattie. Yes, that must be it. He clenched his fists at the vision of his sweetheart and their intimacy being violated by other eyes. He answered the single way any superior would understand, "Aye aye, sir."

Charlie left Cockatoo Island on the waiting small boat to find his men.

On the mainland, women were already lined up along the shoreline, frequently waving their handkerchiefs, but a couple of spirited lasses signaled with lace panties. It was Auckland all over again, except Sydney was huge. Charlie walked along with his hands in his pockets. All he could think of was his sweetheart and their marriage plans. What a desperate fool he'd been to ask her. But he had no choice but to concentrate on finding his men.

He made his way into the main streets of Sydney, poking his head into pubs, sailors' territory.

Charlie's hopes had started to fade when he fortunately caught sight of Vic's head of blond locks crossing the road, his arm riding the bouncing hips of a tall blonde. He smiled to himself and ran after him, whistling frantically. Vic noticed, and then walked on, pretending he hadn't seen Charlie.

"Vic, hold up. We've got orders to return to ship," Charlie shouted.

"What?" Vic's hand slipped further around the girl's waist. "You're joking, right?"

"I'm not. Have you seen any of our men?"

Vic stood there, looking puzzled. "We're all a bit busy now, sir. Have my eye on this pretty girl next to me."

Charlie nodded.

The girl gave a giggle and kissed Vic on the cheek.

"Oh hell, Kinks, can't you see I have business to attend to? You haven't found me. I'll be back at sunset."

Vic walked onwards with his gal, leaving Charlie to wade through the crowd. Feeling dazed with fever, he decided it was useless trying to force his men back. He traipsed haltingly back to the ship.

There was a letter waiting for him from Mattie.

My darling Kinky, I am happy to travel to Australia. Where should we meet? But I checked with the naval department and I need permission to marry you. I am leaving for Dunedin to announce our engagement in the newspapers as they require. I love you and I am sure my parents will, too, when I arrive home and explain just how wonderful you are and what you mean to me. It is better to tell them face to face, although they may not let me go to Australia to marry you. I hope you understand, darling...

Trembling, he picked up his pen. He knew he should have bought her a ring. It all seemed impossible. By the time he let her know where he was and she flew over, he'd possibly be gone. And even if he were able to stay long enough to meet up with her, where should he tell her to go? How stupid of him. How could he do this to her?

It must be my fever, he reasoned. He picked up his pen and wrote:

Darling, Just received your nice letter and it made me very happy to know you love me enough to marry me. You understand what a marriage like ours will mean. But I believe if two persons love each other as much as we do they can be happy anywhere as long as they are together. I'll do everything in my power to make you happy and as soon as the war is over we can be together almost all the time. You can announce our engagement anytime you like. I do hope we have your family's permission and blessing. I'll always try and make them proud they have me for a son-in-law. I can't get you a ring just now for I'll be back in the wilderness almost any day now, and anyhow I would like to give it to you in person. I sure dread the trip back up there for I've had the fever the last few days and more duty up there won't do it any *good. If the Japs don't get me I should be back soon and it would make me very happy if I could see you when I get back. I'll try to write more next time. I would like to hear from you as often as you can write. A letter from a loved one is the best morale booster a guy up at the front can get, so keep me cheered up, will you? Love always, Kinky. P.S. – Enclosed is $140.00. More later.*

He put down his pen, relieved. Now he was ready.

Charlie and his men left Cockatoo Island at 0600 hours the following morning in a small craft, and headed up the coast to Cowan Creek, Broken Bay. To Charlie's surprise, Briggs met them on the beachhead.

"I knew you were coming," said Briggs with his half smile. "That's the *Krait* out there, named after a deadly Indian snake. She's been converted for top secret Operation Jaywick. Sneaking behind Jap lines to raise a ruckus. Hear you're up for the same. They need some extra training on explosives, and these Aussies have bush knowledge you'll need in the jungles up north."

"No sweat. Where do we start?" asked Charlie, looking over at the *Krait*.

"Get ready for night raids in small portable canoes and working underwater in strong currents with limpet mines," Briggs said, walking over to a small craft. He wheeled around, his smile faded. "Australia's getting bombed by the Japs up north of here. We need to act fast."

"I heard. Let's dish 'em out a few surprises," replied Charlie with a grin.

They headed towards the *Krait,* which was sitting in the inlet. "She's an old Japanese fishing tender. A perfect disguise for an undercover raid," said Briggs, shutting off the engine.

Climbing aboard, Charlie remembered his first fishing vessel on the Mississippi. He ran a finger along her old timbers and poked his head down the forward hatch.

"She'll hold six commandos and eight crew," bragged Briggs, "and she has a new Gardner 6L3 diesel in her." He nodded. "See those Corvettes anchored across the bay?

"Yep."

"Tonight, blackened and in balaclavas, get there unseen, two men per canoe, and mark the side with your team number, or better yet bring something back from onboard."

"Got it. I'm sure we can find a souvenir on deck." Charlie beamed.

Vic leaned against the *Krait's* timber bow, about to light a cigarette.

"Hold it," barked Briggs.

Vic heard and stopped.

"No smoking, there's explosives on board."

Vic shoved the cigarette back in his pocket.

"No alcohol and no women 'round here either," said Briggs.

Vic gave a grunt, "Gawd help us."

"We'll be on our way then," said Charlie to his men.

"We've plenty of tents for a few hours' kip before dark," reassured Briggs, pushing off.

They rode back to Camp Z in silence. Australia had a different heat from the tropics, a drier heat, but fierce nonetheless. The men collapsed into their shaded tents, but somehow missed the swaying motion of the *Rigel* in their cots.

Night fell. With blackened faces, Charlie and his gang taught their Aussie counterparts several new tricks: setting explosives and dealing with camouflage netting interlaced with local bush. The Aussies, for their part, were masters at hand-to-hand combat and bush lore. Steadily, the Yanks and Aussies trained and tested one another over the weeks ahead, until they were ready. Silent, deadly teams headed night after night for the unsuspecting Corvettes.

•   •   •   •   •

After they'd returned to the *Rigel,* Vic and the men bounded ashore on their relished liberty. Charlie despaired as he realized he wouldn't get a chance to see Mattie in Australia. Four exhausting days later, the *Rigel* had completed her repairs, converted an LST (Landing Ship, Tank) to a hospital ship, loaded supplies and now sailed up the coast of Australia. As she pounded into effervescent blue-green foam, the full moon's reflections played tricks with Charlie's vision. He visualized Mattie dancing on the velvet-silk waters, waving at him, beckoning to him, like a siren. Dog tired, he finished his watch, and his apparitions unfolded into words:

Darling, Just found out we are stopping a few hours in a port where we can leave mail so I'll try and dash off a few lines. I'm in pretty fair condition so maybe the climate won't get me this time. Anyhow we probably won't be here any too long. I had the midwatch last night. It was a very beautiful night with calm seas, clear sky and a full moon. I did a lot of thinking about you, reliving some of the memories in my mind of the times you and I were together. Love always, Kinky

The next morning, the city of Brisbane unfolded before Charlie's eyes as they sailed at five knots up the river and into the port. The city wasn't as big as Sydney, but it was a very important submarine base. Of course they had kept their arrival a secret.

The *Krait* was berthed over to portside. He thought about Briggs and his mission. It made him proud to know the Aussie's were now headed out undercover to tag Jap ships with his limpet mines. He smiled to himself as he rushed ashore to post the letter to his darling. *I'll be back to Auckland, my darlin'*, he foresaw, *just got a few Japs in the way.*

The *Rigel* loaded critical supplies. Hours later they headed north, back to the tropics. Charlie and his men were rested and ready.

CHAPTER 47

The *Rigel* sailed off the coast of Australia with a full convoy of landing ship tanks (LSTs), coastal transports (APCs), plus the destroyers *Sand* and *Gilmer* as escorts. Charlie chuckled to himself. His old banana boat, leading the charge to the front line. *Well, I'll be damned.*

They anchored in the bite of Milne Bay, New Guinea, near the north shore, a narrow body of water about twenty-six miles long and averaging five miles wide. It was not a tropical paradise. The *Rigel* was a welcome sight in the harbor. It was now flagship to Admiral Barbey.

Already the Navy Seabees had built a base, small docks and ammunition depots. Amidst the mud roads, a small naval hospital had arisen from the muck. There was no Officer's Club, no dance hall, no movie house—just the tools of war. The smooth voice of Tokyo Rose wafted out of the sailors' quarters and work stations, subtly reminding them of a home they couldn't have.

"Seems lousy, a Jap dame with an American accent," said Red, whistling along to the tune.

"I don't listen," snapped Charlie. "She's deliberately making y'all homesick." He tried to change the subject. "Why don't you boys go up topside and watch a movie instead?"

"Yerr, and watch them dames we can't have?" said Vic. "Biggest worry is dodging that bullet with your name on it."

Charlie grabbed Vic and shoved him up against the bulkhead. "You need to get your mind off this fuckin' war. You and the boys go watch the movie." He let him go and walked towards the ladder for topside. He knew his men were getting edgy and totally needed a diversion.

The movies were screened on a large sheet of white canvas. Sailors could watch either side, except on the bow side you saw everything in reverse, kind of like looking in a mirror. Red was making his way to a seat by the bridge.

"Save me a place," yelled Charlie, heading to his cabin to write a letter to his sweetheart first.

The following morning, Charlie entered the wardroom to find the Captain and Mansbach studying a massive pile of charts and documents. The Captain looked up. "Mr Kincaid, tomorrow morning at 0500, you and five of your best divers will depart in a PT boat for Woodlark. Your mission is to blow up any obstacles on the shoreline. This includes coral reefs, and any other steel or concrete welcome wagons the Japs might have left to hurt us. There will be a beachmaster onboard to identify the beach. Your only protection from enemy fire will be to keep your heads underwater, so make sure your rebreathers are in top shape. Choice of explosives is up to you—we have plenty. Good luck and I'll see you here tomorrow night for a debriefing."

"Aye aye, sir. My men are itchin' to get into it."

The PT boat screamed into the morning darkness, pounding full speed towards Woodlark. By midday, they throttled back and engaged mufflers to mutely approach the landing zone.

"Get your men ready. I'll drop you in a line in front of the reef at fifteen knots, one man every ten seconds. I'll be back for pickup in two hours, as agreed," said the PT boat captain.

Charlie and his men were in the water, and in a flash went to work placing charges in the crevices of the reef. They then headed into the lagoon in search of Japanese hedgehogs. Charlie had prepared for these by packing Tetrytol explosive into two-inch rubber tubes, which were wound around the legs of any Japanese obstacles. The men could not resist the temptation, and eventually all had poked their heads above water for a good look. But the beach was completely deserted.

Right on time, the men converged at the pick-up line, and were lassoed back on board the rapidly-moving PT boat. They waited another hour for the timers, and were rocked by a massive display of explosions and water fountains.

"Holy shit, Niagara Falls in New Guinea," said Vic.

"Grab a handful of buckets; we've got fish for dinner." Charlie grinned. The lagoon was awash with enough fish to feed the whole fleet.

Arriving back at the *Rigel*, Charlie reported immediately to the captain in the wardroom.

"What's your report, Mr Kincaid?"

"Captain, mission went perfectly. Beachhead is ready for invasion," said Charlie. "But... be durned if we saw any sign of Japs."

"We scouted both Woodlark and Kiriwina last month, and found no sign of Japs. But you can't tell about those sneaky bastards. Never underestimate the enemy. Well done. The invasion fleet will depart shortly, but you and your divers stay on the *Rigel*. You have much more important chores ahead. That is all."

"Aye aye, sir."

The invasion force pulled out on 30 June 1943 with every usable LST, LCT (Landing Craft, Tank) and LCI (Landing Craft Infantry) plus those borrowed from Admiral Halsey's South Pacific forces, while the *Rigel* remained behind in strict radio silence. Charlie and his divers restlessly awaited word aboard the *Rigel*.

Charlie ran into Mansbach at breakfast the following morning, "Any word from the fleet?"

"Christ! We intercepted one top secret message from the Commander of a LST division issuing invitations to a dinner party upon his return to Townsville, and then—beat this—MacArthur's headquarters makes a radio broadcast announcing the successful landing. But have we heard from the invasion fleet? No!" barked Mansbach.

The next day, Captain Dudley briefed all officers, "Gentlemen, we have succeeded at Woodlark and Kiriwina. No Japs whatsoever, no loss of men or ships. Japs must be busy somewhere else. Congratulations, but do not think it will be this easy on subsequent missions."

CHAPTER 48

It was winter 1943 when Mattie made the long journey to her hometown. *Home*, Mattie grinned.

She stepped onto the platform of the Dunedin railway station and eagerly scanned the waiting crowd.

"Mattie." It was her mother's voice.

Mattie twirled around. Familiar arms embraced her, soft cheeks touched. Best of all, she inhaled the treasured aroma of mother's powder and perfume.

"Why, Mattie." Mary let her go and took Mattie's arm. "Isn't this a happy occasion for you?" she spoke airily. "You'll have to tell me all about your American."

"Later, Mother... later," said Mattie, smiling at her father coming towards them.

"Welcome home, Mattie," said Arthur, as he carried her suitcase with a smile. She laced into both their arms as they made their way to the car.

Mattie needed to quietly contain herself, but Mary filled the car with constant chatter as they drove. When they whizzed past the gravel road to the Leigh overlook—the car fell silent. So many memories came flooding back, Mattie almost wept. She inhaled a deep breath. *I must be strong.*

Arthur eased down the drive to a stop.

Mattie stepped out of the car. "Mother, let's have a cup of tea and I'll tell you both all about Charlie."

It was a steep climb up schist stone steps, past treasured roses and onto a wide wooden veranda. Arthur opened the ornate front door. Mattie tightened the grip on her mother's arm. There it all was—just as she'd left it. The dining table by the window, with two chairs facing each other. The lace curtains obscuring a familiar view of the harbor. The little fireplace glowing warmth into the room, and her mother's poker tilting by the hearth.

Mattie peeked round into the kitchen. "Hmmm, you've been making scones."

"Go and get settled. I'll serve tea," Mary said.

Mattie walked down the passageway taking in each memory, listening to the old grandfather clock chime its way into a new day. The room stood empty, the piano silent.

Those days are gone, Mattie reminisced as she stepped inside her bedroom. The morning sun's rays caught the two lovers in the Marygold painting above her bed, the familiar style of black from an untouchable fantasy. Reliving past moments, she stroked her bedspread, her lip quivering, wishing her sweetheart was with her.

"You'd better tell me about this man, Mattie," said Mary appearing from behind her.

Mattie spun around. "Oh, Mother… he's beautiful. He's had such a sad life, but he's going to be a hero," she said, looking into her mother's face. She knew it would be hard to convince her.

Mary patted her arm, "We'll have to get your father's permission, won't we?"

The word *permission* sparked a mild panic to rise through her chest as they walked back into the dining room.

"My daughter, engaged to an officer in the United States Navy," Arthur said, looking up at Mary. Mattie's eyes darted in defense, from one parent to the other.

"Yes, Mattie… But how can this possibly work, living over there?" Mary's voice trembled with worry.

"Mother, you make it sound like America is an enemy camp. You can visit. I can travel home once a year. What's wrong with you? I thought you were both happy for me."

"We are… aren't we?" Mary looked at Arthur for confirmation.

Arthur sipped his tea.

It always bothered Mattie when he went silent. She leaned across the table towards him, "It will be okay. Charlie totally wants you to be proud of him. He's a good man."

"How do you truly know?" said Arthur. He kept his eyes on the newspaper, refusing to look at her.

"You shouldn't question your father, dear. He knows best."

"Mother," said Mattie, fixing her with a steadfast stare. "I didn't show up here to be reprimanded. I'm quite capable of making my own decisions—and this is one of them."

"But we don't know who he is. We don't know about his background," Mary continued.

"You haven't asked."

Arthur put down his paper.

Mattie stood up, sick with fury. "I'm going to check on the mail." She left them sitting in the room and walked out of the house and up to the back gate to see what was in the letterbox, the bitter cold calming her anger.

Thank God! A letter readdressed with Mrs Frisken's handwriting. She clutched the letter to her chest, watching her breath fog in the morning light. She eased open the back door, nodded at her mother, and walked into the passageway past the bathroom and out towards the sunroom, which ran along the entire back of the house. Mattie sat down in one of the couches and opened Charlie's letter.

Darling, Another letter to let you know that I'm still alright. I've learned to relax quite a bit even though things are rather trying at times. Falling bombs and shell fire doesn't bother me near as much as it used to. I guess I've become sort of used to it and now about the only thing I worry about is when you and I'll be able to see each other.

Somebody sure talked out of turn when we were down South because the Japs know where we are at and what we are up to. About the only good station we can pick up is Radio Tokyo, and the other night Tojo made a speech beamed at us. Here's what he said, "Welcome USS Rigel to CENSORED Bay. We hope you enjoy your stay while there. Anyhow it will be a short one for we are coming in and taking over July 1st" Personally I'm not worrying a hell of a lot about anything he says, and I still think we can shoot the pants off of the Japs anytime they feel like mustering around. If you can go over there, go to Brisbane and I'm sure you'll find everything the same as the time before you and I said goodbye. Love always, Kinky

"Did you get a letter?" Arthur asked.

"Mrs Frisken posted it to me," she said, turning to front on to him. "He's in great danger."

Arthur had a blank expression on his face. "I want to talk to you."

Mattie motioned for her father to sit alongside her but he remained standing.

"Can I see his letter?"

Mattie hesitantly handed it over. He unhurriedly read it. "The contents are a wake-up call as to what you're getting yourself into, young lady." He handed the letter back to her. "You know, Mattie, words are a cheap commodity, they don't always become true. Deeds are precious."

Mattie rose to be opposite him. "I want your permission to get engaged."

"I beg your pardon?"

"Charlie… he wants to ask your permission," she pulled out his previous letter in her pocket inviting her to Australia. "Look, Father," she passed him the letter.

Arthur skimmed over the words. Mattie felt horribly vulnerable, almost invaded; watching him handle her loved one's chosen words.

"He's at war," Arthur said without looking up from the letter.

"But surely, Father, you can give your permission?"

"If God is willing…?" he frowned, now staring at Mattie. "What does he know about God?"

Mattie pressed her trembling lips together for control. "A lot more than most people. He carries his religion right here," she pressed her chest. "I love him, Father."

Arthur folded the letter back to her, and stepped away. "I can see you're determined," he sighed.

"Yes, Father. Australia is so close. I can fly over there."

"I'll make inquiries into this clipper he's talking about. You do what you think is best. It is your life. We won't stop you."

Mattie nervously shuffled the letters. It felt like bombs were falling on her. Arthur laid a hand on her shoulder which startled Mattie; he rarely touched her. "Think hard, it's your decision. But sometimes things are not always as they seem." He smiled.

"Thank you, Father."

•　　　•　　　•　　　•　　　•

The following day Mattie walked into the Otago Daily Times office. The pungent tang of ink laced with grime distracted her, but she forced herself to concentrate. She thoughtfully dictated the notice of their engagement. The same inky oil bouquet greeted her at the second newspaper, the Evening Star. *Mattie Blanc and Warrant Officer Charles Kincaid announce their engagement...*

But when Mattie returned home her mother was waiting for her.

"You slipped out this morning before you could tell me everything on Australia, what's all this about Mattie?"

Mattie knew at once; disapproval was always brewing to stick between them. She realized it was never going to work.

"He has to come here," Mary pleaded.

CHAPTER 49

The amphibious operations were proving exhausting for Charlie and his diving gang. They were underwater more than they were above. Sharks feasted on the sailors' body parts, and nothing seemed to be scarier than the night runs. The Japanese, like the crabs, came out at night and lay low by day.

Charlie and his gang salvaged what they could from the sunken and damaged ships, along with the horror of retrieving dead bodies; tumescent cadavers with bulging eyes floated in every compartment. He'd seen enough to know that a few of the men couldn't cope with the unexpected. He imagined who would survive and who would be snuffed out like a candle. And meantime, all he could think of was Mattie, her face, her touch, and her letters. As long as there was a breath in his body, there was light… and hope for another day.

Back in his cabin at night, drunk with fever, he picked up his pen. He'd write till he died, he loved her so much. He still believed there was a chance they could meet in Australia…

Darling, I haven't heard from you in quite a while, but I'm sure you must have a few letters in the mail for me. It sure is tough loving you as I do and not being able to see you; at least they could send your mail through to me. I've got that damn fever again. I'm taking some pills that are supposed to cure me, at least they are keeping me going. I still get a fever every day or so, and boy does it make you feel lousy.

We had a gruesome job last night picking up several casualties out of about 75 feet of water. It's rather spooky diving at night especially hunting dead guys. I can't see why they want to recover bodies. I'm right in the middle of something big. I'm keeping my fingers crossed and hoping I'll be lucky enough to live through it. If I get through all right I should be seeing you either Sydney or Brisbane. Be sure before you go over to get a written permit from your folks to marry me. Darling, I love you very much and miss you terribly. If there is a God I'll be praying to him to hurry and get us together soon. Answer soon. Love always, Kinky

The fever had the better of him. Doc was the one person who seemed to understand how hard it was to go on when there was nothing but pain.

"Everyone feels like you do," said Doc in a low voice. "I'm giving you a day to get yourself back on top." He handed Charlie a bottle of pills. "No one's getting a break from the jungle. Anything can get you." He patted Charlie on the shoulder. "Take it easy. Hit the sack for a few hours. I'll cover for you."

"Thanks, Doc, you' the best."

Doc smiled at him, "Tell me about your gal."

"If you had all the time in the world, I'd tell you about the best gal a man could ever wish for."

"Bet she is." Somehow Doc was on his wavelength.

Through all the fevers, Charlie must have called out for Mattie. Doubts poured in about his life. He couldn't have her, not yet.

Mattie's subsequent letter was postmarked in Dunedin. He tore it open and grinned when he read about their engagement having been announced. But his smile dropped as he read her words...

Dearest Kinky, our engagement is to be announced in the local papers Saturday, July 24th. Somehow it doesn't feel right that you're not here with me to celebrate our new beginning. And yet I know I shouldn't write like this, but it's how I feel—lost and homesick. I don't want to go back to Auckland, but I have to. It feels hopeless loving you. I want you to know my honest feelings. You asked me to go to Brisbane, but when? How is this going to work? You have to come here. I told you that when we sat on the beach. It makes it so difficult for me. Please understand. My parents want us to get married here. That's all they ask. Please do something... please come back to me...

Goddamn...his throbbing head collapsed into rough hands, elbows firmly planted on his desk. He rubbed his temples and imagined it was Mattie's gentle touch. *How can I get back to Auckland?* He leaned back and stared into the bulkhead, wondering what could get him far away from this hellhole. The sole thing that kept him sane was the engagement notice.

I must stay calm, he determined, *write a sensible reply.* It was like taking care of his men. He had to console her, but also tell her the truth—*if I say no leave, will she stick with me?* It all seemed hard, too damned hard. But Charlie had to remind himself he was in charge.

·   ·   ·   ·   ·

He and his men loaded up their diving boat and headed north with a convoy of landing craft. On the first part of the journey, LCI *226* had instructions to transport a group of natives, sailors, and amphibious scouts to Fergusson Island, a gasoline dump for the PT boats. Halsey had ordered an invasion of Vella Lavella, a small rugged island close to Kolombangara. His intentions were to outflank the enemy and disrupt their supply line. The island was thick with dense jungle, and the beaches were separated by narrow strips of lowland.

Charlie's orders were to head north, where the Japanese forces were guarding a barge station, part of the supply chain into the Central Solomons. His team's task was to blow up the entire northern beachhead at the top of Vella Lavella near Doveli Cove.

But when they arrived at a narrow beach on Maravari, south of their destination, Charlie was horrified to find it crammed with drums, crates, men and bulldozers. He could hear the Kiwi accent for miles. No one seemed perturbed by the stinking, clinging mud and heat, because they knew it would soon be washed downstream in the afternoon's downpour.

"They're sitting ducks," said Red as they pulled up onto the beach. All was quiet, when a scream of engines circled above. A Kitty Hawk dived out of nowhere, with all six machine guns blazing up the tail of a doomed Zero streaking overhead. A loud cheer came from the men standing on the beach as a Zero exploded into flames. The Kitty Hawk rocked its wings, and they could just make out the pilot's thumbs up as it roared across the bay.

"Our boys caught that one," shouted a bystander coming towards them.

"Any chance of a cuppa?" yelled Charlie.

"Shut up, Kinks," said Vic, grimacing at Charlie's cheesy introduction. "You can't be serious."

"Come on over. We've just boiled the pot," said the New Zealander, jutting out an enormous hand. "Eric's the name."

Charlie introduced his gang, and they relaxed under the swaying palm trees, but he warily scoured the sea and sky for any further incoming misery. *Never underestimate the enemy...*

"So you gonna move these gas drums out of sight?" Charlie asked.

"Yep. But we're 35 Battalion army, not packhorses. You here to help us?"

"Nope. We're gonna give the Japs a pile of grief up north," said Charlie, swilling his tea. "Bill Smith... met him in Auckland. Is he around here?"

Eric smirked. "Don't know him." He wiped his mouth on a filthy sleeve. "There's a few of us, you know. All here to clear this shit so you blokes can land. Doubt you'll find him. We all keep our heads down and bums up gettin' these fucking supplies sorted."

Charlie stood up, handing back his cup. "Think I can pick him out of a crowd," he said, winking at his men. "Thanks for the hospitality."

"Suit yourself mate," Eric shrugged.

The assault on the northwest of the island was fated to be tricky. The Kiwis had built a jetty to speed up supply landings at Maravari. When Charlie and the rest of the convoy arrived in their landing craft, it was obvious there was work to do. They set up camp on the beachhead nearby, and began to explode fifty-pound cans of TNT into coral heads four feet under the surface to create a better landing channel. For days they practiced handling their landing craft in the new channel, and blew up any missed coral, until the rough waters of the Pacific were conquered.

On the beachfront, beneath tall coconut palms, Charlie mused at the enthusiastic Kiwi voices. Tension was building with Halsey's orders to speed up the invasion into the northern area. Beat the Japs at Marquana Bay, and force them back to Warambari Bay. Cursing filled the air, as beleaguered men vented frustration at the constant rain and heat, day and night. There was no relief in this war.

Charlie knew which local natives were running scared from the Japs, by the way they acted; and he knew a bit of Pidgin from good old Coco. Coco had warned him, some of them could be dangerous, so when it was time to make the move up to Boro in Doveli Cove, he had a good knowledge of the land and natives.

· · · · ·

Donning their jungle-green fatigues, kneepads, coral sneakers and work gloves, Charlie and his men slipped off the landing craft into the explosives-laden rubber boats, and made their way to the reef edge at Doveli Cove. The night sky hid them as they crawled over the rough coral, splashing through a foot or two of sea, each carrying 40 pounds of tetrytol. They heard a cement mixer grinding, and Jap voices carried in the night air. Charlie scanned the beach. His worst fears were confirmed: a long line of coconut palm-log huts were scarcely 50 feet away.

"We have to blow these cribs up before they spot us," said Charlie.

"We'll never make it, Kinks," said Vic shaking his head.

Charlie crawled a few feet to the adjacent crib. Fingering the connecting wire, he went on, "There's only half-inch trip wires. We should be good. Get the explosives, we're goin' in."

Working fast, they loaded the 120 rock-filled cribs with explosive packs, connecting the charges with yellow primacord fuses. Charlie heard loud voices. *Damn Vic,* he tensed, hurrying through waist-deep water. But it wasn't Vic. *What the hell?*

Charlie froze and listened.

In a perfect English accent, a voice said, "Good morning. Say, Tom, is that you?" But it wasn't morning, was it?

"Bastard Jap," Charlie whispered, grabbing at Vic's arm before he could jump up. "Shhh, we're outa here."

Crouching down to blend with the ocean, they slithered without a ripple into the water. But he caught the rustles… someone was coming after them. Excited voices wafted closer, now speaking Japanese. Charlie triggered the four-minute delay fuses and sank into the water, praying they'd have enough time.

Bullets zipped into the water. Charlie swam and swam, looking around to count his men. "Where's Red?" he asked frantically.

"Isn't he already here?" asked Moult, who was lying on his back. A huge explosion brightened the dark reef in a long-line fireball, blowing coral, bodies, and water sky high.

"We have to go back!" yelled Charlie.

Nobody objected to the return to Doveli Cove. By now, dawn was approaching and gunfire seemed to be coming from another direction. They landed, seeking cover in the dense foliage.

They heard an engine coming out of nowhere. A tank rolled over a hillock and into a clearing nearby to them. The hatch flew open and four sweat-stained men clambered out. To Charlie's astonishment, they promptly lit an alcohol burner.

"Boil that water, we haven't got all day," shouted a Kiwi accent.

They waited undercover, watching the men.

"Goddamn… it's Bill, on a tea break." Charlie stood up.

"Fuckin' hell," said Vic. "No war's gonna stop a Kiwi smoko. I'll be damned."

Charlie noticed Bill looking in their direction. Bill ran for his rifle.

"Bill, it's Charlie from Auckland. How about a cuppa before you shoot me?"

"Heard you were back here. Been lookin' for you," said Bill, watching Charlie walk towards him.

"So's the Japs... 'bout got us last night."

"Thought the Japs might have brought some grief." They smacked hands. Bill handed him a cup, but he didn't have the usual twinkle in his eye. He went on, "Bloody Japs shot one of your boys. I knew it was him. Red. The name stuck on me. Sorry, mate, but we couldn't save him." He handed Charlie the Dog Tags. "We have him up over by that reef." He pointed out towards the ocean.

Charlie looked at his Kiwi friend. They both had tears in their eyes.

•　　　•　　　•　　　•　　　•

It was their first burial on the *Rigel*. With full bugle calls of Taps calling across the waves, men stood solidly on the main deck, remembering the good times with Red. It was a wake-up to their own mortality. They knew any one of them could be next.

Mattie was always there with Charlie in spirit, like a winged angel looking down on him, sending her beautiful letters to soothe him. His black fountain pen flowed precious, calming words onto tissue-thin paper...

Dearest Mattie, I just received three letters from you and enjoyed each one very much. I'm sorry that I haven't written to you this last month. You see I couldn't because I was in the big landing up North and just got back. Right now I'm standing by to go up again.

At one time I was behind the enemy lines. By gollies I never was shot at so much in my life. I can say one thing Almighty God sure was looking out for me that time. One of my divers was killed. It looks like our respective governments don't want us to get married. I tried for leave to travel down there and marry you and was turned down flat and I've been out here almost three years. They say I'm needed up here too bad. It looks pretty bad for us, doesn't it? I don't have any idea how long the war is going to last, but from where I'm at it seems it will last forever.

Write as often as you can and I'll do the same. Love always, Kinky

CHAPTER 50

Mattie arrived back in Auckland after dark. She noticed the curtain was open by the front window as she climbed the familiar steps and opened the door to Mrs Frisken's smiling face.

She gave Mattie a reassuring hug.

"It was so sad," Mattie put her suitcase down and blew her nose. She gave Mrs Frisken a fleeting look, fighting to control the lump in her throat, "I didn't get to Australia. He let me down. There was no word. I felt such a fool."

"Oh there, there, chin up. His ship's probably left Australia. Honestly you two are like a couple of love birds trying to fly when there's war on."

Mattie blew her nose again. "I've got a cold." She smiled through a waterfall of tears. "But when I get better, I can't wait to start my new job."

"That's my girl." Mrs Frisken reached in her pocket. "I have a letter for you." Mrs Frisken moved her suitcase into the corridor. "Let me know the news, won't you?"

Mattie's eyes widened as she viewed the letter. "Can't wait to read it." She carried her bag up the stairs. She felt weary after the travel, but loved being back in her room. It reminded her of their love. Warm memories poured through her. Sitting on her bed, she opened the delicate envelope and noticed a smudged censorship stamp. The back flap was barely stuck.

Dearest Mattie, How are things with you these days? Fine I hope. I'm still alright except I miss you so damn much.

He misses me. Mattie smiled.

The day I had to say goodbye to you was the saddest in my life. It was even worse than that homesick feeling I had the first time I left home. I still don't know when we will get back down there. I sure hope it will be soon. I haven't been on liberty since the last time I was with you. I have worked every day and quite often all night.

Mattie thought, *Poor darling. He's feeling lonely like me.* She put the letter down and stared outside at the dancing trees. A feeling of anger came over her at the unavoidable misery forced upon these men. She went on reading, shaking her head in sympathy.

...a fellow can't realize what a paradise Auckland is until he spends a few months in some of the hell-holes up here. It's worse than being in the worst prison. I wonder if I'll ever be able to enjoy more of the wonderful times you and I had together? To spend an evening with you would be the greatest pleasure. There isn't any worthwhile news I'm allowed to write about so will sign off now. Love always, Kinky.

She put down the letter and walked over to the window. *I love how he writes,* she whispered, '*to spend an evening with you would be the greatest pleasure.*' She trembled with pride, thinking to herself, *I must find the courage to go on. If he can, so can I.* She had a new job, a wonderful place to live and, most of all, a safe haven, something *he* didn't have.

CHAPTER 51

It was January 13, 1944, and the *Rigel* had reached northern New Guinea and anchored at Buna. Charlie ran a comb through his hair, and stared at himself in the small mirror. *I'm as battled-scarred as this old tub.* He grinned. *Get with it, Kinky. Go see Dudley.*

He went to Captain Dudley's cabin door and knocked.

"Enter," called Dudley in a gruff voice. He was sitting at his desk, focusing through a thick haze of pipe smoke. "Up to my ass in battle plans, Kincaid. What's up?"

"My leave, sir. I have to take it. I must see my gal in Auckland."

"Hold it right there, Kincaid. We've been over this before. We have Japs comin' at us thick as flies on horseshit. You and your men are critical." Dudley plopped his pipe into a holder, lit a cigarette and offered one to Charlie. "It's damn tough loving a woman, primarily one like yours. She sounds a winner. If she's anything like you say she is, she'll wait."

Charlie nodded at the praise of her. "Hope so, sir."

"Well then, my son, you've answered your own question. No one's coming in here to take your place, at least not right now. But there are new orders coming up. Looks like we both might be leaving this old relic."

"Why do you say that, sir?"

Dudley shrugged. "Speculation. You and your team do need some time off. Until it happens, we charge on. Do our best each day. Take your men to Buna for a swim day, and don't forget the homebrew. That is all."

Charlie left, elated at the opportunity for recreation. He went straight to tell the news to the boys.

Charlie, Doc, Vic and the others landed their craft and went ashore to a sandy beach. Buna could have been paradise, with a splash of grass, palm trees and a warm sea breeze. But if you walked across to the other side of the bay, it was pure coral—a fool's paradise. But to Vic and the men, it was a chance to strip off and get into the sun and the *booze*.

"Let's hula." Vic laughed, holding up a banana leaf for cover, gyrating his hips like the best Pearl Harbor babes. He cocked a leg behind the leaf to pose for the camera.

"Here, I can do that too," said Jim, one of the new guys. He stripped and grabbed another large leaf. Naked sailors lay in the sand. Charlie rested a few feet from Doc in the shade, still a little dazed and sweaty from the malaria. Beautiful surf rolled in. It was a perfect day.

Thatched huts lined the shoreline, sitting precariously on wobbly poles; nothing seemed structurally sound. The women carried babies on their hips, their bulbous breasts swaying above their waists.

"One breast is for the piglets, and one for the child." Doc grinned.

Charlie remembered his attempt with the T-shirts. Vic noticed and gawked hungrily. Just then a jeep rolled into view down the beach. A native woman was snuggled close to a soldier.

"How the fuck did he get her?" jibed Vic, swigging down a mouthful of homebrew and handing it on.

"It has to be the jeep, 'cause he's one sorry-lookin' tadpole," drawled Crow.

"Kinks, we need to bring a jeep next mission. I got a lotta love to share," whined Vic.

"You Romeos cool off with a swim and finish the homebrew. Then we'll have a wander inland while you can still walk," teased Charlie. He lay back in the sunshine, visualizing Mattie alongside him, in her bathing suit. Her touch, her kiss. *I must get to Auckland,* he said to himself.

Further inland, a cluster of thatched huts on stilts were perched amidst broken-down vehicles lying on the hillside. Another jeep bounced by with a sailor scrunched beside a giggling, half-dressed native woman.

"I like the look of this place," said Vic, walking up to a building. "A bar in the middle of nowhere and boiling hot jeep dates. I can't believe it."

Coconut Grove Bar lodged solidly on a concrete slab. It had a thatched roof with a log for a step, and a grand entrance. On one side was a hula girl picture; on the other side was a sign that read: "Keep Out - Officer Country."

"It's deserted. We'll find another watering hole," Charlie reassured his men.

They walked along another gravel road toward the trees... and then stopped in their tracks. In front of them were rows of simple white crosses in an open field. The men stared. A horrible somber mood settled over them. Charlie removed his hat, and knelt to smooth the dirt near one of the stakes, crumbling it in his hand. Vic knelt aside him, while the others stood in silence. The stark, lonely crosses planted in foreign dirt were a grim reminder of lives instantly snuffed out in this wretched hell. It was a sobering feeling for the men, listening to the frenzied sounds of jungle life and wondering who would be next.

The moment passed, and they walked respectfully now, down the dirt track, past a pile of wrecked planes and back to the shoreline.

The sun was hanging on the horizon, backlighting the natives standing in wooden outrigger canoes, offering them a ride. Each craft was made of a dugout log with bamboo outriggers and a tightly-woven mesh deck, big enough to carry six men. The natives pushed long poles against the seabed, jabbering in Pidgin as they ferried them back to their landing craft.

"Finish the whisky, men. We'll play next time, jeep and all, promise," said Charlie.

That evening, after they boarded the *Rigel*, Doc was worried about Charlie's breathing and gave him a full medical, and then Charlie went back to his stateroom to dream.

●　　●　　●　　●　　●

"We have a meeting with the Captain, at the wardroom," said Mansbach. "New mission."

"As you were, men," said Captain Dudley. "Kincaid, there is a valued Coastwatcher surrounded by Japs up north of here. We need two volunteers to swim ashore from a sub and bring him back. It's a quick in and out."

"I'm your man. I'll take Vic. When do we leave?"

"The sub will get you within 1000 yards offshore, maybe closer. You'll be greased black. Knives only, no other weapons. Out of uniform, so stay clear of Japs. There will be a full briefing on the sub. Get Vic and your gear, and report without delay to the PT boat alongside for rendezvous with the sub. No moon tonight, perfect. See you back here tomorrow with Coastwatcher Harris. God speed."

Charlie and Vic scrambled down the ladder to the PT boat. Her two deep-throated engines blazed them up the coast. A smooth sea allowed their transfer onto the sub's slippery deck, and they were soon below.

"Welcome, Kincaid," said the sub captain. "We've been in contact with Harris: he is hidden near the beach. We can get you within maybe 500 yards of shore. He has critical documents for the war effort. You'll take waterproof satchels for his papers. Get him greased down, into a lifejacket, and back out to us. No heroes tonight. Any questions?"

"No, sir. This will be duck soup for me and Vic, no sweat."

An hour later, the sub was in position. Charlie and Vic slipped over the side with their gear and swam towards shore, while the sub exchanged signal lights with Harris in the ink-black night.

Waves lapping the shoreline masked their splashes as they crept ashore. Just up the beach they saw a fire started in a hut. Japanese chatter filled the air as the Japs prepared their dinner.

Cautiously Charlie entered the jungle with Vic close behind. A bush adjacent rustled and they froze mid-stride. "Aiyyeee!"

Charlie swung around and saw the glint of a sword slashing towards them.

"To your right," grunted Charlie.

Vic spun and grabbed the sword, using it to throw the huge Jap on his back. Charlie jumped on him and shoved two fingers up his nose and a palm over his mouth.

"Get his fuckin' sword and stab him. Stab him!"

"Choke the fucker. He's a giant," gasped Vic through clenched teeth.

Vic struggled with all his might, but this Sumo wrestler was an ox. Decisively, Charlie's stranglehold took effect. Vic forced the sword backward and thrust it up under the Jap's ribs and through his heart.

Charlie and Vic lay panting on the jungle floor, awaiting the inevitable rush of bayonets and bullets. But there was utterly silence.

And then a figure stepped out from the brush. "Great piece of work, guys. This lard ass's been stalking me for days. He's alone. Anybody for a swim?"

"Harris?" Charlie said.

"The same."

"Christ Almighty saved our souls tonight. Get stripped down and greased up. Let's have your documents," whispered Charlie. He signaled the sub with his light.

"I can swim just fine. Don't want any lifejacket keeping me on the surface if bullets start flying," complained Harris.

Like just another shadow, the three blackened figures crawled across the shoreline and slid into the lagoon. Vic and Charlie switched helping Harris with the long swim. An hour later, and their waterlogged Coastwatcher was hauled onto the sub deck.

By dawn they were back alongside the *Rigel*. They reported without hesitation to the wardroom for a debriefing.

"Welcome back, men. Very well done. Heard you had a bit of bother on the beach. Naval Intelligence will be here before long, but meantime pour you a cup of coffee. Eggs are on the way." Captain Dudley smiled.

•   •   •   •   •

The following day, when Charlie was doing his rounds, he saw the Captain in a less cheerful mood. Dudley beckoned to him.

Charlie joined him on the bridge and saluted, "Captain, did you need me?"

Dudley gripped the rail and leaned across into the quarterdeck, toward Charlie, "I'm sorry, son. I thought I was going to be able to surprise you with an officer who was to replace you. But he's only an assistant."

"How could that happen?"

"We're at war. Any unknown crap can head our way," Dudley replied, looking out to the ocean. "You should know that by now."

"Aye aye, sir."

Charlie left the bridge and retrieved another Mattie letter from the mail clerk. He was well aware her support was critical to his state of mind, and knew his reply was meant to be easy but hard loomed, draining....

Dearest Mattie, your letter dated 1944, Jan 18th has just arrived. It took about a month getting here, not bad considering where I'm at. Yes, I'm still at that God-forsaken island and the Japs still leave their calling card almost every day. My luck is still holding out and I never get more than a good scare. I guess I'm still all right except what little spirit and hope I had left has really been put to a test here lately. Remember in the last few letters of mine I spoke of getting relieved soon? Well, that seems to be another great disappointment. Plus I'm on the bottom of the list for rehabilitation leave. Mattie, isn't that enough to make a fellow say what the hell is the use of going on? Somehow, somewhere, though, I seem to find the courage and determination to carry on no matter what life holds in store for me. I'm not licked yet.

I wouldn't mind so very much if I had not fallen in love with you. Life won't mean much to me if I can't have you. It doesn't seem possible that a fellow could be stopped so completely as I am. This is a changing world and the future may not be as bad as it looks. Somehow, somewhere, we will meet again, and the joy and happiness of our reunion will make all this seem as though it never happened. I love you, Kinky.

Weeks of hot, humid repair work dragged on. Then Mansbach appeared in the passageway, beaming ear to ear. "Kincaid, Captain wants to see you in the wardroom."

Captain Dudley dropped his pen as Charlie entered. "You've passed your medical. Doc's report gave you a clear bill of health."

Charlie was puzzled. *Was that why Doc gave me that medical?*

Dudley went on. "You've made it. You're an Ensign, my son. I'm proud of you." He patted Charlie on the back. "Congratulations and well done."

Charlie stood there transfixed. "Thank you, sir," he blurted out.

"Don't thank me, thank the US Navy. It's official. Sorry there'll be no celebrations."

"No sir, I understand. No space for parties."

"Oh, hell, forget all that official crap. Tell me about your gal."

"Well sir, I met her in Auckland. She's beautiful inside and out."

Dudley smiled. "Great gals down there. Hard to get both sides right. Had my fair share of pretty outside, but the inside required some work." He walked towards the door, shook Charlie's hand, and winked. "Don't worry, she'll wait."

Charlie grinned and left the wardroom. He smiled to himself, a proud Navy officer. He had travelled a long way from the faded memories of a dustbowl orphanage.

Vic and the other divers stood gawking, huddled close at hand.

"Hope you're still gonna tend the still," Andy hollered with a smile.

"You'll make the best Ensign ever," said Vic. "This is the moment you've been working for, don't I just know it!"

They stood on the deck for a while. Vic continued with Charlie, "I'll dive for you any day, Kinks, any day. But remember who you are. Don't chase that impossible dream. We gotta job to do."

·   ·   ·   ·   ·

While the men were preparing for another invasion Dudley called Charlie to the wardroom. "New orders. You have been assigned to temporary duty."

Charlie gulped at the possibility of Auckland, his heart racing.

"Don't get excited, Kincaid, it's just a week… and it's top secret. You will proceed via a vessel alongside at 0600 hours on 8 October, verbally designated to report to the Material Officer of our Seventh Amphibious Fleet." Dudley went on, "There'll be no questions asked. Do not talk to your men, and specifically do not write anything about this to that dame of yours. Do I make myself clear?"

"Yes, sir."

"I will make arrangements for your men. You're on sick leave. Prepare for pick-up."

"Aye aye, sir."

CHAPTER 52

Warm spring days enticed the daffodils to peek their heads out in the gardens of quaint villas across the street, framing a grand view down the valley.

Mrs Marshall had now moved her shop into the corner site at the top of Karangahape Road in Ponsonby, offering a new range of services to elite clientele. A vase of apple blossoms welcomed people into the foyer, and a sweet essence drifted from a glass cabinet of products.

Mrs Marshall greeted Mattie with a cheery smile as she entered. "Hello, Mattie. It's your first day. Welcome! We have you half-booked with new clients. The rest of the day you can assist."

As the days passed, Mattie began to feel part of the small salon. Kath chatted constantly. Her intimate, warm nature gave Mattie a comfortable feeling, as if Kath could sense her thoughts, especially when they talked about Mattie's love for Charlie.

"We're going to have so much fun," said Kath, with a twinkle in her eye. "I have the car tonight. Want to come home for dinner?"

"I'd love to, but really, I'm such a bore."

"No you're not." Kath smiled. "Do you good, girl."

Mattie slipped into Kath's car and they drove to Onehunga. The ride was pleasant, the evenings were becoming lighter; but daylight was not much help to Kath's old Dodge as it labored up the hill.

"I'm supposed to take this out only on Red Cross days, but Dad won't mind," she chortled. "Not when I'm bringing a new guest home."

Quadrant Road was home to predominantly weatherboard houses, with balconies under plain eaves. There was none of the Victorian splendor of Huntly House. Kath's home was on a hill over huge gardens, facing Manukau Harbor. A breeze off the harbor caught Mattie's curls as they stepped out of the car and walked up the stairs to the wooden veranda. Kath opened the front door, and they walked inside to the wide passageway.

"Got someone for you to meet, Dad," said Kath, swinging her handbag.

A man who appeared to be in his late sixties, sat hunched by the bay window with a rug over his knees. He seemed to have trouble turning his head; his eyes rotated up and across at Mattie.

"I'm Mattie. I work with your daughter."

"Well, that's nice to hear. We haven't much, but you're welcome to it. Take a seat," he replied, looking back out at the harbor. "They say our supplies are arriving late this month."

"You always say that, Dad," replied Kath, taking Mattie's coat to loop it onto a hall tree. "My family has a furniture shop in Pitt Street," she told Mattie. "But Dad's health is not the best right now."

"Let's hope your Dad is better soon," Mattie smiled, and went with Kath to help with dinner. A clock ticked atop a carved mantelpiece over the stone fireplace, reminding her of home in Dunedin, as they ate.

After dinner, Kath drove Mattie home. Kath interrupted the silence in the car. "Sorry Dad's a bit abrupt. He's had a heart attack, maybe worse—and Mum's taken off with another man."

"Oh, your poor dad. I'm sorry to hear that. How are you coping?"

"I'm OK, just keeping Dad comfortable." She winked at Mattie, "It's war and we have to think of other things."

"Yes, we do."

"But can't all be sad," Kath's face brightened. "We're having a big bash at home next weekend. Would you like to join in?"

"I don't know, Kath. I don't get out much, sorry," replied Mattie, trying to appear interested.

They fell silent for awhile till Mattie motioned at her to drive up the hill to Huntly House.

"Wow, what a mansion. What's it like living here?"

Mattie smiled. "It's wonderful. I'm very happy here."

"I should say so." Kath's warm smiling eyes returned to Mattie. "Go on, Mattie, have a little fun… Your man won't mind."

"I'll think about it," Mattie said with a slight frown. She flushed remembering Charlie's warm, naked body—and jumped out to quell her desires. Before she closed the car door, she said, "Thank you for bringing me home. Would you like to come in for a cup of tea?"

Kath still had the engine running, not wanting to risk a temperamental Dodge. "It's a bit late. I'll get into trouble. Another day?"

"It's a date," said Mattie closing the car door. She stood waving her goodbye and ran up the pathway and closed the door. She walked down the passageway, deliberately looking around to see if Mrs Frisken was still up. She scanned the breakfast room and spotted the letter on the mantelpiece. She leaped up the stairs two at once, clutching the precious letter.

Mattie collapsed onto the bed, her heart racing, eager to read every word. As she opened it, she noticed that again the back flap was moist, wondered briefly why, but couldn't wait to read...

My Dearest Mattie, I just received your letter telling me that you had arrived back in Auckland. I was terribly sorry to know that you have been ill and I wish you could have stayed at home. Honey, you must take better care of yourself. I don't know what I would do if anything should happen to you. I want you to stay the way you were when I said goodbye to you, beautiful and healthy.

He's a sweetheart. Every word was like he was there, stroking her...

Up until now I was in a position where I could get some leave. From the way things are shaping up it looks like all my plans will be shot to hell.

Her face fell. '*Plans... shot to hell...*' She felt his panic turn into her panic.

From a few of the jobs my divers and I have accomplished recently they have decided we are indispensable up at the fighting front. We actually spend more time under water than above it. We now have our own diving boat, and I'm the skipper of it. The thing that is tough about it is we have to go along with the invasion forces and try to salvage what equipment that is damaged in the landing. Our diving boat is equipped with two 50-calibre machine guns and I now have eight divers instead of five. We call ourselves the shoestring divers for our lives just about hang from a shoestring. We may last all the way up, who knows? At least I'm not gambling on it.

I guess I shouldn't write like this but I feel you should have a fair idea of what I've got myself into so that if anything should happen to me it won't be too much of a shock to you. I'm fixing it so that in case I don't get back from one of my trips a shipmate will write you and give you what dope he can. If his letter doesn't arrive and you don't hear from me in about two months after my last letter I will probably have had an accident.

Mattie stared. 'An accident?' What was he trying to say? Mattie had to say the words again, "An accident. Oh, my God! No, Kinky, not you." Her tears disastrously flooded onto his letter, blurring the writing. She collapsed onto the bed, hysterical sobbing taking its dreadful toll. Gradually, she willed herself to a whimper, and then lifted the letter. She had to read the rest of it.

Darling, remember I love you and I hope with all my heart that everything will turn out for the best. I promise to write every chance I get. I believe in that old saying: 'It is better to have loved and lost than never loved at all.' So if I have to go...

He was telling her it was over. Their love was over. Mattie couldn't believe it. She clung to her pillow as though it was Charlie himself. Her eyes darted over his last few words—sad words, on a pathetic piece of paper.

It will be with the consolation that I've had almost everything out of life a man could ask for except a couple of children to carry on my name. My love always, Kinky.

Mattie lay there stunned. A shoestring diver? She reread his words intently, desperately. She closed her eyes: She envisaged him out at sea with his men. Their lives, my life, hang on a shoestring. He wants me to forget him. She didn't have any more tears to cry.

CHAPTER 53

Charlie couldn't believe how swiftly the tides of war had changed. He boarded the tender and travelled across Buna harbor to the USS *Blue Ridge*. He was ushered to the wardroom, where an officer greeted him.

"Good morning, Kincaid, we're glad to have you. Congratulations on becoming an Ensign."

"Thank you, sir." The officer was familiar to Charlie from his last mission. He had no rank and didn't offer identification. He went on, "We need someone to get ashore at two beaches in Hollandia, north of here, reconnoiter and report back. This is past the Japs' 18th Regiment at Wewak, so you'll be deep into enemy territory. The *River Snake* is for transport. It is a purpose-built Chinese junk for commando raids that we've borrowed from the Aussies. You'll be blackened and will sail with a mostly native crew, so you should be able to get right up their noses, no sweat. No uniform; no Dog Tags. If the Japs get you, it will be torture and death. Are you ready for this?"

"I'm ready for anything. When do I leave?"

"Put your personal effects in your cabin, but don't unpack. Everything you need is on the *River Snake*. You'll depart tonight on the PT boat alongside. Leave your uniform with them when you rendezvous; you'll be given clothes. You'll have the latest directional S-phone on the junk, so radio us at once when you finish and are back onboard the *River Snake*. This mission is absolutely critical to the war effort. The Marines are counting on you. God be with you. That is all."

"Aye aye, sir." Charlie saluted, and went back to his cabin.

He settled into his chair, staring at Mattie's letters and picked up her photo. He slipped off his Dog Tags and fingered the little Mizpah medallion. *Mattie darlin', someway, somehow... I will come back to you*, he said to himself.

After steak supper, Charlie stepped aboard the PT boat and they raced north. It was after midnight when he heard the PT boat's engines idle back. Her crew scurried about the decks, making lines ready. Charlie went topside, there was the *River Snake* outlined by the moon, bobbing like a cork in frothing seas.

"Kincaid, stand by to jump when we are close. The seas are too heavy to tie up to her," yelled the PT boat captain.

Moments later, Charlie saw his chance, and leaped. Memories flooded back of a similar jump, long ago, into a Mississippi boxcar. Charlie hurriedly removed his uniform and threw the bundle back onto the fantail of the departing PT boat.

A boisterous Aussie officer handed him a thong and a tee shirt. "Gidday mate, I was hoping it was you."

"Briggs, fantastic. You're a long way from Townsville. Show me your boat."

"She's a beauty, looks like a Chinese junk, but she's loaded with secret compartments in case you're boarded. Follow me."

Charlie and Briggs meticulously worked their way through the boat, uncovering the Oerlikon 20mm, two 50-calibre machine guns, and a few carbines and pistols.

Briggs went on, "But here's the real prize. It's a new S-phone radio. She's highly directional, so just point towards where you want to transmit; no worries about the Japs listening in. Your crew are Aborigines. They're fully trained to run and maintain this boat. The Japs won't know the difference. To them, they're just natives. There's your partner coming on another PT boat. I can hear its engines. Take care of yourself. See you again in Brisbane. We blew the living shit out of a whole pile of Jap ships in Singapore Harbor using the *Krait*. You can do the same. Good luck, I'm jumpin' off now."

The PT boat pulled alongside, and another fuzzy-headed native jumped onto the *River Snake*.

"You didn't think you were gonna have all this fun without me, didja?"

Charlie stared at the black native. The voice and eyes seemed very familiar. A sudden shitbird smile gave him away.

"Vic... you're a sight for sore eyes. Sure as hell needed some help on this one. What gives with the haircut?"

"They dyed us these clown wigs black. Can't wait to try my luck in this with the Buna jeep date."

"No chance for any lovin' now. Let's get below and go over the mission," said Charlie.

They met all the native crew, and deliberately made their way through the boat. The *River Snake* plodded its way up the New Guinea coast, and arrived off Humboldt Bay the following night. Charlie spoke to the head Aborigine. "Well done. We'll slip over the side here. We have all we need in these satchels. Return here at this same time tomorrow night. We'll use a signal light from the beach."

Charlie and Vic slowly swam through the bay towards the inside lagoon. Obstacles glistened below in the moonlight, and they diligently noted everything on their chalkboards. Like jungle pythons, they slithered onto the beach and crawled cautiously towards the dense jungle. Once under the bush, they buried their fins and masks, and changed into wigs and sandals for the journey up into the hills.

"Fuckin' hell, Kinks. I can smell Japs everywhere," whispered Vic.

"Quiet. Keep your head down."

Steadily they made their way through the jungle, staying off trails, until they arrived at an outcrop that overlooked the whole bay.

"OK, here we go. I'll take the binoculars and call out positions. You make notes on the chart," said Charlie.

"Fire away, Kinks, let's get this done. This place is spooky and my wig itches something fierce."

Morning came, and they moved into jungle farther uphill, still with a view of the bay. Charlie and Vic spent the day noting all Japanese and native activity.

A fireball sun was quickly dropping when Vic suggested, "Steak for dinner tonight?"

"Open a can, smart guy. We have two hours before we head down to the beach for pickup. So eat, drink, and crap in a deep hole."

Darkness fell ominously, as thick clouds obscured a golden moon. They cautiously made their way off the hill, staying to the deep gullies and secluded from any other humans. Hours later, arriving at the beach, they recovered their fins and masks, and Charlie signaled with his light. The *Snake* answered from the lagoon.

The Aborigines helped them aboard the boat, and then urgently got underway.

Charlie went to the bridge and spoke to the head man, "You did well, Captain. Now we're headed up the coast to Tanamerah Bay." He knew this man was not a captain, but he did the job as good as any.

"You mean we're not done?" complained Vic.

"One more bay, big boy, then we'll get you the jeep on Buna."

"You think the *Krait* had it this easy?"

"We were lucky, very, very lucky. The *Krait* scored; we can do the same," cautioned Charlie. "Captain, take the long way to Tanamerah. Vic and I need a hot dinner and a long sleep. Be there tomorrow night... same drill."

Charlie went below and radioed *Blue Ridge* their findings for Humboldt Bay. Sleep was difficult in a small boat on the open ocean, but Charlie and Vic were exhausted and they were both seasoned sailors. They awoke late the following morning to the smell of ham and eggs.

"Holy cow, Kinks, get up. We're on a cruise ship."

"Tanamerah Bay is not going to be easy," warned Charlie. "Our subs are reporting that its open kunai grass beyond the beach at this bay. We'll be totally exposed. There's a small beach on the open coast nearby that looks better, but it still has several native huts in the area. Get some rest. We'll need guts and muscle for this one," he told Vic.

Night fell, and they eased their way close to the shoreline. "Captain," Charlie told the head man, "might be good if you can hang around closer to the coast for this one. May need to finish up quick—you never know."

They slipped over the side into the calm, dark sea. They spotted a small fire near the native huts ashore; they headed to the opposite end of the beach. About halfway to shore, the low groundswell boosted them atop heavy breakers, and they were surfing over an unseen reef.

"Vic, are you OK?" whispered Charlie into the blackness.

"What a ride! We won't be bringing any troops onto this beach," answered Vic.

"Don't worry, there's no reef at Tanamerah Bay next door."

Like seals, they swam across the lagoon without another ripple, crawled up the beach and, haltingly, into the dense jungle.

"Bury our gear while I signal the *Snake*. We gotta get up this hill before dawn," breathed Charlie.

By first light, they had again located an ideal vantage point that provided sweeping views of the coast and Tanamerah Bay.

"Vic, pass me the binoculars. I want to check out these boats," asked Charlie.

"Hope our guys headed out to sea. This place is lousy with Japs."

"Shhh... Shit, I see the *Snake*. She's about 3 miles out, and got her poles rigged out for fishing.

"Excellent, fish for dinner."

"Oh crap. There's a Jap patrol boat headed her way. Didn't count on trouble at sea," whispered Charlie. "Make notes on the chart of all the Japs and natives on the mountain, best you can. We may be hightailing it out of here in a hurry. I need to keep an eye on our boat."

Charlie systematically had a look down the mountain, and gave Vic coordinates of enemy positions, all the while checking back on the two boats.

An hour later, Charlie said, "The Jap patrol boat just came alongside and they're boarding. Our crew have their hands up. This is tragic."

"Those Abos are tough. Don't worry."

"They're beating the shit out of our Captain. There's a pile of Japs in the pilothouse. Bet they're trying to start it. Fuckin' hell! They just shot our captain in the head and threw him overboard. Bet he didn't tell about the kill switch. They're herding the crew onto the patrol boat and rigging a line to tow the *Snake*. Shit... there goes our ride home."

Charlie grabbed the chart and started mapping their escape. Vic picked up the binoculars. "Kinks, they're towing her into Tanamerah Bay. Those animal bastards. They're shooting our crew, one by one, and dumping them on the way in."

The Jap patrol boat gradually brought the *River Snake* into the bay. Swarms of sailors ransacked the boat. Both boats lay at anchor, until fortunately, in late afternoon, the Jap patrol boat hoisted anchor and left for sea.

Charlie stared through the binoculars. "Looks like they've finished stealing lord knows what off the *Snake*. There's a couple of Jap guards still on board. We're gonna go down there tonight, and get our boat back. I know how to start it. Are you with me?" asked Charlie.

"Kinks, I'll be at your side no matter what. Reckon I can get us through that kunai on our bellies, just like a Florida gator," replied Vic.

"Good man. We'll take turns watching the *Snake*. We need to be sure who's on board. Check out this Jap. He's got buck teeth and thick glasses, just like in the cartoons."

Darkness fell abruptly. Fortunately, thick clouds hovered for a black night; no stars, no moon.

"Hey Kinks, we're gonna need your night eyes to get us off this mountain," said Vic.

"Yeh. And we're gonna need your redneck nose to sniff out these peckerwoods below us. Pack up. We gotta date on the *Snake*."

Step by step, Charlie and Vic wound their way down the hillside jungle, many times testing a foothold before landing. Not a twig was broken until they reached the large patch of kunai grass at the bottom.

"Ok, gator boy, show me your belly-crawl. Stop when we get to the beach. We'll need to blacken up again," whispered Charlie,

Like prowling reptiles, Charlie and Vic snaked their way into the kunai. It was as if the grass tips were slowly swayed by a breeze. At the edge of the sandy beach, Charlie quietly pulled the binoculars out of his satchel.

"No sign of life on the *Snake*. Excellent. Tide is ebbing. We'll slice their Jap throats, and then hoist the anchor without a sound. The tide will carry us out; we'll start the engine later. Blacken up, ditch the wig, and let's get 'em."

Without the smallest ripple, they moved towards the *Snake*.

"We'll go up over the stern together."

The *Snake* was riding lazily at anchor, the sea's rhythmic wavelets lapping at her sides. Charlie and Vic hoisted themselves onto the stern platform, perfectly synchronized with the boat's natural motion. Stepping over the gunwale, they waited, frozen, for the excess water to drop. Swiftly they crept forward, one up the starboard side, the other portside. Hand signals flowed: they knew where to go, the bunks.

They followed the snoring. The *Snake*'s American steaks washed down with ample sake had put these Japs blissfully into dreamland. Charlie and Vic's two razor-sharp diver's knives sliced their necks. There was a soft gurgling of lungs deflating, and final pulsing of blood.

Charlie and Vic met topside and crept to the bow. Softly, ever so quietly, they worked to pull in the anchor by hand. Any noise from an anchor winch would risk alerting people on shore. Increasingly, the anchor line became almost vertical; but it was well stuck in the seabed.

"Vic, when the bow drops, pull in the slack and tie it off. The boat will break it loose when she heaves back up."

Sure enough, the anchor broke loose, and they silently lifted it. Suddenly there was a flash of steel.

"Uggghhhh…," Vic bellowed as a sword cut through his gut.

Charlie was around and behind the Jap officer in an instant, cutting his neck almost to the backbone. The Jap fell, a limp body with its head hinged backwards, its grisly open neck spouting blood.

"Vic… Oh dear God, not you, Vic, not you." Charlie pulled out the sword. Maybe it was a lucky strike and had missed anything vital. He picked Vic up and carried him down to the captain's cabin. He grabbed the medicine kit, sprinkled Sulpha on the wound, put compresses front and back, and taped him up hard to stop the bleeding.

Charlie rushed forward and properly secured the anchor. The *River Snake* was riding well on the ebbing tide, now almost at the entrance of the bay. He looked back. It was still too soon to start engines.

He went back down below. "Vic, can you hear me?"

"Hey, Kinks, my gut… aspirin…," wailed Vic.

"Aspirin's not a good idea, but I'll give you a shot of morphine. I'm gonna start the engines and get you back to Doc." Charlie jabbed the morphine into Vic, and pulled two blankets over his shivering form.

He shot back up to the pilothouse, reached inside the wall, flipped the kill switch, and the Gardner diesel roared to life. He studied the sky for bearings, and set a course out to sea. The Japs had stripped out the compass and autopilot, taken all charts, guns, and the precious radio, so it was just him and the stars.

Once Charlie was well out of Jap territory, he throttled back, tied off the helm, and went to Vic. Charlie could draw no response from him. He found a mirror and held it to Vic's face. There was no breath to fog the mirror… no pulse. Vic's body was cold, stone cold. Charlie knew his best friend was lost. He used all his strength to carry him onto the deck and placed him on a canvas sail, with an iron vice and old cannonball he found below. He laced this final package together and hoisted it onto the gunwale.

"Vic, I'll miss you more than the Lord allows. My religion is in my heart… right alongside you. I know God already has you on the Buna jeep in heaven. We'll meet again… I know we will," Charlie said, and he lowered his friend into the waiting sea.

His boat meandered, but he knew to head east, beyond range of the Japs. He had no idea where he was. He used the last food scraps as bait and caught several fish, but his fever was building again. He tragically knew he'd lost his mate and their mission was a failure.

·　　·　　·　　·　　·

As days passed aboard the fake junk, memories of his girl faded. Charlie fought to stay alive but, somehow, everything reflected off the calm ocean like a silent wavering movie; his life was slipping away. His mouth grew parched and cracked in the unrelenting sun. Without medication Charlie was soon delirious from his malaria. He lay for days, till a sudden downpour soothed his aching mouth. He had rigged a canvas tarp to funnel precious rainwater into containers.

One afternoon, he saw what seemed at first a mirage, something dancing, waving on the horizon. He had little fuel left, but he altered course towards this ghost. It was starting to look progressively like a ship. Stumbling below deck, he brought up a metal drum and a handful of oily rags. He pushed the drum towards the bow and pulled out one of his last remaining matches. BOOM: the rags ignited with a flare. He crawled for the metal cover… *need smoke, not fire*… and managed to drag the lid half on before he collapsed.

CHAPTER 54

Months had passed without word. Mattie sent letter upon letter with no reply. Simply the warmth of Mrs Frisken's hot tea and kind words of encouragement helped her bear the anguish.

Working at Mrs Marshall's kept her spirits up, and Kath had persuaded Mattie to volunteer with the Red Cross transport, a subsidized use for Kath's otherwise sidelined car. They often went down to the dockside to pick up wounded soldiers on the way home from work. But today was different.

Kath put her arm around Mattie. "Let's hurry, Mattie, I have a few amazing friends you should meet."

The two women hurried to the car. Having Kath as a friend was wonderful. Irene was good, but Irene was family, like a required friend maybe. Kath was becoming a real friend. They drew up by the dockside. This time it wasn't the wounded but a sea of happy faces that peered into their car window.

"How many can you take?" asked one of them. Mattie noticed the thick trench coat of the New Zealand soldier and a shiver went up her spine. She snapped herself out of it and smiled across at the men.

"Shove over, Mattie; we've room for one in the front, three in back, and one in the boot if we're lucky." Kath lit a cigarette, roared the engine, and raced up the hill. They chugged to a stop up Quadrant Road. Kath waited for her passengers to get out and turned quickly, handing Mattie a flask of whisky. "Here, get this down you, girl."

The front door opened and a crowd of faces appeared.

"Hey, Kath, great party you got going on," said a man in uniform. His American accent startled Mattie.

"Sorry, Mattie, I forgot to tell you, the Red Cross dropped off a dozen sailors."

"How do you, ma'am," said the American. Mattie shook his hand demurely. She couldn't deal with his face. His voice only made her sick inside.

It was party time in the main room. Someone on the piano was trying to tinker out tunes, tunes that haunted Mattie. She downed another Scotch and willed herself to relax, *stop being a prude*. She began to tap her high heels to the music and naturally rocked her hips. A welcome hand snaked around her middle.

"Well, who's your pretty friend?" asked a brown face.

"Oh, Mattie darling, this is my cousin, Moana. The Maori Battalion boys let him out for good behavior. He won't harm you."

"Just call me Mo." The soldier winked, with a hungry smile.

Mattie gulped another swig of whisky. The room was swaying to the music, as arms and hands drifted on her. The music stirred something within her. She started to boogie, joining in, and singing to the music. She didn't mind the hot whisky breath warming her neck. One partner blurred into another.

Mattie missed a man's touch. The music set her mind and feet spinning. A strong arm slid around her delicate waist and pulled her into him, gyrating. If she closed her eyes, it all came back to her. She swayed to the beat and her body responded to his rhythm. Her loneliness drifted elsewhere to meet him, welcome him…

Mattie woke up next morning not knowing where she was. She heard *snoring*… A bedraggled soldier was lying across the passageway. She sat bolt upright and froze at the sight of her disheveled clothes. She was still wearing them, although they felt strangely out of position, as though someone else had dressed her. She went to find Kath.

"What happened last night?" Mattie said, rubbing her throbbing head.

"No more hot toddies for you." Kath handed Mattie a cup of warm milk.

"Ugh!" Mattie grimaced.

"It'll settle your stomach. We have to be at work in an hour. You won't make it looking like that," said Kath, bursting into laughter. "Doesn't it make you feel human when you've had a taste of fun?"

Mattie's gaze lingered at her curiously. "Who's that slob in the passageway?"

Kath raised one long penciled eyebrow, and burst into raucous laughter. "I'm sorry, but the look on your face. He's one of your friends from last night. We got drinking and couldn't drive him. Now hurry up, we have to drop him off on the way... can't be late for work."

She had never put in such a long day. Every curler she rolled onto a client's hair with her aching fingers seemed to throb in step with her pounding head. Finally, thankfully, Kath dropped her by Huntly House on her way to dockside. Mattie went up to her room and sank onto the bed.

CHAPTER 55

"Hello, sailor. Wake up... wake up."

"Ohhhhh... my head." Charlie squinted into the bright light. "Where am I?"

"We saw your fire. You're safe on the Dutch freighter *Weltevreden*. Who are you?"

Charlie opened his eyes and stared at a white face above him. He moaned, hardly opening his parched lips.

"We're heading to San Francisco... It sounds like that's home for you, sailor. Right?" asked the ship's medical assistant, lifting Charlie's head for a drink of water.

Charlie shook his head, staring vacantly. He couldn't remember a thing.

•　　　•　　　•　　　•　　　•

Weeks went by before the ship subsequently docked in San Francisco. Charlie was immediately transported to the 12th Naval District Hospital for assessment.

"Hello, sailor, we almost lost you to malaria. What's your name?" asked the Navy nurse.

"My head... I can't remember much of anything, ma'am." Charlie scratched his tousled hair.

"You still have a fever. Hold out your right hand. Let's get your fingerprints away to the FBI so we can see who you are," she answered and left him lying there.

Dazed and incoherent, Charlie lay in his hospital bed, unable to make any sense of the world about him. Steadily, snatches of memories flashed through his mind: dusty roads, cotton fields, underwater compartments, and, most often, a beautiful, blue-eyed woman with silken black hair.

Early one morning, a nurse came running to his bedside. "We found you: Ensign Charles Kincaid. You're a long way from your ship. Navy Personnel have been notified."

"Yes, Kincaid. That might be right. Can I see my records?" said Charlie.

"Navy Intelligence is sending someone over to talk with you. We've been instructed not to ask you about your past. Meanwhile, the doctor wants you wheeled outside in a wheelchair for a dose of sunshine. Security will be here shortly to help." The nurse smiled. "Congratulations... and welcome back."

Charlie felt like a new man in the fresh air and warm sun, surrounded by other patients basking in the floral gardens.

When Charlie was wheeled back, a Navy officer was waiting in his room. "Ensign Kincaid, glad to have you back. Nurse, can we be left alone?" The nurse closed the door and he continued, "You are one of our best navy divers and we thought you'd been lost behind enemy lines. You will gradually start to recall who you are, and what you were doing in the Pacific. As you remember, it is absolutely critical that you never talk about your missions to anyone. I know you're not feeling all that well yet, but you can understand and remember what I'm saying, correct?"

"Yes, sir. That explains my memory flashes of being underwater... and Japs killing like crazy," whispered Charlie. "You can count on me, no talkin'. Can I get some sleep? I'm bushed."

For days the room seemed to move in all directions, until one morning, bright sunlight streamed through the window. Charlie opened his eyes wide, and rose up.

I have to get out of here and tell her, Charlie said to himself.

Charlie threw back the bed covers. He viewed the papers on his bedside table. "Navy orders me to report."

He went to his closet and spotted the new uniform. Gingerly he slipped into everything and adjusted the Ensign cap on his head. He grabbed his orders and headed out the door.

•　　　•　　　•　　　•　　　•

At the Twelfth Naval District Headquarters, the officer spoke in an officious, almost critical tone: "We'll let Naval Personnel know you've reported for duty. Your orders, uniforms, Dog Tags, and personal effects will be here soon from the Pacific. That is all."

Charlie remembered no one was to know about his missions. But by the tone of this officer, he was just another sailor reporting in. He finished the procedure, hastily made his way out of the office, and sent a wire to Auckland, Huntly House, to a Miss Mattie Blanc: *I'm alive.* He tried to make sense of his orders: *You are hereby detached. Proceed to Montauk Torpedo Base.*

•   •   •   •   •

Holding his orders he boarded a train bound for New York. It was the hardest thing to do, to recognize his failure as a man, his failure as a shipmate. He needed to write to the most beautiful woman in the world. But what would she think of him? How could he explain what had become of him? Maybe he could write something about his rescue... but would she believe him?

With his fountain pen steadied, he began to write.

Dearest Mattie: I'm awful sorry that I've been unable to write to you in so long a while. I must have caused you no end of worry...

But his pen dropped and he drifted off into a deep sleep, lulled by the clickety rhythm of railcar wheels bounding over track joints. He rocked and rumbled against the carriage seat, and dreamed he was back in Auckland.

A voice spoke. Charlie haltingly opened his eyes to a white uniform. "Mattie," he exclaimed out loud.

"There's no Mattie here, Mr Kincaid," said an American accent. "You're in Montauk Manor Hospital. You were picked up from a train and brought here according to your orders."

"But I've been lost at sea. I need to find my gal."

The nurse smiled. "Yes... and you need to rest."

Charlie jerked his head and scanned the room. The light almost blinded him. His hand trembled. He gripped the sheets. His body shook, and seemed to lift away from him. Vic was calling him out at sea. *I must go... where is my uniform?* He fell back and tried again. He imagined voices... familiar voices. Then he drifted again, back to his beautiful azure blue sea with beckoning fingers of foam.

When he awoke, he jolted up, startled, and walked over to his desk. He couldn't believe it—his Dog Tags, Mattie's pendant, his fountain pen. Her letters and photos were all intact, even his unfinished letter. He picked up his pen and poured out his heart…

It was not because I never wanted to write to you but I was unfortunate enough to run into a little tough luck. Last January… we ran into a little trouble… I love you so very much… Kinky.

He dressed in his uniform, grabbed his orders, and trudged onwards to find Base Headquarters.

"Ensign Kincaid, welcome to Montauk Torpedo Base. I'm Commanding Officer W R Parker. At ease, as you were. You've been on quite an adventure." Everything about Commander Parker was huge. He gestured to Charlie to sit, offering him a cigar.

Long, tall Texan, Charlie thought to himself, balancing as he eased himself into one of the wooden chairs. "No thanks, Commander." He half-smiled, and took out one of his own cigarettes to calm his nerves.

Parker scanned the pages in front of him and slowly looked up, "So you handle explosives?" He leaned back with a smirk, balancing an arm on the side of the chair. "Quite a record you have, son."

Charlie studied his close-cropped, iron-grey hair and false smile, and watched Parker scratch his wide jaw as he casually chomped on an unlit cigar. He disliked being called son by Parker, and replied, "I've been in combat, sir, for three years. And yes sir, blew up a few Japs." He recalled Vic wincing as the sword pierced him.

"Well, the Navy's having trouble with their torpedoes. Gonna put you in command of the diving tender, YDT-4, so you can help out."

"Thank you, sir… will do my best."

"We need better than your best, Kincaid. See that Stetson sitting on the file cabinet?" Parker grinned.

"Yes, sir, it's a real beauty."

"This war is *inconvenient*, yep, damn right inconvenient. Your job is to retrieve those torpedoes after a test so we can get 'em working and blow the living shit out of anything Japanese. Then I can get back in my Stetson and be home in Texas chasing skirts like I should be. Get it, Kincaid?"

"Aye aye, sir. I get the idea completely."

Parker cut the conversation off and stood up to gaze through the window, jingling the change in his pockets. Charlie rose to join him.

"Better get yourself acquainted with that there Navy resort up on Signal Hill." Parker pivoted. "That's adjacent to your new quarters." His false smile widened, "Complete with indoor movies, shows, dancin'. We got some corralling to do up there, boy... if you like the ladies."

"I'm an engaged man, sir."

"Engaged?" He grinned, inadvertently eyeing Charlie's papers. "Young buck like you should be sowing wild oats."

Charlie ignored his comment. "Aye, sir. Permission to leave, sir?" He saluted and left the office, picked up his belongings and headed up the hill. *What an asshole. Can't wait to get on board my tender.* He smiled inside at the idea of being back on the job.

Montauk Manor seemed to Charlie like an enormous replica of the flash English homesteads he'd seen in New Zealand. Perhaps if he closed his eyes, he could pretend it was Huntly House with her huge chimneys puffing madly. Its stucco walls towered above him as he walked closer to the arched concrete entranceway. An empty wheelchair swung amuck knocking against one of the pillars. He brushed past it. His eyes searched up at the cracked timber of the Tudor ceiling. Down the arched open passageways, he listened to women's American voices. He remembered Roxy for some reason.

He walked into the office, and announced, "Morning ladies, I'm Ensign Charles Kincaid, reporting for quarters."

A young blonde smiled up from behind the high wooden counter. "Mr Kincaid, welcome. We have your room ready."

"Thank you kindly, ma'am." Charlie was momentarily mesmerized by her perfect teeth, and pouty smile. *Parker will be corrallin' behind that counter*, he supposed. He uplifted his keys and kept walking till he came to the end of the hallway. Looking down each archway, he turned right to a door that was slightly ajar. Charlie grinned at his name in the slot and went inside.

The room offered a view of the steep hillside down to the ocean. He dropped his belongings to the floor, walked, almost ran, in a beeline to the window and lifted it open. He leaned out the window and drew in a breath. Charlie knew he would sleep well in the sea air, no matter the temperature. He carefully placed his clothes into the dresser drawers, and hung up his uniforms. He plopped exhausted onto the bed and stared up at the leaded glass ceiling light. *Bet these rooms were waiting for somethin' more fancy than sailors,* he figured.

He dozed in and out of a restless slumber; his lonely heart yearned for Mattie's gentle touch. Was this all a dream?

He lurched upright. How long had he slept? He reached for his pen and paper out of the nightstand drawer, stood up and crossed the room to a desk by the open window. He took a full deep breath and exhaled purposefully with a whoosh. He stared at his opening lines.

Damn it, he said to himself. She's my life, my love. His pen pushed words from his soul. He willfully sobbed as he wrote them. *God how I miss you, Mattie.* When he finished, he fixed his gaze out to sea, his lips soulfully whispering to himself, *Hope you save my place, little darlin'.*

CHAPTER 56

Cerise and white apple blossoms beaconed from Auckland hillsides in a blaze, reminding Mattie of her first day at Mrs Marshall's salon. Her memories flooded from torment to ecstasy as she did her usual climb up the pathway of Huntly House. Mrs Frisken opened the door. Mattie had never seen her like this before.

"I didn't know what to do Mattie."

"Is it… is it him?"

"A telegram arrived today. I didn't…"

Mattie tore open the envelope and they both read the pasted block letters on the yellow form.

Been missing, I'm okay and in America, write soon, all my love Kinky.

Mattie threw her arms around Mrs Frisken. Bonnie burst into a frantic bark fest, and Burt bolted out of the drawing room, holding the newspaper. The commotion was so overpowering that all the borders gathered to hear. Mattie couldn't control herself.

"Now calm down, child," Mrs Frisken said looking at everyone's bewildered faces. "We'll just have to have a hot cup of tea… or maybe an early dinner. We can talk later if you like, Mattie. I'll be in my room."

After dinner Mattie went up to her room. The constant chatter with everyone made her want to take a walk, get a little fresh air. Visit Irene, dear Irene. She grabbed her coat, and peeked her head behind Mrs Frisken's door.

"I'm going out. Don't wait up for me," Mattie said with a smile.

"I bet you are out to celebrate, eh?"

"Something like that."

Knocking on Irene's door brought double excitement when Mattie showed her the telegram.

"Oh Irene, I'm so excited. Charlie's alive and in America… You've no idea what this means to me."

"I know… and you should let your parents know," said Irene, taking her coat.

"Do you mind if I call? I don't like using Mrs Frisken's phone. They'll be so delighted."

Mattie bubbled for joy when she heard her mother's voice.

"Darling, that's good news. You must be home for Christmas. We'll have lots to talk about."

Mattie put the phone down. "They want me home for Christmas…"

Irene raised her eyebrow and folded her arms.

"Irene… you don't look pleased for me. I've waited long enough."

Irene hesitated, "You should have your chance. Let's see what he writes."

Mattie sighed, "It's all a bit much. You're right, I need time to think."

· · · · ·

The letter arrived at last. With trembling hands, Mattie read his words.

Dearest Mattie: I'm awful sorry that I've been unable to write to you in so long. I must have caused you no end of worry. It was not because I never wanted to write to you but I was unfortunate enough to run into a little tough luck. Back last January I was promoted to an Ensign and shortly afterwards transferred to a Chinese junk under our command. We were stationed in the northern part of New Guinea at the time. On a mission out of there we ran into a little trouble, the consequence of which I landed in an out-of-the-way place, unable to let anyone know where I was at. Finally, after what seemed ages, a Dutch freighter picked me up. She steamed for days without making port but eventually put into San Francisco, Calif. As soon as I could get away from the freighter, I reported to the 12th Naval District, who notified the Naval Personnel of my arrival. I had been missing all this time and they seemed a bit surprised that I had turned up still alive and in one piece. Anyhow I was suffering from combat fatigue and had a bad case of nerves, so they ordered me to the place I'm at present for a rest.

Mattie shook her head in sadness. *Oh no, why wasn't I beside your bed? You always begged me to look after you when you needed me. Why was I not there?* She continued reading…

I sent you a wire when I got back to let you know that I was OK, but since then haven't written anyone just been on a spree trying to relax and forget. I'm getting back into shape now. From what I hear will be going back overseas again soon.

Darling I love you so very much, but it looks like I won't get to see you for an awful long time. If I have to go back out there it will be for another three years and that will be awful unfair to you. It's been almost two years already. I wish you could forget that I ever existed and marry some nice young fellow down there, for I'm really a long-shot gamble.

What is he saying… forget him? Mattie couldn't stop shaking. Enraged and crying, she almost tore the letter up. She smacked it on her knee, glaring into the room. *He doesn't know me.* She remained dazed for a while, and then read on with trembling hands. With the next line, he was back, the Kinky she knew…

You are the only girl I've ever loved and there will never be one that can take your place. Darling, I want you so, but everything looks so dark from here. You should marry while you are young and beautiful for I can only bring you misery and unhappiness. In my heart I want you to wait, but it's so unfair to you. I know you love me and I know once you love someone it's hard to forget, specially a love such as ours. I won't blame you a bit if you do decide it's no use. But if you still want to wait that long, that will make me happy. Just the thought that someday you will be mine, if I can live through this turmoil, will keep my spirits up. I'll try and write to you more often. Please let me hear from you soon. Love always Kinky.

Poor darling he's not himself. I must go to him, she sensed. She went to find Mrs Frisken, and glanced into her downstairs office. Mrs Frisken noticed when Mattie appeared.

"Look at this letter."

"You'd better sit down," Mrs Frisken said, peering over her glasses. "Are you sure you want me to read this?"

"Yes, there's stuff in there I don't understand."

Mrs Frisken gave out a huge sigh, and steadied her glasses to go over the pages.

Mattie sat and watched her read. It was a weird, déjà vu feeling sitting there after all these months had passed. Maybe her love affair with Kinky was a dream and she should pursue someone else. Mrs Frisken put down the letter. "What does your heart tell you, Mattie?"

"Find the best way, and marry him."

She smiled. "I think, if you want my advice, you'd better discuss this with your parents. Go down to Dunedin. You owe it to them."

Mattie nodded with tears bubbling in her eyes. "I'll go to the authorities here. I'll need a passport... and I have my father's permission."

"You have indeed."

Mattie rose to leave, "Why didn't he want me to know he was promoted?"

"I guess his missions are top secret, my dear. Are you doubting him?"

"No... never."

Mrs Frisken came over and hugged her, "Always my good girl. Now get that letter posted—and call your parents."

Mattie raced up the stairs. Now it was her turn to take control. She puckered her lips as she always did when she concentrated. She could not write fast enough.

Dearest love, you've no idea how I felt when I read your telegram and now your letter. You poor darling, what you've been through. All those lonely hours lost and then rescued. You must be in so much pain. Of course I'll wait for you. Haven't I always stood by you? I'll never leave you, not until you tell me to. Do you want me to marry someone else? Is that what you're saying? Cause if I do, I'll never be happy. I only want you, so want you, I so.... she broke down in tears but, with shaky fingers, she finished her words, folded the pages, licked the envelope and sent it.

•　　•　　•　　•　　•

Weeks later, another letter arrived. She noticed there were no censorship marks on the envelopes anymore, but still the back flap was barely stuck. *So it no longer matters what I know...*

Dearest Mattie, I received two letters from you today. One was in answer to my last. Darling I'm so happy to know that your love for me is so great that you are willing to wait even if it takes years. I know more than ever my love for you shall never die. And I pray to God that our reunion shall be soon.

You remember in my last letter I said I would probably be shipping out again soon. At present I'm Diving Officer on the YDT4 which is attached to the Montauk Torpedo Testing Range. This is classed as shore duty, but I was warned that I might be transferred anytime. I found out yesterday that I would be here until Jan 1ˢᵗ 1945. After I leave Montauk, there will be no more Diving Officers at this station. There is a fifty-fifty chance I might get another shore duty job somewhere here in the States. I also got the ring size and the next trip into New York City I'll try and get the engagement ring. Darling, answer soon and I promise to write often. Love always, Kinky

Mattie was thrilled at all that was happening for her. She filled out applications for her passport, raced to Peter Pan Studios for her photo, and reported to the Navy Bureau for a medical exam. She was determined.

Her father had to be notified. Mattie called breathlessly. "I want to go to New York," she told him.

The phone went quiet. Slowly and carefully her father said, "Mary and I have decided you need to return home now."

"But…"

"No, it is what we want. You can fly down. I'll arrange the fare."

Mattie put down the phone, and went upstairs to pack. It was the weekend, and Mrs Marshall had given her the day off.

•   •   •   •   •

Arthur was waiting for her at the airport, glancing at his watch as he always did.

"Is everything all right? You look worried," she asked.

He held her gaze and smiled tersely, "We have to talk, Mattie." He lifted her bag to the car. They drove in silence. Mattie didn't mind. She had a lot to think about, driving up Pine Hill Road, past that fateful clifftop ride in Bernie's roadster.

Arriving at Pine Hill Road, Mattie raced ahead into the house. She hugged Mary, but she felt the uncertainty in her parents' voices.

"Please," Arthur directed Mattie across the hallway into the lounge, and sat down beside her. "I'll get straight to the point. We have a number of worries. Arthur looked straight into Mattie's eyes.

Arthur went on. "In fact, Mary and I fear for your safety. We don't want you to return to Auckland."

Mattie tightened her cardigan across her chest. *They got me down here to keep me here. How could they? This isn't about Charlie.*

"But what's that to do with me? I want to go to New York." Mattie felt her heart thumping through her chest. She sensed the tension by her mother's worried expression.

Arthur continued, "Travel is impossible—highly dangerous. Once you go over there, goodness knows what will happen to you. It's a big gamble— you'll be by yourself." He exchanged glances with Mary.

Silence hung in the air. Mattie relived memories in this room that once rang with singing and dancing. What had happened to their lives? Why were they fighting like this? She bolstered with a deep breath and began again.

"Mother, Father... I know what you must be thinking. But I love this man. I want to go to him."

Mary stood up. "Mattie you cannot go."

Mattie dug in her purse and brought out the letter.

"Look, both of you read his words." Mattie threw down the letter.

"I'll go and make some tea." Mary said frowning at Arthur.

Arthur picked up the letter. Mattie wiped her nose on a handkerchief, hoping her sorrow would not acknowledge defeat.

After awhile, her father looked up from the letter. "He's already saying he's returning to war. He's now in Long Island, but for how long?"

Mattie shrugged; she felt her face fill with red rage at her father's intimidating voice.

"Who have you told about the missions?"

"Hardly anyone," Mattie said, perplexed. "Why?" Her bewilderment soon changed to worry.

"He's been involved with something top secret. If any of this gets out, you might get him into trouble. Look," He flipped over the envelope. "No censorship."

"Yes, I noticed that and that's when I..."

"So who did you show it to?"

"Mrs Frisken. But she wouldn't tell anyone."

"How do we know? Does Mrs Frisken read all your letters?"

"Do you think she's some sort of spy?" Mattie remembered how a lot of his letters had been moist, or almost opened. Anyone could have read them. She started to get up.

Arthur put his hand on her arm, gesturing for her to remain seated.

Mattie frowned and blurted, "I don't understand what you're getting at. Mrs Frisken is a wonderful lady."

"Frisken—sounds German. Interesting. Spies are very clever. They fit in. You know yourself the Germans sank the Niagara right under our noses. I nearly drowned. They surround us."

Mary smiled. "Your father has good reason to worry. It's the war. Come into the kitchen for a tea." Mary patted her on the arm softly. "That's why Arthur's so worried about you."

•   •   •   •   •

Arthur called his assistant at Mason headquarters. "Would you check on a Mrs Frisken, Huntly Ave, Auckland, please?"

CHAPTER 57

It seemed like Mattie's letter arrived almost instantly.

Charlie raced to his room. *Why ever did I doubt? My God*, he said to himself. He had to get another letter mailed to bring her over here before the New Year.

•   •   •   •   •

The Navy had completed a massive task of turning a sleepy Montauk fishing village into a full-scale secure facility. The Torpedo Base was artfully hidden under new concrete buildings with 3-foot-thick walls and ceilings, impervious to a German air bomb attack. Sprawling hillsides were now cluttered with solid bunkers aptly sporting painted windows to preserve their idyllic village appearance from above.

Charlie roamed the hills on his evenings off and wondered about Montauk's deep, dark secrets that lay hidden in the aged Indian burial ground aside his Montauk Manor. He smiled when he visualized his fellow Native Americans, the Montauketts, rising up to repulse the Germans or maybe the odd Jap, but most probably the English.

Charlie still felt battered by the after-effects of the malaria, and weary from long days as Commanding Officer of his Diving Tender *YDT-4*. He couldn't wait to tell Doc where he was, but he feared the worst—that contact with the *Rigel* would initiate his return to the Pacific war. He missed Doc and considerably Vic, more than he dreaded another Japanese sword, so he penned kind words to Doc, and this made the night at least tolerable.

It was late October and the Atlantic Ocean became unpredictable, like the war itself. A massive hurricane was headed their way. Charlie noticed the dropping barometer. You're better off at sea, old girl, he thought to himself. Charlie didn't mind that the YDT-4 was unnamed. She was hardly 100ft long, but had a high, seaworthy bow, and wide 22-foot beam.

"Kincaid," Parker yelled, "orders to ride it out at sea."

"Aye aye, sir." Charlie saluted.

He leaned over the bridge rail, hollering to his Chief Engineer, "Make ready to get underway. Hurricane's coming. Top us off with diesel and water. We're gonna need all the ballast we can get. Bring two of those portable de-watering pumps on board from the warehouse ship stores."

He ran down to the galley and found his cook. "We're getting underway to ride out this hurricane. Take two men on the double to the base commissary and get enough food for three weeks at sea. No time for paperwork... call me if you're stuck."

Two hours later, the crew cast off her lines and *YDT-4* headed into the frothing channel. Charlie yelled into the sound-powered phone, "Make turns for ahead full, 10 knots. We'll try to get on the edge of this storm, but I think we're gonna get overrun by the eye."

By sunset, the winds had risen to over 100mph and they were pounding headlong into towering seas.

"Holy shit, these must be 50-foot seas. Keep her headed directly into it. We'll broach if she gets broadside," screamed Charlie. The boat's inclinometer showed she was rolling 52 degrees, shuddering through the mountainous swells. Night fell, and Charlie switched on the searchlight so they could keep their seaway heading, as the growlers crashed over her bow and flooded the main deck.

The Quartermaster yelled, "Captain, we're in the hurricane's path, winds are *125 mph*. We're down to two men in the engine room, and two deck hands."

"We'll take turns at the helm. It'll be over by morning."

The storm continuously eased during the night, and by morning there was a hint of pink behind the angry eastern, grey-black skies. But the sun's energy fuelled the storm, and soon the winds were back up to 80 knots. The radio cackled, "Navy Operations to *YDT-4*."

"*YDT-4* reporting," answered Charlie.

"We have about twenty ships missing in the storm. Are you able to conduct a search and rescue mission?"

"That's affirmative. Winds have dropped to 80 knots, and declining. Send us last-known positions," responded Charlie.

The *YDT-4* spent the following week scouring the seas off the eastern seaboard, but no evidence of any of the lost ships was ever found.

Charlie spoke to his Quartermaster, "Pass the word below, we have just been directed to return to Montauk. See if the cook has a pack of steaks. It will be following seas on the way home. Tell the crew, well done," said Charlie.

People lined the docks and beach as the *YDT-4* arrived back at Montauk, staring in amazement that this little boat had survived a storm that claimed so many lives and ships. Charlie couldn't believe he'd been spared; it was a miracle. He penned a full account of the hurricane to Mattie that night. It was as though she was there, right next to him as he wrote. *Dearest Mattie...We had one of the worst hurricanes in years a few weeks ago. It did a terrific amount of damage. After this, no one can tell me there isn't a God, for it was only a miracle that we were spared. People on the beach could hardly believe their eyes when they saw us come steaming in after the storm...Love always, Kinky.*

After hours, he worked in the carpenter shop, meticulously cutting, chiseling, and gluing the box for Mattie's ring. Nothing would stop him from doing what he so wanted. He was proud of the soft, tawny aromatic cedar, with its grooved sliding cover. It was ready to mail. He set it on the bedside counter and left. New York City wasn't far away.

CHAPTER 58

Charlie strolled the wide streets of Manhattan, looking in the glamorous shop windows. A brisk, cold wind whirled under coats and hats along the avenue. He stopped and stared at a ring in the window of a jewelry store. The shop door tingled with a bell as he entered. Diamonds were shining from every counter. Which one would his sweetheart choose?

He cherished her exquisite hands and the delicate jewelry she wore. A single solitaire gleamed like lightning up at him. It was on its own.

"Can I see?" he asked the jeweler, pointing.

"It's a beauty, all of one carat. It will sparkle now and forever," said the jeweler.

Charlie slipped the ring onto his little finger; he knew it would almost fit her. He slipped it back over the ring stalk. "How much is it?"

"On special today, just $350."

He made an instant decision. "I'll take it… if you'll size it for me, just a tick smaller."

"Can you come back in a few hours? We're rather busy with Thanksgiving coming up. A lot of people like to get engaged during holiday season. Are you new in town?" he queried Charlie.

"Yes, I am."

"Well then, it's only a few blocks to Radio City Music Hall. The Rockettes have a matinee."

Charlie opened the door and grinned. "Be back soon."

His hands in his pockets, Charlie smiled to himself. He had a skip to his step, and a bulge in his wallet. A notice caught his eye. He'd seen it before in the officers' quarters and pictures posted up outside the Auditorium. It was a Cabaret, cancan style—The Rockettes.

Whoopee…wish ol' Vic was here to get a taste of this, he chuckled to himself.

To his surprise he scored a front-row seat. He grinned, listening to the Rockettes overture, relaxed back, and thought about Mattie's reaction when she saw the ring.

An opening chorus of beautiful women burst onto the stage dressed in red and white sparkled shorts and blue sequined jackets, wearing black top hats and carrying walking canes. He gasped: *Roxy...*

He couldn't believe it. She looked right at him, singing through a brilliant whole-face smile. She had the most beautiful voice. He felt uncomfortable thinking about her. *Mattie has a voice like an angel*, he reminded himself. He settled down in his seat, but he wanted to leave. Roxy gave him this funny feeling right down to his stomach. *Is this a dream?* he imagined.

The curtain closed, and intermission gave him the opportunity he was looking for. *The ring... I just have time to get it.* He ran all the way to the jewelry shop as if it otherwise might disappear. The man observed him in a curious way. "You look like you've had a shock. What did the Rockettes dish out?" he asked.

"Yeah, bouncing beautiful dishes. Gotta rush, thank you."

Charlie half-galloped to the station and jumped on a train back to Long Island. He bolted the door and slumped onto the bed, his heart beating, stunned. Had he seen a ghost? Was that a real experience or hallucinations again?

Charlie firmly believed he was not going crazy. He caressed the sparkling diamond, rubbing his finger over its Tiffany prongs. *There you go, pretty gal.* He firmly secured the ring box into his hand-carved cedar masterpiece, and smiled proudly as it disappeared under the sliding lid. *Wish I were there to slide it on your finger, darlin'.* He taped the address to the box and posted it in the next morning's mail.

•   •   •   •   •

A few days later, there was a knock at the door. Charlie opened it wide, excited there might be another letter. He froze... There stood Roxy, wagging a bottle of whisky.

"Did you think you'd never see me again?" she said, pushing her way inside. She leaned back against the desk alongside the window, resting the whisky on the desktop. "Brought your favorite." She rubbed her hands over the polished wood. "It's always the same. You never seem pleased to see me. But you are pleased, aren't you?"

"Roxy, how in the world did you find me?"

"Easy... how many Charlie Kincaid Navy divers do you think are in New York?"

"Roxy, you're amazing. You're everything a guy would want. But I..."

"But you're in love with someone else?" she said, picking up the photo of Mattie. She spun around. "Some gal in the South Pacific? It'll never work."

"Roxy, don't be causin' no trouble now...."

"You're in love with a dream—and you know it." Roxy walked up to him. Her black patent stilettos clicked on the timber floor. "Ain't you gonna pour?" she purred.

Charlie softened in the aroma of her gardenia perfume. He so missed a woman's touch. Her slender, but muscular, perfect legs looked longer than ever. Dancer's legs. She towered over him, as she always did.

Roxy knew the taste of that sweet whisky was just what was needed.

He jolted back to reality. He knew what she was up to. He pushed the bottle aside. "I'm not in love with you, Roxy. I never have been."

"That doesn't mean anything, Charlie Kincaid. Auckland... I know all about that place you were at."

Charlie didn't like her calling New Zealand 'that place'. She was mocking him. But then she had a way with her. She knew how to rile him up. It was happening all over again.

Roxy carefully lifted two small glasses out of her purse and poured. Charlie felt the sweet nectar hit his heart, warm his senses. She took hold of him and clung tightly.

Charlie longed to be held. He was so horribly vulnerable. He kissed her. Her mouth could be Mattie's... soft silken lips... if only he kept his eyes closed. It was all there for him. He'd be loved. He'd never have to say goodbye. What was he doing? He pulled away. "Let me tell you about *that place*. Men lost more than their legs down there. They lost their minds." As he reminisced, Mattie's vision reappeared in front of him as if to defend him. "I lost more than my mind, Roxy. I lost my dream."

Roxy guzzled a mouthful of whisky. He caught she was trying to act serious as she picked up her long cigarette holder. He lit her cigarette for her, and she allowed a cloud to quietly drift along her ivory skin. Perfect skin, so soft... with just a hint of rouge to contrast with her teal-blue velvet jacket. A delicate aroma lingered above the perfume from her rose corsage. She was not the rough Roxy he'd known before. She even had a quiet look of understanding on her face for the first time.

"I'm sorry, darlin'," she said. "I know what you must be going through. I promise I'll be good to you."

Roxy stubbed her cigarette and slowly slipped off her jacket, exposing perfect breasts to Charlie's ready hand. Charlie could not help it; he kneaded her body as Roxy unbuttoned his pants and fondled his manhood. They kissed deeply, gasping, groping into the pleasure.

"Oh Roxy... it has been so long... lonely," Charlie breathed.

"I know darlin'. No more lonely... come to me, feel me." Roxy placed his fingers on her wetness.

Charlie jolted to reality. Shell-shock was like this. He jumped back.

"Oh Roxy, dear Roxy... my mind is wounded. I can't do this." Charlie marveled at her beautiful body, a body he knew.

"Oh darlin' Charlie... remember us... just like before," Roxy approached.

He quivered at the touch of her skin brushing against his face as she pulled him closer. His head spinning, he fell backwards onto the bed. Roxy's fragrance surrounded him. Her lips were on his, kissing intensely. Suddenly he jolted himself up. But Roxy kept nuzzling him, whispering in his ear. He inhaled their whiskey and realized what he was doing.

"I'm sorry Roxy, it's not fair to you. It's the whiskey talking. You need a man... not a drunk."

"Oh darlin', you're no drunk. You just like a bit of whiskey."

"Roxy... stop, please."

"OK lover..." She stood up and intentionally floated her jacket back on with a slow seductive stance. She glided out the door and blew him a kiss. "I'll be seeing you. Keep the glasses for tomorrow," she whispered.

He closed the door and stood thinking for awhile, shaking his head. *Darn gal. She's always been trouble. Like I don't have* enough *to worry about,* he said to himself.

·　　·　　·　　·　　·

Charlie tried to put his thoughts of Roxy and what had gone on between them out of his mind in the morning. He had an appointment with Commanding Officer Parker to apply for Mattie to join him.

"Your request has to go before the Board. You have to provide proof you can support an alien wife," said Parker, looking stern. He continued, keeping his words short, "We have rules for good reason. Men have taken free rein with these gullible foreign women. There's a war on, Kincaid. You have a critical skill; you could be sent back to the Pacific at any time."

Charlie stood stiffly, sensing he was losing this battle.

Parker continued, "How do you suppose she will survive here if you're shipped out? She'll have no job, and no place to live."

"I have my pay, sir."

"Kincaid, this is love-blind bullshit. She's a beautiful gal, from this picture. I'll put the request through." Parker shook his head. "But I've told you before—have a good search around New York. There's plenty of gorgeous blue-eyed, dark-haired dames right here, you know. No need to go looking on the bottom of the planet. That is all."

"Aye aye, sir." Charlie saluted.

Weeks passed. Charlie waited to hear, but there was no word from Mattie. Bit by bit his old doubts crept back. He remembered the evening he first cuddled beside her and poured out his heart, and the doubts he had when she told him about her father. He still hadn't received written permission from him. What if she'd given up? He stabbed his fingers through his hair. It was as much as he could take. He was sick with worry. He'd never been so uncertain, not even on missions.

He panicked and bolted into the storekeeper's office. "Is there any mail for me?"

The clerk responded, "No, Ensign Kincaid, no mail... but there is a message from a young lady."

Charlie snatched the note as if it were his last.

Hi ya doll babe, it's Roxy. I must have impressed you the other day. How about I take you out on the town...

Charlie scrunched the note into a wastebasket by the door and went out. He walked in desperation along the beach. The warm salt spray flooded him with favorite memories.

He was up against a wall. He hated his life here, separated from Mattie. The Officers Club, with all the snide smirks from officers and their wives. He knew what they were saying—damn no-count Injun Mustang, joining our ranks—how dare he? Talking and laughing behind his back, just like back home. He sighed, remembered his empty pockets. *Come on, Kinky,* he heard Vic calling from the sea, *go get 'em.*

My god, I will get 'em—for Vic's sake.

He walked back to his room and sank into his chair. *After all that, she's not coming.* He put his head in his hands, when he saw the gleam of the glass in the sunlight and the whisky bottle luring him. One for Vic, one for Mattie... he poured a full glass and knocked it back... two... three. He was beginning to see the reason why she wasn't coming. She never intended to....

He fell into a dead sleep, so dead he dreamed of Mattie kissing him, holding him, then caressing him into an erotic fervor as solely she could. He was back in Auckland. He woke up with a thud, staring at Roxy.

"My head... What are you doing here? You'll scare a fella to death with that perfume."

Roxy grinned, snuggled closer to him, and moved his hand over her body.

"Now don't be shy. We've had the best night ever," she said, lacing her supple fingers through the hairs on his chest.

Charlie whipped upright and grabbed his head. "Wait a minute. How'd you get in here?"

"We're putting on a couple of shows for you guys. I'm staying here, just down the hall next to the Auditorium. She eased up, naked. "Moved in yesterday. But you were too busy checking your mailbox."

Charlie frowned. It all started to make horrible sense. She was stalking him and his mail. She could have picked the lock, knowing her. He brushed her off and went to the door.

"You tricked me. Get dressed…get out. Now."

"Not so fast, Romeo. I'm still recovering from last night." She smiled warmly.

Charlie watched her gleaming eyes. She had that same expression as when she'd pointed the shotgun many years back. What was she up to? "Roxy, I can't do this."

She pranced over to the whisky bottle and turned, smiling. "You always do things so much better when you've had your whisky. Just like the thing by the sandpit. It wasn't Joe. I lied. It was *you*. And now you're gonna make me an honest gal." Roxy dressed, never taking her eyes off Charlie.

"That's total baloney. Never happened."

"So? It happened last night. And you made two long curtain calls." She smiled hugely now.

Charlie gulped back the panic rising in his throat. "Roxy, please, don't do this to me."

"Well, I'm just down the hall, lover boy." She beamed, swing-walking away. "Jus' close enough for a cuddle."

Charlie closed the door with his back, and leaned against it. He had to think.

CHAPTER 59

Mattie's days at work seemed just that… work, because images of Charlie danced everywhere. When she arrived back at Huntly House, Charlie's letter dated October 14th waited in the mailbox. It must have taken awhile, Mattie thought, puzzled. Why was it still in the mailbox? She stuffed it in her pocket, and opened the door, listening for Mrs Frisken. There was no sound of Bonny's little feet. Her eyes widened at the sight of a small wooden box on the long table. *My God, it's Kinky's writing.* She picked up the box. It had thick white tape wrapped around it with her address and a customs stamp. She brushed her palm over it, and marveled at all the stamps, postmarked November 7th, 1944

She hurried up the stairs, and landed on her bed. With small fingernail scissors, she delicately cut the heavy tape, slid across the delicate lid, and lifted out a black velvet box.

"Oh my God," she said, gasping. Her mouth flew open in amazement, tears welled spontaneously. Fire blazed from a brilliant diamond ring. She slipped it on her finger to a perfect fit. She didn't often pray, but now she sank uncontrollably to her knees and wept. *Poor darling, he carried out his dream.* It was all so surreal.

His letter lay on the floor near her leg. She opened it, half gulping for air, almost hysterical. She began to read his soothing words.

Dearest Mattie, I wrote to you a couple of days ago, but feel I must write again, something that I haven't been doing very regular lately. They sure keep me busy on the new job, but there is one good thing about it—we don't get shot at while doing it. Darling, I miss you something terrible. I keep hoping we can be together, with you as my wife. I've loved you all of my life, even though I didn't get to see you until that day on the tram. You are the girl of my dreams, and someday I hope you'll materialize. The times I held you in my arms and kissed you are the happiest and sweetest memories of my life.

Do you remember when we got the radio how we used to listen to the old classical waltzes on it? To this day those old musical pieces are my favorite. I love to relax and listen for they bring back all the sweet memories I have of you more clearly. It seems as though you are right here beside me. I must close now but I promise to write again soon. Until then, darling, I'll be dreaming of you, Love always, Kinky.

The letter and the engagement ring didn't make sense. The letter was memories… but the ring was their future. *I must go to him,* she decided.

Mattie ran to find Mrs Frisken, calling out her name. Racing downstairs, she rushed inside her room, and noticed a torn envelope lying on her bed but no contents inside. Feeling uncomfortable, she drifted down the corridor, half-listening for familiar sounds in the kitchen, almost colliding with Percy.

"I have some wonderful news," Mattie said, glancing in the direction of the kitchen. "Look," She put out her hand.

"Oh my… all that American kerfuffle came true, eh Mattie?" said Percy, but his face was sad.

"What's wrong? Where's Mrs Frisken?"

"A policeman just came to the door. Mrs Frisken didn't arrive at her daughter's place in Rotorua. She's been reported missing."

"I didn't even know she had a daughter," Mattie quizzed.

"I know. She never talked about her life… only looked after us."

Mattie burst out crying. "What? If she's… No, it can't be."

"Well, they are concerned."

Mattie went back up to her room. She started a letter to Charlie. She knew he'd be waiting for her reply.

Dearest Kinky, the ring is perfect. I got such a shock, my darling. I couldn't believe it. How can I put words on paper when we should be celebrating our life together? I've just returned from Dunedin and everything's gone wrong…

She burst into tears, alone in her room. *Mrs Frisken, oh Mrs Frisken why did you leave me when I need you so? I just can't write and tell him, I just can't…*

Mattie went back downstairs, picked up the phone and called home. She cried when she heard her mother's voice.

"Everything's happened, Mother. Charlie sent the ring. It's beautiful... but—"

"What is it, what's wrong?" interrupted Mary.

"It's Mrs Frisken. She's gone missing... on the way to Rotorua."

Mattie heard the phone click. She stood there stunned, her mouth twisted in painful reality. *The war is here... has been here all along*, she winced. Mattie carefully climbed the stairs.

•   •   •   •   •

Days passed, and eventually their worst fears were confirmed. When Mattie came home from work everyone was gathered in the breakfast room.

"Mrs Frisken's car... it ran over a cliff but no body was ever found," said Percy, he went on. "We'll just have to manage. Her family are sending someone to operate the house."

Mattie threw her hands up in shock.

Jean and Mattie cleared the table from their attempts at making a meal for the boarders, and then Mattie went upstairs to sit and remember her times with Mrs Frisken. Mrs Frisken would want her to be strong. She never imagined her being anything other than genuine. But then, *if someone was a spy, a good spy, they would blend in perfectly... but did she read all Charlie's letters*, she reasoned.

She was ready. She picked up her pen and wrote to Kinky.

CHAPTER 60

Charlie stared at the date of the postmark, the familiar handwriting. *What a darlin'*, he said to himself fumbling with the envelope, deliberately inhaling the beautiful aroma of her perfume...

Dearest Kinky, You'll never know how I felt when I received the ring. It's beautiful just like you. You must have spent hours carving the box. I know you truly love me. The ring shines like our dream. But my God, if you only knew all the heartache down here.

Mrs Frisken had an accident and she's missing, maybe even killed. I can't bear to tell you anymore until I see you. It's all very complicated. I can't write about it.

Darling, we must meet. Please come back to me...

He put down the pages and stared ahead. It was no good. *What's complicated about an accident?* What was hopelessly complicated was getting married during a war.

The following morning, he reported for his weekly debriefing.

"As you were, Kincaid. I hear we're making progress on the torpedoes," said Commander Parker.

"Yes sir, made critical improvements in both guidance and detonation. Won't be long now before we're firing true and steady," replied Charlie proudly.

"Excellent, knew you could do it."

"Permission to speak, sir?" asked Charlie.

"Fire away, Kincaid."

"Any news on my gal... or orders?"

Charlie noticed the change in Parker's expression. "Your gal is not a priority to the US Navy; you are, Kincaid. You have decisively critical skills to the war effort. So no... no word on your gal. Your orders could originate at any *time*... for *anywhere*. We run a top secret facility here. Everything is on a need-to-know basis."

Charlie was amazed at how Parker's tongue could scoot a sodden half-lit cigar from one side of his mouth to the other while he talked. The more excited he got, the faster the cigar moved.

"I can tell you that the Navy is very grateful and aware of your performance. You are being watched. But I don't have the slightest idea what they might have in mind for your orders. You need to be patient. Is this all clear?

"Clear as a bell, Commander. Might be better if I start fuckin' up, then they'll send me to some bullshit shore job." Charlie instantly regretted this outburst, but couldn't help himself. He was thinking he'd be great at Parker's job.

"Don't give me that crap, Kincaid. You do your best for this country... and you do it now. That is *all*."

"Aye, sir, my best... always my best," Charlie saluted, and left.

At day's end, he returned to his room and found the door wide open. His heart missed a beat when he glimpsed a woman's reflection in the mirror. The light was behind her, making of her nothing but a silhouette. But she had a red bow in her dark hair.

"Mattie, is that you?"

"No, it's Roxanne. I've always let you go. I've always made excuses. Kinky, isn't it?"

Charlie knew she'd been reading Mattie's mail. He must keep cool. He turned and smiled, remembering his pride and patience. No one here called him Kinky; only Vic, and he was gone. Why wasn't Vic here to help him? His eyes flashed around the room, till they settled on the whisky bottle. He felt brutal... but he gripped the wall and moved towards the bottle. He poured two glasses of whisky and handed one to her.

"You've always been my rock. I know how much this means to you. Let's celebrate." His heart was torn, but he pretended to sound happy.

"You mean you'll marry me?"

Charlie didn't answer her. He knew she deserved someone who would love her. He smiled at her. "We'll make some arrangements...see if I can stay."

"Where are you going?"

"I can't say."

"If you marry me you can."

"I think the Navy has other plans…"

•   •   •   •   •

The next day Charlie was nowhere to be found, simply his empty desk and a handwritten letter lay on the counter; he knew she'd be in to check on him.

Dear Roxy,

I can't tell you how much I care for you but you have to believe me, don't wait for me. I'm no use to anyone, especially you. My orders are top secret. I'm off to make war.

Love, Charlie

•   •   •   •   •

Charlie sat on a train bound for California. He had a firm grip on his orders, just like always. *Report 12th Naval District San Francisco for further transfer… must be somewhere in the Pacific*, he said smiling to himself, looking out the window. He always kept that perpetual charismatic smile.

CHAPTER 61

Huntly House that had once bloomed with love and kindness, felt empty somehow, with purely the warmth of the sun to comfort her. The radio sounded out tunes, but Mattie reached for the dial and rotated it off. She lay back on her bed, closed her eyes and believed he was there whispering to her, loving her. But he was fading, becoming a lost fading memory.

No... I will not forget. She pushed up, remembering the song and the words in his letter, and reread his last words... *they bring back all the sweet memories. It seems as though you are right beside me.*

Mattie had to go on. She had a job. She reminisced in the tram where they had met, watching the people laugh and chatter. How she wished she could turn back the clock and feel his warm, soft peacoat, stare into those dark eyes once more. A clang of the tram bell and she was out and into the warm salon.

Work was her friend, but she hated leaving at day's end and taking the tram back down the hill to Huntly House. Jean's happy face always cheered her up, and the new manager's meals were delicious, but the nights were brutal. Autumn had arrived early this year and with it the war brought welcome good news but coupled with gloom and disparity. Most newspapers never literally told the truth, Mattie knew, as she tossed the paper back onto the couch.

•   •   •   •   •

One day at work, Kath blithely shouted, "Nan's on the phone. She sounds really out of it. You better come."

"Hi, Mattie. Hey I'm, ahhh..." Nan started.

"Nan, what is it?" Mattie interrupted.

There was silence on the phone, "I think I saw that American, the one you went with. I could swear it was him."

Mattie froze. "Nan, I know you thought I was mad, but please don't play tricks on me. I've never done you any harm."

"I know you haven't, Mattie. I got your job when you left here, and our new girl told him…"

"Told him what?"

"Well the new girl… she told him you don't work here anymore. She didn't know. I'm sorry, Mattie. I'm really sorry."

Mattie put the phone down and burst into tears. Mrs Marshall came in and saw her. "Oh Mattie… slowly to the back room. Please sit, now tell me what's wrong."

All Mattie could see through her tears was Mrs Marshall's kind face, in a blur. She reminded her of her mother. It made Mattie sob for everything she'd gone through. She steeled herself, but refused to give in to grief over an impossible love. She rested her head against Mrs. Marshall and whimpered, "Nan… Nan saw him."

"Saw who?"

"Kinky."

Mrs Marshall bent down and put an arm around her. "There, there, darling, you're imagining things. I'll make you a nice cup of tea. Then I want you to go home, put your feet up and rest… plenty of rest. You haven't talked about him recently. It's not like you. I'm worried about you. Do you want Kath to take you home?"

"No, no thank you, Mrs Marshall. You're very kind. I'll be all right." Mattie sipped the hot tea and took out her handkerchief. The fatigue and loneliness were enough, understandably, but it was the uncertainty. Wartime people lived for the present; the future was just a bullet away.

She stood up, a little shaky. "I'll be better tomorrow. My clients are finished." She smiled and left. Her mind raced, filled with memories. She jostled in a tram onto Queen Street. What if… just what if, for some crazy reason, the *Rigel* was back? She would see it. Her heart thumped as they consciously descended Queen Street.

Mattie jumped off the tram at the bottom of Queen Street. But there was nothing. Nothing but a huge aircraft carrier with a band playing in front of stacked planes on the flight deck, all expertly aligned ready to bring fury upon the nearest Jap. She craned her neck into the cold, brisk wind off the sea. *It's no use… he was only a beautiful dream.*

A bus stopped in front of her, almost knocking her over. Just one last memory… I'll go to the beach, *our* beach. She stepped on the bus, and rode staring out the window at the water lapping against the breakwater, as the bus ambled along Tamaki Drive. A strange nostalgic feeling came over her. Ultimately, the bus stopped at Saint Heliers.

She'd take a walk, back to their spot. There was no harm in reliving, remembering. Besides the sea air would do her good. She buttoned up her coat, removed her shoes and strolled, head down, across the white beach. Her feet slid into the sand, dislodging a blur of colorful shells.

When she squinted at a motion, in the distance a figure was running towards her. The figure tripped, and his hat flew. He was waving, and calling out, but she couldn't hear above the wind.

Mattie stood staring into the cold wind, wiping her streaming eyes. It couldn't be… it was all too much. Please, don't do this to me, she cringed. She dropped to her knees in the sand, and buried her head in trembling hands. *My mind is playing tricks… This is cruel, so cruel.*

She was afraid to look; afraid of her own self, her dreams. It couldn't be. It was not possible. She went on sobbing… but then she felt his warm, tight grip lift her, and she flashed back through her tears into his ink-dark eyes, worn from war. She placed her hand into his. He kissed the ring, and winked at her.

"Did ya think I'd leave my sweetheart behind?" Charlie asked in his slow drawl. He nestled her in his arms. Mattie closed her eyes to the feel and smell of his jacket. This was the man she loved. She couldn't believe it.

"Oh Kinky, dear Kinky, you came!" She was babbling, she knew it, but she couldn't stop.

He wiped the tears from her alabaster skin with the back of his rugged fingers, gazing at her, loving her. Mattie took hold of his hands and kissed them. Then his fingers lifted her chin and warm lips met. They passionately embraced, savoring each other. Charlie had to pull back, hungry for another look.

"Yes, my darlin'. I told you a ways back, they weren't gonna get this Cherokee." He enclosed her in his arms and hugged her, caressed her every feature, so tenderly and so longingly. He looked down at her, reassuring her, "We'll be together. For a long time, remember?"

He gently held her tear-damp cheeks between rough hands, "And baby, this time, no war's gonna stop me. We're gonna get married. It'll be the best wedding in town, you betcha!"

"My dear love... I have waited so long." Mattie clung to him even more now as if he *were* a dream.

"Didn't I tell ya not to worry? I have two weeks leave. I'm goin' back to the Pacific." Charlie watched all the color drain out of Mattie's face. He picked her up, cradled her head against his chest, and spoke softly, "Oh my darlin'. Can I call your parents?"

"Yes, my love. Dunedin... and a church." Mattie could not take her eyes from Charlie.

A wave caught them by surprise. Charlie kept on walking and dipped to pick up his hat with a smile on his face. Everything he fought for was right here, where the sea met the shore.

THE END

The Rigel Affair is inspired by true events,
and the letters Charlie mailed to my blessed mother, Mattie.

About the Author

Lynette grew up listening to her mother Mattie's stories about her WW2 love for US Navy Diver Charlie. She used Mattie's 30 letters from Charlie, and together with her insightful editor/advisor husband, Bud, they completed extensive research to give reality to The Rigel Affair. Lynette has published multiple short stories for NZ magazines. Both Lynette and Bud have completed numerous Creative Writing courses at Auckland University. Lynette is an accomplished expressionist Artist, with works sold internationally.